Rachel Hore worked in  years before moving with her f̶ ches publishing at the Univers d to the writer D. J. Taylor an vels include *The Dream House, T̶ ̶.̶.̶.̶,̶ ̶T̶h̶e̶ ̶G̶l̶a̶s̶s̶ ̶P̶a̶i̶n̶t̶e̶r̶'̶s̶ Daughter*, which was shortlisted for the 2010 Romantic Novel of the Year award, *A Place of Secrets*, which was picked by Richard and Judy for their book club, and the latest *Sunday Times* bestseller *A Gathering Storm* which was shortlisted for the RONA Historical Novel of the Year 2012.

Praise for *A Gathering Storm*

'With a serious eye for exquisite detail, Hore's latest, brilliantly crafted novel aptly follows a photographer, Lucy. She takes a journey to capture past, life-changing family secrets, embracing three generations along the way, across Cornwall, London, East Anglia and Occupied France' *Mirror*

Praise for *A Place of Secrets*

'Sumptuous prose, deft plotting, lush settings, troubling personal histories, tragedy, heady romance and even a smattering of eighteenth-century scientific wonderment mark Hore's fourth novel as her most accomplished and enthralling yet' *Daily Mirror*

Praise for *The Glass Painter's Daughter*

'Another of this year's top offerings [is] Rachel Hore's *The Glass Painter's Daughter*. The main character, Fran has returned home to look after her dying father's glass-cutting business. Overshadowing the central love affair with colleague Zac and an unfolding mystery involving a stained-glass window is the pall of imminent death' *Daily Mail*

The Memory Garden

RACHEL HORE

**SIMON &
SCHUSTER**

London · New York · Sydney · Toronto · New Delhi

A CBS COMPANY

First published in Great Britain by Simon & Schuster UK Ltd, 2007
A CBS COMPANY
This paperback edition published 2012

1 3 5 7 9 10 8 6 4 2

Simon & Schuster UK Ltd
1st Floor
222 Gray's Inn Road
London WC1X 8HB

www.simonandschuster.co.uk

Simon & Schuster Australia, Sydney
Simon & Schuster India, New Delhi

A CIP catalogue record for this book
is available from the British Library

ISBN 978-1-47115-032-6

Typeset in Palatino by M Rules
Printed and bound by CPI Group (UK) Ltd, Croydon, CR0 4YY

For David
and in memory of his father,
J.R.G. Taylor MBE, 1921–2006

We are here to learn both light and dark; without one the other cannot be. Black shows up the white, purple enhances yellow, rough gives value to smooth.

Dame Laura Knight
Oil Paint and Grease Paint (1936)

Merryn Hall, Lamorna, Cornwall, TR20 9AB

Ms Melanie Pentreath
23a Southcote Road
Clapham
London SW12 9BL   *15 March 2006*

Dear Mel,

*Thanks for returning the agreement to rent the Gardener's
Cottage and for the cheque. I'm enclosing your receipt and a
map giving directions from Penzance.*

*I'm looking forward to meeting you here at Merryn Hall
next month. As I said on the phone, I shall probably still be up
in London when you arrive, but Mrs Irina Peric, who looks
after the place for me, will give you the key to the cottage.
Could you ring her a couple of days beforehand on 01736
455836 to tell her when to expect you?*

*I'm sure you will find Lamorna a peaceful haven for your
studies – it's an enchanting place. As your sister will have told
you, I have only recently inherited the Hall and you will see
there is an awful lot of work to be done to the house and
grounds. However, you should find the cottage is comfortable
enough.*

Yours sincerely,
Patrick Winterton

Merryn Hall, Lamorna

Adeline Treglown
The Blue Anchor
Harbour Street
Newlyn   *Easter Monday, 1912*

Dear Mrs Treglown,

My cook, Mrs Dolly Roberts, who I believe to be your sister-in-law, has let it be known that you are seeking a position for your girl and she assures me the young woman is sober, honest and industrious.

I have need of a general housemaid I can also train up as lady's maid, and Pearl sounds most suitable. My gardener, Mr Boase, takes the trap to Penzance every market-day and, should it serve, can fetch her next Thursday from by the Davy statue at twelve noon. I can pay her twelve guineas but keep back 6d a month for her uniform.

I was most sincerely sorry to learn of your troubles.

> *Yours truly,*
> *Emily Carey (Mrs)*

Chapter 1

Cornwall is a great place to lose yourself, Mel reflected with a sense of unease as she turned off the crackling car radio and peered through the rain-lashed windscreen into pitch darkness. She had simply no idea where she was going. Even at a snail's pace, negotiating the meandering country lanes with their steep embankments was like steering on a rollercoaster, the stony hedgerows rearing up in the glare of the headlights with heart-stopping suddenness.

A mile and a half out of Newlyn, turn left past the pottery on the crossroads, Patrick had scrawled in thick-nibbed fountain pen at the bottom of the photocopied map he had sent. But Mel hadn't noticed a pottery sign in the dark and had veered left at what she hoped hadn't been the wrong junction. Why did all these little roads appear to go round in circles, she asked herself crossly, and why were there hardly any signposts?

It was a pity this had proved such a nightmare journey, for Mel had been looking forward to this trip for ages. Ever since David Bell, the Senior Tutor at the college in South London where she was a lecturer in Art History, had suggested she take a term's study leave. His words of warning still rang in her ears:

'If you don't have some time away, Mel, I'm frightened you'll make yourself ill.'

There were more ways than one of losing your bearings, she thought miserably as she steered the car around yet another bend . . . what was *that*! She slammed her foot on the brake as a missile hurtled out of the dark. An owl – she glimpsed a dazzle of shiny eyes above a curved beak before the bird swerved off into the night a second before impact. Mel sat for a moment in shock, then, her heart still thumping, eased her foot off the brake and the car rolled forward once more. Only for her to lurch to a stop again around the next corner: a T-junction. Which way now, for goodness' sake? She wrenched up the handbrake, glanced at the clock – eight-fifteen, it really was dark for an April evening – and stabbed on the navigation light.

In the weak beam Mel squinted at Patrick's map, flexing her neck and shoulders against the beginnings of a headache. Her finger traced the faint lines of roads all running into one another, then along the one she was seeking. It zig-zagged past Merryn Hall, before turning left through the village of Lamorna and down to Lamorna Cove itself.

She wound down the window and leaned out, shivering, peering through the rain for a signpost, a landmark, to match up with the map. But there was nothing. She must be very near Lamorna now, surely, but if she wasn't careful she might be driving around all night. She took her duffel bag from the passenger well and scrabbled about for her mobile, then tapped in the contact number Patrick had underlined at the top of the map. The words 'no network coverage' flashed up on the screen.

I wish Jake were here. The treacherous voice crept unbidden into her mind. Jake had a knack with maps and cars as well as with cats and televisions. Unfortunately, in the end, he hadn't had a knack with Mel. Jake was gone and she would have to get out of this mess by herself.

The thought gave her resolve. It was a nuisance, but she would just have to retrace her route. Hoping another car wasn't going to careen around the corner at this particular moment, she executed a five-point turn in the small space available and set off back the way she had come. Luck was on her side, for after a few minutes she found what she had missed the first time – a narrow road leading off to the left.

Lamorna was in a valley, so her hopes rose when the road started to wind downhill, the hedges towering on either side. After a while the slope became steeper, the twists in the road more regular and every ounce of her concentration was required to keep the car on the road. At least the rain seemed to be easing.

She began to look out for signs of habitation. A short while later, the hedgerow on her side gave way to a low stone wall lined with trees. Soon a pair of gate-posts loomed in the darkness. She slowed the car. Could this be it? She lowered the side window to look. A battered board, half-covered in ivy, hung lopsided from one post. The words 'erryn Hal' were just visible on the cracked paint. Relief flooded through her as she swung the car between the posts.

Pitch black. No, she could glimpse a small blur of light, there, in the distance between the black hulks of trees. The headlights picked out a winding muddy drive full of potholes and lined with great banks of vegetation on either side.

The rain had stopped at last and she bumped the car down the drive for a couple of hundred yards until, before her, the yellow glow of a porch lantern picked out two great columns of a Georgian portal. At its base, three semicircular steps rippled out towards a battered flagstoned forecourt grown up with weeds. The porch light was the only sign of life.

Mel hesitated, then parked at the edge of the forecourt and switched off the engine. She sat for a moment listening, gazing around, trying not to think about all those corny Gothic horror films she had watched as a teenager, the ones in which the heroine arrives at the dark deserted castle on a stormy night, seeking sanctuary, only for the front door to creak open and the terror to begin . . .

Pull yourself together, she thought. There are no vampires in Cornwall.

As far as you know . . . the words, spoken in a creepy voice, as frequently rehearsed by her brother William when they were children, floated into her mind.

Oh, don't be silly, she remonstrated with herself. There is no point sitting here if you want supper and somewhere to sleep. So she pushed open the car door.

The only sound was the dripping of rain on leaves. The house waited in the damp darkness, the glass in the windows reflecting ebony in the porch light. She could just make out a pattern of crenellations in the stone, like castle battlements, high above the porch, disappearing left and right into the gloom. Trees, shrubs and brambles grew right up to the Hall on either side of the courtyard, and indeed across the front of the house so that in the dark she could gain only a limited sense of the scope of the frowning building. The cumulative effect was of desolation and decay, and of something more ominous.

The last drops of Mel's little stock of courage drained away. There was hardly need to knock on the door, for the house was clearly empty. After her long journey from one world into another there was no one to meet her, no welcome. Just this great hulk of a place that almost willed her to go away.

When a cracking noise came from the undergrowth, she spun

round, all senses suddenly alert. She waited; the darkness waited. It must be a bird, she told herself, but her head throbbed with tension. She was, after all, alone in the remotest part of wild Cornwall in what felt like the middle of the night. And she had a strange sense that someone was watching her.

She looked up at Merryn Hall and shivered. What had she expected to find? A pretty cottage nestling in the manicured grounds of a small country mansion? A warm welcome, old-fashioned country hospitality? In his letter, Patrick had prepared her for something a bit crumbly, but not this . . . It was the desertedness and the air of, yes, of lurking menace, that bothered her.

Who *was* Patrick, come to think of it? A friend of a university friend of her sister Chrissie's. Someone Chrissie herself hardly saw now and whom Mel had never met.

Scenes from her nephew Rory's favourite Disney video flashed through her mind. She could be a modern Beauty, coming upon the Beast's castle in a wilderness, seeking sanctuary and finding something quite different. Though in her elderly leather jacket, mud-splashed jeans, and with her red hair lank, she would hardly be first in line for the part of Beauty.

Feeling braver, she pulled her bag off her shoulder and walked towards the porch, intending to try the bell just in case. It was then she noticed something fluttering against the flaked paint of the front door. Up the steps she pulled a folded piece of paper out from under the brass knocker and pinched it open. A message was pencilled in sloping block capitals:

DEAR MEL,

FORGIVE ME. I WAITED UNTIL SEVEN O'CLOCK BUT NOW I MUST
LEAVE TO FETCH MY DAUGHTER. IF YOU DRIVE FURTHER DOWN

THE ROAD THERE IS A LITTLE LANE TO THE COTTAGE. THE KEY IS
UNDER THE MAT. I WILL CALL IN TOMORROW.
  YOURS RESPECTFULLY,
  IRINA PERIC

Mel studied the formal phrases, the carefully drawn letters. On the phone, Irina spoke with an Eastern European accent, stressing the first syllables of words and softly rolling her r's.

The matter drifted to the back of her mind. Her attention was already on climbing back into the car and continuing down the road to find the cottage before she dropped with exhaustion. As she felt in her pocket for her key, she looked up to see the clouds were thinning and a most beautiful moon emerged in a veil of mist to illuminate her way.

It was another twenty minutes before Mel shut the front door of the Gardener's Cottage behind her and surveyed the pile of luggage sprawled across the hallway. Supper in a moment, she told herself, eyeing the carrier bag containing the small stock of food she had culled from her store cupboard at home. Supper then unpack what she needed for the night. That was all she could face now with her headache taking hold. She was weary, bone weary.

She let out a long breath, then, defying cautious animal instinct, she marched down the hall and began to explore the cottage, turning on all the lights as she went. There was a sitting room to the right of the long hall, before the stairs, a room with a polished dining table and chairs to the left; at the back, a dingy kitchen with a round pine table, beige Formica worktops, a fridge, stocked with dairy products, and a washing machine. Overhead, the strip light flickered and hummed. Turning it on and off several times failed to cure the problem. Beyond the kitchen was a stone-floored bathroom with a white suite but no shower.

Upstairs were two bedrooms and a boxroom. All neat and clean, though the furniture was shabby. Making her way carefully back down the steep staircase with its faded runner she noted the chipped paint on the rough stone wall and saw exactly why Patrick had trouble letting the place. It would be fine for her for the next month. Comfortable, shabby but strangely familiar. Today's well-to-do holidaymakers demanded modern fittings, fresh paint and shiny new furniture.

Her plan was to spend the month walking in the footsteps of some of the painters who had settled in and around the nearby fishing town of Newlyn and Lamorna at the turn of the twentieth century, surveying the places they had painted, visiting museums and archives and working up her notes into a book she had been commissioned to write. This she would finish on her return to London. It was a chance to immerse herself in her work . . . and to give herself a break from the troubles of the previous year.

The Gardener's Cottage did feel like home – too much like home, Mel saw as she dumped the bag of food on the kitchen table and opened a wobbly cupboard door to find herself staring at her mother's breakfast china: white porcelain with tiny hedgerow flowers painted around the rim. She picked up a cereal bowl and turned it in her hands. Every morning of her childhood for as far back as she could remember, Mel had scraped her spoon over this pattern . . . and for an awkward minute she was back with her brother and sister in their cheerfully messy Victorian semi in the leafy suburbs of Hertfordshire, rushing to finish breakfast as their mother, Maureen, smart with suit and briefcase, chivvied them to get into the car *now* or they would have to walk to school.

The Pentreaths' china bowls were gone now, the house sold, the pain of letting go of their childhood home a further sorrow after their mother's death nearly a year ago. Mel replaced the bowl and shut the cupboard, leaning against it, as if to lock up the memories. If only it were that easy.

Once again the doubts rolled in. Four weeks in this place, alone with her thoughts, when she was emotionally so fragile – why on earth had she come? Suddenly she longed to be back in her flat in Clapham, looking out on the carefully tended strip of garden where yellow and white spring bulbs would soon be giving way to rich blue ceanothus and purple lilac. Except Clapham didn't seem right any more either. Her flat hadn't felt like home since Jake had left. There weren't enough books to fill the gaps on the shelves, and the pictures he had lifted from the walls had left ghostly shapes behind that shouted their very absence – and his. She knew David had been right – she really did need to get away.

It was three weeks ago that she had been coming out of one of those interminable college faculty meetings in which everything is thoroughly discussed but nothing decided, when the Senior Tutor had caught up with her.

'Mel, do you have a moment? A quick sandwich, maybe?' David looked at his watch. 'I've another meeting at two, but . . .'

They wove a way through the stream of students towards the staff café and soon Mel was picking at quiche and salad, trying to inject some life into her voice as she answered David's routine queries about her work. She mustn't let him know quite how bored she was with it all at the moment, how colourless was the round of teaching and marking – indeed, how dreary everything seemed. She was wrung out. But he seemed to have read her mind.

'Mel,' he said gently. She flinched at his searching gaze, knowing that her eyes were dark-ringed in her tired, pale face.

He smiled, a grizzled, avuncular man, with springy silver hair and lively eyes that belied the fact that he too was feeling the strain. The pressures of providing for increasing numbers of students in cramped conditions and with limited funds were taking their toll on everybody. David was, Mel knew, looking forward to retiring at the end of the summer term, leaving teaching and administration so that he could pursue the historical research he never had time to do.

Now he said, 'Do tell me to mind my own business, but I was watching you in that meeting back there. You looked as though all the cares of the world were on your shoulders.'

'It's listening to John O'Hagen,' Mel tried to laugh, referring to the Angry Young Man of the Arts Faculty, 'banging on about union rules again. I know technically he's right, of course, but we can't threaten industrial action about every little thing. We have responsibilities. God.' She rolled her eyes in a sudden flash of anger.

'Now you're more like your usual self.' David reached over and squeezed her clenched fist. 'A year ago, you know, you would have been talking him down across the table.'

'I would, wouldn't I?' Mel gave him a ghost of one of her most dazzling smiles, then slumped into round-shouldered misery once more. 'I'm sorry, I'm not very good company at the moment.'

'You're always good company,' said David. 'But you've had a bad year one way or another . . .'

'It's not been great, no.'

'How are the family doing?'

Mel pushed a chunk of quiche into her mouth and chewed, which bought her time to consider the question. 'I haven't a clue what my brother William is thinking. He's always been the sort to get on with things. Shuts his feelings out. It's much easier to talk to Chrissie, my sister.' She was silent for a moment, then rushed on. 'It's just not fair, though – the cancer taking Mum so quickly. I keep going over what happened. Did we try hard enough to get her the right treatment? Shouldn't we have noticed earlier that she was so ill? She had been losing weight and getting tired, but I didn't realise—'

'You mustn't feel guilty,' David cut in, picking his words carefully. 'It sounded as though there was little you could do with such a virulent form of the disease.'

Mel looked at her plate. 'That's what the doctors insisted.'

They both ate in silence for a moment, then David said, almost casually, 'And then there's Jake.'

'And then there's Jake,' said Mel, reaching for her water glass and taking a gulp as if it were some nasty-tasting medicine. David knew Jake well. For the irony was that Mel's ex-boyfriend was also a lecturer in the Arts Faculty – in Creative Writing – and she came across him all the time, at the coffee-machine, by the photocopier, in the café. She had taken care at this morning's meeting to choose a seat that meant she wouldn't have to see his face every time she looked up. But even so, she was aware he would be sitting, restlessly doodling crazy cartoon faces on his A4 pad, and she couldn't block out the lazy tones of his voice, once soft in her ear alone, or his comments, as ever acerbic and to the point.

'Mel, I've a suggestion to make,' David said suddenly. 'You're due a term's study leave sometime next year, aren't you?'

'Yes. It'll be five years since my last,' said Mel, who had, like everyone else in the Faculty, calculated to the day when her next paid sabbatical was due.

'What are you working on at the moment? Have you any plans?'

'I do, actually. I've been researching artists in Cornwall,' she replied, 'the Newlyn School of painters at the end of the nineteenth century, and their links with the artists who settled in Lamorna up the coast.'

'Ah, don't remind me. Stanhope Forbes – was he Newlyn School?' David guessed with a look of mild alarm. He was a medievalist and it was a joke in the Faculty that he was only dimly aware of any artefacts that hadn't either been dug up or handwritten by monks on vellum.

'Yes, and his Canadian wife Elizabeth. Then there were Thomas and Caroline Gotch . . . Walter Langley. They're the more famous ones. And then later, in Lamorna, Harold and Laura Knight, Sir Alfred Munnings . . .'

David nodded. 'I know, the one who painted horses?'

'That's right. Grosvenor Press, the art-book publishers, have asked me to write a book about the Newlyn and Lamorna artists and their work. I was planning to finish the research for it over the next couple of months, visit Cornwall for a few weeks after the summer term finishes, and do most of the writing when I get back. The deadline's the end of the year, you see.'

'Sounds an interesting commission.'

'Oh, it is. It's the women I'm particularly drawn to. They had so much personal and professional freedom, but some of them had to struggle so hard. Laura Knight, for instance, found herself a penniless orphan . . .' She stopped, realising she was waving a fork around to emphasise her points, scattering crumbs. David was looking at her, a lopsided smile growing on his face.

'Why don't you start your sabbatical now?' he suggested. 'Take the summer term off, don't wait until next year. If you combine it with the summer break you'll have nearly six months' writing time without distractions.'

Mel's face lit up for a moment, then the light died.

'It sounds fabulous,' she said, 'but aren't I supposed to be taking the "Nineteenth-century Painting" seminars next term? And "An Introduction to Modernism"? And who'll look after my MA students?'

'Mel, I had an email from Rowena Stiles last week,' David said, watching her reaction, and Mel couldn't help frowning.

Rowena had arrived as cover for a term when Mel had been away on compassionate leave eighteen months before. There had been talk about finding her a permanent position, but then she announced she was to follow her banker husband to New York and Mel had been relieved. It was no secret that the two women hadn't got on.

David continued: 'She's back in London for a few months and would be glad to fill in.'

'You'd already asked her, then?' she said, sitting up straight in her seat.

'No, of course not. She had got in touch because she was looking for work. Relax.'

Mel thought for a moment, measuring up the tantalising glimpse of freedom, like a chink of light through a door in a dark room, against the prospect of Rowena taking over her work again. Rowena knew her stuff, all right, but she liked to be in control and had an abrasive manner. Mel was proud of the fact that she herself got on well with her students. Her dramatic red hair and colourful bohemian dress sense gave her a bona fide artistic air, and she was always generous with her encourage-ment and not too hard on those who delivered their work late. By contrast, they had to watch their step with Rowena. And the latter might not be content just to stand in temporarily this time, once she had got her feet under Mel's desk . . .

But a whole term off, starting next week when they broke up for Easter? Then the long summer break? It was tempting – very tempting.

'Rowena does an excellent job, Mel,' David said firmly. 'I know she can be . . . assertive . . .'

'Pushy and manipulative' are the words you're skirting round, Mel thought. She wondered what had happened to that hot job at the Manhattan museum Rowena had boasted about? Well, David was right: maybe her students *could* put up with Rowena for a term – and it wasn't as though she could legally steal Mel's job.

'Are you sure you're not trying to get rid of me?' she teased him, a smile transforming her tired face.

'No, don't be silly,' he said. 'Mel, I'm saying this to you as a friend. If you don't take some time away, I'm frightened you'll make yourself ill. And I won't have you getting to that stage. Think about it over the weekend, then come and see me on Monday.'

The more she thought about it, the more attractive the idea seemed, but there was one problem.

'I haven't got anywhere to stay. It's Easter and everything's booked up.' Mel was on the phone to her sister Chrissie the following Sunday evening. Chrissie, who lived in North London with her amiable civil servant husband Rob, juggled part-time administration for a TV production company with raising two young sons, Rory and Freddy.

'Wait a minute, Rory, darling, I'm on the phone. Sorry, Mel. Where exactly would you want to go?'

'West Cornwall. Ideally in the Penzance area.'

'Ah, the Wild West. Mum used to love that part.' Chrissie sighed. Their parents had met at school in Cornwall, but further east, in Falmouth. They had moved 'up country' to London soon after their marriage, when Tom Pentreath qualified as a junior doctor, the start of a dazzling career as a heart surgeon. 'It's a shame we don't know anyone down there since Aunty Jean died. When did she die, I can't . . . Wait, wait, I've just remembered something. Mel, this is really amazing. You know Patrick?'

'Patrick who?'

'Patrick Winterton. Friend of Nick's?' Nick had been a boyfriend of Chrissie's at Exeter University with whom she had stayed in touch after the romance had fizzled out. Chrissie stayed in touch with everybody.

'No,' Mel said shortly. 'I don't know Patrick.' Chrissie was always doing this, assuming that she, Mel, knew everyone Chrissie knew. And with Chrissie's vast acquaintance this could prove impossibly confusing.

'He studied History at Exeter. Got his own business now. Something to do with the Internet,' she said vaguely. 'He's still the same – funny the way some people don't change a bit . . . Oh Rory, do stop it, darling, you can talk to Aunty Mel in a moment. Anyway, he was telling me he's just inherited this place near Penzance from his great-uncle or someone. I'm sure he said Lamorna – isn't that one of the places you need to go? There's a cottage in the grounds he might do up and rent out. I don't know what state it's in now. Mel, talk to Rory while I find the email address he gave me.'

In the dim glow of the wall-lights with their crimson frilled shades, the sitting room in the cottage looked dingy but cosy. Apart from a huge silver television crouching in a corner like an alien spaceship, the furniture seemed as old as the house. A horsehair sofa with wooden arms, two matching fireside chairs, all with lace antimacassars laid over their backs, were arranged before the small fireplace where a neatly piled pyramid of paper, kindling and wood awaited the touch of a match. A fire would probably cheer up the room, but there was no point lighting one this late. Mel wondered idly where more wood might be stored. Another task for the morning.

She sank down onto one of the chairs. It was surprisingly comfortable. As ever, her professional interest drew her to the pictures on the wall. Instead of the cheap reproductions and mass-produced prints that landlords of holiday cottages often inflict on their tenants were half a dozen fine watercolours of flowers.

She got up to view the one hung above a mahogany bureau. The weak light reflecting off the glass forced her to lift it off the wall in order to study it properly. The words *magnolia sargentiana robusta* were painted lightly beneath the delicate rendition of three pale pink flowers on a woody stem, followed by the initials *P.T.* She noticed the needle-fine detail of the stamens, the light wash of colour blushing deeper towards the centre of the blooms, the gloss of the wood. It was meticulously observed and executed.

She replaced the magnolia and moved to consider the others. There was a creamy *rhododendron macabeanum*, a scarlet camellia, a purple iris and two kinds of rose. Each picture was as exquisite as the last. And each was signed *P.T.* Before she replaced the sixth and last on the wall, she turned it over hoping for a date. But the brown-paper backing was blank.

A plastic travel alarm clock on the mantelpiece, looking as out of place as the telly in this dingy Victorian setting, showed five to ten. Mel went to haul the suitcases upstairs.

In the larger of the two bedrooms the Victorian oak double bed, she was relieved to see, was made up with a plump duvet, rather than old-fashioned sheets and blankets. However, the musty smell was, if anything, more intense in here. She dumped the cases on the floor, wondering where she would stow everything tomorrow. By the door was a rough-hewn chest-of-drawers with a wedge of cardboard under one front claw foot. A cracked jug stood in a wash-ing bowl on top and Mel, clutching an armful of clean underwear, traced its painted pattern of storks with her finger.

With her free hand she pulled at the knob of the top drawer, intending to stuff the underwear in it, but the drawer wouldn't move. She dropped the clothes on the top and tugged at it with both hands. It opened halfway and stuck. Mel peered inside.

Caught at the back was a wad of yellow newspaper which she gently eased out and unfolded. The date was ripped but she held the edges of the tear together until she could read the words *March 1912*. Almost one hundred years ago. Her attention was caught by a short piece about a train-load of unemployed tin miners and their families leaving Penzance to join a ship to the Cape from Southampton. *The stream of emigrants shows no ebb, but still runs on, as fast and deep as ever* . . . the article said.

She turned the paper over. Amidst the advertisements for patent remedies and ladies' fashions was another news article.

TRAGEDY AT NEWLYN

Soon after ten o'clock on Saturday evening, drinkers were alerted to a sudden blaze in the upper storey of the Blue Anchor Inn by the harbour, (proprietress Mrs Adeline Treglown). An alarm was raised, the building evacuated and help came from the coastguards, some of the crew of His Majesty's ship *Mercury*, and fishermen. Although the fire was brought under control, the body of a man has been found in the wreckage. He was later identified as Arthur Reagan, aged 52, a visitor from London. An inquest will be held next week.

Mel read it twice, wondering why someone had kept it. Was it just to line the drawer, she wondered. She refolded the paper and dropped it back in the chest.

As she pulled on an old T-shirt nightdress and brushed her teeth at a little washbasin she thought about events at the Blue Anchor a century ago, imagining that His Majesty's sailors must have been propping up the bar when the fire broke out, and presumably fought the flames whilst the worse for wear. She wondered at the serendipitous way other lives had leaped out of the past and into her consciousness. She had only been looking for somewhere to stow her knickers and had been given a story instead.

Cornwall was one of the most ghost-ridden counties in England, Mel's mother had once told her. There was a time when they were children that William relished reading Mel and Chrissie Cornish ghost stories of headless horsemen, of mermaids and spooky lights luring ships onto wrecks until the sisters lay in their beds at night rigid with fear, unable to sleep. There was one particular favourite of his about the ghost of a suicide buried at a crossroads, which could only be prevented from walking by a spear driven into the chest of the corpse. Little Mel would have nightmares about it, waking screaming, until their mother took the book away. She used to counter the girls' night fears with an old Cornish prayer she had been taught as a child – what was it? Something about being saved 'from ghoulies and ghosties and long-leggety beasties and things that go bump in the night,' ending with 'Good Lord, deliver us!'

Just then, there was a particularly loud creak from outside on the landing. Mel, lying in bed, tensed up, her sixth sense switched onto high alert.

It's just the wooden stairs settling, she soothed herself. As fear slowly receded, the ghouls of doubt and sorrow clamoured for attention instead, and waves of desolation washed over her. She cried a little, feeling as vulnerable as a child lost in the dark. Eventually, as she used to when tiny, she cuddled a pillow for comfort. When she slipped into fitful sleep, she could almost hear her mother's voice whispering, 'Everything will look better in daylight, darling.' She only hoped that without her mother there this mantra would still hold true.

As she slept, the house whispered its secrets.

I lay everything in the drawers like Jenna said except the books Mr Reagan gave me. Then I see the paper in the bottom of the bag. I smooth it out. No need to read it again, I could tell you every word by heart. And what it means. That I've lost everything before I even found it. And because of that I'm sent far from home to this bare attic room with its sight of the early-evening sky. Outside, the rooks whirl in dozens, nay, hundreds, chattering and arguing like fishwives on market-day. Look at them go! Off they swarm to the pine trees on the hill beyond.

A clatter on the stairs. 'Pearl?'

It's Jenna. Quickly I fold the paper, open the top drawer of the chest and shove it inside, just as she bursts into the room.

Chapter 2

The wind got up in the small hours of the night, howling down the chimney, playing chase through the trees, rattling the windows like some demented child-spirit. Mel awoke at three and lay tense and wakeful, hiding out like a small animal in its hole until, at first light, the gale quietened and she drifted into exhausted slumber.

When she opened her eyes next, the room was filled with sunlight and someone was banging on the front door. She sat up in a daze and looked at her watch. Ten past nine – she never slept this late in London. Throwing back the duvet, she reached for her dressing-gown, then, still befuddled with sleep, she stumbled downstairs.

She unlocked the front door and peeped out in time to see a tall, slim woman disappearing back up the track.

'Hello,' Mel croaked, and the woman swung round. Seeing Mel, she hurried back, her dark curly hair blowing about. She was huddled in a zip-up fleece, her arms folded tightly across her chest against the cold. One hand, Mel saw, clutched a car key. She opened the door wider.

'I'm sorry, I wake you up. I am Irina.' The woman was about Mel's age, 37, perhaps a couple of years younger, and Mel liked her instantly. Her eyes were black pools of sadness in her heart-shaped face, but when she smiled, her teeth showed very white in contrast to her olive skin and her face seemed to light up from within. Her voice was higher and clearer than it had seemed on the phone, with a lilt Mel couldn't quite place.

'Oh hi,' Mel replied. 'Don't worry, I needed to get up. Why don't you come in?' She stood back, holding the door, but Irina glanced at Mel's state of undress, must have detected the bat-squeak of uncertainty in her voice and shook her head.

'No, I have my daughter in the car. I only came to see that you'd got here safely. I'm sorry that I wasn't here last night. I had to collect Lana from a friend's house, you see. Is everything all right? You had a bad journey?'

Mel explained about getting lost and how she hadn't been able to phone ahead. 'It was brilliant, you leaving the food in the fridge,' she said. 'I'd have starved otherwise.'

'It was no problem. I don't know what else you need, but there is a good shop in the village,' Irina told her. 'One of the ladies sells food she has cooked herself. Though if you want the big supermarket you must go to Penzance.'

'How far is the village? I'm not sure I can face driving today, especially anywhere that means going back the way I came.'

Irina smiled and pointed along the track. 'It's maybe five, six minutes' walk down the hill. Not far.' She hunched her shoulders and shivered. 'Goodness, this wind.'

Mel took a breath of the salty air. 'It's lovely,' she said. 'So fresh after London.'

'Where do you live in London? I used to live in Wandsworth,' Irina said.

'I live in South London too – near Clapham South tube station. How long were you there?' Mel asked, wondering again about Irina's origins but feeling it was too early in their acquaintance to ask.

'A year, it must be,' Irina said, a shadow crossing her face. 'Here I have been for two.'

Mel opened her mouth to ask where before Wandsworth, but Irina had already moved on.

'Please call me if you need help,' she said. 'I live at the cove – the house with the yellow door. It's called Morwenna. You're welcome to knock on the door if you need anything, or just to have coffee. And of course you have my telephone number.'

'Yes, yes, I do. Thanks. That's really kind.'

Mel watched Irina hurry back up to the road to where she could just glimpse the mud-splashed rear of a red car. A moment later the engine spluttered into life, roared and the car moved away. Patrick had said Irina looked after Merryn Hall, she remembered as she closed the door, shivering. What was she – a housekeeper, perhaps? But surely Patrick wasn't grand enough to have a housekeeper – not from what Chrissie said about him and not if he didn't live here. A cleaner then. Yet that didn't sound right. Irina hardly matched the stereotype of a country cleaner – apple-cheeked and middle-aged with a rural accent. There was something intriguing, exotic about Irina. She had a face full of character, one Mel would have liked to draw. Perhaps this holiday would be a good opportunity to take up painting again. Except, she reminded herself sternly, as she shuffled through to the bathroom, it wasn't a holiday and she should be concentrating on writing about other artists, not becoming one herself. Her mother had been right, though. She definitely felt more cheerful this morning.

It really was the most perfect weather to explore. Mel felt almost jittery with excitement as she stepped out half an hour later, dressed in clean jeans, low-heeled ankle boots and a short russet needlecord jacket. Last night's demented wind spirit was only impish now, shunting puffs of cloud across a sky as blue as a sailor's trousers. Mel closed her eyes, welcoming the warm sun on her face. When she opened them, she was dazzled for a moment, before her surroundings swam once more into focus. She almost gasped.

The grounds of Merryn Hall on every side were a wilderness. She squinted up through the bright light towards the Hall where, glimpsed through sycamore and ash trees, the stone walls were half-covered with climbing plants – wisteria, ivy and Virginia creeper. Vague shreds of memory teased at her consciousness. Long ago when they were children, she and William and Chrissie had played in a wilderness like this – a wasteland near their home with a tumbledown building and *Danger! Keep Out* signs on the broken-down fence. Their mother would have been furious had she found out.

Mel swung round and surveyed the view downhill from her cottage. High banks of tangled jungle rolled out before her, swathed with creeper, bramble and bracken. Like living dustsheets, she mused, through which pushed up the shapes of trees, shrubs and who knew what, like hulks of furniture in a disused room.

In the wasteground where they'd played as children stood an electric pylon. The current had pulsed and sung around them as they played hide-and-seek or made dens in the undergrowth. Once, she remembered, William started to climb the pylon, merely laughing at Chrissie's warnings.

'Get down – you'll die, you'll die!' Chrissie had screamed as the electricity hummed hypnotically all around them, while Mel, at six years old not truly understanding the danger, shared William's excitement, silently urging him to climb higher and higher. Fortunately, a barrier of barbed wire had stopped him.

Now Mel gazed around with wonder at the windblown gardens of Merryn Hall. Last night's first impressions returned. There was no fizzing electric energy here but there was something – mystery, desolation, a sense of watchfulness. In daylight this place didn't feel like the set for Dracula or the Beast's castle, more like Sleeping Beauty's palace, cut off from the world by an evil spell, briars grown up everywhere.

She smiled to herself. A Sleeping Beauty she could cope with. Vampires belonged elsewhere. She would just hope that there wasn't a Beast. And pushing her bag further up her shoulder, she walked up the track to the lane.

Merryn Hall lay nestled in the side of a wooded valley and Mel followed the narrow road as it bucked and twisted downhill through a tunnel of lichen-iced trees. Where the wall bounding the grounds of the house ended came a stone bridge over a stream rushing with water from the recent rain, and then the lane turned sharp left to run above the stream downhill along the spine of the valley towards the sea. This cool green world of tangled trees and water might have been the setting for a painting Mel loved, *Lamorna Birch and his Daughters* by Laura Knight, one of the young girls perched on a branch, the other in the arms of her artist father.

As she walked, Mel tried to view the route as the artists she was studying must have seen it, wondering how much had changed. The valley, she had read in a local history, hadn't been quite so wooded back then. She passed houses and tracks leading up to other properties on the hillside, then a sign to a hotel and, on the left, a pub – the Wink – where, she remembered, Alfred Munnings had stayed. Some of the houses must have been there a hundred years ago, but here and there were more modern buildings.

Eventually, the trees ended and soon she came to a junction and a long granite house with a Post Office sign on the left, set back slightly from the main road, its frontage lined with post-card racks and buckets of fresh flowers, while toy windmills clattered gently in the breeze.

The food can wait, she told herself, her eyes drawn towards the next bend in the lane. She couldn't see the sea yet, but she imagined she could hear it. As thrilled as a child, she almost ran.

Today the water was a deep clear green, with fleeting patches of brown shadow from the fast-scudding clouds, the ripples sparkling in the breeze. Scraping back her wind-whipped hair, Mel walked out onto the quay and leaned over the battered parapet to watch the waves dash against the boulders beneath, then looked out across the water to where a fishing trawler crawled across the horizon. The salt wind and the spray on her face filled her senses.

After a moment she turned to look back at the cove, aware that she would quickly lose the impartial eye of the observer, the outsider. The tide was out, leaving a solitary shabby fishing boat marooned on the great round rocks that edged the sand. Behind, on the harbour wall, lay a pile of nets and lobster pots, which a man in a reflective coat was piling with patient movements into the back of a small van.

A broken arc of grey buildings huddled together below a quarry-scarred cliff. Which was Irina's house? One of the terrace to the right, she imagined. Mel scanned the buildings for a yellow door, settling for a golden cream on the far side.

Lamorna Cove. Familiar from the oils and watercolours of the artists she had studied, its beauty and character struck Mel with the freshness that lured painters to the area one hundred years ago. The view had changed – that modern house with its picture windows wouldn't have graced the hillside back then, and the once stony road had been tarmacked, but the rocky curve of the beach, the strip of muddy sand to her right, now beginning to disappear under the turning tide, the rugged headland, boulders protruding through its motheaten blanket of green, could have come straight out of one of Laura Knight's breathtakingly beautiful landscapes.

After a few minutes she made her way over the rocks to the sand, pulled off her boots and socks, rolled up her jeans and padded across the wet sand. The water was so cold it hurt, the familiar sensation startling.

When they were children, it had been a race between her and Chrissie and William to change into their costumes and run down to the sea first. Usually it was Will who won, but when Chrissie learned to sneak her bikini on instead of her underwear in the morning, she just had to throw off her shorts and T-shirt and rush for the waves. Mel, the youngest, was always last, shouting with helpless rage as she struggled with her clothes, their mother soothing, uselessly begging her elder children to wait for the youngest.

Now, Mel thought as she rescued a little starfish that was lying upside down on the sand, curling its arms in the air, William was still winning, the typical high-achieving eldest child, as a consultant surgeon in the same hospital where their father had worked. Chrissie, however, had never been the confused sibling-in-the-middle. Lucky Chrissie was always unfazed by life and never yearned for the moon. Instead it was baby Mel, who still felt left behind.

Hearing voices close by, she looked up. Two youngish men, wearing wetsuits and clutching oxygen cylinders and flippers, were clambering over the rocks towards her. One was burly,

27

with the well-developed muscles of a weightlifter; the other, lean, more athletic, with cropped black hair like the pelt of a water mammal. As they stopped at the water's edge to put on their equipment, looking for all the world like a couple of otters on hind legs, the slender man lifted his mask, smiled and said hello.

'What are you going to see out there?' Mel called against the wind.

'Mostly fish, I expect. A wreck if we're lucky,' he called back, adjusting the straps of his oxygen cylinder. 'No treasure though, I'm afraid.'

She watched as they waded into the waves, their groans at the cold carrying clearly across the water. Then they sank below the surface leaving only a trail of bubbles.

It was a warm walk back up the hill and a relief to duck under the low doorway into the shop. Inside was small, gloomy, crowded with people buying newspapers, groceries and postcards. A wiry woman in her sixties held court from a stool behind the till. Another, who though well-rounded, could only be her sister, sat behind the glass of the Post Office counter.

Mel picked up a plastic shopping basket and pottered, amused by the sisters' shouted exchanges.

'Mary, my dear,' called the woman on the till. 'Ginger. Have we got any ginger? Mary. GIN-GER.'

Mary, counting coins in the Post Office, shook her head vigorously without looking up from her task.

'No, we don't have any, my duck,' said the wiry woman to her customer. 'Mary,' she shouted again, 'put GIN-GER on the list, will you?'

Mel selected a white bloomer loaf, ham, salad, a cauliflower, some carrots, fruit and a bottle of wine. The thought of cooking for herself, as ever, failed to excite. Here with plenty of fresh local food, she should make more of an effort to eat properly, but she only liked cooking if it was for other people.

`A teenage boy, with the same round face and wide-set eyes as the two sisters, put down his price gun in response to Mel's enquiry and silently led her to a freezer where rows of home-cooked meals in foil dishes were stacked up – Beef Stroganoff, lasagne, fish pie . . . not cheap, but far healthier and more enticing than some of the branded versions. She chose a couple, pulled a newspaper from the rack and joined the queue to pay. As she waited she added a couple of postcards to the basket. David Bell would be wondering how she was getting on, and Chrissie's kids would love the card with the donkey.

Then, weighed down by two heavy carrier bags, she climbed back up the hill.

At the last small stone cottage before the bridge, a grizzled old man weeding in the front garden straightened to rest his back and scrutinised her with faded blue eyes. She smiled nervously and he nodded once in acknowledgement but his face communicated nothing. She walked on, aware of his gaze burning into her back until she reached the bridge, yet when she looked back it was to see him absorbed once more in his task.

After lunch, lassitude set in. She glanced out of the window. The sky was clouding over once more. Perhaps she should explore the grounds before the rain came. Or should she stay in to unpack her clothes. Or try out her laptop connection on the telephone line, organise a work space, or even begin writing . . . but somehow she couldn't summon the energy for anything.

Maybe I'm just tired after the journey, she told herself. Tired and fed up. In her London flat, after Jake neatly packed his possessions in boxes and left, pulling himself up roots and all like a plant ready for a bigger pot, laundry piled up, dirty crockery soaked in the sink . . . she had no energy for looking after herself.

Three weeks after he left, her friend Aimee, who had split up with her man, Mark, a few months before, dropped round unexpectedly. She surveyed the mess and gave Mel a sympathetic hug. 'Never mind, I'll give you a hand. It took me ages to feel like doing anything ever again.' She tossed her small cropped head, 'Now I appreciate having the place to myself. Mark was *so* untidy. I still miss him, though . . .' she ended sadly.

As Mel sat in the kitchen of the Gardener's Cottage, she worked out that it would be two months next Thursday since Jake left. When had it all started to go wrong? It was all too recent to view clearly.

She had met Jake when he had joined the college staff four years before. He had switched careers after years as a journalist, he told her at a drinks party. With two published collections of poetry behind him he was now working on a novel. Mel knew the college regarded it as something of a coup to have persuaded him to enter academia.

'I'm hoping this job will give me more time and focus to write,' he said in his gravelly voice, frowning. He was a tallish man who held himself well; although he was muscular, there was a sense of lightness about him. But Mel wasn't fooled by his laid-back pose. His black eyes flared with intensity as he spoke about his work and he had a nervous habit of ruffling his cropped blond hair and beard that betrayed a coiled-up energy.

'You'll have to learn to say no then,' Mel said, laughing, relaxed and flirtatious after her second glass of red wine. 'It's all too easy to find yourself bogged down with meetings and extra tasks. Never mind all the marking and the forms. But let me know if I can help at all. With how things work in this place, I mean.' Their eyes met and Mel recognised the spark of his interest even then.

And so Jake took to tapping on her door whenever he needed advice – whether with completing one of the endless forms or dealing with a problem student. Both of them tended to work late, long after colleagues with marriages and families had left for the day. He often found her reading or marking essays, curled up on the tiny sofa she'd bought in a junk shop, its worn leather artfully disguised by an Indian throw, and would drop elegantly into the easy chair opposite or pace the little office and chatter amusingly about their colleagues, or challenge her, deliberately provocative, about her scathing views on conceptual art or tease her for getting too worked up in argument ('You're too serious,' he goaded her). Sometimes she made a pot of tea, sometimes he opened a bottle of wine. She learned that he was recently divorced and had two young daughters whom he saw only at weekends.

And so came the day, soon after Christmas, when Jake slid beside Mel on the little sofa, and Mel's heart raced and her voice faltered as he mesmerised her with his caressing flow of words, staring into her eyes, his arm moving across the back of the seat, almost accidentally brushing her shoulder, coiling her hair with his fingers. Eventually she felt herself falling towards him to be kissed deeply, passionately, until she was molten. Only when the cleaner marched in without knocking to empty the bin did they draw back from one another, breathless, giggling.

Dinner at a Thai restaurant later that evening was merely a prelude to a night together. Mel hardly noticed what she was eating.

At one point she couldn't help asking, half not wanting to know, 'Your marriage. What . . . went wrong?'

He shrugged. 'Everything changed with Helen after having

the kids,' he said. 'We both got stressed out, never went out by ourselves, hardly had any time together. Freya – she's the little one – cute as a button, but a real pain – she never slept. And Helen got so wrapped up in them, talked in baby language all the time. It got like she only spoke to me when she wanted me to do something – change a nappy or cook fish fingers. We became strangers.'

'That's so sad,' Mel said, squeezing the hand that held hers.

At the time, Mel only saw his point of view. Looking back later, too late, she realised she should have taken warning from this conversation, but at the time she was too besotted with this gorgeous, charismatic man to worry about anything except the moment. And the moment was delicious.

They quickly became 'Jake and Mel', hardly out of one another's company, and it wasn't long before Mel's Spanish neighbour Cara in the flat above became used to bumping into him in the lobby on her way out to work. He kept on his purpose-built apartment in Kennington, though, which he'd bought after he had separated from Helen. Mel tentatively suggested he let it out and move in with her, but he was reluctant.

'I must have somewhere to write,' he said. 'And I need my books to be in one place.'

But as time passed, he set himself up in Mel's second bedroom, across the hall from the little box room she called her study, and many of his books and a couple of pictures made the trip across South London. In the early days, if it was his turn to have Anna and Freya, he would go back to stay in Kennington, but as their mother came to terms with the idea that Mel was a regular fixture, the little girls would sometimes visit the Clapham flat, regarding camping at Daddy's girlfriend's as great fun.

After a year and a half of the rhythms of this peripatetic lifestyle, Mel began to hint more strongly that they sell their respective properties and buy a house together. She and Jake loved one another, they would find a place with enough bedrooms, so that Anna and Freya could stay and for that hazy point in the distant future when, she dreamed, she and Jake would marry and have children themselves.

But Jake didn't seem so sure. He loved her, he insisted, and he wanted to be with her always, but it was too soon after his divorce to make such a commitment. And it was certainly too early to talk about babies. Maybe when his novel was finished they could start looking at places. He felt he was living in limbo at the moment, unable to make big decisions.

The novel was not going quite as well as Jake hoped. Two years after he met Mel, he completed it and sent it off to Sophie, his literary agent, with high hopes. Sophie said the book wasn't yet in a state for her to feel confident about sending it to publishers. It was too . . . cerebral, too much about ideas and not enough about people and emotions. Would he consider recasting it? After recovering from this blow, Jake locked himself up at weekends and holidays for six months to wrestle with his masterpiece. It consumed his attention. If he wasn't actually writing then he was distant, bearish, and Mel felt sidelined. Suffering for your art was one thing. Suffering for someone else's was another altogether.

Boiling point was reached one Saturday when Helen dropped off Anna and Freya at Mel's flat, expecting Jake to be there to receive them, and there was only Mel. Helen couldn't disguise her annoyance.

'So where is he then?' she asked, retwisting a pink scrunchy onto her messy blonde ponytail, her pretty urchin's face looking more than usually harassed.

'Still wrapped in his creative cocoon in Kennington, I imagine,' Mel said wearily. 'He'll have forgotten about us.'

Helen said nothing, but she nodded slowly and gave Mel such a look of knowing pity, it said more than could a thousand words. That evening, Mel and Jake had their first real row.

'You're never here, you take me for granted,' Mel almost shouted. His answer was to imprison her in his arms and take her to bed.

'Now am I here?' he growled into her damp hair an hour later as they lay hot and exhausted.

Mel shook herself out of her reverie. The one thing she had promised she wouldn't do coming to Cornwall was brood. She would engross herself in her work, learn to be comfortable with her own company again away from the thousand and one interruptions of her teaching job and having to see *him* every day. She got up from the kitchen table, stashed the remaining food in the fridge, in sharp angry movements, and sauntered outside.

The wind had calmed but the sky was still heavy with the threat of rain, tufts of cloud like smoke drifting above the treetops. It was as though the abandoned garden was waiting for something . . .

She strolled across the grass, wondering idly who mowed this lawn. Surely not Patrick? She bent and plucked at a long trail of ivy that was clawing its way across the cropped grass. Several great lengths of it uncoiled from the jungle and she was astonished in a moment to find her arms full of wet weed. She stepped back, yanking at it impatiently and a whole wadge came away, a few strands snapping loudly and a musty stink of sap filling the air. The rest stuck fast, tangled up with the brambles and bindweed. She tossed the leaves back into the ocean of greenery. What was the point? Her feeble efforts seemed to make no difference.

Glancing down, she saw that she had in fact ripped a tear in the shroud of weed. There was a flash of purple in the under-growth, like blood welling in a new wound. She bent down to look. Violets! And a glimpse of creamy yellow proved to be a clump of primroses. Excitement coursed through her.

She crouched down and pulled impatiently at the ivy, trying to see what other treasures its smothering blanket might hide. It came away in long hanks revealing more patches of purple and cream struggling to breathe. What she really needed, of course, was some gardening tools. Perhaps there would be something in one of the outbuildings up near the main house?

Behind the cottage she found a narrow gritty path forging its way up the terraces in just that direction. She zig-zagged through the brambles round the back of the house, past the ruined arch of a crumbling brick wall, until she came to the stable block, set parallel to the front of the house on a small cobbled courtyard. Two of the doors were padlocked, but the third had only a rusty latch that yielded unwillingly, viciously pinching her fingers. Nursing her bruised hand, she heaved open the door with the other and found herself inside a large shed smelling of dust and creosote. Piles of junk lay everywhere on the cobbled floor. Some seemed welded to the ground by cobwebs, looked as though it had not moved for decades – an old ground roller, a rusted mowing machine of unknown vin-tage, several spades and hoes and a small weeding fork that was not too badly corroded. This she seized, coughing, batting at the skeins of dust, together with a stout pair of gloves that looked as though they had recently been dropped down on the elderly trestle table, moulded as though invisible hands were still inside. Her final trophy was a little billhook. Despite flecks of rust, the scythe gleamed keenly. Then, leaning against the door to shut it, Mel returned with her swag to the scene of her excavations and knelt down to work again, slashing at the long grass, digging up the weeds around the flowers, wishing all the while that she had a good pair of secateurs to take to the thick thorny stems of the brambles.

Before long she had cleared a small patch of flowerbed where violets, narcissi and primroses at last had light and air. How long ago had they been planted – or could they have seeded themselves?

It was good to be absorbed in physical work. The scent of flowers, the pungent sap, the smell of the earth were exhilarating. Out here, with new life thrusting through everywhere she looked, it was impossible to dwell on gloomy thoughts. Instead, Mel found herself making plans.

She must take herself in hand or she would waste her precious time here. She would give herself the rest of the day off, enjoy the garden, finish unpacking, eat one of the frozen home-made meals for supper with a glass of wine – but only one – and go to bed early. Tomorrow she would start work on her book.

An hour passed and another. She stood up, stiffly, and stretched her aching limbs, noticing to her astonishment that she had cleared a six-foot width of flowerbed. I've made a difference, she told herself, filled with pleasure as she surveyed the flowers, seeing pale new shoots thrusting their way out of the chestnut-coloured earth. She looked up as a pair of wood pigeons flapped their wings lustily, crashing through the foliage above. Huge and plump, these were entirely different creatures to their scraggy London cousins. High in the sky against the clouds, a bird of prey was coasting on the wind currents and it was as though Mel's heart soared with it, yearning for something she didn't yet know.

As the afternoon grew cooler, she trudged back and forth with forkfuls of weeds, adding them to a heap on a patch of wasteground some way behind the cottage. She was about to pick up the tools when a small ginger cat cautiously made its way round the side of the house. It stopped dead when it saw Mel, crouched tense, not sure whether to run.

Mel stood perfectly still and the cat, encouraged, tiptoed over to the flowerbed, delicately touching a narcissus flower with the tip of its pink nose, then batting it gently with a velvet paw.

Mel made cajoling noises, holding out her hand. The cat sat down and stared at her for a moment, then started to lick its white bib with long languorous movements, its peridot green eyes hardly leaving her face. After a while it desisted and, ignoring Mel, sashayed off down the track towards the road, its tail high. Mel wondered who it belonged to or whether, like herself, it was a stray.

Inside the house she made some tea and ran a bath – whatever else was Victorian about the cottage, thankfully the central-heating boiler and the plumbing were modern. Climbing into the hot water was ecstasy.

The only trouble with baths, she thought shivering, as she yanked at the plug chain with her toes twenty minutes later, was that they tempted you to daydream. All her plans for being positive had trickled away. For once again, her mind had turned to Jake, going over and over the end of their affair.

It was while she was living in a limbo with Jake, hoping desperately that once he finished the second draft of his book he would return to his usual charming self, that tragedy struck. Her mother was discovered to have a rampant form of cancer that had spread to her pancreas.

Whilst Mel, Chrissie and sometimes William between them accompanied their mother on a depressing round of hospital appointments and debilitating treatments, finally finding a place for her in a hospice near home, it was a time of enormous closeness for the family. But it was as though Jake were outside looking in.

37

He was supportive, yes, in the sense that he comforted Mel, showing her immense kindness, but Mel felt he never truly entered her distress. She could see the terror in his eyes on the rare occasions he came to visit the ravaged figure of her mother in the hospice. With Chrissie's husband, Rob, on the other hand, Chrissie's grief was his also. Once, after a particularly harrowing visit when her mother was clearly in a lot of pain, Mel caught Rob weeping in the hospice reception area. She was deeply touched by his sorrow.

'Have we offended Jake in some way?' Chrissie remarked another time when Jake dropped Mel off at the hospice and drove off with a wave. 'Why doesn't he come in?'

'He wants to visit a bookshop,' said Mel, glancing at her sister as they walked down the hospice corridor, wary of her sharp tone. Today, she saw, Chrissie's eyes were red-rimmed and she hadn't bothered with her usual meticulous make-up.

'I mean,' Chrissie said, 'surely he should be here, supporting you.' *Like Rob does*, being the unspoken implication. 'He's quite, well, self-sufficient, isn't he?'

'You don't understand.' Mel snapped back. Chrissie had struck a tender spot. 'He feels awkward coming, that's all. He doesn't know Mum very well, not like Rob. And he doesn't like hospitals – ever since his little sister nearly died of meningitis when he was ten.'

They had reached their mother's ward, so Chrissie merely raised her irritatingly knowing eyebrows in reply.

Maureen Pentreath drifted away in drug-induced sleep on a beautiful day in early May. On the way to the crematorium the hearse passed along an avenue of cherry trees. The blossom fell soft as snow.

In the months after her mother's death, Mel observed Jake

and felt in her heart of hearts that Chrissie had a point. Jake didn't need to rely on anybody else. He loved her, of that she was sure. He had loved his wife, but had allowed her to grow away from him. He loved his children – but sometimes it seemed he could live without them, so absorbed was he in his writing.

'I wonder whether our children would look like Anna and Freya,' she said tentatively one Sunday evening.

He had laughed, uncertainly. 'Not if they were boys. Anyway, Mel, that's the last thing we need at the moment. A baby really would push us over the edge.'

'What do you mean?' she said.

'The disruption. When would I work? When would you work, come to that. I couldn't face all that again for a while.'

'But not never?'

'Not at the moment, is all I'm saying.'

She had felt slightly mollified, but feelings of distress began to build inside her. She was already vulnerable, grieving as she was for her mother, and one of the focuses of her grief, as she confessed to Aimee, was that her mother wouldn't be there when Mel had children of her own. Maureen had not lived to see her younger daughter's children and they would never know their grandmother. The thought was painful to bear.

Early in November, Jake announced that he had finished his book. This time, his agent, whilst still encouraging, sounded impatient. 'It's much better than it was,' she told him on the phone. 'A really fascinating story. But there's something about the tone that still isn't right. And your characters need to be more emotionally engaging.'

'What the hell does that mean?' shouted Jake, after he had

finished the call. 'Emotionally engaging? It's a literary novel we're talking about, not some Mills and Boon romance. What does she know anyway, silly cow.'

'Jake! Why don't you find another agent if you've gone off Sophie,' Mel said. Jake had given her the script to read at the same time as his agent. Privately she was in agreement with Sophie but she certainly wasn't going to say that to Jake. The prose style was brilliant, inventive, playful, the plot ingenious. But was it a little in love with itself? And were his characters – the novel was a satire about the contemporary arts scene – merely talking heads, vehicles for his opinions?

'No,' he said, slamming his fist against the wall. 'It's the best agency for me. She can damn well just send it out to publishers. Then we'll see who's right.'

In the event, however, Sophie and Mel proved to be right. All the publishers Sophie submitted it to sent fulsomely polite rejections. A printed set of them from Sophie's over-assiduous assistant landed on the mat in Kennington amongst the Christmas cards. *But I would be glad to see anything else that Jake Friedland writes in the future*, was a common theme.

And just to make everything worse, it was then the letter arrived for Mel from Grosvenor Press saying that they had read an article she had written for the *Journal of Art History* and inviting her to submit a proposal for a book for their prestigious series about British painters. Mel, of course, was delighted to comply.

Jake entered a deep, black depression.

It was the week before Christmas but Mel hadn't the heart to plan much. This Christmas would be the first without her mother. Would it be forever a season of sadness? She was dreading the day itself, to be spent at her sister's house with William's family invited as well. Jake was taking Anna and Freya home to his parents and frankly, she was relieved.

The week after Christmas, however, she could take the atmosphere no longer.

'Jake, you've got to cheer up,' she said one evening as he slouched morosely around her kitchen after supper. He made no reply. She tried a different tack. 'I know you're disappointed. You've worked so hard.'

He turned and looked at her. His eyes glittered, opaque, unreadable.

'On the book, I mean,' she added, desperate now. It wasn't fair. Why should she put up with this moodiness day after day, week after week, deliberating about every word she said, watching her every move in case she accidentally annoyed him. Anything could make him snap at her these days. A flash of anger crazed through her. She snatched up a mug from the draining board. Its silly laughing pig design mocked her. In a sudden movement she smashed it down on the floor. The pieces flew up around them.

'Mel!' They stared at one another in mutual shock. Jake put his finger to his cheek and touched blood.

'Sorry,' she shouted. 'Sorry, but I can't stand it. It's not fair, what you're doing. I'm only trying to help. I can't live like this any longer.'

He came and put his arms round her and hugged her tight. 'I'm sorry, I'm sorry,' he mumbled into her hair. 'I'm being a bear, aren't I?'

She pulled away and looked up at him. 'I love you, but I need to know,' she said, 'if we have a future together. I hate this hanging on, not knowing. And children. I would like to have a baby, Jake, you know that. With you. I don't want to leave trying until it's too late.'

The expression of stubbornness that crossed Jake's face, the set look of his mouth, made her wish she had kept her mouth shut.

For a month Jake made an effort to be more cheerful, but Mel knew that his distant politeness hid unfathomable depths of misery. Somehow their life together carried on as it had done for the last few years, but it was as though they were going through the motions in their relationship. Then one night Jake just didn't come back after a party at his old newspaper offices.

She knew at once what had happened and confronted him.

'It didn't mean anything. She's not important, I'll never see her again,' he said, but they both knew what it meant. He had taken an axe to their relationship because neither of them could otherwise make the break.

Two days later, he piled his possessions in the back of his car, kissed her with such intensity it took all her will not to plead with him to stay, and went back to Kennington and, she imagined, the first chapter of a new novel.

The next hardest thing was visiting Anna and Freya at their home to explain. She could still see them, she insisted, but although they hugged one another and made promises, all three of them knew it would never be quite the same. And for the second time in a year, Mel went into mourning.

I must write to them sometime, Anna and Freya, Mel thought that evening as she waited for the shop lasagne to heat up in the oven. She ate it at the kitchen table with a novel propped up in front of her. Later, she tried to watch a crime drama on television but, tired of the interminable commercial breaks, switched it off. She sat, curled up in an armchair, wondering what to do next. Ring Chrissie, she decided, reaching out for the phone.

'It's weird,' she told her sister in answer to the questions Chrissie fired off. 'I'd forgotten how dark it gets in the country. It's really cut off. And this place, it's quite spooky. Did Patrick tell you anything about it?'

'Not really,' said Chrissie. 'His family are from Cornwall, like Mum and Dad. The great-uncle left the house to Patrick when he died last year. Patrick says he doesn't know what to do with it, whether to sell it or keep it and move down there.'

'Move? What did you say he did for a living?'

'He runs some Internet business with a friend. Is he down there yet? He goes a lot at weekends, he said.'

'No. At least, I haven't seen him. What's he look like, anyway?'

'Mmm . . . tallish, dark reddish hair. Friendly but, I don't know, doesn't say a lot about himself. Not a city type, more of a jeans and sweaters man, if you know what I mean.'

'What, with reindeer on like Mark Darcy in *Bridget Jones*? Sounds okay.'

'Now, Mel, don't go getting ideas. He's got a girlfriend and I think it's serious.'

'I only meant it as a joke.' Spotting Mel's ideal man was a game of Chrissie's Mel always refused to play. Because Chrissie was cosily married with children she wanted Mel to be happy in that way, too. At the same time, interestingly, Chrissie hadn't seemed all that regretful when Mel broke up with Jake.

Now Mel changed the subject. 'So it's Portugal tomorrow?'

'Tuesday, for two weeks. I can't wait. Oh, I've emailed you our contact numbers.'

'Thanks. Well, have a fantastic time. Bring me another piece of that pretty pottery.'

After Mel had put down the receiver, she sat for a moment, wondering about Patrick. What would he do, living down here in the back of beyond? She hoped, when he arrived, that he wouldn't be the kind of landlord who hung around, interfering. She might be lonely, but she needed the time to work.

She forced herself to plug in her laptop to check she could get a connection. Everything worked beautifully. No point in looking at her college webmail, it would only disturb her, seeing life go on without her. She logged on to her personal email. There was just the promised message from Chrissie and one headed HI FROM THE BIG SMOKE from her friend Aimee, who had been away on a school trip when Mel left.

Hope you've got there safely and that the place is OK. What's it like and are there chocolate croissants within fifty miles? Sorry I didn't see you before you left but we didn't get back from Paris until late Thursday. It went all right – none of the little darlings fell off the Eiffel Tower or into the Seine, anyway. There was only one really bad moment. A little tearaway called Callum Mitchell managed to open a bottle of wine in his dormitory on the last night. Fortunately we confiscated it before too much harm was done, but I had to have a quiet word with his dad. Funny how parents never quite believe it when you tell them that their precious kids have misbehaved. I have to say it was odd visiting the sights with a rabble of fourteen-year-olds when the last time it was just me and Mark. Ho, hum, mustn't dwell on the past. Let me know how you are.

Hi, Aimee, Mel wrote back. *A journey from hell, but I got here. Lamorna is very beautiful, but oh so remote, and no sign of my landlord yet. I think it could get very lonely here, especially in the evenings, but I'll cope. It's a more manageable sort of loneliness than in London where you feel miserable because you're convinced that everyone else around you is having a better time than you are. Here there's no one and nothing except cows for miles.*

Glad Paris went well – I think you're an absolute angel to give up your holidays for the kids and hope the next time you go it will be with someone special – even if it's only me!

Much love, Mel.

She closed the laptop and looked at the clock. Half-past nine. What should she do now? Why was it that lack of deadlines and appointments could sap your energy so?

She sighed and stood up, thinking she should finish unpacking, then noticed that one of the watercolours on the wall was askew. She went over to straighten it. It was one of the roses. She stared at it, seeing what she had missed before, that there was a small honey bee visiting one of the blooms. The artist had carefully reproduced the fine sticky hairs that picked up pollen and the veined gauzy wings.

Yawning, she went out into the hall and dragged the remaining holdall upstairs, where she turned on her radio to ward off the darkness and the ringing silence.

He found me in the garden. Frightened the life out of me, though I have a right to be here. I was doing no one any harm and it's my time off to do with as I please. I tried to shield the paper from him, but he laughed and threw himself down beside me. 'Show!' he commanded, and for certain he is a charming one, for I dropped my hand. He took the paper and gazed for a long time at the flower I had drawn. It was of a rose, white and heavy, at that lovely last moment of fullness before it turns and the petals dull and go brown. He looked up at the bush, searching for the flower. 'It's good,' he said after a moment, 'but where is the bee? You've forgotten the bee!' I laughed, and realised then that I must have been holding my breath, because laughter was such a relief. I looked and, yes, there was a honey bee climbing over my rose, burrowing into the yellow heart. 'Really, though, it's good,' he repeated, returning the drawing to me and jumping to his feet. This was the first time he has spoken to me alone, and I was so overcome I could not say

a word, only watch him walk away with that light step of his. But I have painted in the little bee, and whenever I look upon it, I will think of him.

Chapter 3

April 1912

'Ee mustn't mind Cook,' plump Jenna puffed as they climbed the back stairs. 'She's in a paddy 'cos there's ten for dinner tonight and the missus do ask her to make some fancy mess with the lobsters. Ee best be keeping out of her way. Oh!' She stopped and clapped a dimpled hand to her mouth, though her eyes twinkled with mischief. 'Sorry, I forget. Cook's your aunt, ent she?'

Pearl, dragging her luggage up behind, looked up and smiled at the mock-stricken face above. This had to be a test. She was torn between the knowledge that her future wellbeing in this household might rest on keeping on Aunt Dolly's good side and the desire to be liked by this cheerful young woman, who must be about her own age, eighteen. But tact had always been a well-oiled part of Pearl's armoury. 'She's not really my aunt, I just call her that.' She didn't bother explaining that her relationship with Dolly, her stepmother Adeline's sister-in-law, was so tenuous that, in fact, she had only met her 'aunt' two or three times, on rare occasions when they had come across one another in Penzance on market-day. Even then, Dolly's attention had been on Adeline; she had until now taken little notice of Pearl.

Pearl Treglown had learned early to keep her thoughts to herself. No one could see into her mind and tell her not to be so saucy. Which is what would usually happen if Pearl stopped work to wonder at the shiny scales of the mackerel she was gutting or asked too many questions about one or other of the regulars at the inn that her stepmother couldn't – or more likely wouldn't – answer. Yet in the last month, Pearl had been delivered answers enough to make her head fair spin – and to questions she had never dared to ask before in all her eighteen years. Such as who her true parents were and why Adeline Treglown (whose husband, Cook's brother, had died several years before Pearl was even born) had raised her. And whether she would have to spend the rest of her life drawing jugs of ale and dodging the advances of sweaty sailors in the smoky saloon bar of the Blue Anchor when she had dreams and ambitions far beyond the fish-stinking quays of Newlyn Harbour.

She had discovered the answer to this last question the hard way today, as, after a rough hug and a warning to 'behave yourself' from Adeline, whey-faced and thin from her illness, she had allowed Mr Boase, the weatherbeaten Head Gardener from Merryn Hall, to help her into the back of his trap. There she sat clutching a parcel of books and a shabby holdall containing the rest of her worldly goods, wedged in by several empty baskets and a large slatted crate from Penzance market in which clattered several angry crabs and two lobsters. She was, Adeline had told her, to travel the few miles from Newlyn to Lamorna to be a housemaid at Merryn Hall, where Aunt Dolly was cook. Further than Pearl had ever travelled in her life before.

'That's your bed there, and your uniform,' Jenna said, recovering her breath from the climb. They were standing in a sparsely furnished attic room with a sloping ceiling and bare-plastered walls. The late-afternoon sun poured warmth through the single sash window. 'And you can put your clothes in them drawers there. I be getting back now before Cook kills me.' And she galumphed down the wooden staircase again.

Pearl gazed around her new bedroom. Her room at the inn had overlooked a dark back street and smelled of mildew, winter and summer. Here, at least, it was dry and bright. But, though Jenna had laid out a few things of her own on the other drawer chest – a hairbrush, an animal of some sort roughly carved in wood, a small sewing box – this room was impersonal, so clearly just a place to sleep. Suddenly, it was all too much for her. Here she was in a strange place, starting a new life, and with so many anxieties and regrets crowding in, all she wanted was to throw herself down on her rickety iron bedstead and weep.

Instead, she took a deep sobbing breath and set about unpacking, laying her few clothes in the drawers Jenna had shown her. Her elderly towel she draped on a wooden rail next to Jenna's, her wash bag and hairbrush she left on the chest of drawers. She wasn't sure what to do with the books so she stacked them on the floor together with the paintbox, paper and sketchbook Mr Reagan had given her, to think what to do about later.

There was clean water in the jug on the wash-stand. She tipped some into the bowl and splashed it on her face and neck, patting herself dry with her towel. Then she turned her attention to the uniform. A starched white apron, collar, cuffs and cap lay in a neat pile on the bed. She looked down at the rough brown dress she was wearing and brushed at some streaks of mud with a corner of the towel. That would have to do. There wasn't time to change now and, anyway, she only had one spare work dress.

As she fiddled with the new cuffs, something scraped at the

window, startling her. She glanced up in time to catch a flurry of white feathers as the bird wheeled away. Feeling suddenly stifled, she moved to the window and heaved open the sash, welcoming the sudden cool breeze on her flushed skin.

The attic looked out south-west down the gardens at the rear of the house, although from this angle she could only see the tops of trees, banks of rhododendron just coming into bud, a line of laurels and a rectangular pond with a curious little building to one end. The air smelled of earth and things growing, not the salt and fish she was used to, and apart from the chatter of birds there was silence. At home there had been always the sound of water lapping against the sea wall or the rush of the wind, the eternal cries of seagulls and the shouts of the fishermen.

This new place was miraculous to her: that people should live in such a huge house in the middle of a sort of park. She hadn't seen the main parts of the house yet, but the high-ceilinged kitchen was so light and clean compared with the hot grimy gloom of the Blue Anchor. Even the backstairs up which Jenna had led her were clear of dust, while the staircase of the pub had been cobwebbed and splashed with candle grease even before it had become blackened by the recent fire.

She turned away from the window to survey her new home once more and it was then she noticed the piece of newspaper dropped on the floor. She picked it up and unfolded it, sitting on the bed to read it for the twentieth time . . .

So absorbed was she in her thoughts, the sound of Jenna's boots clumping up the wooden stairs hardly registered. She jumped up, and as the maid burst panting into the room, she thrust the paper in the drawer and slammed it shut.

'Come on now, Cook wants ee something desperate. The missus is home, and Mr Charles, and they've brought company. You're to help Cook take in the tea.' Jenna screwed up her eyes shortsightedly as she looked around the room, noticing the new arrangements. She moved over to the pile of books by the bed. 'Wha's this then?' She picked the one off the top, a collection of poetry by Christina Rossetti, and opened it, a frowning look of concentration creeping across her face. Her lips moved silently, then she shook her head.

She can't read, it occurred to Pearl suddenly, and she gently took the book from Jenna's hand. The other girl's face had a closed look.

'Just something somebody gave me.' Pearl placed it back on the pile then started towards the door. Sharing a room with Jenna was not going to be straightforward. It would be comforting for Pearl to have a friend her own age in this new world where she found herself, but the wariness clouding the other girl's eyes threatened to sour the friendship before it began.

'Where's your cap?' Jenna asked now, brisk, and Pearl, flustered, snatched it from the wash-stand where she'd dropped it and, ducking to glimpse herself in a cracked oblong of mirror on the wall, pinned it to her head. Then without further ado the two girls hurried downstairs to the kitchen.

'But I heard it from Robert Kernow, they're laying off more workers at the mine.' The voice clearly audible through the slightly open door was a young man's, passionate.

'Oh, Charlie, no more politics now, please. Sidonie's bored, aren't you, my love?' a woman's voice protested, as Jago, the trainee footman, knocked smartly on the door and pushed it wide to admit Cook with her laden tray. Pearl, following behind with the silver Georgian teapot and hot-water jug, thanked her stars she was used to carrying heavy jars of cider.

Whilst not daring to stare round, Pearl absorbed with amazement that they were in a blue and white room like a palace with tall windows looking out onto sun-drenched gardens beyond. There was a proper carpet on the floor. When she found the courage to raise her eyes she saw there were three people sitting in the room. A young man in a tweed jacket occupied one of the fireside chairs. A plump matron in a gold tea dress sat in another, close to the white fireplace where flames leaped and crackled. The third, an elegant dark-haired woman, was perched imperiously on a small sofa, stroking a small whippet dog cuddled up beside her.

Pearl was too shy to do more than glance at her. Instead her eyes fixed suddenly upon an enormous painting above the mantelpiece, of a man in a wide hat sitting on a horse. It was only with great effort that she stopped her jaw hanging open. She'd seen a painting very like this before, in one of Mr Reagan's books that must have been lost in the fire. Despite what she had since learned, she still thought of him as 'Mr Reagan'.

The lady on the sofa spoke in the bossy voice Pearl recognised from a moment ago. 'Move the table over here, would you, Jago.' She must be the mistress then. Mr Boase, who had driven her here, had referred to her as Mrs Carey, but being of the strong and silent school had said little else useful. The mistress was still pretty, not young but not old either, fashionably dressed in a pale green gown. Her almond-shaped eyes slid across Cook putting down the tray to scrutinise Pearl, waiting behind.

'Oh good, you must be the new girl,' Mrs Carey said, not unkindly but matter-of-fact.

Pearl wasn't sure if an answer was required to this statement, but Cook decided for her. 'Yes, mum. But the gloves don't fit, that's why she's not wearing un.'

The round-faced matron Mrs Carey had called Sidonie, giggled, but Mrs Carey ignored her. She studied Pearl and nodded, apparently satisfied.

'Never mind, she'll do to wait at dinner. She's tall, that's good.'

Pearl felt her face burn. How dare they discuss her as though she were a dog or a horse. She was aware of the interested eyes of the young man, Charlie, upon her and stared hard at the gold lines bordering the carpet, wishing she and the silver vessels could drop right through it.

Later that night, sitting under the oil lamps with the other servants around the long kitchen table, she was too exhausted to do more than push around on her plate the fatty pieces of lamb left over from the dinner party.

'They ate all that seafood, eh, Mrs Roberts? You should have seen how the mistress's eyebrows shot up when the parson asked for another helping.' Jago – Pearl hadn't worked out whether this was his first name or his last – smiled broadly at Jenna and winked at Pearl across the table. He was sitting in his shirtsleeves, having changed out of the tailored jacket and cravat Mrs Carey insisted he wear at table. The mistress had tried to get him to wear proper livery on occasions such as these, Jenna had told Pearl as they laid the table earlier, but Jago had refused point blank. He was a thin young man with narrow shoulders and a slight limp, possibly in service because he was not strong enough for farming, guessed Pearl. He appeared to have varied duties in and about the house, cycling off to deliver letters to the Post Office, performing odd jobs, polishing the bright Newlyn copper pots, looking after the fires and generally waiting on the family. In the absence of a butler, he, like Pearl and Jenna, answered to Cook, whose caustic comments rarely dented his chirpy manner. Only Jenna's blank ignoring of his clumsy advances seemed to be able to do that.

'At least they left some of that trifle,' said Jenna, greedily licking the gravy from her spoon.

'That's for Family's lunch tomorrow,' said Cook sharply. 'There's the last of the stewed plum for us.' Jenna groaned. 'Then you can finish the pots in the scullery, sweep the floor and stoke the range. Pearl can help Jago clear up in the dining room then she had better go to bed.'

Through her veil of tiredness Pearl felt a flash of gratitude at this small act of kindness. After Pearl had helped serve tea, Cook had tossed her a large coarse apron and worked her in the kitchen without a moment to sit down. With ten to dinner it had been all hands to the pump, Cook barking orders like a sergeant major. Pearl had peeled vegetables, fetched supplies from the storeroom, washed up, cleaned floors, stirred pots and basted the joints. Dolly Roberts had praised her for none of her work, but neither had she chided her. She supposed this had to be good enough. What had been missing, though, had been any note of sympathy for Pearl, though Cook had asked after her sister-in-law and shook her head in a grim fashion when Pearl described how weak Adeline Treglown was growing.

As Jenna had shown Pearl how to arrange the place-settings with their complicated array of cutlery, the kitchenmaid didn't stop asking questions. Pearl described the bare facts of her situation. That she could remember no other home but the Blue Anchor, that she had been to the Board School in Newlyn but, despite being praised by her teacher, had been taken away when she was fourteen so she could work in the inn twelve hours a day or more, chambermaiding for any overnight guests, serving behind the bar, cooking, tidying up, cleaning, breaking up fights, all unpaid.

Then calamity had struck. Four weeks ago a fire, probably started in an unswept chimney, had destroyed most of the inn's upper storey and killed a guest – Arthur Reagan. Pearl couldn't talk about it without her voice shaking. Then, where they were staying with neighbours shortly afterwards, Mrs Treglown suffered a seizure and it became clear she was ill with some progressive disease.

'She wrote to Mrs Roberts,' Pearl told Jenna, 'asked her to get me a place. And she's sold the inn – or what's left of it – and is moving in with her sister in Penzance. But there's no room for me there.'

'That's hard,' said Jenna, clearly shocked by Pearl's story. 'You poor duck.'

Jenna's sympathy made Pearl wish she had the courage to tell her the rest of it. But what Adeline Treglown had revealed to her hadn't sunk in yet, didn't seem real. She wanted time to get used to it, and to grieve for what she hadn't known before was hers to lose.

It had been two days after the fire, after Adeline had attended the inquest into Arthur Reagan's death as a witness. Usually a brisk, matter-of-fact woman who got on with the job in hand, Pearl had been shocked to find her stepmother hunched over a bar table in the devastated inn, crying.

'It's losing this place that's done it,' she said, through her sobs. 'And what happened to that poor man.'

Pearl swept the soot off the bench opposite and sat down gingerly. She stared around the bar. Although the fire hadn't reached this room, there was soot and cinders on every surface and rubbish floated in pools of dirty water on the uneven floor. The room stank of smoke and stale beer.

'It's not your fault,' was all she could manage to say. She wanted to tell Adeline that she missed him, too, that with his death something special – not just the man himself, but a glimpse of another world, a way out – was gone.

Mr Reagan had been a periodic guest at the Blue Anchor for as far back as Pearl could remember. He was a painter and would visit Newlyn for a few weeks at a time, once for several months. From the age of about six or seven, when she could escape school and Adeline's clutches, Pearl would run down to the new pier or along the cliffs, wherever he had set up his easel, and watch him sketch and paint. Sometimes he would talk to her about what he was doing – about recreating the precise mood of the sea that day or how to represent boats far away on the horizon. Sometimes he told her about his travels. He had visited painters' colonies in France and once spent a year in Italy. Seeing her interest, he showed her books about these places or catalogues from exhibitions.

'They don't get across how bright the colours are,' he complained of the black and white plates as he tried to describe the visual shock of works by Vincent van Gogh or Paul Gaugin.

Pearl knew Reagan was married. His wife lived in Kent and they had five children, but he didn't talk about them very much. She had the impression that his wife wasn't happy about his visits to Newlyn and she certainly never came too.

There was something melancholic about him, she thought, studying his gaunt face with its dark beard. He never seemed to eat properly and his shabby if well-made suits hung off him as though they had been tailored for a different man, one sleeker and happier.

Sometimes he was cheerful because the Academy or the Watercolour Society had accepted one of his pictures and it had subsequently sold. 'It isn't so much the money,' he would say, 'but that the Academy approves what I've done.' From that she assumed that he had some other income, although she couldn't imagine what. Everyone she knew always seemed to be in need of money.

He was a lonely figure. Sometimes he sought the company of other painters who had settled in Newlyn, for a time sharing an old fishloft as a studio with two others. But mostly he kept himself to himself. He didn't seem to mind sitting on his own, smoking endlessly and staring at the sea like an old sailor dreaming of past voyages.

Adeline, Pearl was surprised, seemed fond of him. She always made an effort with the cooking when he was staying and sent Pearl up every day to clean his room, while other guests would receive more cursory attention. And then, just as suddenly as he had arrived, he would be bidding Pearl goodbye, off back on the train to London – but always promising to be back 'as soon as I can square it with Lena', his wife.

Now, in the wrecked bar of the Blue Anchor, Adeline's crying had turned to a long exhausting coughing fit. When she was calm again she sat, twisting a handkerchief in her fingers and staring, watery-eyed at the floor. After a while she said, 'Arthur Reagan was your father.'

For a long moment, Pearl could not breathe; the blood stood still in her veins. When the attack passed she said nothing, too long-schooled in suppressing her reactions.

Adeline went on, as though she had spoken, 'Yes, I know I told you your parents were dead.' She had said her father was a fisherman lost at sea one stormy night, that her mother, a maid at the Blue Anchor, had died giving birth to her.

The bit about her mother, apparently, was true. 'Maggie were a pretty lass, but no better than she did belong to be. She did wind that poor man round her little finger. She knew he be married but it made no difference to her. She would have him. I were all for throwing her out when she started to show but she begged me. Then you was born and she took sick and died.'

Pearl still couldn't speak for shock. Adeline began to cough into her handkerchief again, long hollow coughs that Pearl was shocked to see brought up blood. Finally Adeline said, 'He used to give me money – to pay for your keep. Not much, mind, but it was something. Now that's all gone.' She looked about her. 'And so's this place. I don't know what will become of us.'

Pearl sat in silence, gazing at her fingers, grateful for the 'us', but struggling to reinterpret her whole life.

Not only had Arthur Reagan opened her eyes to a wider world beyond the possibilities of a fisherman's daughter, lending her books and teaching her about drawing and painting, but he had belonged to her and she to him in a way she had never suspected.

'Why didn't he tell me?' she whispered now, looking up at the wretched Adeline.

'He said not to. Too many here knew him. What would he have done if it got back to his wife? It was her family had the money, see, and if she knew about you . . .'

'I'm glad you've come, my dear,' Jenna chattered, interrupting Pearl's thoughts. 'Since Joan went off to Africa last month to marry her boy, it's been a parcel of work for the rest of us.'

'Africa?' Pearl asked.

'Yes, he sailed from Plymouth a twelvemonth ago, to the mines. Then he sent for her and she's off like a dog after a rabbit. She promised she'd send us a message to say she'd got there, but she ent yet.'

'Maybe it takes a long time for letters,' said Pearl, standing back to survey their work. 'These flowers,' she said, nodding at the arrangement of irises and narcissi, 'they're so pretty. Who does those?'

She began to copy Jenna, who was laying out glasses from trays on the sideboard, several different sizes and shapes for each place-setting.

'Mrs Carey's in charge of the flowers.'

'Who else lives here then?'

'Master, of course,' Jenna said. 'He owns the land where my pa and brothers farm. He works in the office here or goes out and about,' she added vaguely. 'Sometimes he rides to Penzance or Jago has to drive him.'

'Is Charlie their son?'

'Mr Charles to you. He's Mr Carey's nephew. Lived here for a few years now, since his own ma and pa died. Mr and Mrs Carey only have girls. Miss Elizabeth, she's sixteen, and Miss Cecily is fourteen, I reckon.'

'What does Mr Charles do then?'

'Well, he's supposed to be learning 'bout the estate but he don't seem that fussed. Goes about with Mr Carey sometimes, works in the office. But he do like painting pictures. And the garden – you'll always see him out there.'

'Are we allowed in the garden?'

'If Cook do give you a moment's peace and the family aren't out there, yes.'

Pearl nodded with pleasure at the thought of walking in those beautiful grounds and followed Jenna out to the hall to fetch some more chairs.

Past six, just before the guests were due to arrive, Pearl was filling a pan with water from the scullery when Jenna called her. 'Mistress is wanting you, my dear. I'll take you up.'

Pearl threw down her apron and washed her hands. They hurried up the back stairs and scampered along a carpeted corridor as guilty as two bad mice, arriving outside a door to a room at the front of the house.

'Don't be nervous,' hissed Jenna. 'She don't bite.' Which just made Pearl more jittery. Jenna knocked and at a 'Come in,' cuckooed from within, she opened the door and almost pushed Pearl into the room.

In this bedroom the carpet was soft, blue and gold curtains hung at the windows where, beyond, the front gardens were falling into shadow. The air was heavy with perfume. The mistress was sitting at a dressing-table between the windows, a jewel box open before her. She had been trying on earrings in the glow of the oil lamps, but now she laid the pendant jewels down on a lace-edged mat and half-turned.

'Ah, good. I need you to do my hair.'

Pearl moved forward to stand behind the mistress and, hesitantly, began to draw the pins from Mrs Carey's thick tresses. Earlier, in the sunny drawing room, the crown of hair had reflected chestnut, but in the fading light it appeared dark brown, threaded with white. It fell past her shoulders and Pearl began to brush with the silver-backed hairbrush the mistress passed her, in long languorous strokes.

Mrs Carey closed her eyes and began to hum. She looked, thought Pearl, watching her in the mirror, as though a hundred and one thoughts were passing through her mind. There were dark shadows under her eyes, and her skin was dry and tired. She smiles a lot and frowns much, too, Pearl decided, reading the lines written on her face. She looked up at her own reflection in the mirror, scrutinising the oval face, the strong straight nose. She was pleased with her large round dark eyes, the lines of her eyebrows like a painter's sure brushstrokes, but thought her mouth too wide. Under her white cap, the unruly dark hair, trained back in its bun, blended into the shadows.

Her young rosy face above her age-pale mistress's in the mirror looked like an illustration for a lesson on the fleeting nature of time, and clearly this struck Mrs Carey too when she opened her eyes. She stared for a moment at the contrast of mistress and maid before her and snapped, 'That's enough now. I'll show you how I like it to be.'

But as she taught Pearl how to lift, roll and pin the coils of hair into a flattering halo, she grew kind.

'You're gentle, that's good. Joan was neat but she did pull so.'

'I used to do my stepmother's hair,' Pearl ventured. 'It would calm her.'

'She is ill, Cook told me. I'm sorry. How is she?'

'The doctor says it could be months or only weeks. I . . . I don't know.'

Mrs Carey nodded sympathetically. 'We will pray for her. We have prayers after breakfast, you'll know. And attend church up at Paul on Sunday mornings – all of us.' Paul was the village a couple of miles away, towards Newlyn. 'There's a chapel here in the village and it's your business if you go there as well in the evening. Some here do.'

'Chapel people didn't like us selling the drink.'

'Ah,' said Mrs Carey, 'I have to say I wasn't sure about the inn myself, but Cook was sure you were a good girl. I expect you to prove her right.'

Pearl raised her eyebrows in surprise as she met her mistress's firm gaze. Aunt Dolly had always betrayed so little interest in Pearl when they met and now, it seemed, the woman must have argued her case. And yet, she thought, remembering the previous few hours, Cook seemed terse with everyone. It must be her way.

Mrs Carey opened a blue velvet box and passed Pearl the delicate diamond choker within. As Pearl fastened it around her mistress's neck and made small adjustments to her hair, the older woman patted the powder puff to her face one final time.

'One of the artists died in the fire, I hear,' Mrs Carey said. Pearl forced herself to carry on her task without even catching her breath. 'Not someone Charles knew, I gather.'

'Beg pardon, madam?'

'My nephew is a painter, did you know?' But before Pearl could answer there was a rap on the door. It opened and a burly middle-aged man in shirtsleeves stomped in. 'Fix these damn cuffs, will you, my love?' he barked at Mrs Carey, looking Pearl quickly up and down. 'Who's this then?'

'This is the girl from Newlyn I told you about, Stephen,' Mrs Carey explained to her husband, as she threaded a cufflink. 'You may go now, Pearl,' and Pearl fled.

Pearl wasn't asked to serve in the dining room that night, but to watch how it was done as she hurried back and forth for Jago and Jenna, weighed down with entrée dishes and vegetable bowls, piles of dirty plates and fistfuls of empty bottles.

As she blew out her candle and lay on her lumpy bed waiting for sleep to overtake her, exhausted but her mind racing, the memories of the day tumbled together in her mind. The jingle of the horse's harness, the swaying of the cart on the potholed road, the clang of kitchen pots, the rich cooking smells, the steam and heat of the kitchen, light twinkling through fine crystal, the scent of flowers, skirls of ladylike laughter, the wine on the men's breath as she helped with the coats.

All this was a hundred miles away from this morning, hurrying past the fish spread out on the beach, last night's catch, men and women haggling, seagulls squabbling for scraps and the sea a brooding monster after the night's winds, crashing on the shore.

And yet, despite all that she had lost, she had a hope that she could be happy here in Merryn Hall, that there was kindness, beauty, and the succour of daily work to heal her.

She felt under the bolster and her fingers closed around the little paintbox her father had given her. Then rolling over, listening to the hoot of owls, she slipped into sleep.

Chapter 4

It wasn't until the following Friday that Patrick Winterton arrived, although every day Mel listened out for a strange car in the drive, wondered if today he would come.

She spent a productive week, engrossing herself in her work. On the Monday she visited the Victor Pasmore art gallery in the old fishing town of Newlyn, though the beautiful small building itself had been of more interest to her than the modern conceptual artworks currently showcased within. It was easy enough, standing alone on the wind-bludgeoned cliff, staring across to St Michael's Mount, to sense the appeal of the place for the artists of a century ago. Today's fishermen wore luminous waistcoats rather than traditional Guernsey sweaters and woollen hats, and a single company now dominated the distribution of the fish at a modern covered market, where once fishermen and their wives had cried their wares on the shingle, but the place had the same sober sense of purpose that it must have done one hundred years before, and memorials of recent tragedies bore witness to the continued dangers of bringing in the harvest of the sea.

Tuesday and Wednesday she studied paintings in Penlee House art gallery in Penzance and spent hours reading in the

Morrab Library,. It was fascinating to discover how the local fishing community had seemed to accept the invasion by painters from the Midlands, London and elsewhere in the last quarter of the nineteenth century. Indeed, many had become models for the sometimes tragic tableaux the artists created – *In the Midst of Life We Are in Death* was the title of one painting, *A Hopeless Dawn* another. Mel supposed the modern equivalent was being filmed in your daily routine for reality TV.

By Friday, she realised that she had hardly spoken to anybody for days, unless she counted asking a librarian for a book or the man on the meat counter at the supermarket for sausages. A walk down to the beach is what I need, she thought, and I'll see if Irina is in for a chat.

Apart from several hurried visits to the shop for papers and milk, she hadn't been near the cove again. The day was bright and sunny, and Mel found herself noticing things she had missed on her first walk – late daffodils growing wild, a crumbly old millhouse, the millpond, despite recent rain, little more than a stagnant pool. When she reached the tiny village hall, she saw a poster advertising an art exhibition. After a moment's hesitation, she went in.

It was warm and light inside, the high roof and the many windows giving an exhilarating sense of space. The walls were crowned with bright modern prints of Cornish scenes represented by flat blocks of colour. Not great works of art, but they were lively and decorative.

There was no one else in the room, though she could hear the hiss of a kettle and a chink of china from through a side door, so she enjoyed walking dreamily around by herself, taking time to look at all the prints. The final few pictures were different: half a dozen photographs of the sea hung by themselves in a corner. Unusual, dramatic. She liked them.

'Sorry, I didn't hear you come in.' A young man in a crumpled Oxford shirt and shabby cords emerged from the doorway, bearing a steaming mug. He frowned slightly, narrowing his dark eyes. 'Do I know you?'

'I don't think so,' said Mel uncertainly then remembered. 'Unless . . . yes, we have sort of met. You were one of the divers, weren't you?'

'Down at the cove last week – yes, that's where I've seen you.'

'Did you find anything?'

'Nah,' he said cheerfully. 'Like pea soup down there.' He placed his mug on the trestle table by the door, his lips curved in what might be a smile or just a natural quizzical expression. He was of average height, aged perhaps thirty, with a small dark face and a lean, compact figure. Mel remembered him in his wetsuit. She could imagine him emerging from the water, sparkling water droplets sliding off his short dark hair. Sleek as a seal or a merman. In a graceful movement, he slid into his place behind the table and selected a typed catalogue, which he held out for her with a theatrical flourish.

'Is this your work?' she asked, looking around at the paintings.

'Just the photos. The paintings are by a friend of mine,' he said.

'The photos are good,' Mel said, peering again at the sea pictures. 'Specially that one with the boulders.'

'Thank you,' he said. 'It's a hobby really, though I'd like to spend more time on it.'

'What's stopping you?'

'Oh, everything else I do. My job, the diving, surfing.'

'What's your job?'

'Work at a surfing shop in Penzance. I kip in a mate's flat over the shop. But I was brought up in Lamorna so I'm here a lot.

Mum's on her own now, you see. She runs a hotel up the road and always needs help. What about you? On holiday, are you?'

'It feels a bit like it, but I'm meant to be doing research.' She explained about her work.

'People are always asking about the artists,' the young man said. 'But you're actually writing a book about them. Wow!'

'Not as glamorous as it sounds,' she said with a grimace. 'It's unlikely to be a best seller. I think you're so lucky to have been brought up here surrounded by the scenery the artists painted.'

'Can't argue with you there,' he agreed. 'Beautiful, isn't it? But West Cornwall's pretty cut off. Most of my schoolmates have moved away, up country. There weren't proper jobs for them here.'

'I suppose there's work in tourism.'

'Yeah, but the trouble is, it's seasonal. There's not much farming now either, or fishing, and the mines are nearly all gone. Anyway, my mates don't want those kind of jobs any more. Everything's changed. Take this valley, for instance. So many houses belong to incomers – retired people or second homers. Mum says the sense of community has gone.'

Mel glanced down at the catalogue he had given her – Tobias Walters, the artist was called – and went over to look at the pictures she had liked best, higgledy-piggledy cottages from the Newlyn back streets, and the photographs. After a moment she returned to the table and handed back the catalogue.

'Your friend has a good sense of colour.'

The man laughed. 'I take it that means you're not tempted,' he said.

'Not today,' she said, judging him to be someone who appreciated honesty. 'But I really do like your photos.'

'Thanks, that's nice, especially from an art historian like yourself. Well, if you're in Lamorna for a while, perhaps I'll see you around. Where are you staying?' When Mel told him, he became animated. 'Really?' he said. 'Mum's always going on about that old place. There's some family link from way back.'

'Do you know Patrick Winterton, the man who owns it? I haven't met him yet, you see.' She explained who Patrick was.

'I heard the old bloke had died. Mum will be interested to hear who lives there now. Look, my name's Matt. Matt Price. You're . . .?'

'Mel. Melanie Pentreath.'

'A Cornish name.'

'Yes, my parents came from near Falmouth. But they were part of the great exodus you've talked about, I'm afraid. They moved to London in the 1960s. I've never lived here myself.'

'Ah well, I hope you have a great stay. Good luck with the book. Maybe we'll bump into one another again.'

She was still thinking about Matt when she reached the Post Office. There she met Irina coming out, a straw shopping bag on her arm and a shy-looking girl of about eight in tow.

'I've been wondering how you were getting on,' said Irina, brushing her hand quickly across Mel's forearm in a warm gesture. 'Have you time for coffee? This is my daughter, Lana.' She drew the small girl forward.

'Thanks, I'd love some. Hello, Lana. Are you on holiday from school?' Lana nodded, her dark eyes huge and liquid in her small pointed face. She was a more solemn miniature version of her mother.

From the outside, Irina and Lana's house was a fisherman's cottage like any number of others, but inside, a bright modern pine kitchen and breakfast room contrasted sharply with the living room crammed with elderly furniture. Irina had disguised the shabby upholstery with coloured cushions and, here and there, were intriguing hints of her origins – an icon on the wall, a couple of painted wooden dolls on the mantelpiece, a photograph of a smiling middle-aged couple, the woman with a headscarf tied under her chin, in front of a stone-built house with green shutters.

Mel leaned back in a deep leather armchair, hugging a cushion. The scent of the rough wool material reminded her of her father's overcoat, and her earliest memory of him rushed back. Her three-year-old self swept up into his arms and hoisted high in the air until she screamed in joyous terror.

She was returned to the present by Irina coming in with the coffee. Lana slipped in, catching her mother's eye as she stole a glass of squash from the tray and disappeared upstairs.

'You were looking at the photograph. My parents,' said Irina, nodding at the couple. 'Taken in Dubrovnik, before the troubles. They look so . . . contented, don't they? My father still lives there in our hotel, but now the tourists are coming back it is very busy, too much for him. He wrote to say my brother has become the manager.'

'And your mother?'

'She died five years ago after being ill with her diabetes for a long time.' Irina concentrated on the ritual of pouring coffee and offering Mel milk and sugar.

'I'm sorry to hear that,' said Mel quietly. 'My mother died last year.' She brushed at her eyes, astonished as ever by the sudden tears. 'Cancer. It took her fast.'

'How terrible. I am so sorry.' Again, the other woman reached out and touched Mel's arm. 'And your father? Is he still alive?'

'Yes,' she said, suddenly encouraged to confide in Irina. 'He's a heart surgeon. Or rather, was. He's retired now. But my parents divorced when I was five. Dad lives near Birmingham with his second wife. We – my brother and sister and I – hardly saw

him after he went. I think it was difficult for him, he felt guilty.'
That was how her mother had explained it and so Mel had built
a wall in her mind to keep her feelings shut away.

'I wasn't able to go back to Croatia for my mother's funeral.'
Irina's eyes narrowed. 'I was married then, here. It was complicated. A shaggy dog tale, as you would say.'

'How did you end up in Lamorna?' asked Mel.

Irina stood up and walked over to the window, looking out
across the bay. She turned, and Mel couldn't see her face against
the light.

'I came here to get away from London. My marriage was over
and Lana and I, we were living somewhere horrible. Bars on the
doors, rubbish everywhere. I read in a magazine about a job. The
old man, Mr Winterton at Merryn Hall, wanted a housekeeper
and when I told him about Lana he said he liked the idea of a
child about the place. And it was by the sea. I missed the sea,
you know. In Dubrovnik, well, my parents' hotel is right on the
harbour.'

'When did you come?'

'Two years ago. Mr Winterton was unwell for a long time.
After I had been there a year there was talk of him moving to a
nursing home, but he wouldn't go, so Nurse Wright came and
we both took care of him. He was a big man and it took the two
of us to lift him. It was a bad time watching him die, bad for
Lana, too. He had been very kind to her. He was in a lot of pain.
And then, after he had gone, we found he had looked after us.'

'Looked after you – what do you mean?'

'He left us some money. It was very good of him, I am so
grateful. It meant we could find the deposit to rent this house
and pay for Lana's music lessons. What about you, Mel? Are
you married or . . .?'

'No, I've never found the right person,' Mel said, carefully placing her empty cup on the tray. 'My family despairs of me.' And she explained briefly about Jake.

'I thought I'd found the right one,' said Irina sadly. 'Two times. But it was not to be. So, now I'm happy with Lana, just Lana and me, aren't I, darling?' she said, spreading her arms to hug her daughter who had sidled back into the room, her hands busy knitting together long strands of coloured plastic that Mel remembered from her own childhood.

There was something about the child, thought Mel, a sort of wariness, a vulnerability. She looked delicate, troubled.

'Can we ring Amber, Mummy? I want her to come and play.' She was as light as a bird, Lana. Mel watched her weave the lengths of plastic with her long sure fingers.

'In a little while, angel.'

'Where do you go to school, Lana?'

'At Paul,' the girl said. 'Amber lives there, too.'

Yes, thought Mel, Lamorna was beautiful but, as Matt had said, very isolated. Living here must be difficult for a child yearning to belong.

'I haven't asked you,' said Irina. 'Are you finding the cottage comfortable?'

'Oh yes,' said Mel. 'I'm getting used to it now. Though it's very cut off, isn't it, particularly when there's no one at the Hall?'

Irina nodded. 'That's what I felt. Lana and I lived in your cottage for a few months, before old Mr Winterton became so ill.'

'I thought there was a ghost, didn't I, Mum?' said Lana.

'It was just the furniture creaking, darling. We never saw anything,' said Irina firmly. 'Patrick asked if we would like to live there after Mr Winterton died, but I preferred to come here to the cove.'

'You do at least have neighbours around.'

'Mummy didn't like the garden either,' piped up Lana. 'It was so—'

'Come now, Lana, ssh. You'll frighten Miss Pentreath.' She looked at Mel. 'The garden feels a little desolate, that's all. We liked helping Mr Winterton when he was alive, but now it suits us better here, doesn't it, Lana darling?'

'And the view is lovely,' said Mel, standing up to look out of the window. 'Do you feel Lamorna is home now?'

'More so than we did. I have a reception job at one of the hotels, and I clean for Patrick and look after two of the holiday homes here. You know, clean after people have left, sort out problems. It is not easy to make friends, though. Many of the houses here are just for holidays and there are no families. More live up at Paul where Lana goes to school.'

'Such a change after London,' Mel murmured.

'London was the loneliest place in the world for me,' said Irina. 'Here I feel free.'

Which do I feel – free or lonely? Mel asked herself as she walked back up the hill to Merryn. She might still be held captive by her grief but at least, in Irina, she had perhaps found a friend.

She didn't see the metallic blue sports car parked in front of Merryn Hall, sparkling in the sun.

Chapter 5

That afternoon, deep in her task, Mel didn't notice the tall figure of a man coming down the path from the Hall.

'If you'll excuse the gardening pun, what on earth are you doing?'

The voice right behind her sounded amused rather than angry, but Mel, crouched in her flowerbed, levering out an ivy root, was so startled she missed the root and flipped soil in her eyes. The weeding fork clattered on the stones and she staggered back on her heels, blinded and crying out.

'Oh blimey, I'm sorry,' said the man. 'Hang on, I've a hanky somewhere. Here I didn't mean to creep up on you.' The handkerchief was soft linen and smelled of wool and soap. When, through her tears, Mel could focus on its owner, it was to see him hunkered down beside her, a concerned frown creasing his forehead. He was broad-chested with hazel eyes and a squarish, cleanshaven face, too pale, as though he spent all his time indoors. His red-brown hair was neatly cut but for a cowlick that fell boyishly across his forehead. He was dressed in an elderly Barbour jacket with a wool scarf looped round his neck.

'You nearly gave me a heart attack,' she breathed as he helped her up and pocketed the handkerchief. 'I was miles away.' She bent and picked up the fork, then smiled at him. 'There's a garden under here,' she said. 'Let's say I'm liberating it.'

The man gave a reluctant lopsided smile and regarded the results of her work, arms folded across his chest. 'I admire your energy,' he said, 'but I'm afraid I'm reminded of King Canute trying to hold back the sea.'

'Perhaps you're right. But that's no reason not to try, is it?'

The smile was replaced by a look of resignation as he gazed out across the jungle. 'It'll take more than one woman – even a very determined one – to clear this garden. An army of mechanical diggers and the team from Heligan, I reckon. It's a wreck, isn't it?'

When he turned, she noticed his sweater – an inoffensive plain blue – and remembered her joke about Mark Darcy's reindeer design. The penny dropped.

'I don't suppose you're Patrick, are you?' Mel said cautiously.

'Yes, sorry, should have introduced myself.' He put out his hand to shake hers. 'And I know you're Mel. You look so much like Chrissie.'

'No, I don't,' she said indignantly, almost dropping his hand. 'We're completely different. She's fair-haired and two inches shorter. And . . . everything.' She stopped, realising she sounded petulant.

Patrick's laugh was uneasy. 'Sorry. I shouldn't expect you to be like Chrissie, should I, just because you're her little sister. Not,' he added hastily, his glance taking in her five feet nine, 'that you look little . . . It's just you have the same smile and . . . I don't know.' He peered at her. 'Cast of features, I suppose. Anyway,' he changed the subject, noting Mel's frown, 'how are you finding the cottage?'

'It's great, thanks. I'm glad it's not restored to within an inch of its life like so many of these places. It feels . . . comfortable.

Well, except there's no teapot. And the light in the kitchen has a horrible hum and flickers. Drives me crazy.'

'I'll give it a twist for you. That usually fixes them. And I'm sorry about the teapot. I'll see if I've got a spare. Anything else?'

'No, just the garden that needs attention.'

Patrick looked down at what she had done, then, choosing his words carefully, he said, 'It's very good of you to have a go, but I shouldn't worry too much, if I were you. That's my problem, I'm afraid.'

He paced up and down, hands in the pockets of his cords, then turned to look up at the big house. Mel saw gloom settle on his features. It was as though he had forgotten she was there. From his expression she gauged that Patrick was seeing not the romance of the old house but the financial liability. Some of the slate roof-tiles were missing, others, thick with gold lichen, were broken. Many of the windowsills looked rotten, and here and there between the all-embracing creepers, she could see the mortar was crumbling. The house looked sad, today, rather than brooding. Abandoned, full of echoes.

'How old is it?' she asked, after a moment. 'Georgian?'

'Mmm, 1819, according to the deeds. Built by a chap called Carey. Made a packet out of mining and bought the kudos of being a big landowner. He snapped up a lot of farmland round here, by all accounts.'

'An ancestor of yours?'

'No, not at all. My great-uncle bought it from the estate of a Miss Cecily Carey in the late seventies, but its glory days were long gone then. The house had been empty for a couple of years and Uncle Val picked it up for a song.'

'What are you going to do with it? Live here?'

'You're certainly as direct as your sister,' Patrick commented.

Mel had to laugh. 'I love her dearly, but she's not forward

74

about holding back, is she?' she said, having frequently fallen victim to Chrissie's interview technique.

'Well,' said Patrick, 'if you must know, I'm still thinking about it.' He suddenly looked at his watch. 'Look, I'd better get on. There's a surveyor due any moment to advise me whether the place is about to fall down. See you soon.' He started to walk away. Then checked himself and turned around. 'Tell you what, are you busy this evening? Come and have a drink about six. Uncle Val left rather a good cellar.'

Feeling annoyed and slightly crestfallen, Mel watched Patrick disappear around the side of the Merryn Hall. He hadn't noticed her at all, not the real Mel, but had fallen into that easy trap of misjudging someone because they appeared familiar. When he looked at her, he saw not Mel but Chrissie, she was sure of it. She thought of all those times as a teenager when she had had to interrupt callers midflow who had mistaken her voice on the phone for her mother's or for Chrissie's. As she grew older she became more resigned to the family likenesses. But at that age she had rebelled, wearing outrageous clothes and choosing troublemakers for friends.

Now she looked down at her well-cut jeans and buttondown shirt and picked up the fork with a sigh. Patrick hadn't appreciated her efforts. All her pleasure in the garden was spoiled. It was a pity. Before Patrick had interrupted, she had been happily comparing her situation to Irina's, congratulating herself on having discovered a task that cheered her up, freed her from herself. Oh well.

She really ought to sort out some of the notes she had made yesterday. Jabbing the fork back into the soil, she went inside. Then, as she switched on her laptop she remembered Patrick's invitation. And despite everything, she looked forward to seeing him again.

Chapter 6

'I've never been given flowers before. Especially from my own garden.'

For a moment Mel worried that she had made a mistake in presenting him with the narcissi, but a look of shy delight dawned on Patrick's face and all was well. The flowers' fragrance filled the gloomy hall. Jake, a man of grand gestures, had taught her about the joy of giving and receiving unusual presents, once giving her a couple of live crabs which she proved too squeamish to cook!

'And here's a vase,' Mel said now, passing Patrick a glass carafe she had found at the back of a cupboard.

'Great, I wouldn't know where to look for one here,' he said, taking it from her. 'There are these babes, of course.' He nodded at a pair of large brass jars on either side of a console table, one of which was doing service as an umbrella-stand.

'I wonder how long it is since the garden grew flowers grand enough for those,' said Mel, imagining the lush displays that must have decorated the rooms in the heyday of the house and garden. She looked around the high cold hall, feebly lit by its single electric chandelier, noticing how the yellowed paint peeled off the walls. A spindle-railed staircase ran gracefully up one side to a small viewing gallery.

'So elegant,' she murmured, aware he was watching. 'What horrors did your surveyor unearth?'

'I'm glad to say the place won't fall down tomorrow. There are a few small problems with tree roots, and a new roof is in order, but I can deal with those. Quite a relief, I can tell you.' He smiled and she realised that he was certainly more relaxed, friendlier than he had been that morning.

'I can imagine,' she said.

'Come through to the kitchen a moment and I'll get us a drink. Do you like claret?'

As Patrick decanted the pungent contents of a dusty bottle and located two glass chalices, Mel unwrapped the flowers and splayed them in the carafe on the kitchen table. Then she followed him through to the drawing room, which looked out onto the garden at the back. A wood fire crackled beneath a marble mantelpiece, the scent of the smoke not quite masking a sinister whiff of damp. She gazed around her. The room was an unhappy mixture of decorative styles. Chipped anaglypta wallpaper gave off a ghastly pale-green glow in the early-evening light. Around the fire huddled a modern reclining armchair and a pair of baggy sofas patterned with huge roses.

Patrick noticed her interest.

'I'll show you round later if you like,' he said, putting down the bottle and glasses on an ugly tiled coffee-table. 'But it's warmest in here. Try Uncle Val's throne,' he said, gesturing to the armchair. 'It's really very comfortable.' He set a glass of wine on what was probably a plant stand by her side and settled into the sofa opposite.

'Here's to Val,' he said, raising his own glass to her, 'and to

you, of course. I'm glad you've come. I don't get many visitors.'
He gulped at his wine, too quickly.

He looked tired, Mel noticed, and sort of sad.

'And are you finding here a good place to work?' he asked.

'Oh yes,' she said. 'Did I tell you anything in my emails about the book I'm writing?'

'Only that it was about the local artists.'

'It's all about the Newlyn and Lamorna Schools.'

She told him how she had visited some of the locations they painted and discovered some papers in the Morrab Library. 'A diary and a memoir. A local history expert in Newlyn has given me some other leads. What I need to do is visit St Ives and have a chat with an art historian who knows the period well. Guy called Jonathan Smithfield.'

'Where are the main archives?' asked Patrick, lifting his glass to admire the effect of the firelight shining through the ruby wine.

'Oh, all over the place. Cornwall, Birmingham, London, America. All much easier to track on the Internet these days, of course.'

'The Newlyn Group has been written about a lot, am I right? I vaguely remember going to an exhibition round here years ago.'

'Yes, but they're not fashionable now. They were into social realism – the kind of Victorian painting of ordinary working folk with a moral. You know, stoicism in the face of tragedy, the glorification of hard work and suffering.'

'Ah, yes, fishermen's wives sobbing in the dawn because their men have gone down in the storm.'

'Exactly.' She was gratified that he pretended to have at least some interest in her subject. 'Dozens of artists came to Newlyn in the last quarter of the nineteenth century,' she went on, 'and many settled for some years, made it their home.'

'How does this tie up with the ones who came to Lamorna?'

'That was a bit later, really. There was John Birch, a man from a fairly humble background, who came here in the early Edwardian era. He became known as Lamorna Birch to distinguish him from another Birch, Samuel.'

'I'm sure Uncle Val used to talk about him. He married a local girl, didn't he?'

'Yes. And then there were the Knights – Harold and his wife Laura. Laura is the better-known painter. And Alfred Munnings joined them at one point.'

'Oh, yes. The bloke who painted horses.'

'That's right. A larger-than-life character, by all accounts. The locals were shocked by his raucous behaviour. But there were others, too. Many of them started off in Newlyn but came to Lamorna as well. Even Augustus John visited later on.'

'But no more maudlin moral tableaux?'

'No. This generation was more influenced by French Impressionism. They wanted to capture the beauty of the area. Theirs were happy pictures, often with a holiday mood.'

Patrick reached for the bottle to top up their glasses. 'I think I know the sort of thing,' he said. 'And what angle particularly interests you?'

'The women, I suppose. The obstacles they had to deal with to become successful painters. I'm still fine-tuning my arguments,' Mel said. 'Are you sure I'm not boring you?'

'Not at all. It's fascinating.'

Mel plunged into an explanation of her theories about the women painters, the subjects they chose to paint, their relationships with the men and how they had different obstacles in pursuing their careers.

'Some of them came from quite privileged backgrounds,' she said. 'Nineteen hundred was still a time when it was very difficult for a woman of no means or social standing to develop artistic talent, unlike some of the men – Lamorna Birch is a great example of a man who pulled himself up by his bootstraps. Laura Knight was left in near poverty after her mother died, but she was a middle-class girl with education and connections. She still needed enormous determination, though, to become a painter.'

'Sometimes a working girl became a model and married the painter,' Patrick suggested.

'Well, yes,' she said, 'that did happen. But of course,' she added quickly, 'the husband might not encourage her talent, and then children would start to come along. She would have to be very strongminded to practise her art in that case. She would have to make sacrifices.'

'And you?' Patrick said, leaning forward and carefully placing his wine glass on the table. He sat back, his hands clasped behind his head, and considered her seriously. 'Do you make sacrifices? Chrissie told me you work much too hard.'

'I enjoy my work,' Mel replied. 'It's challenging and creative. So what else has my wretched sister been telling you?'

'Nothing terrible, I assure you,' he teased.

'What about you, what is it you do?' she said. Somehow he had got away with asking all the questions.

'I sell inventions.'

'You're an inventor?' She looked at him with curiosity.

'Not exactly. My partner and I run a website for inventors. We help them sort out patents, which is a complex business, and try to find firms to develop and manufacture their ideas. We take a cut if it works out.'

'What inventions have you sold?'

'Quite a range, really. A new kind of rotary clothes-line, ergonomic chairs, gardening tools. There was a children's toy that was a nice little earner a couple of Christmases ago – a remote controlled cat that climbed curtains.'

'I remember – it was cute. My boyfriend's kids had one. Ex-boyfriend, I mean.' She stared at the ugly whorls on the carpet to hide her confusion. Boxing Day, three Christmases ago, the four of them together in Jake's flat, little Freya bouncing with excitement as she ripped brightly coloured paper off present after present, her laughter at the antics of the funny little robot cat.

'. . . plenty of less interesting things, too,' Patrick was saying. 'Widgets that reduce friction in engines, new types of packaging. And a lot of ideas that waste time and never come to anything.'

'How long have you been going?'

'Five or six years. It started when Geoff and I were at uni. We had a deeply boring job picking blackcurrants one summer, and we thought up a gadget to help. In the end, about eight years ago, we got a manufacturer to take it up, but he ripped us off, designed his own version and did very well with it. Never gave us a penny. We didn't want that to happen to other people so we started up the business as a sideline. It just grew and grew. On the whole I like the job. I was in high finance before and, quite frankly, I was getting burned out. It's flexible, there's some travel involved and you never know what you'll be dealing with next. It's amazing trying to gauge which idea is going to take off. But Geoff's pulling out now, selling me his share of the business. I'll be free to do what I want with it.'

Mel nodded. 'Will you need to be up in London all the time?'

'That's one of the things I'm considering. I'm going to keep my flat in Islington, and I can always travel up when I need to. But I want to take advantage of the break and get this place sorted out.'

'Chrissie said you have family down here.'

'Yes, my parents live outside Truro. My brother and I were brought up on the family farm, but neither of us wanted to work on the land – Joe's a schoolteacher locally – so Dad sold the lease when he retired.'

'And Uncle Val?'

'Ah yes, dear old Uncle Val. Look.' Patrick fetched a framed black and white photograph from a table by the window. 'I found this in his bedroom after he died. It must have been taken in the early 1960s. He was around thirty-seven or thirty-eight then.'

Mel took the picture and angled it towards the light. It was of a fleshy, youngish man, half-turned to the camera, caught mid-conversation at a party. He had a wing of dark, jaw-length hair and sideburns, and was bringing a glass of wine to his full, smiling lips. The photograph was signed *Valentine Winter* in a scrawl very similar to Patrick's own.

'"Winter" was his stage name. He was my dad's uncle,' said Patrick, going to sit down once more. 'Though there was only ten years between them. He was my great-grandma's unexpected gift, you see – the much-spoiled late baby.'

'He certainly doesn't look like a farmer.'

'Let's say he was the black sheep.' Patrick grinned.

Mel gave a snort of laughter. 'Nor is Valentine a typical name for a farmer's son.'

'The story goes that he was Great-gran's last chance at having a daughter. And he was born on the fourteenth of February. The combination was irresistible. It's hardly surprising he turned out the way he did.'

'He looks as if he enjoyed life.'

'Oh, he did when he was young – the original playboy, outrageously flamboyant. The family were scandalised. He started out as a TV actor, and went on to create some very successful comedy series. Made a lot of money out of it. But he developed multiple sclerosis in the late nineteen seventies, gave it all up and moved back to Cornwall. Spent the rest of his life here all by himself. Hardly saw the family or his friends. So sad.'

Patrick dropped another log on the fire, then picked up a poker, crouching down to prod the embers. Mel watched him coax the flames into new life.

'But he chose to leave the place to you,' she pointed out. 'He must have been fond of you.'

Patrick rose and turned to look at her, the poker still in his hand, the other arm resting on the mantelpiece in a proprietorial manner, as though he belonged.

'I was always a favourite of his. We understood one another at some level, had the same sense of humour. He could be difficult, bloody-minded, but to me he was always good company. He liked a gossip, and I enjoyed listening to his stories. He didn't become incapacitated with MS until the last few years. I would drive over whenever I was home and we would look through his scrapbooks and he would talk about the old days. I can show you newscuttings of him with famous people – Barbara Windsor, Joe Orton, even the Beatles. He missed that world, but he hated being ill, losing his looks, growing old. I think he felt ashamed.'

'Poor man. Irina sounded fond of him. He left her money, she told me.'

'And to the nurse, yes.' Patrick sat down once more. 'They were devoted to him, despite his fussiness. Even when he was dying he could be charming, amusing. I was the only beneficiary in the family – not that there was much money left after the taxman had taken his tranche – just this place really.'

Mel wanted to ask whether the rest of the family minded Patrick inheriting Merryn, but felt this question to be too intrusive.

'Come on,' Patrick said, putting down his empty glass. 'If

you'd like me to show you round we'd better do it now, before it gets any darker.'

He led the way out of the drawing room and across the hall, where he threw open the double doors of a dining room. The huge walnut table was battered and chipped. An assortment of chairs was pushed back against the sides of the room. The walls looked like those of a classroom after the end of term, when all the work has been taken down, for it was studded by drawing pins that still held the corners of torn posters.

'Soldiers were billeted here during the war. They obviously used this as their operations room,' Patrick explained. It was almost as though the soldiers had left only yesterday. 'It's astonishing that the last Miss Carey left it untouched. Val hardly came in here. Sometimes he and I sat at opposite ends of the dining-room table for our meals when we fancied pretending to be grand. We would slide the salt and pepper up and down like shot glasses in a Western saloon bar and bark silly comments at one another like mad Regency squires.'

Mel laughed.

Patrick showed her a big office down a corridor where several dented filing cabinets sagged next to two huge desks and a wall of empty shelves.

'What do you suppose this was before?' Mel asked, gazing round. On one of the desks, Patrick had installed a computer. On the other he'd dumped half a dozen boxes of papers.

'Probably the estate office. I read in the solicitor's files that the Careys owned hundreds of acres of farmland round here. Most of it was leased out to tenant farmers, so I imagine a lot of the work was only admin, but until after the First War they kept a dozen acres to farm themselves.'

Closing the door of the office, Patrick led Mel back up the corridor and into a small sitting room at the front of the house.

'It's lovely and sunny here in the mornings,' he said. 'Val used it as his den – until he was bedridden and couldn't get downstairs.'

The room looked as though it had last been decorated thirty years before. Orange and brown paper in a geometric design bubbled with age or damp. There was a low flat sofa with wooden arms, a scallop-backed cane chair with a stained cushion and, by the fireplace, another reclining armchair, clearly the partner of the one in the drawing room. The grate was obscured by an old-fashioned, double-barred electric fire. Shelving units bearing books, photographs, an old hi-fi system and a large vinyl and tape collection filled the two alcoves.

'Like being in a time warp, isn't it?' Patrick said, stabbing at a button on the hi-fi. The lugubrious tones of Leonard Cohen filled the air and he quickly pressed the stop button.

'Weird,' Mel agreed. She looked out of the window to where Patrick's gleaming new ultramarine sports car brought her firmly back to the present.

'You know, I think of this house,' he said, escorting her through the kitchen to see the larder, pantry and scullery, all painted a sludgy olive green, 'being like a dowager duchess, dreaming of the gracious past, too frail to shrug off the monstrosities of post-war decor.'

Mel eyed the beige Formica cabinets, of the same ilk as those in the Gardener's Cottage and nodded. 'All in the name of progress,' she sighed.

'Wait till you see the avocado bathroom upstairs,' he grinned suddenly.

Mel laughed. 'It's strange, isn't it, how people reach a certain period of their lives and get stuck. Your uncle decorated this house in what was the latest fashion when he moved in and stayed with it ever after.'

'The only thing he updated regularly was the television. Do you want to see upstairs or have you had enough?'

Upstairs didn't take long. There were six bedrooms on the first floor, sparsely furnished, and two attic rooms above.

'I gave Irina some of the furniture,' Patrick said, 'and I moved some things over to the Gardener's Cottage when I decided to rent it out.'

'Did anyone live there before?'

'Val let it out to a local couple, until a few years before he died. But there was some argument about money and they left. Then Irina lived there for a bit with her daughter.'

'And the pictures,' Mel said, thinking about the flower paintings. 'Where did the pictures in my living room come from?'

'I found those by accident,' said Patrick, as they walked back into the corridor, 'all packed away in newspaper in a hidey hole in one of the attics. There was one more, which I've got in my bedroom. Hold on, I'll fetch it.'

Mel, waiting just outside the door, wondered why Patrick had taken for himself a stuffy small bedroom at the front of the house rather than, say, Uncle Val's bigger room. The curtains were still closed, and through the crack in the door, she could see that the bed was unmade. Patrick switched on the light. A few books were sprawled across the floor, and Mel, who liked to learn about people from their choice of reading matter, peered at the titles. A literary crime thriller, a politician's autobiography and a couple of popular science bestsellers.

'I like this room,' Patrick answered her unspoken question, as he emerged bearing a canvas a yard square, 'because it reminds me of my room when I was a kid.' Mel followed him back into Val's room where he propped the canvas up on the mantelpiece. They stood back in silence to look at it.

P.T.'s seventh picture was quite different from the others, an oil painting of a young man standing in a walled garden in summer. The flowerbeds were a riot of colour and the plants so carefully painted Mel could identify delphinium and lupins. A white rose rambled across an arch above a wooden gate. The young man, smiling slightly, was smartly dressed in a light jacket, waistcoat and trousers, but his white shirt was open at the neck and his head, unusually, was bare. He was holding something in one hand that might be a pen or a pencil. She stepped back a little to bring it into focus. No, she couldn't see it clearly and this fading light was no help. She liked the painting. It glowed with summer warmth – she could almost hear the humming of bees – and the whole was dappled with sunlight falling through leaves.

'What do you think?' Patrick was saying, almost anxiously. 'I find it . . . draws you in.'

'It's wonderful,' Mel said. 'There's something about the light. It's so uplifting – ecstatic, almost.'

Patrick nodded, slowly. 'That's how it takes me, too.' They stood in silence, studying the painting.

'His clothes look Edwardian. I suppose it's the turn of the twentieth century,' said Mel, after a moment. 'It's not unlike some of the more famous Lamorna paintings.'

'Oh? In what way?'

'The loose brushwork, the idyllic treatment of the subject. I'd need to see this in better light. It is definitely by P.T., isn't it? Yes, look, here are the initials. Do you know who P.T. was?'

'Absolutely no idea.'

'Was there anyone in the Carey family with those initials?'

Patrick shook his head. 'No one I've come across. Perhaps he was one of the artists passing through, or a drawing master here.'

'Might have been a she,' Mel said absently. 'The garden is this one, isn't it? Look at the shape of the arch here. We must be looking at the old Flower Garden.'

'Yes,' agreed Patrick. 'In its glory days.'

Mel moved over to the window and looked out. The sun was sinking behind the valley, throwing the garden into shadow. After a moment's hesitation, Patrick came to stand beside her. There was a new easiness between them now. Together they surveyed the wilderness.

'Are you a gardener?' he asked, glancing at her. 'I'm afraid I know more about crops and vegetables than flowers. Though we used to grow bulbs on the farm.'

'Mum was the gardener. She was a botanist, in fact, so a brilliant person to learn from. I'm the only one who inherited her green fingers.'

'I was sorry to learn about your mother's death,' said Patrick. 'I only met her once. She came down to Exeter to see Chrissie. Chrissie was going out with Nick then, and your mother invited me along to lunch as well so Nick wouldn't feel outnumbered.' He smiled. 'I was very shy and awkward, didn't say much but I remember being impressed because she supported Watford F.C. and they were doing pretty well then. She could remember the result of every game in the division that season!'

Mel laughed. 'She would.' Her voice was a little shaky. 'She supported them for the rest of her life, you know. One of the last big outings she had was when my brother took her to a home game last spring.'

She was silent for a moment, remembering their large garden in Hertfordshire. It backed onto a railway embankment, the sound of the trains only slightly muffled by a belt of trees. The end of the garden was a deliberate wilderness where she and her brother and sister played hide and seek or squabbled over whose gang should take a turn in the rough wooden treehouse they had cobbled together in a huge old apple tree. The lawn had been a muddy patch for ball games – only after her children left home did Maureen succeed in coaxing it into a smooth green sward – and the rest of the quarter-acre plot was their mother's. A rockery, a shrubbery through which their mother would vanish for hours on end into the vegetable garden beyond.

'We all had our own little flowerbeds when we were kids,' remembered Mel. 'But I was the only one who was really interested. Now, I've only got a long thin strip of garden in Clapham but at least it's south-facing and gets the sun.'

'I'm not sure where to start with this jungle, to be honest,' said Patrick.

'What about taking some professional advice?' Mel suggested. 'Getting in one of those landscape architects, perhaps.'

'I've thought about that. Maybe I will.'

Back downstairs again, she picked up her bag with a sense of reluctance. Going back to heat up the contents of a foil dish for supper in her lonely cottage suddenly had no appeal.

Patrick watched her and said, with effort, 'You know, I feel I started off on the wrong foot this morning. You're nothing like Chrissie really, are you? You are yourself.'

Is that a good thing or a bad thing? Surprised, Mel almost opened her mouth to ask this question, but Patrick said, 'Wait,' and disappeared into the kitchen. 'You'll need this, city girl.' He handed her a small torch. 'I'll walk you round now, if you like.'

'Very gallant.' She smiled. 'But no, keep it – it's not even properly dark yet. I'll try not to fall down any rabbit-holes on the way. I'm used to the dangerous city streets, remember.'

He laughed, but as he said goodbye he seemed a little distracted, sad. He held the door open for her, then a phone started to ring deep in the house and he closed the door with an apology before she reached the bottom step.

As she made her way back round the great brooding bulk of Merryn Hall she passed the ruins of the walled garden, the ragged contours silhouetted in the misty dusk. The brick half-arch rose above like a giant question mark. A light breath of wind passed, so the coat of vegetation shivered like the fur of a sleeping animal and the leaves sighed in the trees.

She was relieved that she had accidentally left on her kitchen light, for it gave her the comforting feeling of going home.

He lets me use the oils in his studio by the stables and shows me what to do. I like the soft buttery feel of the paint, the smell of linseed oil. At first I painted fruit and flowers and pots and garden tools but now I'm trying faces and pictures of the garden. Nothing pleases me and I paint over the canvases when they are dry. He says I'm too hard on myself, but I'm sure he's only being kind.

Only Jenna knows how I spend my Sunday afternoons when they're all away visiting their families or going to chapel. She's seen my sketchbook, but she promises not to tell. She doesn't ask about Master Charles – does she know?

'Is that all you do – draw? That's lonely,' she said. 'You must come home with me sometimes. My ma would be pleased to see you.'

So I went once, to their bare cottage, and ate tea with them. They were friendly but there are so many of them and they argue and tease each other without mercy and I can't hear myself think. I can't chatter like Jenna, and the oldest brother mistook my silence for high and mighty airs, I can tell. I won't go again. I would rather paint and see Charles.

Chapter 7

Rain fell all the next morning and a curtain of mist hung over the garden. Mel sat at her computer, trying to shape the introduction to her book, but the sentences seemed clumsy, the ideas too banal. After an hour of this she sighed impatiently and looked at her emails instead. There was an automatic message from the St Ives art historian, saying he was away on holiday for a couple of weeks. That was a nuisance. One from Aimee, sighing that school was starting again next Tuesday and complaining about a dinner-party last night where she had been sat next to the spare man who had not asked her one single thing about herself all evening.

Mel stared at the screen for a moment. Already, London seemed another world. But rather than have to return to her writing, she called up her college webmail and typed in her password, dreading the list of round robins that she would have to scroll through, but concerned not to miss any real messages.

True to form, she deleted message after message about guest lecturers, computer network problems and the squash ladder, catching some information she had wanted from an American college librarian, an email about David's planned retirement in June, before the name *Jake Friedland* popped into the box. INVITATION, the message was headed. Heart in mouth, she clicked on it, knowing even before it opened that she would be disappointed. And she was. It wasn't even a message purely for her but a group email inviting Faculty members to attend a talk by a visiting writer. Stabbing the Delete button, she closed the webmail site.

And sat, with her face buried into her hands. Why did Jake's name still have the power to disturb her so deeply?

After a while she slipped outside into the rain and relieved her feelings with half an hour's angry weeding, ripping ivy and bindweed as though she were scratching her ex-lover's flesh.

She was making a sandwich for lunch when a piteous mewing started up outside the kitchen door. She opened it to find the ginger cat padding up and down in the drizzle. An offering of a dead mouse lay upon the mat.

'Thanks for that, cat.' She picked the little corpse up by the tail, whilst the cat watched her curiously. What should she do – drop it in a dustbin or throw it into the undergrowth? No, it would have to be properly buried. She found a trowel and, using last night's foil dish lid as a bier, walked up a path she had not tried before, searching for a patch of bare earth.

A tangle of high trees that might mark the boundary of the garden were as far as she could go. Below these, a belt of rampaging rhododendrons began. She stooped under one huge bush, cleared the dead leaves and dug a shallow grave in the damp earth, then, still crouching, found herself looking through a new world of gnarled trunks and roots spreading out all around. It was like a playground for children – or for Cornish piskies, she thought – low boughs for sitting on or swinging, secret dells for dens and hide and seek where the rain didn't reach, all bathed in a magical greenish dusk.

Wobbling suddenly, she shot out one hand behind to balance herself, and hit something sharp. She snatched her hand back and examined the cut on her palm, already welling with blood. With her other hand she brushed away the dead leaves until she found what had hurt her – a thin shard of metal sticking out of the soil. She pulled it out and examined it, sucking her cut. The stick was T-shaped, blackened, with patches of green. Turning it over, she considered its flatness, its pointed tip. A plant stick, she guessed. Copper probably, judging by the green, and topped with some lumpy design that formed the rough cross of the T.

Back in the cottage, she calculated the date of her last anti-tetanus injection as she dressed the cut and cleaned up the plant stick as best she could under the kitchen tap. The cat, as though remembering her annoyance at the mouse, was still reluctant to come in, and sat on the doorstep licking its haunches with long rasping strokes.

'Look, cat,' she said, holding the plant stick up. 'A mermaid.' There was no doubt. The handle of the stick that formed the cross of the T was a swirly-haired woman with a fish's tail.

The cat stopped washing and sat, one hind leg in mid-air. It stared at the stick without interest, its eyes today as mysterious a blue-green as the sea.

It's the first time he's given me a present. Apart from paint and canvas, of course. I will cherish it for ever.

'A friend in Newlyn made it for me,' he said, 'as a joke, I think, because I love gardening. But it's not much use in the garden – it'll spoil. You have it, I'd like you to have it.'

It is so pretty, the little copper mermaid. Her hair flows all around her serene face like seaweed, her bare breasts are masked by the mirror she holds . . . I must hide her, though. It wouldn't do for anyone to know. And I mustn't think about the heat that spread through me when our fingers touched or wonder whether he guessed.

'Where did you say you found it?' Patrick had appeared early that afternoon.

Mel, fed up with her own company, spotted him from out of the side window of the kitchen and leaped up to open the door.

'Well, if you're making yourself some,' he said in answer to her offer of tea, 'then yes, please, though I haven't found you a teapot yet. Even mine's broken. I came to fix that kitchen light if now is a good time.' He stepped out of his wellingtons and stood them next to her ankle-boots by the back door. His feet were bigger than Jake's, Mel noticed, and his boots dwarfed hers – menacingly or protectively, she couldn't decide.

As she poured boiling water onto teabags he threw his thick gardening gloves on the table and climbed up on a chair. She watched him twist the fluorescent bulb, and obediently pressed the light switch when he told her to.

'That seems all right now,' he said, stepping down.

'Thanks,' she said as he turned the chair round to sit down. She passed him the mermaid plant stick. 'I found it in the rhododendrons.' She explained about the mouse. 'Whose cat is it, anyway?' she asked. The animal didn't seem to mind Patrick's presence and was lazing on the mat, inside the open door.

'No idea,' he said. 'Perhaps it's a witch's familiar.' He poured milk into the tea she passed him.

'Does that make me the witch? Ha ha, thanks very much.' With a mock scowl she plumped the sugar packet down on the table. 'Perhaps it knows I can't resist cats.'

'It looks well fed, doesn't it? Must belong to someone round here.' He took a sip of tea. 'Are you busy? Only I thought it might be fun to look for the Flower Garden. Try to work out where that painting is set.' He patted the pocket of his jacket. 'I found some secateurs in a drawer and we can use some of the tools you found.'

The rain had dwindled to a light drizzle as, armed with the billhook, a large fork and the secateurs, they marched up the path. Ripping and trampling their way through brambles and bracken, they clambered over piles of fallen bricks to where the half-arch hung – today sparkling with raindrops like a broken rainbow.

'If this is indeed the arch in the painting, we must be at the entrance to the Flower Garden,' said Patrick, testing with a practised hand a rusty hinge that hung from the brickwork. 'And over there,' he indicated a fallen wall further down the garden, 'might be where they grew vegetables. It would make sense. Convenient for the kitchen.' He bent down and fossicked in the undergrowth below until he dragged up part of a rotted door, across which woodlice scuttled in all directions. He threw it to one side and rubbed his forearm. 'Ouch, these are killer nettles.'

A couple of minutes later he had hacked a way under the arch and they found themselves standing at the edge of an overgrown path gazing across the remains of a large enclosed garden. Here and there, sections of the wall still stood, peeping through trees and creeper. In one or two places, especially in the long walls at right angles to the arch, whole lengths had cracked away and keeled over like a child's Lego, to become engulfed by the greedy greenery. In the rain, everything looked lank, swimming in a dark green sea.

'It's difficult to believe it was once full of flowers,' Mel said mournfully. She walked further down the path then turned, mentally measuring her distance from the arch. 'I think P.T.'s young man must have been standing about here. Which means over there was a flowerbed, and there would have been fruit trees trained against that wall. I suppose there must be a greenhouse somewhere under all that mess.' She nodded towards the wall on one side of the arch where a flowering plant like a huge furry blanket hung down. It shrouded the skeleton of a crouching building like an ill-fitting hide. Through it poked a tangle of trees.

'Difficult to tell, isn't it?' Patrick parted some of the vegetation. Underneath, the remains of a wooden frame could be glimpsed. They ducked inside the doorway to see. One of the window frames, its glass long gone, hung down shivering in the breeze. On the side against the wall, bunches of shrivelled black beads were embalmed by dense cobweb.

'A vine, I suppose,' said Patrick. He unfolded a small penknife and stabbed the blade into the wooden frame. It cut through like butter. 'Completely rotten. We'd better be careful the whole thing doesn't fall on us.' He looked troubled.

'How long do you think the garden has been like this?' she asked, as they ducked back through the doorway.

'Decades,' he said. 'I don't know. It was certainly in this state when Val bought it. He had no interest in gardening. The couple who rented your cottage cleared some of the ground around and grew flowers and vegetables but Val did practically nothing.'

'Who mows the grass down there now?' she remembered to ask.

'Oh, an old bloke called Jim who came round asking for work. I felt sorry for him. Strapped for cash, I think. Says he used to work here once, but his accent is strong and he mumbled. I couldn't make out everything he said.'

Mel nodded. 'I suppose it might be worth quizzing him

sometime though.' She turned and stared round at the wilderness that seemed to stretch in every direction. 'It's sad, it must have been so beautiful once. Have you found any photographs or maps of the place?'

'I looked into all that when we wound up Val's estate.' He explained that Cecily Carey's solicitor had been helpful. When the house had been requisitioned during the war, most of the contents of the estate office had been packed away in one of the attics for safekeeping. Then when Miss Carey had died, the solicitor had sorted through a lot of the material with her great-niece – and sent most of it to the Cornwall Records Office in Truro. 'So I think that is where I have to look. When I have time, that is.' His sigh was impatient.

Mel looked around the devastated Flower Garden, fascinated.

'Come on,' called Patrick, striding off towards the far end. 'I'm going to see what's down here.'

'It is definitely a shed of some sort,' said Patrick half an hour later. They were surveying an L-shaped wall of brick against a main long wall. 'The potting shed, I think – look.' In one corner, a great rack of earthenware pots had once collapsed and sunk to the ground, the pots falling forward, still lying where they had smashed.

Mel caught her foot on something that clinked. Shuffling the undergrowth she uncovered a rusted half-moon, the blade of a turfcutting tool, perhaps. There were more plant sticks, too, twisted and unreadable, but none of them decorated like her mermaid.

The previous half-hour had seemed like a dream. To Mel it was as though they had passed through a magic veil – the miasma of the past. Jake, Chrissie, her life in London . . . could all be another universe. It was partly, she decided, being within these walls that shut out the activities of the modern world. Here, she and Patrick were hidden; here, they were part of the plans and visions of other times. What had these walls overheard? The sound of hard industry, metal on stone, secret conversations, tears and laughter. Here, if you knew where to look, under the briars, were arcane signs to be read in the earth – the shapes of flowerbeds, the sketched lines of a busy household.

A cross of paths had once quartered the Flower Garden – a few minutes ago, walking across the centre, Mel had nearly wrenched her ankle when the vegetation gave way under her.

'I think you've found the dipping pool,' said Patrick, helping her to her feet. 'Water for the garden. Look, there's the pipe. I wonder where the water came from.' But the pipe ran into the ground, preventing further investigation.

'There's the stream running near the bottom of the garden, down the valley to the sea. Perhaps they pumped water up here?' Mel said, still rubbing her ankle.

'There was a leat,' he said suddenly. 'I remember one of the neighbours complaining once to Val.'

'What's a leat when it's at home?'

'An artificial stream or channel. It would have come from a reservoir further up the valley, then run down by the side of those trees and fed one of the millponds below.' The owners of Merryn apparently had a duty to maintain the leat so that one of the mills could operate. Val, of course, wasn't bothered. The mill was no longer in use by then, but a neighbour had a garden that relied on the leat flowing properly and had threatened to take Val to court over it. Val had grumbled about paying a firm to clear it.

'So the leat would have fed Merryn's garden, too.'

'Together with the stream, I expect, yes.'

Shortly after that, they found the remains of another greenhouse against the south wall, the pinioned arms of long-dead fruit trees half-shrouded by the nettles that reached to Mel's chin. Here and there, scalloped glass panes remained, held in by ancient putty.

'It's extraordinary that it's survived a century of storms,' said Patrick. 'I got an SOS call from Val after one five or six years ago. He lost about twenty huge trees, several falling right across the drive. I managed to find a tree surgeon – Val was useless at dealing with problems like that at the best of times, and he was quite ill by then. We're still burning the last of the wood, you know.'

Patrick scrunched his way to the far end of the ruined potting shed where there was a gap in the garden wall. 'I'd no idea this was all here,' he called back. 'Here's the Vegetable Garden. And another hut.' And he disappeared through the gap. Mel followed.

The hut was better preserved than the potting shed, most of its roof was still remaining. It smelled of damp earth and wet ashes. Patrick had ducked through a crumbling brick doorway halfway along and she heard his excited cry.

'Mel, come and see this.'

She peered through the half-darkness of the hut to see where he had gone. When she reached him he was wrestling with the doors of a wall cupboard, on the right of which was a small fireplace full of rubble. Amazingly, a rusted kettle still stood on the hob.

'This must be the Head Gardener's hut,' he said, yanking open the cupboard doors. They both stared at the contents – rows of glass jars of seeds and a large oilskin-wrapped package. Patrick slid the package out from the cupboard and placed it on a desk in the corner of the room. Gingerly he opened it and pulled out two large ledgers. The top one, when he opened it, immediately tore at the spine, so he closed it again.

'Logbooks, I think. Let's take them back to the house.'

As they made their way back across the garden, Mel realised that the rain had stopped. A gust of wind soughed across the leaves. 'It's as if the garden is sighing,' she said. 'It's starting to tell us its secrets.'

Patrick rolled his eyes. 'You'll be telling me next it has a soul.'

She wrinkled her nose. 'Don't be silly.'

But as she followed him back through the arch, she turned to take one more look at the heartbreaking desolation and felt that it was calling her back.

In the kitchen of Merryn Hall, Mel sat at the table and wiped the ledgers carefully with a duster as Patrick stuffed teabags into a cracked Brown Betty teapot with a saucer for a lid.

'It starts in 1911,' she said, turning the cover of the first book. 'Look, it's a sort of diary.'

Patrick peeled off his jacket and sat down beside her. As he poured the tea she was suddenly very aware of his closeness, the oily smell of raw wool. 'Here's your tea.' His body twisted towards her as he passed over the mug, then he leaned closer to look at the ledger, one hand nursing his own drink. He had large, strong hands, Mel noticed, with neat, square-cut nails. A worker's hands, but smooth, not callused with cracked skin as his farming ancestors' hands must have been. She turned her attention back to the logbooks.

The Head Gardener in 1911 was a man called John Boase, who had written his name and job title on the front page of the first ledger. He appeared to have supervised a core of four men, with the occasional help of others, though as the years went by the names changed. The diary was a careful record of which men had turned up each day and the jobs they had been given, together with anything of note that had happened in the gardens.

18 October 1911

John Martyn (planting potatoes, swedes, turnips), John Tonkin (preparing beds Flower Garden), Peter Hawke (help me to remove diseased oak by south-east wall), William Simpson (30 minutes late to his duties clearing leaves).

6 May 1912

John Tonkin (pruning laurels), Zachary Hawke (clearing pond by summerhouse), John Martyn (preparing flowerbeds), James Tresco (rockery). No frost for two weeks. Rhubarb ready.

8 July 1912

John Tonkin (spray roses for greenfly), Zachary Hawke sick, John Martyn (prune fruit bushes), James Tresco (mowing), Martin Tresco (general assistance). Peaches good this year. Mistress sends compliments for Hamburgs.

27 December 1912

Terrible storm yesterday afternoon. Worst any can remember. Many trees lost including Master Charles's beloved handkerchief tree. Early crocus shredded, many shrubs destroyed. Statue in pond by summerhouse smashed. Mistress distraught. All day has been spent in general clearance. Thanks to God for our borders of fine trees for all might be worse.

'What on earth is a handkerchief tree?' asked Patrick.

'A rare Chinese specimen discovered by a missionary called Father David,' replied Mel, her brow wrinkling as she tried to decipher writing on a page infringed by damp. 'Its blooms look like white handkerchiefs. Plant-hunters died searching for them and they're difficult to grow here. Master Charles, whoever he was, must have been devastated.'

After the excitement of the storm, she turned the pages expectant of further drama, but all remained routine until the end of 1914. Then, suddenly, next to Zachary Hawke's name in October of that year was written the word *enlisted*, underlined in the faded black ink. At the beginning of 1915 and the start of the second ledger, it was John Tonkin's turn. *Enlisted*. Barely a week later, by James Tresco's name was written, *Martin Tresco has enlisted. Aged seventeen last week.*

After that, with only one regular man helping him, a note of strain began to enter the tone of John Boase's normally factual comments.

Buryan Feast, May 1915
James Tresco (Vegetable Garden). Master says we are to turn the Flower Garden over to vegetables. The vines and the peaches must look after theirselves, there is too much else to do. Next winter we grow potatoes on the lawns unless we wish to eat grass. Last night as I walked in the fields I saw a white hare, which gave me troubled sleep. The news from the Front is bad, very bad. I fear for my young men. How terrible to see this time when men give thanks if they are old and have no sons.

1 June 1915
The blow has fallen. Jem Hawke sends word Zachary is killed in action. The Lord be with Jem and Susan for he is their only one.

5 September 1915
Martin Tresco reported Missing Presumed Killed. James did not work today so Jago helped me pick apples. He is very distressed about Martin and ashamed of his own weakness of

the chest that meant he was passed over for service. I tell him not to be daft. We will need men like him to build a new land when this war is done.

Then, in July 1917, came unexpected news.

Master Charles reported Missing Believed Killed. All the glory of man shall fall as a flower of the field. Will there ever be an end to this business?

Mel flicked through the remaining entries. The ledger ended in August 1917.

In the second book, the entries were even terser, the range of tasks attempted more narrow. Boase had little help, it seemed. Few flowers were grown and no exotic fruit. He recorded the death of his employer, Mr Carey, in 1920.

'It's easy to get the picture, isn't it?' said Mel, closing the second book and leaning back in her chair. 'The war ruined the garden as it destroyed all those young lives. Without a team of men, the Head Gardener must have struggled to perform the important tasks.'

'And everything else was left to go hang,' agreed Patrick, standing up and going to the window. He stood at the sink, looking out on the sleeping ruin of the garden before him. 'It's fascinating,' he said. 'To think of what might be out there, under all that wilderness.'

Mel went to join him, close but not touching, one arm folded, with the other twisting a strand of her hair.

'We know there's a summerhouse and a pond,' she said dreamily.

'Maybe still with a broken statue,' added Patrick.

'And laurels and a lawn. How can we find out what else?'

'The Records Office,' he said, almost to himself. 'I really must go when I've got some time.'

'You seem to be getting quite excited by it all.'

'The garden, you mean?' He turned to look at her, and she hadn't seen his face this alive, intent. 'Do you know, I think I am. I'd love to restore it all – I really would.'

'That sounds a wonderful plan,' Mel said. 'A lot of work, though.'

'And money, no doubt. Not that I'm impoverished, but you could pour tens of thousands into this place to little avail if you weren't careful.'

'I don't mind helping while I'm here,' said Mel, 'with the plans and whatnot. But I tell you what really interests me, and that's finding out more about the mystery painter. It could be that there's some connection to the Lamorna Group, and I'd like to find out what.'

'I've no idea how you should go about that,' said Patrick, frowning.

'I've got an appointment to go to the Records Office next week,' said Mel, 'so I'll root around in the catalogue and see if there's anything useful there. I'll take a quick look at what's in the Merryn collection as well.'

'That would be very helpful,' said Patrick, clinking their empty mugs as he placed them in the sink. 'Then I can have a proper look some other time. Now the question is, is five o'clock too early for a glass of wine?'

'It's not too early for me.' Mel watched Patrick select another dusty bottle from a rack in the larder.

'Let's try this Château Neuf. Tell you what,' he said. 'Stay for supper. I stopped off home on my way down from London and my mother gave me a joint of lamb. There's too much for just me.'

'Sounds lovely, thanks,' said Mel, as the rich aroma of the wine filled the kitchen. 'If I change out of these damp clothes I can come back early and help you. I'm useless at proper gravy, but I can peel vegetables for England.'

He laughed as he handed her a glass. 'Just for Cornwall tonight, my dear,' he said in a broad local accent.

Chapter 8

Rounding the top of the stairs of the Gardener's Cottage after her bath, wrapped in a towel, Mel was brought face to face with another woman. The door of the wardrobe in the spare room had swung open and for a second she froze in shock to see her reflection in the long mirror.

Since Jake had left, she had avoided looking at herself with much attention. If he hadn't loved her enough to stay, had thrown her over so easily, perhaps there was something lacking in her. Perhaps she was grown faded, unremarkable.

Now she saw with fresh eyes that this wasn't true at all. Her legs beneath the short towel were long and shapely, her shoulders rose white and flawless. Her pale oval face beneath the tails of wet hair glowed out of the half-light like a Renaissance madonna's. For a moment, though, she was a female Narcissus, innocently entranced by her own image.

Mesmerised, she stepped inside the doorway. The towel slid to the floor.

If anyone had asked Mel which part of her body she liked most and which least, she would have said she was happy with her hair and her legs, but that her breasts were too small and the swell of her tummy put her off wearing close-fitting skirts and dresses. But this evening, in the weak light of the overhead bulb, in the dreamy solitude of this house, she could see that the woman in the mirror was beautiful. Her breasts were high and firm, the nipples slightly swollen from her bath, like tiny pink cherries. The pear-shaped curve of her body – so like her mother's – was full and luscious; her bush of dark red hair an ornament against her creamy skin.

Her eyes met those of the girl in the looking-glass. Tonight, the blue irises were indigo, the strongly drawn nose a contrast to a soft red mouth, lips slightly parted, almost bee-stung from the steam. For a flash she imagined Patrick was looking at her. *Perhaps I am desirable*, she told herself in surprise.

In harsh daylight, she knew she would see slight crow's feet at the corners of her eyes, etched lines arching up from between her eyes and from her nose to the edge of her mouth, lines that Time's pencil would score more deeply as the years slipped past. But tonight she looked perfect. The insight was a gift.

As she stared at herself, it was as though something heavy was shifting itself in her chest, at the base of her throat. To her dismay, tears began to well in her eyes. She blinked them away.

Suddenly, she shivered in the cool air. She bent, picked up the towel and wrapped it round her, flinching at its dampness. She glanced again in the mirror and this time saw a flicker of movement. She turned round, puzzled. Nothing. A trick of the light. Or maybe the mirror had wobbled. But there was something else – that feeling of being watched again. By whom? She didn't know, but a picture came into her mind of a tall woman with a halo of dark hair. Then it was gone.

Mel pushed the wardrobe door shut and hurried back into her own bedroom, her mind already taken again with the question of what she should wear tonight. It felt good to have someone to dress for again, she thought, pulling on a flattering pair of trousers and a pale blue cashmere jumper. A necklace of stones the same blue as her eyes completed the outfit.

She had only met Patrick two days ago but, she had to admit as she plugged in the hairdryer and started to finger-dry her long wet tresses, there was something intriguing about him. He was nice-looking rather than handsome, she decided. She liked the way his hair fell across his forehead. She wanted to reach out and push it back. And his remoteness, the things he concealed, lent him an air of mystery, fascination.

She dusted some blusher across her cheekbones and squinted in the little wall mirror to apply eye-shadow and mascara. Whether he was attracted to her, she didn't know. But she did sense his growing interest in her as a person, and that was flattering after the months of loneliness. She wondered about the girlfriend Chrissie had mentioned. Patrick hadn't said a word about her yet.

She went downstairs, pulled on her leather jacket and stepped outside, taking care to leave the hall light on to guide her way home. The evening was dry, with a warm breeze that carried the bittersweet scent of early may blossom. Up the track, a pair of eyes glinted in the gloaming. She froze. Was it the cat? The eyes blazed, then the animal swung away and leaped into the undergrowth in a shock of dark brown. A fox then, loping off into the secret world of the garden. She locked the door and made her way up towards the house.

A rustle of leaves – someone's coming . . . No, it's only some beast slipping away through the ferns. It's the first time we've agreed to meet after dark. Aunt Dolly thinks I'm upstairs turning the covers. I'll only be a minute, that's all I dare. I see the glow of his cigarette ahead in the shadows where

the door of the studio stands ajar. 'There you are,' he rasps, and grabs me,
pulling me inside.

'I meant to ask, how did you get on with your writing this morning?' said Patrick as he sloshed red wine into the rich dark gravy simmering in the roasting dish.

Mel, laying out knives and forks on the wooden table, looked up, amused at how at home he appeared at the elderly stove, where he was peering under saucepan lids, checking the browning potatoes, a tea towel slung over one shoulder, singing along tunelessly to some jazz tune pouring out of a sound system he had rigged up.

She sighed as she pulled out a chair and sat down. 'The writing's not flowing at the moment,' she said. 'I know roughly what I want to say but I need a fresh focus, some way into the subject-matter that can be a touchstone for the book.'

'Surely there's plenty to say about these painters,' encouraged Patrick as he poured the gravy into the blue and white striped jug warming at the back of the stove.

'Yes, but wouldn't it be fantastic to discover something new instead of reinterpreting existing evidence.'

'Some hot lesbian affair, do you mean?'

'If only.' Mel laughed. 'No, it's likely to be more boring than that. I mean finding a lost painting or discovering that a known artwork was misattributed, or uncovering an unusual source of inspiration . . .'

'Mmm, the lesbian affair does sound more fun.'

As she helped Patrick decant the leeks, carrots and potatoes she had prepared into the faded serving dishes of Val's elderly dinner service, Mel tried to bring to mind the picture of the young man in the garden. 'That's partly why I'm so interested in P.T.'s work,' she told Patrick. 'The picture upstairs, it's from the right period, or slightly later, judging by the man's clothes. But I can't think of any local artist with those initials. Still, I am intrigued.'

Sitting at the table watching him carve the joint, an idea occurred to her. 'Do you suppose the Carey descendants might have other works by P.T.? Or know who he or she was? I'm assuming the pictures belonged to them, rather than being something your uncle bought?'

'Not Val's cup of tea, I assure you, despite him knowing about Lamorna Birch. It's possible they might know something,' he said, and frowned slightly as he passed her the plate. 'I've got an address for the family's solicitors somewhere. I'll dig it out and contact them if you like. There we are,' he said, refilling her glass. He raised his own. 'Here's to the garden – and P.T. – the success of two projects.' They smiled at one another and drank.

Later, Patrick reached into the fridge for a bottle of dessert wine to drink with the early strawberries and clotted cream.

'Just half a glass, thanks,' Mel murmured, feeling distinctly mellow after a huge first course and the heavy red wine.

One arm along the back of an empty chair, Patrick poured with the dexterity of a *maître du vin*. She watched him lazily, admiring his relaxed enjoyment of the moment. Despite the air of aloofness, he was a peaceful man to be with, entirely present for her.

He looked up and his eyes crinkled in a smile. 'Here you are,' and for a moment, their fingers touched. There was no spark exactly, but they looked at one another appraisingly and there was vulnerability in his eyes. She felt a rush of warmth towards him and smiled back shyly, then lowered her eyes, glad to turn her attention to the strawberries. They were small and slightly tart, despite the coating of sugar.

'I was thinking,' she said after a silence. 'Stop me if I'm getting too keen.' His eyebrows rose and she felt her face grow hot. 'Go on,' he said.

'When I'm at the Records Office next week, if there is anything useful for you about the Carey family and the gardens here – old maps or photographs – I could order copies and we could work up a sort of master-plan of the garden.'

'That would be great, Mel. Would you really have time?'

'It depends how much there is, doesn't it? But I'll try.'

'You know,' said Patrick, stretching back in his chair, that now familiar teasing expression on his face, 'it seems to me that you're getting as excited as I am about Merryn.'

'An historian's interest,' she said, worried that he might think her intrusive, 'fired by the Flower Garden and looking at the diaries this afternoon. The place weaves a strange spell on you, don't you think? The sense of a lost world in an enchanted sleep. Waiting to be woken.' She remembered something. 'Do you know that Lana talks about the place being haunted?'

'I know they felt uncomfortable about living in the cottage, but I thought that was because it was too isolated for them.'

'There is an atmosphere. I'm not sure that it amounts to a haunting. Just a strong feeling of the past.'

'Yes, I know what you mean. It's surprising, though, given that the Careys mean nothing particularly to me. They weren't family.'

'No, but that doesn't matter. It's funny, you know. It's a difference between people – what they see. Take Chrissie and me. When she was helping me look for a flat, ages ago, she would walk into those lovely old Victorian places and be looking to change them all around to suit. You know: "If you knock down that wall you'd have a walk-through living room" or, "Pave over

111

the garden and build a conservatory". Whereas I would be happy with places as they were, even if they were inconvenient. Chrissie says I have no imagination but I don't think she has enough sometimes.'

'You mean you look at a place and see the layers of the past and she looks at it and sees the needs of the present and the possibilities of the future?'

'I suppose so, yes.'

Patrick said reasonably, 'Yes, she's very practical, isn't she? Perhaps, ideally, one should be both. After all, our ancestors weren't so sentimental. They would raze buildings to the ground and build new wonders. Look at Castle Howard, for instance.'

'I wonder whether you'll decide to come down here permanently?' Mel asked now.

Patrick looked confused for a moment, then he said, 'Until recently, I had decided to make it my home. A family home.'

A home for a family. His family. His children. 'Oh,' said Mel.

'But not now.' He picked up the bottle of dessert wine. 'Have some more.'

Mel placed her hand over her glass in a sudden, defensive gesture.

He put the bottle down again and turned it, studying the label intently as though it were of sudden absorbing interest. He was silent, so Mel asked gently, 'What happened?'

'An all-too-familiar story of love's labours lost.' He stopped then growled, 'I'm not really up to talking about it.'

'Sorry.'

'No, it's me that's sorry,' said Patrick, taking another large gulp of wine. 'It's selfish of me. Chrissie told me something similar had happened to you recently.'

'Oh, did she?' said Mel. So Chrissie had been as indiscreet as

112

she feared. But suddenly she couldn't bear for the evening to descend into an alcohol-fuelled morass of self-pity and gloom. 'It did, but I'm trying not to think about it. Let's have some coffee. I'll make it if you'll show me the right cupboard.'

After that, the conversation returned to safer pastures – Patrick's upbringing in a rambling farmhouse in the central part of the county, arguments about books they had read and films they had seen.

When it was time to go, Patrick turned down Mel's offer of help with the washing-up and reached for his jacket as he came with her to the door. He looked tired and slightly the worse for wine.

'I'll walk down with you,' he said.

'No, I'll be fine. Look, I've bought the torch.' Mel pulled it out of her coat pocket.

'I have to go back to London tomorrow,' said Patrick, as he opened the front door.

'Oh.'

'But I'll be down again Friday evening, if I can.'

'I'll have had half my stay by then,' Mel said softly.

'Mmm,' said Patrick, then paused. 'It's not let after you go, you know. I keep forgetting to do something about an ad.'

'Oh,' said Mel.

'So you can stay on if you like.'

'How kind,' she said formally. 'I'll think about it, whether I need more time here.'

'Well, you know you're welcome.'

'Thanks, and thank you for a delicious meal,' she said, her voice a little too bright. 'Perhaps I can return the favour some-time.'

'Sure, maybe next weekend.' He gave a mock bow and watched her go. 'Oh, and good luck at the Records Office.'

'Thanks.'

At the corner of the house she glanced back. He was standing on the steps, arms folded, staring out across the drive, looking so dejected she almost stopped and walked back.

Chapter 9

Sundays, Mel reflected the next morning, padding downstairs in her nightgown, her head throbbing from too much wine, felt different from any other morning in the week. Perhaps it was the quiet. Even the birds hadn't woken her this morning. Of course, in London, the difference was more marked. The build-up of cars began later on a Sunday, there were no workmen's drills, no doors slamming followed by urgent footsteps echoing down the street at 7 a.m.

So the rev of a car engine, heard through the open bathroom window, came as a rude interruption of the peace. She listened to the sound recede; 8.30 Patrick was already on the road back to London. She was alone again. She splashed cold water on her skin and buried her face in her towel for comfort.

As she dressed, she tried to rationalise her feelings. You're in a vulnerable state, she told herself severely. Just because you have a moment of – what was it, friendship, closeness? – with Patrick doesn't mean he owes you anything or that it's going to turn into more than a passing acquaintance. He's obviously in no state to start a new relationship and neither are you. You've been on your own plenty of times before and survived, and you've just got to get used to it. All over again.

For there had been other men before Jake, of course there had. The longest-lasting had been Steve, with whom she had lived for five years in her twenties. Early passion cooled to something more comfortable and then they came to take each other for granted. Mel loved him, he was kind and easy to love, but in her heart of hearts she knew that wasn't enough, and after thinking about it for many sleepless nights, she told him it was over. Afterwards she wondered whether she had done the right thing, whether a pleasant relationship with a good man was all she could realistically expect. Perhaps she was turning out like her father? Not a stayer, once the romance was gone . . .

It had been hard starting over again. It was the year she turned thirty and, Saturday after Saturday, so it seemed, she had to turn up alone to friends' weddings, to wish them well and scatter confetti with a cheerful smile on her face, before returning home to her shabby rented flat. After a few months she bought her own place and tried to exorcise her loneliness by burying herself in her work and social life, spending all her spare time decorating and making curtains and cushions, choosing furniture, having people round to dinner endlessly.

In retrospect it was not an unhappy time, but a period of adjustment, learning to rely on herself, having her own space, focusing on her job, being free to go where she wanted when she wanted. For a while she feared she was walking a psychological tightrope and mustn't look down, but then her confidence returned.

She should, in time, be able to enjoy being single now, after Jake. But, brushing her hair in the mirror and snatching at several silver threads that glistened in the cruel daylight, she was suddenly weary of it. Meeting new men could be exciting though, as Aimee frequently told her, she treated the whole business too seriously, expecting relationships to deepen quickly or, the opposite fault, not bothering to try to get to know someone if they didn't attract her strongly from the outset.

Where did Patrick fit into this pattern? Was she just latching on to the next attractive man who came along for fear of being alone? Would she have been drawn to him if they had met in London? She tried to imagine bumping into him at a party, perhaps thinking he was attractive, quietly charming, but not someone who would have struck an instant spark like Jake. Did that make her a superficial person? She hoped not.

There was something about Patrick that touched her. She remembered the gentle curve of his mouth, his strong hands working the penknife or opening a bottle and pouring wine in a steady movement, thought of his stillness when he listened to her. Yes, she already looked forward to his return. She laid down her brush and went downstairs.

When she was filling the kettle, a familiar miaowing began outside the back door. She turned the key in the lock and yanked open the door.

'Just you and me again, cat,' she said. Seeing its hesitancy she stood back from the doorway. The cat placed one paw over the doorsill then the other, and looked around the kitchen carefully. Then it lost courage and daintily withdrew once more. 'Make your mind up, can't you?' Mel said mildly, going back to the sink. But she left the door open on account of it being such a sunny day.

A pile of books lay on the table from yesterday and as she waited for the toaster to pop she slid one off the top and started flicking through it. It was a catalogue of the works of Laura Knight. She turned the pages and it struck her not for the first time how much painting from this fruitful part of Laura's long career represented the holiday side of Cornwall. Young

Edwardian women in loose flowing dresses perched on a clifftop gazed out at the glorious shining sea spread out below; chubby children played on a beach dappled by a tracery of sun and shadow; sun-worshippers, daringly half-naked, basked on rocks. A Golden Age, before the wings of war cast their dark shadow. Once again she was struck by the liberating contrast to the sober moral realism of the Newlyn painters.

Mel frowned as she stared at the picture on the clifftop. There was something in the choice of palette, the texture of the paint, the Impressionistic way heat and light seemed to radiate from the scene that reminded her of P.T.'s painting of the man in the garden. Which of the many artists who had passed through Lamorna at the time could P.T. have been? How could she find out? It would mean rereading the memoirs of other artists, combing through papers related to the house, digging amongst documents of local history.

After breakfast she worked in the garden. The size of her flowerbed was expanding fast, but today she tore away at the undergrowth in a half-hearted manner, feeling tired and clumsy. With a sigh she picked up the heavy garden fork and plunged it into the space she had uncovered. It bounced off something hard with a clunk. She crouched down to see what she had hit, scrabbling through the surface layer of dead creeper and leafmould with her gloved fingers. To her surprise, the entire layer peeled back like a piece of matting, revealing a path of hard-packed earth lined with gravel and white sand. A path to where?

Her interest was tinged with sudden frustration. There might be a whole network of paths lying buried under this jungle, a secret pattern waiting to be discovered. But it needed more than her pathetic efforts to find them. To reclaim this garden Patrick needed to organise a whole taskforce of people equipped with proper tools. One woman with a fork and an ancient pair of secateurs was hardly going to make much impact.

She stood up to go, jabbing the fork into the earth, where it stuck quivering.

Later, she walked down to the cove and then west up a dry narrow rabbit-path that scampered along the edge of the cliff. The coconut smell of flowering gorse blended with the scent of grass and the salty tang of the air. The sun was beating down now and she was soon panting with the effort of the climb, having to watch her every step on the stony earth.

Before long she came to a large cairn, a pile of boulders raised high above the rocky promontory that jutted out into the ocean below. The disturbing feeling came that she had seen it before – of course she had, in paintings. She peered over. To one side a faint path zig-zagged down to rocks now half-covered by the tide.

She sat for a moment in the shelter of the boulders, gazing out across the sea, her eyes instinctively searching for some detail, some solid object on the restless, shimmering surface. How many an anxious woman had waited here over the centuries, watching for the fishing boat or the merchant ship that carried her loved one home, hope failing as the hours passed. She closed her eyes. Or what must it be like up here in a storm, watching a ship being sucked helplessly towards the rocks below, unable to help the screaming, struggling sailors? She shivered and opened her eyes once more, glad of the warmth of the sun on the rocks and the present calm of the shimmering water below.

A yapping noise startled her. Someone called, 'Hello!'

She swung round to see Matt standing below on the cliff path. An elderly white wire-haired terrier puffed up to snuffle at her feet.

'Hi, Mel. Sorry about him. Stinker – leave,' he said sternly, climbing the slope and grabbing the dog's collar.

'Oh don't worry, I don't mind dogs,' she said. 'Is he really called Stinker?'

'It's Tinker, really, but you don't want to be in a closed room with him for long after he's been at the beer. He belongs to my mum, but she doesn't have time to walk him. Getting a bit tubby in your old age, aren't you, Stinker, old boy?'

'Wonderful up here, isn't it?' She turned to look back at the sea.

'Wait till you see it with lightning flashing through the sky. It's breathtaking.'

Mel shivered, imagining again the watchers in the storm.

'Which way are you going?' Matt asked, casual.

'Oh, I don't know, just back to the cove, I suppose. Home.'

'Why don't you come with me, try a different route.' He gestured behind him across the thicket-covered cliff. 'Through the field there's a path goes past Mum's hotel and, if you want a bit of a walk, on up to the Merry Maidens.'

'The Merry Maidens?'

'You haven't seen the Maidens? You should. But come and have some coffee at the hotel first. Mum would love to say hi. She's always interested to hear what's going on at Merryn.'

'We've only just met, you and I,' Mel said, her eyes sparkling, 'and you're already introducing me to your mother. Maybe I ought to question your motives, young man!'

Matt smiled uncertainly, and she wondered if she had struck the wrong note. She followed him up the cliff path and inland through the bracken. Tinker lolloped fatly ahead, stopping to bark occasionally at gorse bushes.

'Why does your mother want to meet me?' she asked Matt, who had waited for her to catch up.

'I said, didn't I? Because of the house – Merryn Hall. She's always been fascinated by it.'

'Why in particular? Though I agree, it is fascinating.'

'Some family reason. Great-great-aunty someone or other used to live there, I think.' He shrugged. 'Mum's gran was one of eight so I get easily confused. You'll have to ask her.'

'Matt will fetch us some coffee, if you wouldn't mind, Matt, my dear. I'll come and join you both, but I must have a quick word with Chef about tonight's fish.'

Matt's mother was in her fifties and as stout as her dog. She had serene dark eyes and her son's black hair, with hardly a trace of grey, though hers was curly where his was straight. Matt's delicate bone structure and mercurial movements must have come from some other part of the family, Mel decided. In the proprietorial way she stood in the hotel lounge, hands on hips, and the way she measured every word she spoke, Carrie Price seemed as solid as Cornish granite.

'Back in a moment.' Matt twisted away from his mother who was ruffling his hair. He vanished through a door behind the bar. Carrie walked back into the hall like a sailor on a swaying deck.

Mel settled into her comfortable fireside chair and looked around. The hotel was designed like an Edwardian country house, the panelled walls hung with oil paintings of cherubic children and gracious behatted ladies cradling roses. The lights were Moroccan-style lanterns, and two Knole sofas were festooned with embroidered cushions. Old-fashioned genteel comfort.

'Matt tells me you're staying at Merryn,' said Carrie, returning and lowering herself with a little, 'Oof,' into an armchair opposite Mel. She had a soft country accent, burring her r's, unlike her son, who appeared to have exchanged his somewhere along the way for ubiquitous Thames estuary.

'Yes. I've been here a week now. Three more to go.' And she told Carrie a little about her research.

'I used to see Lamorna Birch's daughter about when I was young,' said Carrie. 'And Cecily Carey. I remember her, too.'

'Matt said you had a connection with the family, or the house anyway.'

'Yes. My mother's mother had a sister older than her, worked there as a maid. Way back, we're talking about, before the First War. Before she married. Great-aunt Jenna's long dead now, of course, but I remember her talking about the parties they had. Lovely affairs, she said, with lights and music and fireworks. In those beautiful gardens.'

'The gardens must have been wonderful once. What did she say about them?'

'Oh, I don't really remember, except there was a cave – a grotto, she called it. Full of candles, it was, hundreds of them, like Christmas.'

'Lovely. Have you always lived round here, Carrie?'

There was a break in the conversation as Matt emerged from the bar with a tray, and poured them all coffee with hot frothy milk.

Carrie adjusted her cushion and nestled more comfortably into her chair. 'Phew. What a morning. It's nice to be waited on for a change. Yes, to answer your question, my dear, I was born up the valley in Paul village. Matt's father inherited the hotel from his own parents and we've been here ever since we married, though Matt's dad passed on five years ago.'

'I was born in the Honeymoon Suite, as Mum never tires of telling me,' Matt put in, rolling his eyes.

'It was a quiet time of year and I'd always loved that room,' explained Carrie. 'Anyway, I heard Mr Winterton had got Merryn, but I haven't ever met him. Do you know what he's planning to do with the place? It's terrible it's so rundown, such a lovely house.'

'I've only just met him, as a matter of fact. But I believe he wants to live there himself.' A thought struck Mel. 'Did your great-aunt ever talk about an artist connected to the house back before the wars? Someone with the initials P.T.?'

'P.T.? No, that doesn't mean anything to me. Aunt Jenna used to talk about the family. There were Mr and Mrs Carey and two daughters. Then there was some relation, a young man – the girls' cousin, I reckon – lived there for a bit, too. But he blotted his copybook somehow. Got sent away.'

'That's intriguing, Mum,' said Matt. 'What did he do? Catch Aunt Jenna behind the rose-bushes or steal the teaspoons?' He twinkled wickedly at Mel, who smiled back.

'No, no, I'm sure it was nothing like that.'

'I suppose we'll never know,' said Matt. 'Too long ago and everyone dead.'

'Norah's still alive – Jenna's daughter. Not that I see her much. Lives up near Truro. Ah, that was lovely,' said Carrie, putting down her empty cup. 'It's nice to see you, my dear, and I hope you'll call in again, but I'd better get back to work. We're full this weekend. Matt, can you stay and wait at dinner?'

'Sure, Mum, but I won't stay over. I'm on early shift at the shop in the morning.'

'I'm always telling him,' Carrie confided to Mel, 'he ought to live here. I really need his help, and then, when I retire, this place can be his.'

Behind his mother, unseen by her, Matt grimaced. One would always be second string working for Carrie, Mel imagined.

'I ought to be getting back myself,' she said, trying not to laugh. 'Thanks ever so much, Carrie.'

She walked with Matt out towards the front door and stopped in surprise. A familiar figure now stood behind the reception desk.

'Irina! I didn't know you worked in *this* hotel.' The woman looked tired and her eyes seemed rimmed with red.

Irina looked from Mel to Matt, who was lurking behind, waiting to say goodbye. 'And I didn't know you knew Matt,' she said. 'I've worked here some months. Carrie is kind and allows me to come when I can.'

'I've been meaning to ring,' said Mel, 'to see if you wanted to meet up for lunch one day.'

'I'd love to, but I can't this week, I said I'd be here. How about the evenings? Maybe you would like to come to supper at my house. Thursday or Friday?'

'Thursday would be good,' said Mel. 'Thank you.'

As she hurried down the steep path to the road she thought about Irina and about the maid, Jenna, and secrets locked in the past. Then she remembered how she had intended to walk on to the Merry Maidens, whatever they were. That would have to be for another day now.

Tuesday was the day Mel had arranged to visit the Cornwall Records Office outside Truro. As she was locking up the cottage, she heard a vehicle bumping down the track, its gears screaming. A small open truck rounded the corner and stuttered to a halt. The man who climbed out of the cab looked as ancient and weatherbeaten as his rusted transport, his square face so brown and wrinkled he might have been the spirit of an old gnarled tree.

'Lovely morning,' he said, nodding at her. He walked stiffly to the back of the van, where he lowered the tailgate and hauled out a large battered petrol lawnmower. Mel recognised him suddenly – he had been working in the front garden of one of the houses near the beginning of the village on her first morning.

'Are you Jim?' she asked, remembering what Patrick had said.

The man nodded and touched his cap, but he was looking past Mel to the flowerbed she had cleared. A look of concern crossed his face.

'You're the one doing that thur?' he said, suddenly fixing her with watery blue eyes.

'Yes,' she said. 'Is there something wrong?'

'No, not wrong,' he said uncertainly, 'but thur's a powerful pile of work you set yourself thur.' His accent was very thick and Mel had to ask him to repeat himself.

She remembered Patrick saying Jim had worked here previously. 'Did you know this place when it was a proper garden?'

The man was silent for a moment. 'Before the soldiers come,' he said. 'Parking thur tents on the lawns, trampling everything down. My dad, he wur a gardener hur awhile. Sometimes I do help him.'

'Was that the last war? What was the garden like before?' Mel asked eagerly. 'What do you remember about it?'

'Well now,' the old man said, straightening up from his task. He looked out down the garden, lost for a moment in thought. Then he turned and gestured up towards the house. 'Up thur, see, that wur grass with a sundial. Here, whur you been digging, well that wur flowerbeds, but thur wur a big hedge to hide yur cottage. The soldiers ploughed that up to get their trucks and whatnot past.'

'It's all rhododendrons over there, isn't it?' Mel pointed over to the far side of the garden where she had buried the mouse.

'Yus, and further down, laurels.' He shook his head sadly. 'There wur a rockery, too, and a kind of cave. But that had been all grown about. The gardener, he wur an old man then and thur wur just the old lady, Missus Carey, and her daughter. When the soldiers took the place they do go to live with the other daughter up Fowey way.'

'Wasn't there a pond, with a statue?'

'Ay, its head fallen off – down thur, see, where thur's all the trees. Thur was what the old lady called the ravine. Wild as Bedlam. Good place for hiding, though, if you're a young tacker like I are then. And the gardens at the front, too. A ruddy jungle.'

He sighed and bent down to his mower once more as if the memory weighed heavy. Then, one hand on the ripcord, he looked up and said, 'If you want my advice, you don't go digging and disturbing. She's still hereabouts, see. She watches you.' He shook his head and muttered. A twist of a lever and a tug of the ripcord and the mower leaped into noisy life. 'Better get on now, my dear,' he shouted.

'What did you say?' shouted Mel. 'Seen who? *What?*'

But he was engrossed in his task. Mel looked round the garden again, trying to picture it as the old man had described. It was frustrating. She would have to speak to him again. Then she and Patrick could perhaps draw up a plan of how the garden used to be. But what did he mean by, 'She's still hereabouts'? Another mystery to join the others.

'The Careys,' said the young woman in the Records Office, once she had checked Mel's registration credentials. 'Yes, we do have a collection from Merryn Hall. If you'd like to look through the catalogue here . . .'

Over a hundred documents were listed, relating to the history of the Hall since it was built in the early nineteenth century. A large number, it seemed, were property agreements and accounts related to the farm estates. What sounded more relevant was a selection of photographs of the house and gardens and of the occupants. Mel made a note of these, together with the references for the tithe map of 1891 and an Ordnance Survey map of the estate dated 1909. There were also listed several ledgers of household accounts covering the late nineteenth and early twentieth centuries. After a moment's hesitation, she added the ones that covered 1900 to 1910 to the request for material for her own research, the diaries of a female Newlyn artist from the period.

While she was waiting for the first batch of material to arrive, she had a sudden thought. Perhaps the information she was looking for about P.T. might be found in the 1901 Census. She found a computer station free and called up the site.

There were eleven names for Merryn Hall. The family consisted of Stephen Carey, the head of the household, aged thirty-nine, his wife Emily, thirty-one, and their two daughters Elizabeth, five, and Cecily, three. The staff included a cook, Dorothy Roberts, an unmarried governess by the name of Susanna James, a housemaid, a kitchenmaid, a butler, the Head Gardener, John Boase, and a coachman-cum-groom. There was no one with the initials P.T., no Jenna and no sign of Master Charles, whom the Head Gardener had mentioned in his logbook, or of Jago, come to think of that, whoever Jago was. Mel sighed with frustration. The next census date was 1911 and she knew the information from that wouldn't be in the public domain until 2011, an arrangement designed to protect respondents' privacy.

Her documents arrived and she carried them over to her desk. The best part of an hour later, she reluctantly arrived at the conclusion that the artist's diaries were mundane, all too often merely recording trivia of her daily routine. Mel closed the notebooks and sat for a moment in contemplation. Then she turned to the batch of photographs from Merryn.

There were about thirty in the packet, each wrapped in acid-free paper and labelled. A family group on the lawn was dated *'around 1880'*, as was a photograph of the house from about that period. Mel was surprised by how bare it looked, no sign of the creeper that smothered it now. The forecourt was neat, without a weed.

Soon after came a photograph confidently marked *'June 1900'* that made her heart leap. It was taken from the back of the house looking over a portion of garden, the central section. A small blurred terrier dog sprawled out by a sundial on the lawn, a lawn that swept down past a rosebed to a long thin pool with a summerhouse at the far end. In the pond was the statue of a boy or a very young man. To each side of the pond was a high hedge that hid the garden beyond. In the left-hand corner Mel wondered if she could make out the lines of her cottage. It was out of focus, difficult to tell.

Most of the remaining pictures were more recent. Studio portraits of different Careys, a group of Army officers milling about smoking, a jeep on the forecourt, the house behind patterned in red and green by Virginia creeper.

She stopped as she came upon a snap of a young man and two girls, lolling on a lawn. The girls were almost women; one wore her hair up. Both were dressed in white. The younger girl was playing with a dog, this time a small greyhound or a whippet. She turned the photograph over. *Mr Charles Carey, Miss Carey and Miss Cecily Carey, 1912* it said, in faded italic handwriting. So this must be Master Charles and his cousins. She stared at them in turn, but particularly at Charles. The latter's hat was tilted slightly back to show a long, handsome face, carefree, smiling beneath his moustache. Yes, she concluded, it could be him, the man in the painting Patrick had shown her. Charles Carey.

Mel laid this photograph to one side, together with the one taken looking down the garden, and the Ordnance Survey map that showed the boundaries of house and gardens. Of these she would order copies. Then she focused her attention on the accounts books.

What am I looking for, she wondered. She turned the pages slowly, her eyes occasionally alighting on some unusual item – a satin dress or a peacock-feather fan or a new cooking range – but mostly it was a meticulous and relentlessly dull recitation of every item of household expenditure from candles to clear starch, all in Mrs Carey's neat copperplate, now a faded sepia. Every Quarter Day were listed the servants' wages with careful deductions for any uniform bought. After a while, Mel felt her interest drift. She didn't know what she was looking for and she was starving hungry. She was just considering what kind of sandwich she might buy for lunch from the superstore nearby, when her eye fell on a name – '*Pearl Treglown*'.

P.T. It was part of a list of names of servants who received their wages in June 1912. And there were other names she recognised – Jago from the Head Gardener's logbook – John Jago, it said his name was here – and Jenna Penhale, who must be the maid Carrie Price had mentioned.

But Pearl was surely a red herring in the search for an artist? She was, after all, only a servant. Mel flipped the pages, noting references to payments to Pearl. They continued into early 1914, and then stopped. Her name vanished from the records.

129

Chapter 10

August 1912

'Pearl? Get out there quick, girl. The wind's up.' Aunt Dolly stood at the window, her dough-caked arms raised as though in horror.

Pearl, polishing the last of the silver knives, glanced out to see a white nightdress coiling itself around a tree like a ghost in agony. She dropped her rag, threw off her dirty apron, rinsed her fingers and ran out through the scullery, snatching up the linen basket as she went. A rush of wind took her breath away and the back door banged to behind her.

The sunny August day, as still as the millpond earlier this morning, had lured the maids into draping the whites from yesterday's wash over shrubs and bushes behind the kitchen to air and bleach in the sun. Now, whirling dervishes from who knew where had ripped up the pillowcases, chemises, slips and collars and cast them about the garden under the darkening sky.

Pearl ran hither and thither, disentangling a lace handkerchief from a rosebush, lifting an embroidered tea cloth carefully from a flowerbed lest it soil, stowing everything in the basket she carried.

One of Cecily's hair ribbons had flown up into a tree and got caught around a branch, just out of Pearl's reach. She leaped up several times, her outstretched fingers only brushing it. Then, gathering up her skirts, she placed a boot on a nubbly foothold on the trunk to swing herself up.

A man's laugh. She removed her foot.

'Well, you get it then if you're so clever,' she snapped, turning and expecting to see Jago, but the young man watching her, arms folded, appreciation in his eyes, was Master Charles. Her mouth formed a wordless 'O'.

'Yes, ma'am,' he said, mock saluting, stepping forward and, reaching up easily, unwrapping the ribbon with one deft movement. 'Here,' he said, then laughed as she put out her hand and he jerked it up out of her range again.

'Very funny,' she muttered, glaring at him and reddening up at the thought of the figure she had cut, leaping like a deer, her skirts flying up. She turned her back on him with a stamp of her foot and picked up the basket.

'I'm sorry,' he said, close behind her, as he pushed the ribbon into the pile of clothes. 'Here, I'll help you.'

His sharp hazel eyes sought out several more items flung by the wind and she watched him negotiate prickly shrubs and eye-poking branches to collect them. He waved a pair of female drawers suggestively at her and she rolled her eyes in embarrassment, one arm crooked on her hip. Fat drops of rain began to fall as she snatched the drawers from him with a barely audible, 'Thank you, sir,' and flounced inside without a backward look. As she slammed the scullery door, did she hear laughter, or was it the wind?

'You'd better finish up there and get them irons hot.' Aunt Dolly nodded at the abandoned silver, still kneading her dough. Pearl placed a pair of irons onto a hotplate and set about tidying away the silver. They were shorthanded for an hour or two as Jenna had been sent off to fetch more eggs from the farm.

'Was that Master Charles you were talking to?' Pearl was still for a second. She knew Aunt Dolly missed nothing and so she nodded and went to take out the ironing board. Dolly didn't usually like to gossip, but the peace of the house without Jenna and the mistress, who had taken the girls to stay with friends at Fowey, must have lowered her guard.

'Reckon there'll be a wedding in the family before too long,' Dolly said.

Pearl looked up, surprised.

'Watch that Miss Elizabeth,' said Dolly, looking satisfied at the effect she had caused. 'And that young man come to dinner again last night, Sir Francis whassername's lad.'

'Oh, but I thought . . .' started Pearl, then stopped, knowing her aunt didn't like being contradicted. Pearl had waited at table last night and had noticed the youth in question. Julian Styles was little more than a boy, with his long lanky figure, his moustache still a shy blond shadow on his short upper lip, giving him a slightly rabbity look. He had certainly seemed entranced by sixteen-year-old Elizabeth, who sparkled with the zest of being treated as grown up, and self-consciously walked around the garden with him after dinner when the others were playing cards. But Pearl had thought that during the meal, Elizabeth's glances rested more often on Charles than on awkward Julian Styles.

As for Charles, he remained deep in conversation much of the evening with the squat dark stranger Jago had introduced to the company as Mr Robert Kernow. She heard their talk as she collected up the plates. Kernow uttered phrases in a language strange yet oddly familiar to her – Old Cornish, he told Mr Carey.

'How do you know that's how it's pronounced,' growled Carey, motioning to Jago to pour more wine. 'It's dead and gone. We're all English now.'

It was obviously the wrong thing to say. Kernow replied irascibly, 'If a people loses its language, they're dead. We must revive it. There's enough still speak some words to determine the accent. And if we're to look after our interests well, we must rediscover our identity as Cornishmen.'

Charles leaned forward, listening intently, one finger stroking the side of his moustache, a habit Pearl had previously noted. His eyes were dreamy. 'We mustn't lose the old stories, our history,' he said, 'that's for sure. This is one of the beautiful places of the world and we must fight to keep it ours.'

'Times are bad here,' argued Mr Carey, 'for farmers like ourselves. The mines are failing, too, and the fishing. We need strong representation in London, not old words.'

'Only if we band together as a people, a nation, will we see a rise in our fortunes,' said Kernow, playing with his unused cutlery. When Pearl took away his plate she saw he had arranged the pieces of silver in the shape of a cross – or was it a dagger?

She glanced at Kernow's face as she moved round the table. She'd seen that expression before, on the face of a travelling Methodist minister in Newlyn. This was a man with a mission, the sort who wouldn't let anything or anyone get in his way.

'It'll be good for the farm, marriage with the Styles,' continued Dolly now, cutting her dough into small loaves. 'That young master will inherit his father's farm and marry it with this. It'll be a weight off Mr Carey's mind.'

'But what about Master Charles? Isn't he supposed to have this farm?' Yet she had seen Charles listen to his uncle declaim on the drop in the milk yield or the falling price of vegetables, always polite, but with a glazed look on his face.

'That's what they say. But what they do will be another matter,' Dolly said enigmatically. 'He ought to look to where his bread and butter's coming from, did Master Charles.'

In the scullery, away from the smuts, Pearl pulled a blouse out of the basket, tested the heat of the plate on a corner and began to iron. They all seemed to disapprove of Charles, she mused as she worked, and yet he was so charming, so interesting, so . . . passionate about his Cornish roots.

Today's incident hadn't been her first encounter with him alone. A few weeks ago, Mrs Carey had announced in the middle of the day, when Jenna and Pearl were up to their elbows with the laundry, that Bijou, the nervous little whippet, had fleas and should be bathed and powdered at once.

With some grumbling from Jenna, who needed the hot water for the copper, Pearl drew off several buckets and heaved them upstairs, one by one, to the bathroom where the mistress insisted the deed should be done. She didn't notice Charles passing the top of the servants' staircase until she had to swing the bucket to avoid him and splashed water over his shoes.

'Sorry,' she gasped, looking up into his surprised face. She put down the bucket and delved into her apron pocket for a cloth.

'No.' He stayed her with a gesture and pulled a handkerchief out of his jacket, crouching down quickly to repair the damage. 'No harm done,' he said, smiling. 'Now where's this going?' Then, 'This I must see,' laughing, when she explained about Bijou.

He picked up the pail and lugged it to the bathroom where Mrs Carey, all togged up in a housewife's overall, waited with the wretched beast.

In the end, the bathing of Bijou brought pity rather than amusement to all observers – the sight of the skinny creature, bowed and shivering in the cooling rose-scented water brought to Pearl's mind the half-starved cats of Newlyn that challenged her with eyes that were pools of anguish before turning tail and vanishing into shadow.

Then, last Sunday, the family had taken luncheon at a neighbour's house. Pearl had spent the afternoon in the Flower Garden, sketching roses, and he had crept up on her unseen and cajoled her into showing him her work. Was it an accident today that he had come across her alone?

'Mistress wants a party for Master Charles's birthday next month,' Dolly called through the scullery door as she shut the oven on her loaves.

'A party?' echoed Pearl, dragged roughly from her daydreams.

'He'll be five-and-twenty,' Dolly went on, bringing out the dirty utensils and dumping them in a sink. 'A parcel of work for us, I tell you. Seventy guests or more, she says. With dancing and supper. We'll be needing some extra help then, I says, and she says all right we'll have it.'

'I've never seen a party here,' said Pearl, looking up from her ironing, eyes shining. She was imagining the women in their beautiful clothes, the men polished in dinner-jackets and white cuffs, the sounds of music, the scents of the garden and the ladies' perfumes. And the dancing. Dolly gone back into the kitchen, she swayed gently behind the ironing board, humming, eyes half-closed. Imagined herself dancing with Charles, one warm hand with the long artist's fingers resting at her waist, pulling her close, the other imprisoning hers.

She was aware that she watched him – did he realise? She hoped not. Sometimes she saw him in the garden, when Aunt Dolly sent her to pick herbs or to ask Mr Boase for more lettuce for a picnic.

Once she passed him sitting on a low wall, frowning as he sketched a group of girls, Elizabeth and Cecily among them, lounging on the lawn in pretty summer dresses, Elizabeth twirling a parasol.

Pearl stood back in the shadows of some trees, watching him draw with his strong quick movements, the cigarette caught between the first two fingers of his left hand serving dual use as he squinted along its stub to measure the lines of the garden. Until she heard a gentle cough and glanced over to see Mr Boase watching her and she stumbled away towards the rosemary she'd been sent to cut.

Overhead, against the sun, she glimpsed the dark shape of a bird of prey, floating on the wind, then poised, ready to drop. This was a garden of watchers. Pearl turned back to the kitchen with the herb. There was Cecily, for instance. A pretty girl of fourteen, but awkward beside her bolder elder sister. Sometimes, when she wasn't with her tutor at the Askews' house up the hill she would follow Pearl and Jenna around the house, stalking them, always at a distance, never saying a word. It gave Pearl the willies, to be cleaning a room and hear a creak in the corridor outside, seeing the door shiver when there was no draught.

'Pearl.' She was reaching into the linen basket for the last tray-cloth to iron when Dolly's voice broke through her thoughts once more. 'Soon as you've finished, go and ask Mr Boase for more tomatoes. Some of these aren't ripe.'

Mr Boase – there was another watcher. Pearl returned the iron to its partner on the range, took a shawl against the rain from a hook in the scullery and let herself out into the garden.

'He were a soldier once.' Jago had looked admiring when he said this about the Head Gardener. Pearl glanced at the foot-man's too-thin body, the underdeveloped chest. It would be natural for Jago to envy physical prowess. 'Fought they Borrs in the African war. They say he were shot in the stomach and when they patched him up and sent him home his hair had turned white.'

'How old do you reckon he is then?' Pearl had asked him.

'Maybe near fifty summers,' hazarded Jago. 'Same age as my pa, anyway, I reckon.'

The rain was falling steadily as Pearl hurried down the path, waved at the postman clunking over the cobbles on his bicycle, and ducked under the rose-studded arch into the Vegetable Garden. She found Boase sitting in his hut, making careful notes in a large leather-covered book. On seeing her, he stood up slowly, a craggy man with sinewy limbs and unblinking blue eyes, and when she announced her request, without a word he led her over to a greenhouse where he found a clean enamel bowl which he filled with deep red tomatoes.

His large frame and measured movements defined him as a countryman, and as she observed him gently press the fruit to test for ripeness before picking it, she almost couldn't imagine him as a fighting man. He loved to grow, not to destroy.

But there was steel there, too. She had noticed also that he directed his small team of 'boys' with firmness. Even cheeky Martin avoided disobeying 'old Boase', despite mimicking the older man behind his back. For to cause Mr Boase's steady blue gaze to cloud with displeasure was punishment enough. He never stormed, but in Boase, they sensed the truth of the phrase 'still waters run deep' and forebore to test him and risk awakening some raging beast within.

Mr Boase's fingers brushed against hers as she took the bowl from him and he withdrew them quickly as though he'd crossed some forbidden line. Perhaps the Head Gardener was shy of women, it occurred to her, though she guessed there were those who would have found him handsome enough. Jago, who bored anyone who would stop and listen about his unrequited passion for Jenna, had repeated some confidence Boase had shared with him in return, that he had never married because he had never seen a girl he wanted enough.

There was something about the tender courtesy with which he treated her that made Pearl feel special, honoured. When she was with him it was as though she held a dish of water that quivered, full to the brim, but that she didn't dare let overflow. Her eyes lowered, she whispered thanks for the tomatoes and walked away in as elegant a fashion as her burden would allow.

In the scullery, she ran water over the tomatoes, dried them and carried them through to the kitchen. There sat Aunt Dolly at the table, a letter in her hand. Standing behind her, twisting his cap in his hands, was Jago. They looked up as Pearl walked in. Dolly's face ravaged with shock, Jago's furrowed with anxiety.

'What's happened?' asked Pearl, but she already guessed.

'Adeline,' croaked Dolly, clearing her throat. She dabbed at her eyes with a tea towel. 'She passed away yesterday.'

Pearl put down the tomatoes, concentrating her mind on their vibrant glow. She took the proffered notepaper, a letter dictated to a neighbour by Adeline's sister, and read it.

She held on after the tide had turned, then her soul left her body, sweet as a bird. I swear I saw it fly through the open window and out to sea . . .

Pearl felt the blood drain from her face and passed the paper back to Dolly without a word. Then, turning, she placed one foot slowly in front of the other until she reached the privacy of the scullery. There she stared sightlessly out of the window and waited for the news to sink in.

As the shock wore off, a cyclone of thoughts began to whirl

in her mind, faster and faster, until she feared her head would burst. With a violent movement she swung round then ran, out into the rain, gasping as the now heavy drops soaked through her clothes.

Men's rough voices. Mr Boase's boys were sheltering in an open stable. She ran from their catcalls, slipped into the Flower Garden and hid herself in one of the greenhouses. As she leaned against the lime-washed wall, huge sobs began to tear out of her.

Adeline might have been distant, sharp, lacking in tenderness, but she was the only mother Pearl had ever known and now she was dead. The girl had never felt so alone. She couldn't rely on Aunt Dolly. The memories of her father were dissolving fast. The whole of her life in Newlyn at the inn, the children from her school, fishermen bartering their catch on the beach, the smell of oil and paint and tar, all these experiences were suddenly sucked into the past as though they had never been. She had nothing to go back to, only this life here and now.

Eventually, all strength gone, she slid down the wall, uncaring of the white dust on her uniform, and crouched there on the floor of the greenhouse, wiping her nose on the back of her sleeve, her head throbbing. When she opened her eyes the sodden garden was visible only through a latticework of leaves.

Footsteps, a shadow falling across the floor, then the door opened . . . Enveloped in oilskin and with watering can in hand, there stood John Boase.

She scrambled to her knees in confusion, suddenly aware of how ravaged she must look, her hair torn from its pins falling across her tear-stained face. 'I'm sorry, I didn't mean . . .'

In his face she saw surprise and tenderness. He crouched down before her, the rain dripping from his cape. He said, very gently, 'They're looking for you, you know.'

'I . . . had some bad news. My stepmother . . .'

'Aye,' he said, shaking his head. 'She's gone. Jago just told me. Here.' He stooped and picked up a hairpin and handed it to her. 'It's a great shock,' he said, 'but you've your life ahead. You must look to yourself. There's happiness to be sought.'

Pearl was astonished. These were more words in one go than she had ever heard the man utter in all the months she had been here.

'A moment,' he said and, leaving the greenhouse, he hurried back through the rain towards his office. She quickly smoothed down her uniform, wiped her nose on the back of her cuff again, tucked the worst of the escaped hair back into its knot and pulled on her cap.

When Boase returned he held out to her an umbrella with a carved ivory handle. She stared at it, then out at the rain. He was being kind, she knew, but something in her didn't want to be beholden. She shook her head. 'It's stopping. I'll be all right now.'

She lowered her eyes and he stepped back to let her go. Before she passed under the arch she looked back. He was still standing there in the doorway to the greenhouse, regarding her, the umbrella held across his open palms, all nobility, like the picture in one of her father's books of a knight of old offering up his sword.

Chapter 11

'Patrick! I didn't think you'd be back till tomorrow.'

It was Thursday after lunch. Mel had just put down the phone to Irina, who had rung to confirm supper that evening, when she had heard his knock.

They stood at the door smiling stupidly at one another. Over the past few days, the details of his face had blurred in her mind, but now she reacquainted herself with his hazel eyes, the way his hair fell down over his forehead, the strong lines of his square face.

He stood, almost shyly, one hand in his jeans pocket, the other cradling a lumpy brown-paper package.

'I finished everything earlier than I expected,' he explained, then he held out the package. 'A present. Careful, it's breakable.'

'Thank you,' she replied, taking it, surprised. 'Why don't you come in?'

They went through to the kitchen. When she opened the bag she had to laugh. It contained a little teapot, decorated with flowers and garden tools.

'I saw it and thought of you, or whatever the ad says.'

'I didn't mean you to go to the trouble of buying something

special,' she said, peeling the plastic protector off the spout. 'But thank you, it's so pretty.'

Patrick leaned against the worktop near her as they waited for the kettle to boil, then picked up the mermaid plant stick that she had left propped up on the windowsill. She saw him turn it in his large hands as though it were something fragile and extremely precious.

'There's a local mermaid legend, you know,' he said. 'West of Lamorna there's a Mermaid Rock. The original story is lost in the mists of time, but it's said a mermaid with a comb and mirror may appear there as warning of a storm. She sings especially plaintively if there's going to be a wreck.'

'A useful mermaid then.'

'Not entirely. Her siren voice lures young men to their doom.'

'Ah, the woman's to blame as usual.'

'The spell of female beauty gets us every time.' He smiled lazily at her and she laughed. He replaced the mermaid on the window-ledge.

'Oh good, it just does two cups,' she said, pouring out the tea. 'So how was your week?'

'Okay,' he said, taking the mug she held out. 'I am now the sole owner of the business. Geoff has his money and the deal is done. The only awful bit has been telling the staff that we're dispensing with their services.'

'I thought you were keeping the business going?'

'I am, but I've finally decided. I'm moving it down here.'

'Are you? Isn't that very sudden?'

'Not really. I've been toying with the idea ever since Geoff announced his plans.'

'How many people do you have?'

'Only two. One isn't too disappointed. She's going to use her redundancy money to go travelling. The other was quite angry,

142

but I think he should find another job without too much trouble. Still, it's not fun telling them.'

'No, of course not. So what now?'

'Well, a small office unit in Penzance has just come free to rent. That's the other reason why I've got back early. I have to go and see it this afternoon. If it's right, I'll instruct my solicitor, get things going. I must also find someone to handle the admin side of the company.'

'Couldn't you have run the business from here – the Hall, I mean? You could convert one of the outhouses. That stable with the hayloft looks—'

'Hey, stop, stop, you're being like your sister again,' he warned, wagging his finger at her. This time she laughed.

'I agree,' he went on, 'it would be more convenient in some ways, but I like the idea of being in the town. It'll be near the station for visitors and, anyway, it's better for me to at least try to keep work separate from the rest of my life. I find I end up doing nothing else otherwise. Never mind that I value my privacy here.'

Mel nodded, her eye resting upon the mounds of paper on the kitchen table, a dirty breakfast bowl nestling amongst them.

'I know exactly what you mean about work overwhelming your life.'

'Did you have a useful week?' he asked.

'I went to the Records Office on Tuesday,' she said. 'And somewhere under here . . .' she scuffled amongst her papers '. . . is my notebook.' She told him all about the photographs and the plans and what she'd discovered from the accounts books.

'It sounds as though the photos and the plan will be useful for the garden. Have the copies arrived?'

'They should be here soon.'

'Good.'

'Oh, and I spoke to your gardener chap, Jim,' she said. 'He told me how the garden looked just before the last war. Tell you what, if we go outside, I'll try and describe for you what he said.'

The sun had come out and Mel stood for a moment, feeling its warmth, as she looked out across the wilderness. She was intensely aware of Patrick close beside her as she pointed to where the old man had indicated the site of the rose garden and the pond and the ravine.

'And over there was a laurel grove, he said.' After a moment, they walked the width of the garden to where the rhododendrons flowed up into the trees like a great green wave, now breaking gloriously into crests of white, pink and red.

Patrick, who had been listening to her talk, turned to her suddenly, his face animated. 'You know, I feel we're starting to get somewhere with this garden,' he said. 'On the basis of the plan and the photographs and what Jim says, we can try some reconstruction.'

Mel nodded. 'Let's go and explore for ourselves.' She ducked her head and entered the tunnel of rhododendrons once more, its strange, secret undergrowth. The wild gnarled trunks and roots everywhere put her in mind of an ancient faery forest. 'Watch your head here. Ooh, it's like an Arthur Rackham painting, isn't it?'

'Or, more sinister, Tolkien's Mirkwood,' suggested Patrick as they twisted and crawled their way through the cool green otherworld.

'Let's hope there are no giant spiders.'

'You're not keen on spiders?'

'No way.'

'Not even little ones?'

'I had hypnotism once, so I don't scream any more, I can deal with it, but no, not even little ones. Oh!' Suddenly Mel, bent nearly double, tripped and would have flown forward except for Patrick grabbing her arm. She swung round to face him, both of them half-crouched under the low canopy.

'Are you all right?' he asked in a low voice.

'My foot,' she said, screwing up her face against the pain. 'Don't worry, just a slight sprain, I think.' When he took his hand away she missed its warmth.

Soon, strands of laurel mingled with the rhododendron, and after a while thick tangles of the dark shrub made progress impossible.

'Let's try round this way,' suggested Patrick, and he surged deeper into the banks of rhododendron. Mel limped to where he had forced a way through the bushes. Now she was lost in thick shiny green leaves that scratched her face.

'Patrick,' she called, 'where are you?'

'Here,' he shouted back, and she shoved through the greenery in the direction of his voice. Dry branches scraped her face and leaves rattled. She was blinded. 'Patrick, tell me where you are!' His answering voice seemed further away. The greenery seemed to be pressing in on her like some malevolent creature. She tripped again and nearly fell. Panic welled. 'Patrick!' she cried again.

'Mel? Come on,' he said, somewhere up ahead. 'I've found something.'

'What? Ouch. Where are you?'

'This way.' And suddenly, she emerged into a small clearing. There he was, sitting on a little bench, and it was all right again. The laurel rose around them like green walls of a castle keep, open to the sky. The bench was made of stone, with scrolled arms and a low back.

'Is there room for me?' she asked, and squeezed thankfully onto the seat beside him.

'How's your foot?' In a hesitant gesture he put his arm around her.

'Not too bad.' She felt herself relax into him.

'Good.'

'Where on earth are we?' she said. 'I completely lost my sense of direction.'

'A secret world at the centre of a maze. No one in the world knows we're here. Fun, isn't it?'

They sat together in companionable silence, listening to the birds singing, noticing the distant cracks of twigs and the rustle of the wind in the leaves.

'No giant spiders, thank God,' remarked Mel.

'That grab you and wrap you up tight,' Patrick joked, and hugged her quickly. She gave a little scream, and this immediately started up the urgent *chik chik chik* of several blackbirds. Then an eerie silence.

Mel and Patrick sat frozen, all senses alert. The shadow of a cloud fell across the grove and the air turned chill. Patrick removed his arm. Mel shivered, then remembered something.

'Patrick, your gardener said something odd. I wonder whether he was hinting that someone was buried in the garden. I'm not sure – I couldn't make him explain.'

He looked at her, perplexed. 'That's weird. What did he say?'

'Well, it's not exactly what he said. Just that "She's still hereabouts" and he told me not to go digging.'

'Who was he talking about?'

'An old Mrs Carey, I think, but I'm not sure. As I say, I couldn't get him to explain. Perhaps he'd be more helpful with you.'

Patrick stood up; his face looking troubled. 'This place is suddenly giving me the willies,' he said. He glanced at his watch. 'Heck, I've got to be in Penzance in three-quarters of an hour. Come on.' He reached for her hand and pulled her up. For a moment they stood looking at one another. Then he squeezed her hand gently and said, 'Shall I go first again?'

He said to meet him at the bench in the laurel maze, but I've waited and waited and he hasn't come. Now the shadows grow long and it's getting cold. I'm tired of pacing up and down and Aunt Dolly will be looking for me. But what can I do? Evening is falling and this secret place is full of eyes. Why hasn't he come? The scrape of boots on gravel. Leaves clink. Is this him at last . . .

When they emerged from the rhododendrons they saw the weather had changed. The sky was steel-grey, the wind was up. The air rang with the threat of thunder.

'May I . . .' Mel reached up to pull a twig from Patrick's fleece.

'Thank you,' he said. But he seemed distracted.

'Is something the matter?' she asked.

He shrugged. 'Not really. I was thinking about what the old bloke said. And . . . just the strangeness of it back there. Like passing into another time. I'm glad we're out.'

'Me too,' she said, stuffing her hands into her jacket pockets. 'There is a strong atmosphere about this place. It's as though someone is here . . .'

'An echo,' ventured Patrick, turning to look up at the house. 'That's what Val used to say. He had a favourite theory about ghosts. That perhaps we can leave a kind of imprint of ourselves. But perhaps he just spent too much time alone.'

Perhaps we do, too, thought Mel sadly, thinking that she and Patrick were haunted by their ex-pasts.

'What are you doing later?' asked Patrick hesitantly.

'Having supper at Irina's,' replied Mel. 'What about you?'

'I was half-thinking I'd go to see my parents. Stay the night. Yes, perhaps I'll do that.'

She merely nodded, disappointed. Perhaps he wouldn't have gone if she had been free.

'Well, I'll see you very soon then,' he said.

'Yes. Hope it goes well in Penzance.'

'Thanks,' he said, and, slowly lifting one hand, he made a motion as though to brush her cheek. Then he turned the gesture into a wave. 'Goodbye,' he said simply.

She watched him walk away to the house as though he had already forgotten her very existence.

Chapter 12

That evening, when Mel walked down to the cove to have supper with Irina, she hardly noticed the silver mist-wreathed beauty of the valley; her mind was occupied with thoughts of Patrick and of the unquiet atmosphere in the garden.

After Patrick had left she had retreated indoors and sat down at her laptop to reshape the opening paragraph of her book, but she felt too muddled. She sat in a daydream remembering his arm around her again. Had he just been friendly? And had the sudden shift of mood in the garden merely been a change in the weather?

When she reached Irina's cottage, her knock was answered so quickly she was taken unawares.

'Are you all right?' said Irina. 'You look . . . dazed.'

'Do I? Sorry, I was woolgathering.'

'What?' Irina asked, baffled. She still looked tired and strained, Mel saw.

'Daydreaming,' Mel explained. 'Too much time alone with my thoughts. I'm becoming thoroughly unfit for human company.'

'Oh, I'm sure that's not true. Come in, please.'

Mel handed over the bottle of wine she had brought.

'Thank you. Come into the kitchen. Lana has her friend Amber here. They've been helping me with the cooking.'

The two girls were sitting together at the table scraping out a mixing bowl with teaspoons. Lana looked up and smiled at Mel with her spaniel eyes. Where Lana was dark, Amber was Nordic blonde, with skin so fair the veins showed through the delicate lids of her pale blue eyes. An ice queen, perhaps. But no, Amber's 'Hi,' was warm enough. The fragile princess on the pea then.

'We've made torta,' said Lana, licking her spoon.

'I hope you've left some for me,' said Mel.

Lana laughed. She seemed less wary, more like a normal child today. 'It's in here,' she said, and a blast of hot air filled the tiny room as she pulled open the oven door to reveal a cake rising.

'Close it quick, Lana dear,' called Irina, who was pouring some wine, 'or it won't rise properly. Now, why don't you take Mel into the sitting room while I finish here.'

In the sitting room, Mel was instantly drawn to the window to stare out at the darkening cove. What a wonderful view it was, even on a foggy evening like this. No moon was visible tonight. A light from a passing boat twinkled through the mist. She shifted position to see the quay and the cliffside better and knocked into something metal and spiky, sending papers drifting to the floor.

'Sorry,' she said, righting the music-stand and bending to rescue the scores. 'Is it you who plays the violin?' she asked Lana. She remembered Irina talking about music lessons. Lana, curled up on the sofa, nodded.

'She's really good,' cut in Amber. 'Aren't you, Lana?'

Lana shot her friend an embarrassed frown but told Mel, 'I've got my exam soon, so I've got to be good. I've been practising for simply hours and hours.' She rolled her eyes in theatrical fashion.

'I'd love to hear you play, Lana. Would you?'

'Okay.' She said this clearly, without either the airs or the reluctance that most children exhibit if asked to perform for their elders. A violin case was pulled from under a cabinet by the mantelpiece. Taking out the instrument, Lana tuned it with quick fingers.

The *thwuck thwuck* sound took Mel back to school days, her brother sawing away at his instrument behind the shut door of the dining room but, as Lana placed the instrument under her chin, closed her eyes and began to play, Mel was amazed. Instead of the expected wail of a strangled cat that constituted William's usual performance, a beautiful voice leaped from Lana's instrument, in some wild folk dance that expressed first laughter then yearning, tragedy and finally, exaltation. It was an astonishing performance.

When the music finally ceased, she and Amber clapped until Irina's voice sounded from the door. 'Well done, Lana.' Her tired face was transformed by pride in her daughter. 'That's the best you've played it.'

'She's really good in front of other people,' Amber confided to Mel. 'I go all wobbly on my recorder when all the mums and dads are there.'

'I don't notice them once I start,' shrugged Lana, some of her watchful reserve returning. 'I think about the music.'

Later, after their meal of peppers stuffed with meat and rice and the delicious chocolate torta, Irina suggested to the girls that they take a 'midnight' feast of sweets from the store cupboard and put themselves to bed. When they had said goodnight and tramped upstairs, Mel watched Irina make coffee in a brown pottery jug before joining her at the table.

'I don't know what to do about Lana,' she said, lighting a

151

cigarette. 'Sorry, do you mind? I try not to, but tonight I feel like it . . .' She sighed.

Mel shook her head. Although she had not smoked since her early twenties she secretly still liked the smell and she was surprised by a sudden desire for one. She resisted. Irina poured syrupy black coffee into two tiny cups.

'What do you mean, do about Lana?' prompted Mel.

'You heard her play before supper.'

'She's incredible,' said Mel.

'Yes. I want to be encouraging – not pushy, you know. She herself wants to play, she really does. But she must have the right opportunities and I don't think she can find them here in Lamorna. It's the one thing that worries me about being here.'

Mel, sipping her coffee, nodded slowly.

'She has a good teacher at the moment,' Irina went on. 'Mr Winterton – the old man who died, I mean, not Patrick – bought the violin and, I told you, left money for lessons. Soon I'll have to find the money myself, but it is difficult, and there will be a time when she needs a better teacher.'

'Mmm. Surely there are bursaries for promising pupils? What does the teacher think?'

'The same as you. But there are expenses, even if she was lucky enough to win a scholarship to a school or college where she would get special tuition. And we might have to move up country. Nine is still very young, but maybe next year or the year after.' Her voice had been passionate but now it turned leaden. 'Her father might pay.'

'Her father?' It was hard for Mel to keep the curiosity out of her voice. 'Does Lana see him?'

Irina shook her head violently. 'No,' she said, stabbing out her cigarette half-smoked in an ashtray and immediately lighting another.

Mel waited. Irina's vitality had drained away. Her skin appeared sallow, dull. She picked at the cuticles of her nails which, Mel had noticed earlier, were bitten down to the quick. Eventually she looked up.

'I met him in Dubrovnik, during the fighting. There were . . . reasons why I could not stay. He – his name is Gregory – an Englishman. He was wealthy, had powerful connections. He helped me escape, took me to London. He was in love with me, he said. I thought he was safe and I was grateful to him. I loved him a little, too.' She laughed. 'He is very good-looking, very . . . he has charisma. It was more than a convenient marriage. I wanted to stay in England, yes, but I wanted to stay with him.' She took a long pull on her cigarette.

'So – we married and lived in a nice house in London, in Chelsea. He had rescued me and looked after me and I was grateful, though I missed Dubrovnik and my parents. Then Lana came along. Everything seemed all right – a happy ending. But I must have been in shock all that time, I think, because one day I woke up and realised I didn't love Greg at all. I had discovered the kind of man he was. He was kind to us, yes, but he could be ruthless, too. It was like he was two people. He became very dominating, very jealous. If I went out he would want to know where I was going, who with. I don't know what he thought – that I was seeing another man? And we started to argue and then I told him I didn't love him and after that he knew he was losing me. He would try to control everything I did. Sometimes he would lock me in the house. He didn't ever hit me and he never touched Lana, thank God, but I feared all the time that he would. He seemed to think he owned me, that he could do what he liked because he had rescued me. It was a terrible time, but I was so afraid to leave him. I spoke little English. I thought Lana might be taken away from me and that

I would be sent back to Croatia without her. That's what he threatened would happen.

'Many months passed and I – is this right? – I came to my senses. We took Lana to the doctor's once for her injections and when I used the bathroom there I saw an advertisement about women like me, women who are afraid of their men, and one evening when Greg was out at a business appointment I rang the number. And so I found people to help me leave Greg and begin life without him.'

'Irina. That's so terrible.' Mel reached out and laid her hand over the other woman's, stilling her nervous play with the plastic lighter on the table.

What must it be like, being alone with a young child in a strange country, trying to find the means to survive? Mel wondered fleetingly why Irina didn't go back to Croatia, but as she was framing the question Irina rushed on.

'At first we stayed in London. My lawyer couldn't get Greg to send us any money and I was terrified anyway that he would find out where we were. For a month we lived in a hostel in Wandsworth and then the council found us a flat. It was a horrible place, horrible. People had to put bars on their front doors because of the break-ins. I was so lonely. I could not work much because Lana was still so young and I was frightened to leave her with neighbours. She was all I had. I went to a class to learn better English when Lana was at school. I cleaned people's houses – anyone who didn't mind Lana coming sometimes. Then, after about a year, a very nice lady I worked for, who wanted to help me, showed me a magazine with jobs. I saw Mr Winterton's advertisement.'

'But it was so far away. That was brave of you.'

'I didn't realise how far Cornwall was. Though it's not that far, really, after Croatia. But it said the house was near the sea, and when I spoke to Mr Winterton on the phone he sounded so kind and paid our train fares to go to see him.'

'And he gave you the job and you moved down here. That must have been a relief.'

'It was, I can't tell you. To live in a beautiful place like Lamorna and to feel safe.' She stopped, then said quietly as though someone else might be listening, 'Greg doesn't know we are here.'

'Does he pay anything for Lana's upkeep?'

'No.' Irina smiled, but it was a tired smile. 'I get anxious sometimes,' she said vaguely. 'The past. It is never easy to escape – it leaves a mark.'

Mel's eyes were drawn to the hand now toying with the lighter. Across the palm, reaching along the underside of her wrist and up her forearm, where it disappeared under her sleeve, Mel saw stretched a long white scar.

'How . . .?' started Mel but, suddenly self-conscious, Irina pulled the sleeve right down.

'I did it to myself,' she whispered. 'It was when I was bad, very bad. 'Not any more.'

Mel was lost for words. Despite all the bad times in her own life she had never felt self-destructive, suicidal. Somehow she had coped and she felt humble at the realisation. She accepted more coffee and the two women sat in silence for a while, each lost in thought.

Then Mel remembered where the conversation had started.

'So how did you discover Lana's musical talent?' she asked.

'Her class teacher, Miss Thorson, noticed she was quick at learning the recorder, very quick, and let her try the school piano. She discovered Lana has perfect pitch and when she played easy pieces to her, Lana could play them again, straight off. Mr Winterton paid for some piano lessons for her, but then

Lana asked to learn the violin instead, and so he bought her one for her birthday. He was a saint, that man. Patrick's been so kind, too.'

'Is musical talent in your family?' Mel asked, trying to ignore as unworthy the stab of possessiveness she felt at the mention of Patrick's name. He hadn't alluded to helping Irina, but then why should he have talked about it?

'My brother played the violin very well. And my grandfather, he was a professional in an orchestra.' Then Irina stubbed out her cigarette and said, 'But I have been stupid.' And she began to cry.

'Irina, what on earth is the matter?'

'Two weeks ago, I wrote to Lana's father asking him for money. I have explained about her music, that she will need money for music college, a bigger instrument. Well, we had had no contact since the divorce. Nobody has ever managed to make him pay us much money – he is clever like that. He wanted to have Lana stay with him at weekends, you see, and I wouldn't let him and so the money stopped.'

'Did you ever have to go to court about all this? Wasn't there an arrangement when you divorced?' Mel was beginning to feel lost in the twists and turns of Irina's explanations.

'Yes.' Irina hung her head. 'He was supposed to see her. Because he never hurt her, you see, I had no argument. Maybe I was wrong to take her from her father, I don't know. He never harmed a hair of her head. It was me, he blamed me for everything. And perhaps I was selfish. Well, I thought I should stop being selfish, that he could visit Lana here, help her – pay for her lessons, maybe for her to go to the right school.'

She looked up and her eyes met Mel's.

'How does he make his money?' Mel asked casually. What had Greg been doing, a businessman in a foreign war zone?

Selling weapons, it occurred to her. The thought of Lana's education being funded by other children's misery was too ghastly to contemplate.

'Buying and selling things,' Irina said, then saw Mel's expression. 'Oh no, nothing dreadful. Businesses. Finance stuff.' She waved a hand, dismissive.

Relieved, Mel whispered encouragingly, 'I'm sure you believed you were doing your best for Lana, always.'

Irina smiled slightly, then the smile vanished. 'On Monday a letter came. I gave a Post Box address so he does not know where I am. He says he will give money for her but only if he can see her regularly. Have her to stay with him sometimes. I don't know what to do, what is best!' This last was almost a howl.

'What does Lana think?' said Mel, not knowing what, if anything, to advise.

'That's just it. I haven't dared tell her yet. I am frightened of what she will say.'

There was silence in the kitchen. Floating down the stairs came the sounds of chattering and giggles. Amber and Lana were clearly not settling down to sleep, but they sounded relaxed, happy. Two little girls enjoying a sleepover, unaware of the black clouds of adult care. And so it should be, sighed Mel.

'Irina,' she said softly, 'if it's meant to be, there will be help for Lana, I'm sure there will be – without involving her father. Can you contact your family in Croatia?'

Irina shook her head violently. 'I can't. My father is not well and my brother, we quarrelled and he won't want to hear from me,' she half-sobbed.

'Then there will be scholarships. Grants and so on,' Mel said hopefully. Music wasn't an area of education she knew much about. 'And it's still early days. She needs to be doing well at school, at all the other subjects.'

'Yes,' said Irina. 'I know, of course. But I've messed up so much else in my life. She's all I've got. I want the best for her.'

'You are doing the best for her, I'm sure,' Mel said. 'Making a stable home for her, giving her a happy childhood. That's more than many children ever have.'

Irina's eyes were bright with tears now. She reached out and clasped Mel's hands in both of hers. 'You're right,' she said. 'Thank you for saying that.'

Mel glanced at the kitchen clock and was surprised to find it was after eleven. Upstairs, the children were silent now. She yawned suddenly.

'I really must go in a moment. There is something I wanted to ask, though. It's something Patrick's gardener – Jim who cuts the grass around the cottage – said. I don't know, he might just be a confused old man. But did Val ever say anything about someone being, well – buried somewhere in the garden?'

'Oh, no! No, I never heard anything about that. Though I told you, there is an atmosphere about that place. Who knows what might have happened there.'

'I expect he was just rambling. Never mind.'

When she walked back up the road to Merryn it was pitch dark, apart from the lights from houses, and Mel was glad she had remembered her torch.

But after this afternoon's experiences, it couldn't save her from feeling the hairs on the back of her neck rise and her body shake as she slipped through the velvet darkness down the path to the Gardener's Cottage. Only the welcoming light in her kitchen was on, as she had left it. Merryn Hall, on the other hand, she could sense was empty, rising up in the darkness. Patrick must indeed have gone to his parents. As she let herself into the cottage, she felt terribly alone.

Chapter 13

Two days later, Saturday morning, the end of the first fortnight of her stay, Mel was sitting at the kitchen table sorting through a batch of post. It included the photocopies from the Records Office and a big packet of letters which her London neighbour Cara had sent on. This contained mostly brown envelopes and circulars but there was a postcard from her father from the South of France. *Magnificent rolling fields of budding sunflowers,* ran his spindly italics, *and some marvellous restaurants. Stella finding the heat difficult so she plays the mermaid in Derek and Viv's pool. Trusting this finds you well. Love, Dad.* Mel was just musing how typical a communication this was from her father – no phone call for two months and then an uninformative postcard; who on earth were Derek and Viv? – when a knock came at the back door and she looked up to see Patrick through the glass. She let him in.

'Sorry if you're busy,' he said. He seemed a little nervous. 'Perhaps I should have rung from the house. What are your plans for today? I wondered if you'd like to come to the beach with me. I've got the makings of a picnic.'

'What a great idea,' said Mel, instantly dismissing her intention to write. 'Give me twenty minutes?'

Later, they walked across the forecourt to his sports car. 'Oh, lovely!' she cried, seeing that he'd lowered the roof.

'Will you be warm enough?'

'Yes, I expect so.' Just then, there was a flash of white in the trees. 'Did you see that?' she asked.

'What?' Patrick said, closing the boot on their picnic.

'A bird of some sort. Pure white. What would that be?'

'No idea. A dove?' He held her door open for her then went to get in his side.

'Smaller than that.'

'I don't know. Didn't see it, I'm afraid.' He reversed the car in one sudden sickening turn. Mel clutched involuntarily at her seat. 'Sorry,' he said, his face mischievous. 'I'll go carefully.'

'Thanks,' she breathed. 'I'm more used to cars you have to coax gently into life.' He laughed.

'Did you get back last night?' she asked innocently. She had in fact lain awake for what seemed like hours, listening out for his return.

'No, only an hour ago. I meant to come back yesterday, but Dad needed help putting in a new bathroom and we didn't finish until late.'

'Bye bye, avocado?' she said.

'Oh, they left that house years ago. No, Mum needs a bath that's easier to get in and out of. With her arthritis, you see. So they took the opportunity to change the whole suite.'

'Ah,' said Mel.

He drove too fast, but skilfully, west along the winding narrow road to Porthcurno, where they walked around the Minack Theatre built into the cliff and ate their picnic. Later they rested by rocks in the secluded cove, Mel running the pale gold sand, made of crushed seashells, through her fingers, as she laughed at Patrick's stories of what he, Chrissie's old boyfriend

Nick and their other friends got up to at university, trading a few tales of her own.

Out of the wind it was really very warm and soon they fell silent, lulled by the rhythm of the waves, idly watching a small group of surfers in the distance.

Patrick amused himself by trickling sand over her bare feet. 'Get off,' she giggled, slapping him. He laughed and rolled onto his back, feigning sleep, so she dumped sand on his stomach until he mock-growled and twisted onto his knees, pushing her down onto the sand, crouching astride her, imprisoning her arms, Mel protesting, both of them laughing, then falling quiet. Looking at one another for what felt like a long time but was probably only several seconds. Something deep inside her turned molten.

The klaxon squawk of a seagull made them both look up to see it strutting on the rock behind them, and it was then that Mel became aware of a tiny boy with gold curls and a spade in one hand, standing inches away, staring at the bird. The enchantment was broken. They both laughed and Mel said hello to the toddler, but he was more interested in the gull.

'Come along, Archie, sweetie,' said a woman's cut-glass voice, and the child was led away.

Patrick released her, pulling her up to sitting and clumsily helping her dust the sand from her hair.

The tide had by now receded, leaving a passage to the next cove.

'Come,' said Patrick, taking her by the hand. They walked round the rock dividing the coves, the water painfully cold around Mel's bare ankles. Surfers there were trying to ride the giant waves and they stood and watched their efforts, not even trying to talk against the crash of sea on shore.

I could be happy here for ever, thought Mel. The warmth of

the sun made her feel she was unfolding like the petals of a flower. The unceasing pounding of the waves banished the sense of time passing. She felt washed clean of any care.

The direction of the current swept the surfers nearer and nearer to where they waited. One, it began to dawn on Mel, looked familiar. She wasn't certain until, after a few minutes, Matt waved to his companion and waded towards the shore, pushing his board ahead of him, passing near to where they were.

'Oh, hello,' he called in surprise.

'Hi,' returned Mel, thinking how beautiful, slim and sleek he looked in his wetsuit. 'We've been watching. You're good. Isn't it absolutely freezing out there?'

'It's great!' said Matt. 'If you keep moving, that is.'

'Matt, do you know Patrick?' Mel asked.

Patrick had wandered off to lean against a rock. Now he came forward and the men looked one another up and down warily.

' Hello. Patrick Winterton.'

Matt shook the outstretched hand, apologising for his wet one. 'Matt Price. My mother runs the Valley Hotel. You're from Merryn, aren't you? Good to meet you.' He shouldered his board and said, 'I'm off to change now. Do you guys fancy hot chocolate at the café in a few minutes?'

Mel glanced at Patrick, who shrugged in a non-committal fashion. She couldn't gauge what he thought and it irritated her. There was no need to be unfriendly. She said, 'Good idea, why not?'

They watched Matt stride off across the sand to the car park.

'How is it you know him?' asked Patrick, a little frostily, as they set off up the beach towards the café.

'Just keep bumping into him about the place,' said Mel. 'And I've been to the hotel to meet his mother.'

'I see.' Patrick said hardly anything on the way to the café. Can he be jealous of Matt, she asked herself, or is he just reserved?

'Is there any water sport you don't do, Matt?' Mel said lazily, taking in the way the blue of his long-sleeved shirt perfectly suited his colouring. They were sitting at a table on the veranda of the café, looking out across the bay and drinking frothy hot chocolate.

'Mmm, aqua-aerobics? Synchronised swimming?' joked Matt. 'I've tried most things though. But surfing I like best of all. Just me, the board and the sea. The nearest thing to flying, really.'

'Skiing's like that,' said Patrick, nodding agreement. He was still frosty.

'Not much of that in Cornwall,' said Matt. He kept glancing from Mel to Patrick as though trying to work something out.

''Fraid not,' said Patrick, stirring his cup. 'It looks like my main hobby here will have to be gardening.'

'I gather you've a big job on your hands there with Merryn.'

'You haven't seen the place?' Patrick's tone was sharper than the question warranted and Matt said hesitantly, 'No – well, only from the road.'

Mel took refuge in her hot chocolate, embarrassed by Patrick's jealousy. But then he seemed to relax, 'I'm still deciding whether it's a gift or a curse,' he said. 'But, do you know, Mel, I really want to get on with clearing the garden now.'

'Fantastic,' said Mel. 'When shall we start?' She had meant it as a joke and was surprised when Patrick took her question seriously.

'I've borrowed an electric saw from a neighbour of Dad's. I can make a start at least,' he said. 'Why not tomorrow? The forecast's good. Do you mean "we", Mel? Do you really want to help?'

'You bet. Just tell me what to do.'

'I'll come if you like,' broke in Matt. 'It'll be a change from washing up.'

'That's a good offer, but I'm sure we'll manage.' Again, that wariness.

'No, seriously, I mean it,' Matt said.

'Well, all right, that's great.' Patrick still sounded unsure.

'What will we do first?' asked Mel, to move the conversation on.

'What about the Flower Garden?' said Patrick. 'Not so many big trees to deal with there. I'll need proper machinery for trees. And skips. And trucks for carting skips around. And diggers . . . In fact, professional tree surgeons. What am I starting?' But there was a light of excitement in his eyes.

'So this'll be slashing and burning tomorrow, will it? Fantastic,' said Matt, rubbing his hands. 'I love a good bit of destruction.'

'It's supposed to be creative,' Mel teased, then a thought struck her. 'Patrick, wouldn't it be best to draw a plan first? I mean, you want to be careful we don't destroy clues of how the garden used to be, or any plants worth saving.'

'You and I could do that when we get back,' said Patrick, glancing at his watch. 'Anyway, the two things run in tandem, don't they? I mean, we won't know what's there until we start clearing. Though the photocopies from the Records Office will help.'

This reminded her. 'Matt, there's something else I must ask your mother. Would her aunt, you know, Jenna the maid's daughter, be up to visitors, do you know? I would love to meet her and find out what she knows about Jenna's life at the house.'

'Aunt Norah? I can ask,' said Matt, scraping back his chair and pulling his sunglasses out of his pocket. 'I don't think she's ga-ga, but I haven't seen her for years. Mum will know. Look, I must get back now. What time do you want me round tomorrow?'

'Ten?' hazarded Patrick.

Matt nodded, scooped his keys off the table and said goodbye. Was it Mel's imagination or did his lingering look mean something?

Patrick finished his drink. 'Brief look at Land's End?' he said to Mel. 'It's very near.' He held out his hand.

'You bet,' she answered, taking it.

They were driving back in the late afternoon and Mel, whilst trying not to break any confidences, was telling Patrick about Irina's anxieties for Lana.

'There must be something we can give her in the way of practical advice,' she said. 'She won't know the education system here.'

'I can't say I do either. She did bring me some prospectuses for music colleges a couple of months ago, asking what I thought. But Lana is too young for them at the moment. She's only, what, eight or nine?'

Mel sighed. 'Nine, yes, but I can see why Irina is worried. After all, if you have a gifted child then you want to map out a future for them. Make sure you're pointing them in the right direction at every stage.'

'She's having lessons with an excellent teacher, by all accounts, and should listen to her advice. I don't know, it's none of our business but I think Irina is getting wound up unnecessarily. She says she is not being a pushy parent, but I wonder.'

'Your Uncle Val helped them. Do you think that is why she came to you?'

'Yes, I suppose so. After Val's death I felt a little responsible for them. I couldn't afford to go on employing her as house-keeper – I don't need or want one – and she didn't want to rent the cottage, so I arranged for her to come and clean regularly and look after the keys. It pays her something and it seems to work with her job at the hotel. And it helps me.'

'She's very nice, isn't she? But a bit lost. The sort of person someone would want to look after.'

'Yes, I suppose so.'

Mel glanced at Patrick. There was an edge to his voice. Had there been something between him and Irina? His expression was unfathomable.

'You sound hesitant.'

'Not really. It's just you can't live other people's lives for them.'

'Of course not. But someone in a strange country, a single parent, coping on their own with no family support . . .'

'Mmm. I don't know, Mel. I am happy to help them up to a point, but I don't want to get too involved. We don't know everything – about Lana's father, for instance. Or even how good Lana really is. We have to leave it up to the professionals to help, the violin teacher and the school. I don't mind helping to fill in a few forms, but it's not right to try to give advice.'

'No,' said Mel slowly. Then: 'Oh look, the Merry Maidens!' as they passed a sign near the brow of a hill. She remembered Matt mentioning them.

Patrick slowed the car. 'We'll stop if you like,' he said. At the next opportunity he turned the car quickly, then drove back to park in the layby near the sign.

They climbed a stile to find themselves in a small field of cropped grass enclosed by hedgerow. In the middle stood a large circle of stones, all waist-high.

'How many are there, I wonder?' Mel said as they passed into the circle. When she turned round to start counting, she was dazzled by the sinking sun.

'Nineteen,' Patrick concluded. 'The story, so old Jim told me, is that they were young women who dared to dance on the Sabbath. This was their punishment, to be turned to stone. And sometimes at midnight, even now, they dance.'

'They do look a bit like dancing figures, some of them,' she said, noticing the way the stones around them leaned and twisted, as though dipping and bowing to some unheard tune. 'But they must have been very small girls.'

Patrick laughed. 'There are the pipers as well,' he said. 'Another pair of stones, but bigger. In the field across the road there.' He pointed.

Mel shivered. 'It feels so primeval, doesn't it? Do you think we're on some ancient leylines? You're drawn right back into the distant past standing here.'

'The Cornish are Celts, don't forget,' Patrick agreed. 'And sometimes it does feel as though that old pagan world is still going on around us. The Romans never really made it here and the established Church only had a tenuous hold. There are times when it seems as if the intervening centuries hardly happened, have scarcely touched this place.' He ambled across to one of the stones and laid a hand on it as though it were sacred, thrumming with energy.

Mel closed her eyes. Sun spots moved across her retina. For a moment she imagined some force whirling around her, weak but still disturbing. Whether these stones really had been happy maidens defying the new Christian authority and being punished for it, or whether, as was more likely, they had been planted by some ancient peoples at the time of Stonehenge on this high place in the sight of the dying sun, it was a place of deep power. How would it feel to be here in the gentle light of dawn, in a midday thunderstorm? In the dead of night? It would be a place of many moods.

She opened her eyes.

'Here,' said Patrick. She walked over to the stone where he stood. 'What are these?' A scattering of tiny red beetles scurried across the top of the stone.

'No idea,' she said. She moved to the next stone. 'They're here, too, and here. They're on all of them.'

A movement in the corner of her eye. A rabbit had ventured out at the far end of the field. Insects, rabbits. These creatures took no notice of ancient spirits. New life burgeoned. The past was gone.

'Are you all right?' said Patrick, touching her arm lightly.

She turned and looked up at him, so close she could see flecks of green and dark brown in his hazel eyes, the length of his soft eyelashes. He scanned her face, a flicker of tenderness crossing his features, and smiled gently. Then he put his arm around her and pulled her close a moment. 'Come on,' he said. 'I'm going out later, so I'd better get back. But there's ginger cake for tea.'

Chapter 14

The next morning, Mel woke early with a feeling of anticipation. It was how she felt as a child on the day she went on holiday, for example, or on a special birthday. Not the dread of the day of an exam or a difficult interview. Nor was there any trace of the depression of varying intensity that had descended most days over the last eighteen months. She was astonished to conclude that she was happy.

Sliding out of bed, she threw on the oldest clothes she could find – jeans, a fleece jacket and a stained T-shirt she pulled out of the dirty washing pile. How long had she been here now? Two weeks and two days. She was running out of clean clothes. She bundled up the pile and took it downstairs to sort for the washing machine.

It was the thought of starting work properly on the garden that was part of the reason for her happy feeling. Sure, she had worked on her flowerbed, had helped Patrick cut a way through the jungle to discover some of the secrets of the old walled gardens, but none of that had done more than to make the sleeping wilderness turn slightly in its slumbers, before sighing and falling again into unconsciousness. Today they would properly begin the task of reawakening.

The other reason for her happiness was Patrick. She remembered their day out yesterday, and how they had spent the early evening before he had had to go out to meet a friend.

'You seem almost as fired up by this project as I am,' he had joked as they worked together on the long dining-room table, poring over a strip of lining paper anchored down by books, drawing as accurate a representation as they could of the gardens of Merryn Hall. This wasn't easy, but at least the map gave them an idea of the proportions of the garden and they could fill in some of the features that old Jim had described.

'It's wonderful, rebuilding a garden. Sort of life-affirming, don't you think? And then there's the mystery – what will we find underneath all the weeds?'

'Not a grave, I hope,' said Patrick soberly.

'No.' Mel felt troubled.

'I still need to ask old Jim about that.'

Mel appraised the plan so far. To one side of the central shape of the house was sketched the rough shape of the Flower Garden, gates, sheds, greenhouses and trees all marked. Then the Vegetable Garden, the as-yet unknown boundaries a dotted line. The banks of rhododendron were next, followed by the laurel grove. Mel had sketched in the little seat they'd found and, in a moment of amusement, a giant spider. Patrick had looked at her intensely over the top of his reading glasses and made a stern face. 'This is serious business, Ms Pentreath, and I won't have any messing about.' So then, sitting close to him at the table, alert to the times he brushed against her, she pointed out where he should draw the long pond, the sundial on the now-vanished lawn, the rockery and the ravine.

'I'm sorry about having to go out this evening,' Patrick said, unhooking his glasses, his face for a moment seeming naked and vulnerable until she got used to it again. 'I met an old schoolfriend, Tom, when I was up seeing my parents, and he goes back to Bristol tomorrow. I'd ask you to come, too, but . . .'

'I know, it'll be one of those "Do you remember when Old Squiffy let off the stinkbomb?" evenings.'

'Exactly. Why on earth did I say I'd go?' he said gloomily.

'Don't you enjoy that sort of thing?'

'Not really. I never seem to have the same memories as other people. I suspect everyone was having more fun than I was. I didn't really start enjoying myself until I went to university. I've loved life most since starting work and can do more of what I please in my own time rather than someone else telling me what to do.'

That was one of the most revealing things Patrick had said, it occurred to Mel now.

At a quarter to ten, she was hanging up the last of the washing on the line at the back of the cottage when she heard the doorbell. She picked up the empty basket and hurried round to the front to find Matt lounging on the doorstep in long-sleeved T-shirt and faded jeans. Under one arm he carried a fusty old jacket that looked as though it had been left for years forgotten in some outhouse.

'You're in good time,' she said. 'Come in for a moment while I put this away.'

He seemed too full of energy for the little house. When Mel showed him into the living room, he threw himself onto the sofa, then kept standing up to investigate things – the TV remote control, the pictures on the wall, a magazine. Mel went out to the kitchen and he followed her, watching her tidy up, and was instantly drawn to the pile of books and papers she had left out on the table.

'Laura Knight,' he remarked, flicking through the pictures.

'Everyone still goes on about her around here. By the way, I talked to Mum and she's going to ring Aunty Norah for you.'

'Thanks, that's great,' said Mel. She felt curiously self-conscious with Matt here, who was like a lively dog that wouldn't leave her alone. She pulled open the back door. 'C'mon, let's go up and find Patrick.'

Patrick seemed a little taken aback when he opened his front door to see Mel and Matt together, and Mel felt she had to gabble an explanation of how Matt had called for her on the way.

In the musty dining room, Patrick showed Matt the plan of the garden. Mel listened, privately amused, as Patrick and Matt discussed how to treat the greenhouses as though they were planning a military campaign.

'There's a strong chance the greenery on this one is all that's holding it together. We'd better go carefully,' said Patrick.

'Leave it till last then?' put in Matt. 'We can start clearing the beds today.'

Another sharp pain shot from the top of her arm to her shoulder. Mel straightened and stretched, dropping her machete onto a heap of mown nettles. The smoke floating up from Matt's bonfire made her eyes water. She squinted at her watch. Just after midday. They'd been clearing the Flower Garden for nearly two hours now, a merciless sun steadily climbing overhead. It was time for a break.

Looking about, she was amazed to see how much inroad they had made into the jungle in such a short time.

For argument's sake they had started from the dipping pool, she and Patrick swathing away side by side, she with her machete, he with his new Strimmer, and Matt carting away barrowloads of detritus to burn further down the garden. The great fog of smoke, for the vegetation was very damp, had impeded progress until the breeze had dropped. They had worked without talking much, all of them involved in the rhythms of their tasks.

Now Mel watched Patrick swap the Strimmer for the electric saw to fell a sapling. He turned to grin at her.

'You just love doing that, don't you?' Mel observed.

'Yup. It's the roots that are boring,' he grumbled, grabbing a big garden fork and levering away at the base of the narrow stump without much success. She smiled to see his tousled hair, the streak of mud across one cheek.

'Here,' she said, grabbing some pruning shears and snapping away at the roots he'd exposed. 'The rest will come up when we dig over the garden. Look, we're doing well, aren't we?'

They both gazed around them, surprised by the fact that they had effectively cleared an area the size of a tennis court.

'I'm worried that we haven't noticed anything worth keeping,' said Patrick, wiping at his face with the back of his sleeve. 'You don't suppose we've gone at it too hard?'

'A lot of the flowers would have been annuals,' said Mel. 'And many of the perennials wouldn't have survived the weeds. It really is going to be a matter of clearing it all and starting again, I'm afraid.'

'What'll we plant?' he asked, leaning on his fork. 'What would work here?'

'Mmm, well, Mum used to grow lupins, cornflowers, clarkia and nigella, sweet william and delphinium.'

'Sounds a good start.' He smiled, watching her. 'You'll have to tell me when and how to do it all, though.'

'Of course,' she said lightly. 'While I'm here. Only another couple of weeks now,' she added heartlessly, and watched him press his lips together in a rueful manner.

173

'How was last night, by the way?' she asked.

'Oh, with Tom? All right, actually.' Patrick grinned. 'In fact, I might go skiing with him and his wife at Christmas.' He returned to levering his stump.

Christmas. What will I be doing at Christmas? Suddenly, Mel felt shut out. Patrick would go skiing with his friends and she might not even know him any more by then. All the energy she had felt this morning drained away. Picking up her machete from the nettles, she dropped it safely amongst the other tools, then walked off towards the cottage. 'I'll bring us all drinks,' she shouted back in explanation.

When she returned, Patrick and Matt were resting, deep in a conversation about cricket, which had apparently provided them with some bonding at last. Mel was glad. She sat down on part of a fallen brick wall and sipped at her squash. Her shoulder was still bothering her and she had a deep scratch down one arm from a rose briar, but she was pleased that her good mood had returned.

'I feel properly alive in the garden,' her mother used to say, when people teased her about the large amount of time she spent on her knees in the earth. Mel now knew exactly what she meant. She gazed up at the tall trees bordering the garden – presumably at some point a deliberately grown shelter belt. She understood how trees could be sources of comfort, a protection against the world. Listen to them sigh and creak, as though whispering secrets as deep and eternal as the sough of the waves on the beach.

How many generations had sat here, where she was, in this once-lovely garden, hearing the wind in the trees, the call of the rooks, finding succour in this mellow walled haven filled with the scent of flowers ... She looked down, shuffling the bindweed under her feet.

Then two things happened at once.

Her foot snared itself in some wire.

And someone called, 'Ah, here you are.' It was Irina.

'Hello,' Mel called, bending and pulling the wire off her foot. It was the skeleton of something metal. An umbrella. The curved handle was covered in slime and when she rubbed it with her glove it gleamed yellow. Ivory, perhaps.

She raised her head and was struck to see Irina's expression. There was something wrong. Irina looked . . . anxious, hurt. The woman darted little looks from Patrick to Matt, to Mel.

'I was on my way back from taking Amber,' Irina addressed Mel in a small voice. 'I came to see if you were in.'

'Patrick thought we should start on the garden.' Mel held the umbrella skeleton towards her. 'Look, treasure,' she said, and laughed. Irina looked uncertain.

She feels left out, thought Mel suddenly. Or is it that I'm here with Patrick? She glanced at Patrick who fortunately caught her meaning.

'Fancy helping?' he said pleasantly. 'There's plenty to do.'

Irina smiled delightedly.

'It's nearly lunchtime, actually,' Patrick went on. 'I've got some bread and cold meat . . .'

'Then I can cut us all some sandwiches,' Irina said happily.

'Sounds great,' said Matt. 'I didn't have breakfast.'

'Didn't get breakfast,' said Irina in a mock-horrified voice, hands on hips. 'You should never miss breakfast, you know.'

'What is it about women?' moaned Matt to Mel. 'They can't stop trying to be my mother.'

'It's because you're such a boy,' said Mel, laughing.

Later, as the sun began to sink, Matt and Irina left at the same moment, Matt to walk back down the hill to the hotel to help serve dinner, Irina to drive up to Paul to collect her daughter from Amber's house.

'I expect I can come next weekend if you want me,' Matt had said. 'I enjoyed it.'

'And me,' said Irina. 'I will try to come, too.'

'You are mad,' Patrick said. 'Completely crazy – I'm so grateful to both of you.' He watched them go then turned back to Mel. 'And you. You've been a real trooper,' he said. 'I can't believe we've achieved so much in so short a time.'

'Nor me.' Mel was exhausted. 'A hot bath for me, I think.'

'Me, too, after I've put all those tools away. No, no, you've done enough today.'

They stood looking at each other, hesitant. I can't ask him what he's doing later, she thought. I've already taken up a lot of his time recently. He'll think I'm chasing him.

Patrick said very tentatively, 'I was going to drive down to Penzance this evening for a change. Find a pub or somewhere to eat. Would you like to come? Don't worry if you're busy.'

Mel tried her best to look as though she was weighing up whether she could spare the time from her non-existent schedule to go out with Patrick. After a moment she said with a smile, 'Yes, I'd love to.'

Patrick gave her a broad smile back. 'Okay,' he said. 'Come up to the house about seven?'

'Great,' said Mel, her spirits soaring.

Patrick shifted the tools and vanished indoors. Mel had almost reached the cottage when she remembered her jacket, which she'd left hooked onto a tree, so she returned to the Flower Garden.

She looked around at the wounds they had gouged today in the old garden. They had scraped off the scar tissue of many years of neglect, revealing the fresh earth underneath. What were they awakening in this special place? She picked up the rusted skeleton of the umbrella, spreadeagled like a great dead bird on the pile of rubble where Irina had dropped it, and studied the ivory handle. The flowery carving shouted feminine ownership. A parasol then. Difficult to say, with no scraps of cloth remaining.

She moved over to one of the greenhouses and lobbed the metal skeleton into a corner inside amongst the nettles, out of harm's way. What a medley of clues this place was yielding up. The mermaid plant label, the ledgers, the oil painting of the Flower Garden and now a parasol. Think of the stories they might weave if they only knew how to read them, these memories of a far-off time. A garden of memories, it occurred to her suddenly – that's what it was. As though these clues had been laid out on purpose by someone who wished to communicate a secret. A ridiculous fancy, she knew.

Was it really just over two weeks she had been here? It was beginning to feel like for ever, that she belonged, somehow. She hadn't even thought about Jake much recently, had she? Imagine Jake down here doing actual physical work. He would be horrified if someone handed him a spade and expected him to work himself up into a sweat digging a flowerbed. He didn't even like gyms. Jogging round the London streets occasionally was his limit. He preferred his car.

Instead she pictured Patrick again, hacking doggedly at a tree root, strong, determined, focused. Chalk and cheese, Jake and Patrick.

Chapter 15

At half-past seven they stood gazing up at the statue of Sir Humphry Davy, inventor of the lamp that saved so many miners' lives, where he looked down Penzance High Street to the promenade beyond and the sea. Above, in the gloaming, a few seagulls circled.

'Bet you wish you'd handled Sir Humphry's portfolio,' said Mel. 'Where's your office? Is it round here?'

'No,' Patrick said. 'It's a few streets away, beyond the park. There's a tiny industrial estate with workshops and offices – it's one of those.'

They walked slowly down a side street lined with restaurants, leading to the great bulk of St Mary's Church overlooking the bay and eventually, after peering into windows and scanning menus, they selected a small Italian restaurant.

'Something filling is what we need after all that gardening,' Patrick said as he pushed open the door. Even on a Sunday evening it was half-full, but the waitress led them over to a corner table by the window.

When Mel peeled off her short coat and scarf and handed them over to the waitress, she couldn't help noticing Patrick's appreciative glance at her gauzy blouse cinched with a heavy silver buckled belt over a gypsy skirt. He chose to keep on his black moleskin jacket and she thought how smart it looked against his white grandad shirt.

They ordered wine and pasta and Mel said, 'Would you really have come out on your own to eat – if I hadn't been here, I mean?'

'Sure, why not?' He shrugged. 'It's much nicer to have company but I don't mind being on my own. I'd have brought a book.'

'I wouldn't like it. Of course, I've had to sometimes, if I've been away on a research trip, but I always feel so self-conscious, as if everybody is looking at me and thinking I'm a bit sad.'

'That nobody loves you, you mean? Do you suppose people think that about men on their own?'

'I don't,' said Mel, taking a gulp of the wine the waitress had poured for them. 'I assume they're on business or that they're on their way somewhere and need to eat first. Silly, isn't it?'

'Well, let's face it, some men are unashamedly predatory. When they see an attractive woman on her own they regard it as an opportunity.'

'That must be it. Women are frightened of that.'

'How are you finding being down here, locked away in the country when you're so used to the city?'

Mel bit into a breadstick and considered the question. 'It is lonely,' she said finally. 'It's partly the quiet and the darkness – it gets very dark, doesn't it, when there's no moon?'

'I love it,' Patrick said fiercely. 'It's so wild, so elemental. I go out walking sometimes at night. Only places where I'm sure of the way, but it's amazing what you see. Badgers and foxes, yes, all sorts of animals, but also the shape of the land in the moonlight. And sounds carry. Not just natural sounds, unfortunately. You can hear a car engine miles away.'

'Don't you miss other people?'

'Do I feel lonely? Sometimes, yes – yes, I do. Especially since . . . well, there can be too much time to think. But I'm used to being by myself. I've lived on my own in London on and off for years. And being brought up in the country I'm used to everything being remote. London crowds in on you, forces you to look upon everybody else having fun, paired off, going out somewhere noisy "for a laugh". And yet there are so many truly lonely people there, people who hate going home because there's nothing for them there, people who are frightened of being beaten up if they walk alone from the bus stop. Not that the countryside is crime free or that people aren't lonely here, it's just my own experience. I feel . . . in touch with myself, to use that horrible phrase.'

'You must have deep inner resources then,' Mel laughed. 'If we're talking horrible phrases.'

'I think a lot and I read. And there'll be the garden, especially over the summer. And I do know people down here. I have family – Mum and Dad, and my brother Joe over near Truro. And there are a few other friends from school scattered around the county. I suppose I must invite one or two over sometime when I'm more organised.'

Their food arrived and they were silent for a bit as they ate. After a few mouthfuls, Patrick looked up and smiled at her. 'I have to say, I've not felt at all lonely lately, with you living in the garden,' he said shyly.

'You make me sound like a fairy!'

'You're supposed to be flattered.' He touched her hand in a tentative movement.

'Oh, I am,' she said hastily.

'We have a lot in common, don't we?' he said. 'The garden, a sense of the past, all sorts of things.'

And our own pasts, she thought, struck by his air of sadness. She wondered what had not happened for him, whether it was only his broken relationship that had made him retreat down here, to lick his wounds.

'What is it you intend to do down here?' she asked suddenly.

'*Do?*' he said, narrowing his eyes, defensive. 'My work. Live quietly, rebuild the house and the garden. Enjoy the peace and see what happens. Why, what do you want to "do" where you live?' He poured them both another glass of wine.

'Only, shouldn't life have more . . . purpose?'

'Do we need to be useful, do you mean?'

'Well, yes, possibly. Or creative.'

He thought, then nodded. 'There are many different ways of doing that. They don't all have to be done as part of a community, do they? I'm not really a group person.'

'Perhaps you're right. Do you feel your way of life is fulfilling?'

He put down his fork and considered this. 'No,' he said simply. 'Not at the moment. I suppose I'm in limbo or undergoing some sea-change. I'm waiting to be carried by the next tide.'

'Yes,' she echoed, feeling the sudden weight of her grief. 'That's a bit like me.'

The waitress came to clear their plates. Mel licked ice cream from a long-handled spoon while Patrick drank cup after cup of syrupy espresso, watching her. A noisy crowd claimed the table next to them and they gave up trying to talk much. Finally Patrick asked for the bill and when it came the waitress left a small bowl of *amaretti* – almond biscuits wrapped in tissue paper.

It was dark when they stepped out into the still evening, munching their *amaretti*. Patrick gently clasped her hand and they walked downhill past the church, towards the sea. They stood on the promenade, looking out across the bay to the lighthouse winking in the far distance and the lights of little ships slipping through the distant darkness. All was quiet except for the whisper of the waves below.

Patrick leaned over the railing, staring down into the black water, deep in his own thoughts. 'Do you ever feel as though it's sucking you down, drawing you in?' he asked quietly. 'They're treacherous, these seas.'

'And thrilling and beautiful, some of the time,' she replied, thinking of how exhilarated she had felt at Porthcurno only a couple of days before. The sea was much calmer tonight.

'And like the powers of hell in a storm,' he said. 'But today they're just lurking, biding their time.' There was something bitter in his tone. It was beginning to rain now, very slightly. Fired by some angry energy, Patrick grabbed her hand and pulled her back up the hill. She could hardly keep up with him. 'Patrick, don't. Wait,' she gasped. 'My shoe . . .'

'Sorry.' He stopped under a streetlight in the marketplace and waited for her to slip the strap back over her heel, his breath coming hard. She looked up and was fascinated by the pulse beating wildly in his throat.

'Sorry. What a brute I am,' he whispered, and took her hand more gently this time, leading her up along the road to the car.

He didn't speak as he drove, far too fast as usual, back through the narrow lanes to Merryn Hall, and Mel didn't like to break into his thoughts for fear of disturbing his concentration. Why was he like this, a man who could be so peaceful and then suddenly tormented? She was slightly frightened, yet drawn to him at the same time.

By the time they bumped down the drive of Merryn Hall, the rain was falling steadily. 'Come on in,' urged Patrick as they hurried across the courtyard. She huddled under the porch as he fitted the key into the lock. Deep inside she could hear the telephone. The door swung open, *ring ring*, louder and louder, *ring ring*, and he crossed the hall into the kitchen to answer it.

Left in the hall, Mel tried not to listen, but her hearing did that trick that dogs have, of tuning into a sound that interests them, even through a cacophony of others. She knew she ought to walk away, into the drawing room, but she froze, her face reflected ghastly white in a mottled oval mirror.

'No, it's difficult to talk,' came Patrick's voice. The kitchen door started to close as though pushed, but then swung open again by itself. 'I've got someone here . . . The person who's renting the cottage.'

Someone. The *person*? Tears prickled.

'Look, you'll be okay. Take some deep breaths . . . yes, that's right. You've got to ring him, you must. Right away. As soon as you come off the phone. I'll call you in the morning. Are you okay? . . . Don't be like that.' This, gently. 'No, that's not fair . . . I'll ring you back, promise. Look, for goodness' sake call him then go to bed. I'll speak to you in the morning . . . Goodnight.'

Mel found she could suddenly move and slid inside the drawing room just as Patrick emerged from the kitchen. She sat down quickly on one of the sofas. The room was dark, cheerless, smelled of ash. The grate was cold.

The door opened and Patrick walked slowly in. Mel stared at him, noticing at once his agitation. He passed a hand over his mouth, then seemed to recover.

'Sorry about that. Now – would you like some coffee or something stronger?'

'Patrick, are you all right?'

'Yes – yes, of course. Why?'

'You don't seem it.'

'I'm fine. Honestly. I was going to open a bottle of wine myself.'

'I'd rather have a cup of tea, I think.'

After a moment she followed him out into the kitchen, pulling her cardigan close against the chill in the air. Patrick was standing by the stove. In one hand he held a bottle, but he hadn't bothered to look for the corkscrew. He was staring into the distance. When he saw her he checked himself and yanked open a drawer. 'Would you mind putting the kettle on?' he asked, his voice toneless.

'Patrick,' Mel said, drawing up her courage. She walked over and touched his arm. 'What's happened?'

He shut the drawer slowly and put the bottle down on the table.

'Really . . .' he started to say, looking away, then in a forced voice, 'It was Bella on the phone.'

'Bella? You mean . . .'

'My fiancée. *Ex*-fiancée, obviously. I suppose Chrissie has told you all about her?'

'I don't think Chrissie's met her, Patrick, so no, she hasn't told me anything.'

His eyes met hers at last and she saw he was a hair's breadth away from tears, his face pale and pinched. He pushed impatiently at the hair falling across his forehead like a small boy, so she gently put her arm around him, as she would do to comfort a child. They stood like that together for a moment, she gently rubbing his shoulders, feeling his body quiver with distress.

'Oh Mel,' he said, raising his head. 'I'm sorry, this is pathetic.'

'It's all right,' she said soothingly. 'It's all right.' But the words seemed useless. 'What did she want?'

'She was having a panic attack. She gets them occasionally, especially when she's on her own.'

'On her own where?' The Sahara Desert?

'She's in her flat. In Clerkenwell.'

'Oh,' Mel said flatly.

'I know. It sounds odd, but I'm used to it.'

'Look, sit down, let's open this bottle.' Mel fished the corkscrew out of the drawer and passed it to him then went to lift a glass, no, two – forget about tea – glasses out of the cupboard. She sloshed wine in both and pushed one towards him. 'Drink,' she commanded, sitting down opposite. 'Now tell me all about it.'

It was a familiar tale. A man approaching forty, ready to settle down, meeting a woman ten years his junior who is flattered by his attentions.

'Bella works for Connyngham and Hall – you know, the estate agents? We met through a mutual friend. I thought she was an extraordinary person. I still do. She's so warm and lively, interested in people. We had similar backgrounds – do you know, her father was a farmer, too, but in Devon. We were good together – or so I thought. And she is very lovely.'

Here he hesitated, then pulled out his wallet from his inside jacket pocket and leafed through the notes and cards, finally drawing out a small photograph, which he passed to Mel.

She gazed at the pretty tanned face, the fine, naturally fair hair pushed back by the pair of dark glasses on her head. Bella was relaxed, laughing, a soft sweater tied loosely round her shoulders. She might have been on a yacht, or drinking iced tea after tennis. A Grace Kelly girl. A sort men fall for hook, line and sinker. Mel laid the photo on the table between them without a word.

'I knew I had finally met the right person. Isn't that odd? How wrong one can be.'

185

'What happened?' She felt overwhelmed by this golden vision of Bella.

'She didn't, in the end, feel the same certainty I did, I suppose is the answer. You know, we had talked everything through. The life we wanted together. We both agreed we hoped for children – or so she said – but she didn't want to work all the hours of the day that she had to with her job and have to combine that with kids, so we talked about downshifting. Moving out of London, her getting a less demanding job. Then, eight months ago, Val died, and suddenly this place entered the equation.' He gave a shuddering sigh.

'I brought Bella down here. It was wrong from the start. She was horrified at how remote it was, how much needed to be done to the place. I said we could keep a house in London, why not? Do up Merryn gradually as a second home until we felt sure about it.'

'It would have been quite a culture shock to move down here if you weren't used to living in the wilds,' Mel admitted. 'I know it would be for me.'

'Yes, I appreciated that. But she had been brought up deep in the Devon countryside. And, if you think about it, she'd be nearer her family here than when she was in London. Anyway, it wasn't as though I insisted on us moving here. I'd have sold it if she had said the word, but she just wouldn't make up her mind about anything. This place became a catalyst – it forced certain decisions about our relationship.' He paused and took another large gulp of wine, as though to anaesthetise his feelings.

'And then she told me. She had met someone else. Actually, she had re-met him – an old flame from law college.'

Mel was touched by the lines of pain and tiredness etched into his features. The light flickered and she looked up. A moth was dashing itself against the bare bulb.

Patrick didn't notice. He was staring sightlessly into the dark shadows of the scullery. 'What was most awful was that she couldn't decide between us. I couldn't stand it, I felt . . . stripped of my sense of self. In the end I broke it off. It was the only way to keep sane.' The expression on his face was almost crazed now, desolate, hopeless. Mel fought to think of any words of comfort. With a moment of sudden clarity she remembered the phone call.

'Has she accepted your decision?' she whispered. 'Is it hers also?'

'At the time she agreed it was the right thing to do,' Patrick said dully. 'I know the other bloke has moved in with her. But he works late sometimes and she hates being on her own . . .'

So she's got the best of all worlds, thought Mel scathingly, but she kept her mouth shut. Patrick would have to see this for himself. But then Mel could hardly talk, could she? She asked herself what she would do if Jake contacted her out of the blue, suggested that they start over again. Damn, was it the wine or Patrick's misery that was making her cry, too.

Her chair jerked back with a teeth-jarring squawk as she went over to the sink and yanked a wad of kitchen paper off a roll lying on the windowsill to blow her nose. Against the black hatched glass she could see the hideous underbellies of a dozen crawling insects, moths, flies, beetles, drawn by the light. She shuddered.

'You're freezing,' said Patrick, half rising from his chair.

'No, no, I'm fine,' she said, but he picked up their glasses and touched her elbow.

'Let's turn on the electric fire in Val's sitting room,' he said. 'It's a bit late to make up one in the drawing room.'

They moved through and Mel stood watching him fiddling with the switches on the double-barred fire until it began to glow red. Where should she sit – the chair or the sofa? The strange misery rose in her chest, threatening to choke her.

He solved the problem for her. 'Come next to me here,' he said, sinking onto the sofa, so she sat down as close as she could without touching him and took her glass.

'Would you like a blanket?' he said anxiously, seeing her shiver despite the fire now blazing away. He leaned towards her, put an arm around her shoulder and pulled her close, rubbing her arm vigorously to warm her.

'No, I'm all right,' she said quietly. After a while, he was still again and almost without thinking she laid her head onto his shoulder.

They were silent for a minute, then Patrick said in a low voice, 'Thank you for listening. It was a shock, her ringing like that.'

And you've got to ring her back tomorrow, thought Mel, but she didn't feel like reminding him.

'I . . . I know I shouldn't ask about your situation, what happened to you. Chrissie just said your relationship had broken up.'

'I know it's only fair that I tell you,' she said in a tight voice. 'We were together four years. Jake's a lecturer at the college where I teach. It . . . it got to the point where we had to decide. About getting married, I mean, having kids – the whole show. And there we stalled. He'd done all that once, you see, and he wasn't ready to try it again. I suppose that's it in a nutshell.'

'Poor you.' Patrick squeezed her arm gently. She lay, eyes closed, resting on his shoulder, enjoying the warmth, the peace, waiting for the misery to ebb away. It didn't. Talking about Jake made her long for him again, brought home the fact that the fascinating closeness of Patrick didn't feel like Jake. Patrick seemed bigger, fleshier, more reassuring, whereas Jake's coiled-up energy was challenging, exciting. Even Patrick's jacket smelled different – not unpleasant, just as if it had been kept at the back of an airless wardrobe. They took getting used to, these differences. She sighed and her warm breath on his neck made him turn his head towards her, then he shifted his whole body. He regarded her, calm now, and gave a sleepy smile. It was strange seeing someone's face this close. How naked and vulnerable he seemed, how touchingly unfinished were his features.

It would be so easy . . . to let him lean forward and kiss her, to allow him to run his hands over her body. She wanted to, badly, but somewhere inside a voice cried, 'No, it's no good, not like this.'

With a great effort of will she smiled at him and moved slightly, to put a little distance between them.

'You are beautiful, you know that?' She watched the soft movements of his lips as he slurred 'beautiful'.

Beautiful. Belle. Bella.

'Thank you,' she said, her smile feeling pasted on. 'And now, I really must stop drinking.' She leaned forward to place the glass on the table.

'Me too,' he said wistfully, crumpling back against the sofa with a sigh. Then he laughed. 'What a sorry old pair we are.'

'Aren't we?' she said. 'You know, I ought to be getting my little old self off home to bed.'

He reached out and squeezed her hand. 'Thank you,' he said again simply. 'For putting up with me.'

'Oh, you're impossible to put up with.' She had to make it into a joke or she was lost. When she stood up, she found she was drunker than she thought, but she waved away his supporting hand and stumbled out into the hall.

'Shall I walk you round?' he said.

'No,' she said, scrabbling in her bag. 'No, really. I brought the torch, look. I'll find my own way.'

She staggered around the side of the house to the Gardener's Cottage, the torch beam waving wildly. At first she jiggled the lock with the wrong key, then fumbled the right one until the door opened. She slipped inside, shutting it firmly behind her.

Teeth chattering, the aftermath of drink and emotion, she threw her jacket over the back of a living-room chair and looked round the room. Tonight it gave off a sad, abandoned air. Even the flower pictures seemed lifeless behind their gleaming glass. The silence was sinister.

In the kitchen she drank a lot of water, then dragged her weary body upstairs. Throwing herself upon the bed she pulled the duvet over her head and gave way to her misery.

'Any moment,' a little voice inside her said hopefully, 'any moment he'll follow you, come down and knock on the door and take you in his arms and comfort you, which is what you wanted him to do all along, wasn't it? You would have comforted each other.'

But would that have been right? How would they have felt in the morning? Two unhappy, hungover strangers, probably. The risk was too great. This wasn't a man to trifle with, a one-night stand. He was special. And so, she reminded herself, was she. Still, that didn't stop her wishing that he would come.

But he didn't come. And eventually she fell asleep.

In the night she woke to see black shapes leaping outside the window. Just wind tossing the trees, she realised after a moment's terror, and got up to close the curtains. Drifting off again she dreamed of being lost in thick fog. Her mother was calling, but when she tried to call back she could make no sound. She fought her way to the surface, waking to feel a terrible sense of grief gouging her throat. She turned on the light, then rolled out of bed to go to the bathroom.

From the side window in the kitchen she could just see part of Merryn Hall. As she sipped some water and contemplated its stern bulk, on the first floor where Val's bedroom must be, a light came on and Patrick's upper body was briefly silhouetted in the window.

She wasn't really alone. He was awake, too.

Chapter 16

On a Monday morning, eight days later, the sound of clanking and grinding dragged Mel out of troubled sleep. She opened her eyes to bright daylight flooding through the gap in the curtains. Rolling onto her back, which ached after too much gardening, she lay awhile, staring at the shadows flickering across the ceiling.

Only five more days at Merryn – well, six, if she counted Saturday, but she ought to leave before nine to miss the traffic, so five really. And after that she might never see Patrick again. A thought which brought back ragged trails of last night's dream, something about running and getting nowhere . . . no, it was gone.

There was another clunk, a *whoosh* of airbrakes and the teeth-jarring sound of metal being dragged across stone. She sat up, remembering what it was. The skips Patrick had ordered must have arrived.

And she must get up if she was to make her appointment in St Ives at ten.

Since that miserable Sunday evening, Patrick had thrown him-self into a frenzy of activity. Mel watched from the sidelines, where she felt firmly placed, acutely aware of his unhappiness but unable to breach his wall of polite friendliness.

First he arranged for the landscape architect to visit, then he rang round several firms of tree surgeons. He told Mel he had earmarked the front garden of the house as the next area for clearance, which would involve serious industrial work, and finally decided on a roofer who, depending on the weather, would be starting work during August.

Mel comforted herself that leaving really was for the best. Merryn might not be a peaceful place to stay and work for long. On the other hand, the cottage would be empty. Patrick told her he would not be trying to let it to anyone else if the estate was going to become a building site. It would stand vacant, and the thought saddened her.

But there was another reason why it was sensible to go.

Since that moment of intimacy over a week ago, their relationship had undergone a profound change. It had become self-conscious, forced, though they had tried to carry on as normal. She had helped Patrick in the garden several afternoons and they had worked in silence or talked about safe subjects – how Patrick should go about reconstructing the greenhouses, or what the school was like where his brother Joe taught. There was an unspoken awareness of something between them like a great solid lump that couldn't be touched or, it seemed, even mentioned. All the physical ease they had shared had gone, too. He would stand back courteously if Mel passed him in the kitchen and deliberately take an armchair if she sat on a sofa. Either he was repulsing her, or something else was going on. Maybe he was protecting her or himself.

Part of her was readying itself to leave now, to escape this dreamy backwater and to dive back into the busy currents of normal life, but another part of her knew she would be leaving something valuable behind.

Now she was simply trying not to dwell on this, to be businesslike. Last week, she had worked hard on the early chapters of her book. She had visited the Records Office again and would meet with the art historian in St Ives this morning, finish the remaining bits of research she needed to do in Lamorna and go. The detailed plan for her book was ready. She even had a title: *Radiant Light: The Artists of Newlyn and Lamorna*. She would write it in London over the coming months.

'I had an email from Jonathan Smithfield last night,' she had said to Patrick yesterday afternoon after another hard bout of gardening. Matt had been helping, too, but had left in response to a summons from his mother to help with a large party of German tourists. Now Mel and Patrick were lolling in a couple of rickety old steamer-chairs that Patrick had found in a stable, and drinking ginger beer. 'You know, the art historian who lives in St Ives. I'm going to see him tomorrow. Shall I show him your paintings – P.T.'s, I mean?'

'That's a good idea,' said Patrick. 'Which ones would be best?'

'I thought your oil and two or three of the flowers. What I'm hoping is that he's seen other work by the artist. Or, at least, he might be able to cast some light on P.T.'s identity, or have a suggestion about how to find out.'

'I wish I could come with you,' he said casually, crushing his drinks can in a single, cruel movement, 'but I don't have the time. The computer man's coming tomorrow.' Mel watched him toss the can in a perfect over-arm movement to land on a pile of garden rubbish and wondered why she felt as if she were the can.

As well as all his work in the garden, Patrick had been making progress with his new office, installing equipment and interviewing two candidates whom the local Job Centre had sent along for the post of administrative assistant.

Considering how much time he had spent at the office it was amazing really that they had achieved as much as they had in the garden.

It was a warm day for the tail end of April. Mel finished the dregs of her drink and looked around. Most of the Flower Garden was cleared now and Patrick had been digging hard in preparation for planting. They had bought dozens of trays of bedding plants, pots of herbs and seedlings, from a local garden centre. Already, Mel had bedded in several rows, which she regarded with satisfaction. Now she leaned back in her chair and closed her eyes, enjoying the sun on her face.

When she opened them again, it was to find Patrick sitting up, arms folded over bent knees, watching her, an expression of such unhappiness on his face that pity surged through her. She smiled at him and he smiled back then looked away, suddenly distant again.

She remembered this now as she ate breakfast, and considered what it might have meant. What were his feelings for her really – deep down? He was impossible to read.

He hadn't mentioned Bella again. Had he rung her back the following day as he had promised? Mel hadn't dared to ask, but once during the week she wondered whether she had interrupted such a conversation. Hearing his car in the drive – she guessed he must have been at the office all day – she had walked up to the house to give him a parcel the postman had left with her. When Patrick answered the door he was on the portable phone, halfway through some intense conversation. He finished the call quickly but he seemed distracted as he took the parcel from her and thanked her formally. She hadn't stayed.

Jonathan Smithfield lived in a terraced house near the new Tate Gallery in St Ives, in a road overlooking one of the beaches. Out of his back window Mel could see some of his sculptures, stone figures, reclining like sleeping Buddhas, frosted by the same yellow algae that touched the roofs of so many buildings in the little town.

Jonathan himself was a tall, gangly individual in his mid-fifties, who gestured enthusiastically with his long arms when he talked about his lifetime's study of Cornish artists, his own creative work and his involvement with the community of artists in his native town.

For a while they discussed the Lamorna painters and Mel was relieved when he was able to corroborate certain parts of her theory about one painter's influences, suggesting new lines of enquiry for another, directing her attention towards one or two of Laura Knight's less well-known paintings.

Then she brought out P.T.'s pictures, first the two flower studies she had taken from the cottage, and then the oil painting of the young man.

Smithfield dismissed the flower paintings with a, 'Nice.' But he was interested in the oil painting. 'This is quite distinctive,' he said. 'Not by someone who's been classically trained, I should say. But there's a naturalness here, a *joie de vivre*. And the *impasto* – the brushstrokes . . . I can see why you might think there is a link with Dame Laura. Though it's not, of course, by her at all,' he added. 'There's not the draughtsmanship.'

When Mel pointed out the painter's initials and spoke of Charles Carey, Smithfield tapped his fingers thoughtfully on the table. 'Yes, Carey is a name I recognise,' he said, 'though I don't think I've ever seen anything by him. But this . . .' He set the painting up against a wall and stood back to look at it from a distance. 'I like it. It has something, don't you think?'

He listened attentively as Mel explained about her find in the archive, the reference to Pearl Treglown.

'It seems unlikely, don't you think – a servant who painted? But not impossible. I tell you what, are there any other papers belonging to the family from the period? I know you've searched the archive, but maybe there's something they've kept back.'

'I am fairly sure there isn't anything in the archive.' Mel thought for a moment, remembering her visit last week in which she had combed the collection again, taking some more photocopies of documents relevant to the garden. 'I think Patrick has written to the family's solicitors to ask, but I don't believe he's heard back yet.'

'It's the right line of enquiry. You'd be surprised what turns up sometimes in the loft amongst the broken birdcages and Great-Aunt So-and-So's love letters. Well, I'd have to say good luck with everything, my dear. I'd be pleased to cast an eye over the proofs of your book in due course.'

'Oh yes, I'd be so grateful,' said Mel. 'If it's not too much bother.'

'It would be a pleasure. And if your friend Winterton needs a dealer to look at this picture and give an opinion, tell him to be in touch and I'll suggest one or two names. Not that I feel it would be worth a lot, mind, but it might have a market.'

'Thank you,' said Mel. 'I will.'

Patrick was still out when she returned to Merryn at lunchtime, so she brought the pictures in from the car then made herself a large cheese sandwich, which she took out into the garden by her flowerbed. The grass had been cut, she noticed suddenly, breathing in the lovely smell. The old man must have been again while she was out.

After the sandwich and a cup of coffee she must have dozed off in her chair, because when she came to, it was to realise with a shock that someone was standing a few feet away watching. It was a relief to see it was just Matt.

'Oh, hello,' she said, sitting up and running a hand through her tangled hair. 'How long have you been there?'

'Only a moment,' he said softly, hunkering down before her. 'I didn't want to wake you.' He plucked a grass stalk and slipped it between his teeth. White, even teeth, she noticed for the first time. 'I've a message from Mum. She's busy all this week at the hotel, but when she's free, Aunty Norah can see you both any day except Thursday.'

'Oh, thanks.'

He plunged on. 'Also, I was on my way to Porthcurno beach again. Wondered if you wanted to come along?'

Their eyes met. He was close enough now that she could see the faint dusting of freckles on his smooth tanned skin. He was smiling slightly, but there was a tension there too. If she wanted, she could put out her hand and discover the feel of his short spiky hair, explore the dimple at the side of his mouth. He was lovely, this young man, full of life but at the same time disarmingly vulnerable, his dark eyes shy beneath the long lashes. A boy. So different from Patrick. Or Jake.

A long, long second passed and it was Patrick who reasserted himself in her mind. What, after all, did she and Matt have in common? They were worlds away from one another.

She said carefully, knowing a thoughtless word would crush him, 'Normally, I'd have loved to have come with you, Matt, but I promised Patrick I'd help him here this afternoon. I don't know where he is, actually, he's late.'

'Oh, that's a pity.' Matt slowly stood up. 'Another time then.'

'Yes, another time. But, Matt, listen, I won't be here much longer. I'm going back to London on Saturday. In fact, tell Carrie it looks as though I won't have time to visit your great-aunt after all.'

'I see. That's a shame. It's meant something to me, coming here.'

'You can still come. Patrick will need lots of help.'

'I didn't mean that . . .'

'Matt . . .' He looked at her and she shook her head very slowly. He stood up and, was the sudden brightness in his eyes her imagination?

'Okay,' he said. 'I'd best be getting along.' But he loitered forlornly, looking around at the garden.

Mel watched him and said, 'Matt, what's wrong? You're not your usual self at all.'

'Oh, nothing,' he mumbled. Then, when she waited, he turned round and added, 'Oh, I'm just kind of confused at the moment.'

'What about?'

'I'm not sure which way life is pulling me. Mum needs so much help here, and I'm bored with the shop. I don't feel it's getting me anywhere. It's funny – I didn't used to mind, but recently . . . Then last night, Toby – you know, my friend the artist?'

'Oh yes.'

'Tells me he's getting married. Toby . . . I can't believe it.'

'I expect it'll happen to you sometime.'

He shook his head. 'You know, there's never been anyone serious. I've always thought life's supposed to be fun, but just now it seems full of responsibilities. And then you came along, and . . .'

They looked up at the sound of a car in the drive beyond the house.

'Patrick,' said Mel, standing up quickly. She forgot what Matt had been saying now, busy as she was shuffling on her shoes. Damn, her hair needed a good brush. 'I hope I'll see you before I go home, Matt.'

'I'm sure you will.' Matt's tone washed over her like an icy wave. She looked up but he was already walking away. What was *that* all about? she thought, but deep down inside she knew.

'Mel.' Patrick was hurrying down the garden. He caught sight of Matt disappearing up the lane and slowed his pace. His expression hardened.

'Matt came to give me a message,' Mel said, too quickly.

'He's always popping along, isn't he?'

She shrugged. 'I thought you liked him.'

'He's not a bad bloke.'

'Then what's the problem?'

'There isn't one.'

'Isn't there?'

Patrick said nothing to this. Instead he sighed impatiently and said, 'Sorry I've been so long. Complications with the damned website, as ever.'

Mel fetched him a can of beer from the fridge and then sat down, wary. But while she was inside Patrick seemed to have shaken off his bad mood because he said, 'How did you get on this morning?' and she described her meeting with Smithfield briefly, allowing a certain coolness into her voice. He had no right to be jealous of Matt; she was free to do as she liked. But Patrick didn't seem to notice her frostiness so she gave up.

'Not much then about the pictures,' he said. 'A pity, but I suppose I didn't expect anything.'

'No,' she said. 'The whole thing is still a mystery.'

'Have you been up to admire the skips then?' he said.

'Not yet,' she yawned, forcing herself up out of the chair, her limbs suddenly heavy. 'I meant to – I forgot. Come on, I suppose we ought to get to work.'

'Are you sure you want to this afternoon?' he said. He reached out and brushed her shoulder quickly and it was as though he was deliberately breaking something forbidden.

'Yes, why not?' Her voice thickened at his touch and she couldn't help but turn towards him. 'You've only got me here for a few more days, so you'd better make the most of the fact.'

'I know.' He was studying her. 'Don't imagine I haven't been thinking about it. Mel. Please. You can stay on, you know, as my guest.'

'You've said. That's kind,' she said lightly.

Their eyes met, unreadable emotions struggling in his face. 'Mel, I can't stop thinking about it, to be honest. I . . . I wish you would stay. Do you need to go back yet? I mean . . .'

'Patrick, I have commitments. I have to visit some libraries, see my friends and family.'

'But there's nobody . . .'

'Special?'

'That's right.'

'You know about that,' she said in a flat voice. She stepped away from him, as nervous as the ginger cat.

'It's just a thought,' he said, his smile rueful. 'I . . . love having you here. It feels good, just knowing you're here. Mel, I'm sorry I made a fool of myself the other night . . .'

'Having me here?' Mel snapped, unable to stop herself. 'Like a next-door neighbour?'

'No, no, more than that. You know I mean more than that. I'm not putting it very well, am I?'

'Patrick . . . what are you saying then?' *What about Bella?* she wanted to ask, but found she couldn't. He shrugged.

'I'll think about it,' she said unhappily. 'Come on, let's go and look at the skips.'

'Don't you love the sound of breaking glass?' Mel was feeling more cheerful after two hours of physical hard work.

Patrick had just torn away a great net of creeper from the biggest greenhouse and, as they had feared, half the structure fell inwards.

'Completely rotten,' he grunted, jabbing the pruning shears into the frame. He picked up a shovel and began hacking the joints apart. Mel, glad of her thick gloves, trudged to and fro, hefting loose beams into the giant skip that stood beyond the tumbledown wall.

They had hardly spoken to one another for the previous couple of hours, but they hadn't needed to. The silence had not been uncomfortable, it was just that each was involved in their own private thoughts. Often, though, when Mel glanced at Patrick it was to find him looking at her in such a way she felt she wanted to drop what she was carrying, walk over and wrap her arms around his neck.

Why had her resolve to leave been so easily shaken?

Here, working in the shelter of the walled garden with Patrick, the place cast its spell over her once more. London life was receding. A voice inside kept asking, what would she be missing if she stayed here a little longer, a week, a few weeks? Why would it matter?

On the practical side, there was money coming into the bank – the college were paying her regular salary throughout the sabbatical. Cara upstairs was keeping an eye on her flat. The garden would be a wilderness, but a few weeks wouldn't make that much difference. Her friends, her family, what about them? They would still be there for her. Then there was the matter of her book. She had to admit, she could just as easily write it here. In fact, if she stayed down here she might find out more about P.T., and have new material to include. The whole thing might also, of course, turn out to be a wild-goose chase, but it would still be fascinating to see how far the trail took her.

Much more worrying was the question of the paintings' owner. She straightened from her task of shovelling debris into a wheelbarrow. This had to be the most important thing to consider. Patrick, too, might be a wild-goose chase, yet another man leading her astray ... 'But from what?' came the voice. In London, she had felt bewildered – cut loose by the loss of her anchors, her mother and Jake. Merryn was a haven, so why shouldn't she stay? But had it now done its work? Havens were for the short term. She had to set sail again sometime, get on with her life. Should she stay and risk her peace of mind, or was it time to go back?

She glanced at Patrick, who had moved over to the wreckage of the gardener's shed and was beginning to pull away a fallen roof. He looked up from his task and smiled at her with such warmth she felt suddenly giddy. This afternoon she had felt so comfortable with him again. But there was also something secret, unknowable there. Merryn was a haven for him, too. He was like an animal that had come to a place of safety to tend its wound, a deep wound, she knew now. But whereas she would eventually have to return to her normal life, he had decided to stay here, to hide away from the world.

It might be dangerous to stay, to be swallowed up ...

A bird's warning cry.

She just glimpsed a shape flying across the garden into the dazzle of the afternoon sun. 'Look!' she cried.

This time Patrick had seen it. 'Extraordinary. A white bird. Not a gull.'

'Or a pigeon or a dove?'

'No, smaller than that. There it is again!' He pointed through the gateway to the Vegetable Garden, to where it had perched in a bush.

Mel crept over to look. It was a bit bigger than a budgerigar, but with a straight orange bill.

'It's a blackbird, surely,' she whispered.

'But it's pure white.'

The bird once more gave a stuttering cry, and took off in the direction of the rhododendrons.

A shadow streaked across the garden. Mel shaded her eyes against the sun. High above circled the silhouette of a bird of prey.

Patrick was off after the white bird, trampling a way through the Vegetable Garden, cursing as his shirt caught on brambles. Mel watched him disappear beyond the ruins of the far wall, then leaned her shovel against a wall, deciding to walk the sedate way round to the rhododendrons. She found Patrick crouched amongst the dead leaves under a tree in spectacular pink flower, staring intently into the gloomy greenery.

She sank down beside him.

'It's there,' he whispered, and she caught sight of a flash of white flitting away through the bushes. 'I saw it quite close for a second. It is like a blackbird, but white and with pink eyes.'

Patrick put out his hand to pull Mel through the thickening undergrowth after him. Past the little stone seat and through the hedge at the other side, the bird's cry of alarm still sounding ahead of them. Mel, blinded by the foliage wrapping itself round her face, was glad of Patrick's strong warm hand to steady her. Suddenly the hedge released her and she opened her eyes. She was walking over a springy bed of dead leaves and straw, then a crunch of broken something. To the right the ground rose suddenly in a hummock, about shoulder height.

Patrick stopped, dropping her hand. Then he edged forwards, peering ahead into the dense undergrowth, listening. 'I've no idea where it's gone now,' he said, leaning against the hummock, arms folded.

'What was it, do you think?'

'I think an albino blackbird.'

'Oh.'

'It's rare a bird like that has survived into adulthood.'

'You mean because they're easy prey, standing out like that.'

'Exactly. You saw the hawk.'

'Is that what it was?'

'Yes, you can tell by the wing shape.'

'One of your boyhood interests?'

'As a matter of fact, yes, I was fascinated by birds.'

'The feathered ones?' she asked in mock-innocence.

'Both types,' he said, and she laughed. Then something caught her attention, where his shoe had scuffed the ground cover.

'Don't move,' she said, and bent to pick up the piece of white and blue. 'Look, it's china – porcelain, in fact. And here's another bit. From a plate or saucer, look.' She scrabbled about in the leaves, but her search revealed only two or three more pieces. Not enough to fit together into something recognisable.

'I wonder which part of the garden this was,' said Patrick, brushing a hand over the mound's pelt of moss and ancient ivy. He grabbed a hank of ivy and pulled. Underneath was rock. Several beetles scuttled away. He yanked at some more creeper.

'Looks like we've found the rockery,' he said. 'It's quite extensive.' He pointed out how it sloped up towards the boundary of the garden.

'You'd have thought the rockery would have been over in the ravine, the other side of the garden,' Mel said. 'I think that's what your old gardener man said.'

Patrick was pulling at the ivy again. 'My mistake. It's actually one huge piece of rock,' he said. 'Probably too big ever to have been dug out and moved. So they just left it here, made a feature of it.' Resting his right hand on it he began to force his way round it, stamping down brambles as he went. 'There's a bit that sort of juts out here,' he said after a moment. 'Like a cairn. Wait.' He was almost out of sight now, hidden by the rock. Then, 'Hey, Mel, come and look at this!'

Mel made her way carefully along the track he had trampled and round to the other side of the rock. For a moment she couldn't see him, and then she did. He was crouched in a hollow under a great lip of rock. Around him, on several ledges lining the sides of the cave, was arrayed a number of assorted small pots, several dozen perhaps, and he was examining one in his hand. She knelt down beside him. There was room for both of them side by side on the sandy floor which was crisscrossed by tiny rock plants. The pot she picked up contained a small stub of candle and when she scratched the foggy surface she saw that the pot was glass.

'It's the grotto,' she said, gazing across the arch of the roof. 'Carrie mentioned this. What was it? Something her aunt said.'

'A niche in a rock, filled with candles?' Patrick's tone was unimpressed. 'Looks more like a shrine.'

'It does a bit,' she said, looking about. 'But imagine it on the night of a summer party.' She sat back on her heels, trying to picture the scene. 'It must have been magical to a generation that hadn't seen movies or holograms. Even now, there is something special about candlelight, isn't there? The sense of awe. Fire against the primeval darkness. And the intimacy, the way it picks out the essential shapes of things and softens them. Bathes them in beauty.'

Patrick carefully replaced the candle pot on the ledge and sat with his back against the rock. 'They must have generated considerable heat, too, a few dozen candles.'

'We could do it, Patrick. We could clear a path here and fill the grotto with light again.'

Patrick regarded her with amusement, through half-closed eyes. 'That's going to take longer than the rest of the week.'

She laughed, slightly uncertainly.

'Please stay,' he said, reaching out and grasping her hand. He looked so serious, his face intense. 'Please. I'd miss you if you went.'

She sighed. 'I don't know,' she said. 'There's a risk. I might get too attached to this place, to the idea of hiding away here.' Blood suffused her face. 'And there are things I have to do, a whole life in London.' She loosed her hand and staggered to her feet.

But he was next to her, grabbing her hand again and swinging her round. Tears of confusion threatened and she tried to turn away, but he imprisoned her other hand, too.

'Look at me,' he commanded, but gently. She raised her eyes to his face. How troubled he seemed, his eyes dark, unhappy. 'It's not just this place, is it? Say it isn't. Is it me who is the risk?'

She nodded once and he dropped her hands but instead pulled her towards him, squeezing her hard and burying his face in her hair.

'I'm sorry, I'm sorry,' he whispered, his hot breath almost sobbing into her ear.

She struggled, pushing him away from her so she could look at him.

'What are you sorry about?' She was angry now. Was he

manipulating her? Why couldn't he be clear? She'd had enough of being messed around.

The energy went out of him. 'That it's a risk. That I'm a risk.'

'It's still Bella, isn't it?'

'It's difficult getting over her, don't you see?' It was he who was angry now. 'It's difficult trusting someone else again. Making myself vulnerable. *I* would be taking a risk with *you*. Why do you think I came down here? It's to start again, to grow strong. And now you're here. All I know is that I want you to stay. It might be selfish of me, I don't know. And yes, there's a risk. There's always a risk . . .'

'But you can't just shut yourself away from life, Patrick. You can't be an island.' A rock, an island, feeling no pain, she thought, remembering the song. One hand brushed the grotto that had stood untouched by time, by change, by storms, for what – a hundred years? And she? In a fortnight's time, she remembered, would come the first anniversary of her mother's death. It felt like an invisible barrier through which somehow she and Chrissie and, yes, stoical William, would have to pass. It would mean they would have completed a whole year, all four seasons, with all their anniversaries and birthdays, without Maureen. She would have to be with Chrissie that day, she knew now with certainty. Go back to London.

And Jake's selfishness – for she felt it was selfishness – was still too much to bear. He hadn't wanted her enough to want to make a child with her – what greater rejection of her could there be? And yet she had to look forward, she knew that. Chrissie had Rob and her children. She herself had so much in life to enjoy. She loved her job, loved being in London, and maybe, who knew, there would be someone in time who would stay for her.

She turned. And yet here he was. Patrick. She wanted him so

badly, she knew now, but maybe this was the wrong place at the wrong time. He was a risk, but was he a risk she was prepared to take?

Suddenly she felt reckless. 'Okay, I'll stay. I don't know for how long.' And relief flooded through her. 'I've got to go to London for a few days, though. There are things to do . . . But I'll come back.'

'You will? That's fantastic.' Patrick was staring at her, a look of joy on his face.

'Mr Winterton! Mr Winterton, sir – are you there?' It was a man's country voice some way away, up the garden.

'Bugger. It's Pascoe,' said Patrick, remembering. 'The man with the digger. I forgot he might be coming today.' He began crashing through the undergrowth back the way they had come. Mel stood there for a moment, her mind reeling, then followed after.

They emerged from the rhododendrons. 'Will I see you later?' Patrick said in a low voice.

'This evening?' she said.

'Yes.'

'Look, why don't I cook for a change? Is seven-thirty all right?'

'That would be lovely if it isn't too much trouble.'

When she returned to the cottage, it was to find a phone message from Rowena from college. Would Mel act as second marker for the students' essays this term?

'Like heck I will,' said Mel out loud as she banged down the receiver. Real life was the last thing she wanted to think about at the moment.

Chapter 17

September 1912

'Another over here, girl,' ordered Mr Carey's fat friend the lawyer, waving his empty wine glass.

Pearl passed among the party guests in the silvery twilight with a tray of drinks while still managing to keep an eye on Charles and the fascinating group of unconventionally dressed visitors standing apart, near the fountain. His birthday party had, in the end, had to wait until the harvest was over and now, well into September, there was a distinct chill in the evening air and some of the guests were drifting inside. The artistic contingent, however, seemed impervious to the weather.

The lively woman in the bright green dress was Laura Knight, she knew. Mrs Knight was exchanging banter with a tall, wide-shouldered, narrow-hipped man in a loud checked suit, throwing back her head to laugh uproariously. That must be Mr Munnings, then – A.J., as Charles called him – the one living at Mr Jorey's in the village, who painted horses and amused everybody by singing hunting songs. Pearl pressed her lips together, remembering last Sunday afternoon at her drawing lesson when Charles described to her the people she might expect to see, making her laugh by mimicking Munnings's flamboyant gestures. He had, she saw now, got Munnings to the life.

'Who's that one behind them?' she whispered to Jenna as they stood together at the edge of the crowd, nodding towards an intense-looking man with greying hair sitting gloomily on the concrete rim of the pond, trailing his empty glass in the water.

Jenna screwed up her eyes. 'Mr Knight, I should say. And that talking to him now . . .' for a big, handsome man with an easy, friendly manner had wandered over to Harold Knight, who sat up straighter and instantly became more cheerful, 'is Mr Birch – they call him Lamorna.'

Pearl saw the mistress beckoning from the crowd and nudged Jenna, who went across with her tray. Left alone, Pearl's eyes moved to Charles, something uncoiling inside her as she admired his long, lithe figure propped languorously against a pillar of the summerhouse where he flirted with a young woman with a cloud of fair hair. She glanced back to Mr Birch. She had seen him before, she remembered now. Up on the cliffs near Mousehole where she had strolled on an afternoon off with her sketchbook. He'd nodded to her as he stood aside to let her pass and after a moment she had turned round and gazed at his tall, upright frame striding back towards Lamorna Cove.

'Come on, girl, don't moon, fetch the other tarts and look sharp about it.' Cook, bearing a huge tray of pies – apple, blackberry and redcurrant – swept past across the lawn towards the trestle tables laid out with white cloths on the terrace, and Pearl moved her remaining full glasses to Jenna's tray and hurried back to the kitchen with the empties, butterflies of emotion fluttering in her throat.

It was all as exciting as she had thought it would be, this party. Dozens of beautifully dressed guests, with Elizabeth looking as fresh as a snowdrop in the white off-the-shoulder gown

Pearl had laced her into earlier, before encasing Mrs Carey in a flattering dark blue gown with an Empire neckline which she had ordered specially from London. Her husband had insisted on squeezing his middle-aged spread into his ancient black evening suit but, despite not being able to do up the buttons on the jacket, he cut a distinguished enough figure as he roamed the house and garden.

But it was Charles's artist friends who fascinated Pearl the most. They were in a category by themselves, not acting like gentlemen and -women quite, but not like ordinary working people either. It seemed that all that sort of thing didn't matter to them. What united them was their passion for their work, their ambition. Charles was encouraging her to have that ambition, too. He'd been giving her drawing exercises for some weeks now, ever since he'd found her in the Flower Garden that Sunday, building on what her father had taught her about the rules of perspective, shading, the art of seeing. Charles was a natural teacher. Already her drawings of flowers and faces, the views from the cove, were transformed. But he wanted more for her, she knew.

Shoving open the scullery door, she caught sight of Milly, the skinny young cousin of Jenna's brought in to help wash up, cramming the scrapings from a meat-pie dish into her mouth. Milly started and there was a crash and a muffled wail as pieces of pottery flew across the flagstones.

'Here, quick,' Pearl said, shaking the snivelling girl to her senses and shoving a broom in her hands. 'I won't tell. Just get it cleared up before Cook sees or she'll skin you.'

She tiptoed her way through the mess into the kitchen and picked up a tray of tarts and clout cream. 'Dump the bits behind the stable and I'll bury them later,' she called through the doorway. The girl nodded through her grimy tearstained face. Pearl made a *moue* of sympathy and rather than risk slipping on the slimy fragments with her tray, decided to go back through the house.

The hall was empty, but the door to the morning room was half-open. She heard a man's voice – a young man – husky with passion. 'I know it's him you want, your cousin, but you will have me, you will.' A scuffling and a scream. 'No, Julian!'

Pearl froze. *Elizabeth*. She nudged at the door with her tray and it swung open with a creak. Two heads turned, revealing a tableau of living statues. The young man had pinned Elizabeth against the opposite wall; one of his hands was pushed down the bodice of her dress. The spell broke. He let her go and she staggered, crying. Pearl swung the tray aside as Julian hurtled past her towards the drawing room. Pearl called into the morning room, 'Are you all right, miss?'

'Yes. Leave me alone. Go away!' Elizabeth hissed, picking herself up and, holding the torn straps of her dress, she too hurried past Pearl, but in the direction of the stairs.

Pearl watched her stumble, wondering whether to go after her, then swung round as another figure scurried out of a hiding-place in the shadows of a corridor and went off upstairs in pursuit. It was Cecily.

Her heart banging in her chest, her mind whirling, Pearl stood a second to recover herself. Then she shrugged and continued through the drawing room, arms aching with her heavy burden, and stepped into the garden.

In a single moment of surprise she forgot all that had just passed, for during her short time in the house, all daylight had gone from the sky; now great milky stars shone down and Jago had lit all the Chinese lanterns around the garden. A tiny row of flickering lights picked out the path up past the laurel maze, making her long to follow where it led.

Instead she hurried dutifully over to the tables where Dolly and Jenna unloaded the pies and cream. 'What kept you, girl?' snapped Dolly. 'Been to Newlyn and back?' and bid her help serve out dessert.

'Pies, more pies,' quipped a teasing voice. 'What do they say? If the devil came to Cornwall·he'd be put into a pie.' It was Munnings staring down at her, his face under his fringe almost white in the lantern light, his expression mischievous, challenging, hard.

Dolly, who had made her views of the artists as spongeing time-wasters perfectly clear to Pearl, pressed her lips together and riposted, 'Nobody else is complaining.'

'And nor, in truth, am I,' he said, giving Pearl a wink as he turned away with his plate full.

Inside the drawing room a small group of musicians in evening dress were now tuning up. As Pearl passed the open windows with a pile of empty plates, she saw Elizabeth and Charles standing together talking. For a moment she locked eyes with Elizabeth and was shocked at the girl's cold glare.

Later, after the dancing, as Jago was fetching coats and opening the doors of carriages, and Dolly was fussing over where to put the remains of the food, Jenna filled Milly's pockets with little parcels for the family and Pearl escaped, ostensibly to collect up forgotten glasses from around the grounds. She slipped past the Flower Garden where the dahlias and chrysanthemums slept, across the edge of the lawn and up the path by the laurels.

Then she stopped, captivated. As if to reflect the great stars overhead, the rockery was aglow with little jar lanterns, each containing a candle. Some were dwindling, a few had gone out, but those that remained made the rows of sea shells studding the stone glitter and gleam in the still air. Inside the tiny cave, two dozen points of light twinkled through coloured glass. She had never seen anything so lovely.

A footstep behind her. She spun round. It was Charles. He came up beside her, touching her lightly on the elbow in greeting. She looked up at him in surprise. He was close, very close now, the edges and planes of his handsome face softened by the candlelight. She felt his warm breath on her cheek and could make out the separate hairs of his moustache. When he smiled, his eyes sparkled and she glimpsed the tip of his tongue against his teeth. Fascinated, she stared, hot blood pulsing through her body.

A voice – the mistress – called from the house. 'Charles? The Knights are going now.' And the moment passed.

'Your sketchbook,' he said.

'What?'

'I came to ask. Can you fetch it for me, quickly now? Knight said he'll take it to look at.'

'Will he?' she said, amazed. A real painter who had shows was going to look at her work? 'Thank you,' she said and, after a pause, bobbed an odd sort of curtsey. 'Thank you. Thank him for me.'

She slipped away and ran up the back stairs to her room to fetch the book from the drawer.

Chapter 18

The eight-thirty news bulletin started and Mel, who had already heard the headlines at seven-thirty and eight, snapped off the radio.

Where on earth was Patrick?

She had started cooking soon after seven, frying the onion and the mince for spaghetti bolognaise, adding tomatoes and mushrooms, herbs and stock, stirring as it simmered. Now she moved the pan off the hob and contemplated the pan of water for the pasta. No point in doing anything about that until he was here. She looked around the kitchen. The table was laid, the salad mixed, Parmesan grated, a bottle of red wine waited open on the side. But there was no Patrick.

She had said her place, hadn't she? She looked out of the window up at the house. Faint light glowed through the lower-floor windows. Impossible to tell whether he was in. Perhaps she ought to go and see?

No, she must leave him to come in his own time. It was an artificial situation, this, living so close to one another but knowing each other so little, needing to preserve the boundaries.

She sat down at the table, wondering whether to start on the wine, just one glass, but that might lead to a second – and what

216

if he arrived stone cold sober? What if he didn't arrive at all, had regretted what happened earlier? Her resolve ran out. She poured herself half a glass, turned out the kitchen light and moved into the living room, where she was struck with immediate satisfaction at how cosy she had made it – the curtains drawn and a fire crackling in the grate.

Some wine splashed on the mantelpiece as she put down the glass and she hurried back to the dark kitchen to grab a cloth from the draining board. A point of light outside caught her eye, moving far across the garden. It shone steadily, disappearing now and again, then the point becoming a shaft of light, bobbing up and down. What was Patrick doing out there in the wildest part of the garden at this hour? Assuming it was Patrick.

The beam of light was coming nearer now. She could see his boots, then his legs. She fled back to the living room with the cloth, not wanting him to see her watching him, and caught a glimpse of her face, eyes glittery, in the mirror above the mantelpiece as she scrubbed at the wine stain. After a moment, there came his special knock, three short light taps and one loud one.

Her relief as she wrenched open the door turned to anxiety again, for he wasn't standing by the doorstep waiting to come in but hanging back, as if to deliver some excuse that he wasn't coming to supper after all. The large torch lantern and the Barbour jacket suggested a night exercise rather than a cosy night in.

His words only mildly reassured her. 'Is the food at a crucial stage? I've something to show you.'

'What?'

'You'll have to come and see.'

'Hold on a moment.' She shrugged on her jacket, pulled on her boots and stepped out into the cold garden. There was a faint moon glowing through veils of cloud.

Patrick had already vanished, she thought at first, then she saw his dark shape separate itself from the shadow of a tree and the torch came back on. 'Over here,' he said, and started towards the rhododendrons.

'Patrick, where are we going?'

'Have patience, woman.'

'But it's pitch black. Shine the light over here. Ouch.'

'Here, take my hand.'

They tripped and stumbled through the undergrowth, branches grabbing their throats like the hands of assassins, leaves slapping against their faces like knives.

'This is crazy,' Mel moaned. 'Ow, that was my toe.'

'Sorry. Just keep going. Through here – look, there's the bench.' He swung the lantern. 'Duck down now. This way . . . and we're almost there.'

They had finally reached the trampled undergrowth by the rockery; the rock itself, an invisible presence, dulling sound in the darkness. Patrick flicked off his torch.

'Patrick . . .?'

'Ssh. This way.' Her hand was warm in his.

As they edged round the rock, she became aware of its silhouette – but its golden aura wasn't the moon. It was a warmer, yellower glow than that. And then Mel saw why. The cave was full of tiny dots of light from candles burning on every ledge.

Like votives, she thought, immediately seeing the church where her mother's funeral had taken place, how the children had been drawn to the flames, their high voices clamouring to light candles for Granny, the air pungent with incense.

'It's beautiful,' she whispered, her hand still in Patrick's.

'I found a bag of nightlights in a cupboard and waited until it was properly dark. It felt like a ritual, laying them out and lighting them.'

'What did you pray for?' she asked.

'Funny you should say that. I thought about the people who had lived here, who had created this garden. And Val. And now . . . me, you.' He squeezed her hand. 'It was a strange, elemental feeling out here. As if there is only some thin crust separating us from the layers of the past.'

Patrick moved behind her, snaking his arms around her waist, and they stood together in silence, Mel absorbing the fact of his warmth, his cheek on her hair, watching the lights leap and flicker.

After a moment, he removed one arm to delve into his coat pocket. 'I kept a couple back,' he said, showing her two tablets of wax. 'Shall we light them?'

They crouched down by the grotto, Mel touching a flame to her candle first and standing it on the lowest ledge, then Patrick placing his next to it. He looked dreamily into her face. The words 'for us' passed through Mel's mind, but he didn't actually speak them. She stared at the flame of her light, yet not seeing it.

After a moment he stood up and stepped back. 'There's something else,' he said, and took her hand again. 'Come and see what I found when you were out.'

He shone the torch into the tangle of bushes opposite the grotto, further down the garden and along a rough pathway, recently trampled. Then he guided her down the carpet of undergrowth, the moon obligingly emerging from cloud to illuminate their way.

A minute later, a blanket of ivy rose up on their left. Patrick shone his torch upon it and through the leaves Mel glimpsed solid stone. The wall of a small building.

'Round here,' said Patrick, and they turned the corner to squeeze through a gap where he'd hacked through creeper and bramble. 'There's a door here somewhere.' He felt across the building until she heard a handle rattle, then a click. Soft amber light fell across Patrick's arm, then across his face as the door opened inward and they almost stumbled into a little room.

The source of the light was immediately apparent – a hurricane lamp stood on an upturned metal pail at the further side of the stone-walled hut where a double door seemed firmly sealed.

'It's the summerhouse, isn't it?' she said, her voice unnaturally loud in the small space. It smelled fusty – a collection of rotting deckchairs in a corner might be the cause of this – but the air was surprisingly dry and the wooden floor mostly intact. The shuttered shapes of windows were apparent on each side wall and to either side of the double door.

'There must be a remarkably good damp course,' Patrick said, banging one heel on the wooden floor. He shone the torch up at the tiled roof. 'The whole building is in good nick, isn't it? Perhaps Val had something done to it, I can't remember now.'

The only pieces of furniture, apart from the useless deckchairs, were two director chairs from the house and a small picnic table laid with a cloth, a bottle of wine and two glasses.

'Don't tell me these have remarkably survived the years here, too,' joked Mel.

'I thought it might be fun to have a drink in a secret den,' Patrick smiled, a flash of white teeth in the half-darkness. He looked as dark as a Mexican bandit in the light from the oil lamp, the planes and shadows of his strong face somehow thrilling and dangerous.

'It is like a children's gang hut, isn't it?' she laughed. 'Perhaps we need a password and nicknames.'

'Sounds fun,' he whispered. They were facing one another now, close, quite close, their figures throwing up great shadows on the back wall. He smiled down at her, studying her upturned face in the glow of the lamp. 'So,' he said, his voice turning low, sinister, his eyes narrowing, leering at her. 'If you want to be in the gang, you need to prove you're worthy.'

'Oh, yeah?' she riposted. 'What are you going to make me do then?'

'Mmm,' he said, looking around as though for inspiration. 'How about this?' And very slowly, he bent down and touched his lips upon hers. 'Will that do for a start?' he said softly.

'You'd better try again to make sure,' she said, her voice shaky. This time the kiss was deeper. Their mouths slid over one another, licking, nibbling, devouring. She tasted the smoky flavour of tea mixed with spearmint and an indefinable tang that was Patrick himself. His kiss felt different from Jake's, rougher yet softer, and part of her felt inestimably sad. Then as the kiss went on she relaxed into it, squeezing her eyes tight shut against dark thoughts.

The world seemed to spin and she staggered slightly, almost pulling him over, tipping up one of the chairs.

'Oops,' he said, dropping her suddenly and catching at the wobbling oil lamp. 'And this is before we've had the wine.' He settled the lamp and, stepping back, righted the chair.

They stood looking at one another almost shyly, and to break the moment, Mel said, 'Why don't we have a drink?' So he picked up the bottle and sloshed an inch of wine into a glass. He swilled it round, and took a mouthful, his swallow audible in the stillness. 'St Emilion,' he said. 'Definitely one of Val's finest.' He half-filled both glasses.

'Here,' he said. 'We need a gang toast.' And they linked arms and drank around the crooks of each other's elbow, giggling.

'You know, it doesn't feel like my idea of a summerhouse,' said Mel, sitting down. Patrick took the other chair, one leg crossed horizontally upon the other, ankle to knee.

'Well hardly,' he said, 'it being the middle of a chilly April night.'

'It's not just that. There's something about it being made of stone. Wouldn't it feel cool and dark in summer? And it faces the wrong way – east. That's odd, too.'

'I suppose, to face the house. Or else it's another mystery to add to the rest,' said Patrick, leaning back in his chair.

They were silent then, feeling the warmth of the wine run through their limbs, listening to the wind rising in the garden outside. How cut off they were here from the rest of the world. It could have been fifty years ago, a hundred. The wick on the lamp needed trimming, for the flame was leaping and dancing like firelight. It felt spooky rather than cosy in their hideaway now.

Mel jumped at a spider running over her hand.

'It's only a little one,' Patrick teased.

'It might have big brothers,' she retorted, brushing at her jacket to make sure the creature had gone. She shivered.

'Are you chilly? We can go if you like.'

'There is supper waiting,' she remembered, pulling herself up from the chair. 'I'm hungry.'

'So am I,' whispered Patrick, standing up and taking her into his arms.

'You're so lovely,' he said later after their meal, as she sat curled up in his lap on her sitting-room sofa. He stroked her hair and kissed her yet again. 'All red and brown and gold, like autumn. I couldn't believe it, that I'd find someone like you down here in the back of beyond. I was worried I would end up being grumpy and lonely by myself.'

'Nor did I think I'd find you,' murmured Mel, nuzzling her face into his smooth-shaven neck, feeling the warm skin against her eyelids. 'I feel safe here, safer than I've felt for a long time.'

'Poor you,' he whispered and they both fell quiet, sunk in their own reflections, as though they sensed danger in too much intimacy too soon. Then he kissed her again.

'I don't ever want to hurt you,' Patrick breathed into her ear.

'Then don't,' she replied, immediately regretting the sharpness of her response for he was quiet again and she was frightened that she had wounded him.

'Patrick?' she said, a flutter of fear in her throat.

'Mmm?' But his eyes had a hard, faraway look.

'What are you thinking?'

'Nothing,' he said. Again, she felt unease. Another man, another planet, and he was deep, this one. Could she really face embarking on this voyage of exploration all over again? Yes, she could.

And when, later, she took him upstairs to her room, the air seemed thick with the presence of the past, not just the past of this house, but all the other times she had ever made love.

A week and a half later, Mel drove back to London. But ten days after that, she was down at Merryn once more.

Chapter 19

Four more weeks passed at Merryn, the days and nights with Patrick slipping past like gleaming pearls on a string, Mel's life in London but a hazy dream.

One rainy June morning she sat at her kitchen table in the cottage, absorbed in her writing. The book was growing steadily now, more than half of it done.

It was during this period, she had just typed, *that Laura Knight began work on* Daughters of the Sun, *shocking local people by using professional models from London who posed nude, sunbathing on the rocks below Carn Barges or swimming in the sea. Laura, fascinated by the effects of the light, made study after study . . .*

Mel looked up from her laptop to riffle through her notes, before copying down Laura's own words: 'How holy is the human body when bare of the sun (*Oil Paint and Grease Paint*, 1936).'

Had she got the quotation right? She looked for her pencil to scribble a reminder to check it, but it had gone. When she spotted it under the table she fumbled for it with her stockinged foot, accidentally prodding the sleeping cat, which shot across the kitchen to the door.

'Sorry,' she sighed, and picked up the pencil to write – what?

Her concentration was broken. Anyway, it must be nearly time to go. She looked at her watch. Ten. Another half an hour and Carrie would be here.

They were finally going to visit Aunt Norah today to talk about her mother, Jenna, who had been a maid at Merryn before the First World War. First Norah's husband had been ill, then Carrie had been too busy at the hotel. Now, in mid-June, there was a slight, unexpected lull in the trails of visitors, and Carrie had phoned the night before to ask Mel if she was free.

The cat stretched and meowed to be let out. When Mel opened the door it slipped into the pouring rain, keeping close to the house for cover, and vanished round the corner. Where did it go? It never ate the food Mel put out or, for that matter, the little corpses it continued to drop at her feet. It must be getting fed somewhere else. 'It's like you,' Patrick had breathed in her ear last week. 'It just arrived and made itself at home.'

'Oh, you.' She tried to twist away, but he held her too firmly. 'I seem to remember you begged me to stay. I'll go if you want.'

'Don't you dare,' he growled, moving his hands down her back and up her tight jumper. 'There are things I want to do with you.'

She stood for a moment, eyes closed, remembering this, a slight smile on her face as she breathed in the fresh air of the garden, listening to the pattering rain, the flapping of wood pigeons in the trees, these sounds overlaid by the vibrations of some distant farm vehicle and the occasional roar of a passing car.

A gull's harsh cry startled her and she glimpsed the bird wheel and vanish behind the trees in the distance. How different was the scene before her from even six weeks ago, she thought. Her flowerbed was coming alive with summer colour – the lobelia she had planted, marigolds, white alyssum – and buddleia and sistus were beginning to burgeon. But beyond, she and Patrick had cut vast swathes into the tangled wilderness, uncovering the path to the summerhouse, clearing the ground to prepare for grass, as the landscape architect Patrick consulted had suggested. During the last few days they had set to work to rescue the pond from its covering of brambles and to dig out layers of silt.

Another picture – Patrick working the little mechanical digger 'like a boy with a shiny toy', as she had teased him yesterday when he had worked late into the evening, gouging out mud and dead vegetation, dumping it in a skip. 'Completely obsessed.' Patrick had laughed, a carefree laugh of pure pleasure.

This morning, lying asleep, the early-morning light falling through the curtains across his face, he had looked very young, too, she thought now, the worry lines on his forehead and around his mouth ironed out, his skin glowing. She had watched him for a moment, learning the strong planes of his face, the soft lashes, the tender set of his mouth, before she fell back once more into slumber. When she woke again, he was kissing her goodbye. She touched her hand to her cheek, remembering. His fresh-shaved jaw had been cool against her sleep-warmed face.

'Oh, don't go yet,' she had murmured, pulling him down to kiss him properly, breathing in the fresh lime smell of his shaving soap, but he had brushed his hand teasingly against her breast, causing desire to shoot through her once more, and pulled away, laughing.

'Nine o'clock meeting, I'm afraid,' he said. 'And I've got to look at the paperwork first.' And he was gone, stumping down the stairs. A moment later, the front door banged and his footsteps receded across the gravel. A car door slammed, the engine roared away and in a moment there was silence. Only the tick of the alarm clock and the echo of his recent presence. She listened to the furniture settle and mourned.

Why did she feel this, this fear of losing him?

Sometimes, after making love, he held her so tightly it was frightening. 'What is it? What is the matter?' she would ask.

'Nothing,' he would say. 'Nothing's the matter. Just . . . sometimes I can't believe that this is happening.'

'Why can't you?' she would whisper, hugging him back, but he wouldn't answer, and sometimes a great tremor would go through him as though he were repressing some feeling building up inside.

It was amazing, she thought now, shivering as she shut the kitchen door, that they had known one another for – what? less than three months – in this secret place shut away from the world. In some ways it seemed like a lifetime.

There were other occasions, Mel thought, as she washed up the breakfast bowls, when Patrick seemed to her unfathomable, when he would retreat deep inside himself, turning distant unhappy eyes upon her when she begged to know what was the matter.

'Nothing's wrong,' he would mutter. 'Don't nag at me.'

And she would turn away quickly to hide the tide of panic rising in her chest, until he would see that he had hurt her and would wrap his arms around her in that frighteningly desperate way, murmuring, 'I'm sorry, I'm sorry, it's not you, it's never anything to do with you. I'm sorry.'

It might be just his nature, these periods of loss of energy, of introspection. She had met his parents and his brother Joe and had been struck by the strange kinks of inheritance.

Frank Winterton, Patrick's father, was a straightforward man in his seventies with a light manner and a firm handshake. His hair grew in a tuft in front like both his sons' did, but was a shock of silvery-white now. Mrs Winterton, Gaynor, was more intense. Not a happy person, Mel thought, with pity, noticing the stiffness of her arthritic limbs.

'I suppose you're vegetarian or something,' was her first comment to Mel, when she and Patrick arrived at their converted farmhouse for lunch two Sundays ago. 'You all seem to be faddy these days, your generation.'

'No, I'll eat anything,' was Mel's mollifying reply but she could sense that Gaynor felt she was being tested.

When Mel praised the pretty farmhouse-style kitchen, Gaynor looked pleased but said, 'I don't suppose it's as sophisticated as you're used to.'

'It's beautiful, I love it,' reassured Mel, and Gaynor seemed to relax a bit, but was still anxious serving up the food and took no compliment at face value. Perhaps she had passed some dark streak of unhappiness on to Patrick, her elder son.

Joe, on the other hand, had clearly taken after his father, happy to be living where he had grown up, a teacher married to another teacher, completely at ease tending to the demands of their eight-month-old son Thomas who, as the first grandchild, was the centre of attention.

It was so illuminating meeting people's parents, Mel mused, as she sat down at the kitchen table again, staring at her laptop where the white doves of her screensaver now soared across the screen in never-ending flight. Now she knew where that funny gesture came from, that Patrick had sometimes of stroking the back of his neck. His father did exactly the same thing. Or the way he would stand hands in pockets – that was like Joe. Those were just superficial things, she knew, but there was something about the way he and his brother vied for their mother's attention. What did that presage for his relationship with women in general, with Mel? She shrugged, pressing the touchpad on her laptop and causing the doves to freeze before they dissolved into some secret limbo inside her computer and her document appeared.

White birds. From time to time she and Patrick had glimpsed the albino blackbird in the garden, but never as closely as they had that day six weeks ago in the Flower Garden. It was so distinctive she was surprised it hadn't succumbed to some predator, even in this garden haven. Every time she saw it she sent up a silent prayer for its survival.

As she moved to close her document, warning of an email pinged onto the screen. Chrissie was asking what she wanted for her birthday in four weeks' time.

Mel smiled. Typical of her sister. It had never occurred to her to surprise Mel with a choice of present in her life. She pressed Reply and tapped out her answer: *No Marks & Spencer for miles here, so tokens no good. How about some earrings, say silver studs, if that's OK.* She thought for a moment then typed, *Hope to see you soon.*

She had last seen Chrissie and her family nearly six weeks ago when she had journeyed up to London on the train just before the anniversary of their mother's death. They had spent the heavy day together, the two of them, visiting the graveyard where Maureen's ashes were buried, threading her favourite white lilies into the vase holes on the small gravestone. Later, she had stayed for supper with the family and they had spoken to William on the phone. She had felt too worn out with emotion to go on to her flat that night, so had slept in the spare bedroom with Rory's fluffy polar bear for company.

It was strange returning home to Clapham the following day. When she unlocked the door, the flat smelled musty, and black dust from the street had settled in a fine layer on everything, separating her like a symbolic veil from her own past. The garden, too, looked abandoned, the grass a meadow, the beds a riot of nettles. Her neighbour, Cara, had gone back to visit her parents in Spain, so there wasn't even the comfort of footsteps and opera music overhead.

She had only been in Cornwall for a month or so, but now, her mind full of Merryn and Patrick, she felt like a visitor in London. In those few weeks, she had bedded down in another world, put down thirsty roots, found underground water that slaked her sadness. On the phone to Patrick that night from Clapham she became overwhelmed by a longing to be back in the cold moonlit garden with the sound of running water, the great silent stars looking down overhead, the past whispering its secrets and the wilderness creeping its way to the door.

The following couple of days, Mel visited the city's libraries to check a whole sheaf of queries she had compiled so far during the writing of her book. She also met up with Aimee and a number of other friends. Aimee had met a man she really liked.

'Do you remember Callum, the boy I told you about, who came on my Paris trip? Well, it's his father. He's called Stuart.'

'Are you allowed to go out with your kids' parents, Aimee?' asked Mel.

'Mmm, not sure of the etiquette on that one. But I'm only teaching Callum this term, so I think it's all right. I told you I had to speak to Stuart after the incident with the wine in Paris? Well, he came in to see me after school one day for a longer chat. It turns out he split up from his wife last year and Callum's found it difficult to deal with. Then I bumped into him at a neighbour's party. It went on from there, really.'

So Stuart was on the rebound, too. Like Mel and Patrick. 'I'm really pleased for you, Aimee,' Mel said, hugging her friend, 'but don't get hurt again.'

'I could say the same to you,' answered Aimee, who had heard all about Patrick, but she looked so happy that Mel knew at this point Aimee didn't care.

She called into college where people greeted her with warmth, yes, but also with surprise. She was supposed to be having a term off, so what on earth was she doing back?

Once, an office door opened and Jake came out. They stared at one another for a long moment of surprise, but she was being talked at by Rowena, who was gushing on about a problem with one of the units she was teaching, and he merely raised an arm in greeting as he ushered in a waiting student, and when she finally escaped Rowena the door was closed. She stood outside, her hand raised to knock, intending to interrupt with a breezy, 'Hello,' in brazen demonstration that she was over him, that not only was she surviving without him, but that she was living well on it, the ultimate revenge. But she couldn't quite muster the courage.

Ten-thirty. Carrie would be here any moment.

Now she finished up her email to Chrissie: *Why don't you come and stay sometime in August? Patrick has plenty of room and I'm sure he wouldn't mind, much love, Melxxxx*

The kisses were to make up for the argument she and her sister had had on the way back from the churchyard. Mel had confided in Chrissie about Patrick and had been astonished to find that Chrissie disapproved.

'Nick's told me Patrick is in pieces about Bella. Do be careful. Never mind the fact you've just broken up with Jake.'

'It's fine, Chrissie.' Said through gritted teeth. Why couldn't her sister be pleased for her? 'I'm quite capable of looking after myself.'

She was even proud of her behaviour when she arrived back at Merryn and turned on her computer, freezing in astonishment as an email from '*Jake Friedland*' popped into the Inbox. She had stared at it for a moment. 'Delete it, go on', said a quiet voice in her head. 'Not without reading it first,' said another, sinuous voice. She double-clicked on it.

Hi, Mel. Sorry we didn't get to speak when you came in today. Just back in harness here after the holiday and haven't stopped to take breath. I'd heard you're on sabbatical! Good for you. Hope all goes well. Freya was asking about you yesterday so I send one of her best princess kisses.

Cheers, Jake.

Cheers? *Cheers*? After everything that had passed between them? This time she did delete the email, but the following day she rescued it from the Deleted box. She must be more adult about this. Cool. She tapped Reply.

Hi, Jake. Great to hear from you. I'm in Cornwall for a few weeks, as you might know, in a beautiful place, and my book's going really well. So sweet of Freya. Give them both big kisses from me.

All best, Mel.

She closed down the laptop as if frightened that the message would decide to try and come back. That was the way to handle him. Except she felt a bit ashamed of mentioning her book, which had a publisher when his didn't.

The next day, however, there was another message from him. This one moaned about disorganised students and the lack of time to write, and she felt oddly guilty. This time she wrote back one line and hoped that that had got rid of him for the time being.

Now, as she heard Carrie's car coming up the drive, she reread her concialitory email to Chrissie, added two more kisses for the boys to the end and pressed Send.

Chapter 20

'Just opposite the church, it is,' said Carrie, as the car swung round another bend in the lane, the trees overhead dripping with the recent rain. A granite tower came into view on the right. 'There.'

Mel felt the wheels plough into the muddy verge. 'Oh yeuch,' she said as she climbed out into the sludge. She tiptoed round and opened the door for Carrie to ease her bulk out, then lifted the seat to rescue the pot plant Mel had brought as a present for Aunty Norah.

'We must take Norah as we find her,' Carrie had explained. 'She'll be eighty-six now and I couldn't get much sense out of her on the phone, she's so deaf.'

'She is expecting us, though?' Mel asked.

'Oh yes, I had a word with Cyril, her husband. Dear Cyril. Doesn't say much, though.'

Unlike Carrie, who had talked non-stop the whole of the hour's drive from Lamorna to this little hamlet outside Truro where Jenna's daughter lived. Carrie had described Norah's three, now middle-aged children, and recounted the names and exploits of their own grown-up sons and daughters until Mel's head spun. She then told Mel about her upbringing in Penzance, where her father had worked as a railway guard, and about her dead husband Neil, over whose memory death had cast a golden glow. Mel thought he sounded a quiet and malleable foil to Carrie's considerable energetic presence, the backroom boy in the hotel where Carrie played front-of-house. But like the leit-motif in a piece of music, her attention periodically returned to her son Matt.

'I worry so much about him,' sighed Carrie. 'He lets life drift by. He's a good boy, coming home the way he does, but he has no sense of purpose. Doesn't know what he wants to do with his life. I suppose it's partly my fault. I always organised everything for him, you see. He was my only one. And so when Neil died he was all I had left. Oh, you need the middle lane here, sorry, my love.'

Mel swerved right on the main road, cutting up a shiny navy saloon car which hooted urgently. She was feeling vaguely guilty about Matt, whom she had hardly seen in the last few weeks. Carrie chattered on.

'He misses his father, of course, though he doesn't say so. Neil was a good man, but he wasn't firm enough with Matt. Never made him take responsibility for anything. They used to potter about together. Neil did all the hotel cooking, you see, and Matt would help him. And they'd go fishing together when Neil had a couple of hours off.'

'I'm sure he'll find something to interest him,' Mel said, feeling compelled to comment when Carrie drew breath. 'What about his photography? I thought his pictures were very good.'

'Oh, that's just another hobby,' moaned Carrie. 'He's never wanted to make a career out of it. It's just something else he fits around all the other things he does, the diving, the water-skiing. What happens when he gets married and has children, I ask you? How's he going to pay for everything?'

Mel laughed. Was Carrie, like Irina, another over-ambitious mother? Or was it mere concern to see one's child settled and secure. Maybe she wouldn't understand the Carries and Irinas until she had a child of her own. If she ever did . . . She slowed behind a trundling farm vehicle and even Carrie fell silent as they watched fruitlessly for the chance to overtake. But Mel's mind was ticking over.

She was half-glad she had never had this parental pressure. Her mother was a strong example to her daughters without trying too hard, unlike Carrie; a strong, positive person who knew what she was good at and what she needed to do. Mel remembered some words of a conversation she had had with her mother when Maureen lay in hospital after an early bout of exploratory surgery.

'I was never concerned over Chrissie and William,' Maureen had told her. 'William was like his father – knew what he wanted to do and got on with it. And Chrissie – she sails through life. It was you, Mel, wanting so much to try things but anxious about them, lacking in confidence. I'm so glad you found something that suits you, dear.'

What is it that makes us so different, one from another, even within the same family, Mel wondered. And how much can we really blame our parents, as Carrie was now blaming herself.

Again, she was surprised by that image of her father lifting her up as a toddler, high in the air. Then he had gone.

They had visited their father regularly in his new life. A weekend once a month, a two-week holiday with him and his new wife Stella every summer until they were teenagers and could refuse to go. When had she last seen him, come to think about it? Christmas. And before that, at her mother's funeral. He had come without Stella and stood alone, away from the large family party in the church as though afraid someone might hiss at him to go away, say that he was unwelcome. Though they would never have done that. Mel knew that his guilt at leaving them all still weighed him down. Because of this guilt he had never reforged his relationship with his children – it had never been natural again.

Yet there was William, turning into a carbon copy of their father, without any seeming awareness about it. Strange really, since William's relationship with his father was formal at best. Did William still see the man as a role model, or was this singleminded determination to become a surgeon, his brilliance at chess, his tendency to live on his nerves, merely to do with DNA? Let's hope that the likenesses didn't apply to William's attitude to marriage, thought Mel, picturing his sweet caring wife, who had given up her own medical career to bring up their children.

Carrie was quiet still and Mel wondered whether she hadn't responded enthusiastically enough to what she had been saying.

'I'm sure it will work out for Matt. He seems such a nice, talented person,' she said. She pictured his neat tanned features, the quirky mouth, twisted in a perpetual smile, the short sleek hair and his lean, graceful body, and remembered the way he had looked at her that day she had got together with Patrick. Matt would be all right.

She glanced at Carrie. Why was the woman looking weirdly at her?

'I'm sure that is what he thinks about you, my dear,' said Carrie gently.

Mel gripped the wheel tighter. 'Really?' she said faintly.

'He's become very fond of you.'

'I'm sure not. I've hardly seen him recently.'

Carrie must have absorbed her meaning because she said, 'There's no hope there, then?'

'No,' said Mel.

'Oh. Well, don't tell him I talked to you about it.'

He'd be absolutely mortified, thought Mel, herself red with embarrassment. Just at that moment the farm vehicle pulled into a layby and she relieved her feelings by slamming her foot down on the accelerator and roaring past.

'Watch out, you've missed the turning,' cried Carrie, then as Mel slowed down to turn round, 'oh no, you're all right. It's coming up.'

The subject of Matt's lovelife, it seemed, was closed.

As they drove into deep country they passed a sign to a National Trust garden.

'Matt was telling me about all your work on the Merryn garden. Norah would be interested to hear about that. Will he open the place up, do you think?'

'Open it? You mean to the public?'

'There's several that do in Lamorna. There'd be a lot of interest. Brings visitors to the area, that sort of thing – with the right advertising, of course. I'd support it – keep leaflets in the hotel. And he'd need permission for the developments, of course.'

'What developments?' Mel was lost.

'You know, a tea room and a car park. Lavatories.'

'I don't think he's anywhere near that stage yet,' said Mel, bewildered.

'That was the road to Norah's,' said Carrie suddenly, as they shot past a narrow turning.

'Don't know that I'm going to be much use to you, dear,' said Norah, looking Mel up and down in an admiring fashion as they sat drinking coffee in the front room. She had a high-pitched voice cracking with age. 'My mother's been dead these twenty years now.'

Mel put down her cup and leaned forward. 'I'm trying to find out anything I can about an artist I've come across,' she said, speaking clearly for Norah. 'At Merryn Hall, where I'm staying, there are some paintings signed with the initials P.T. I'm sure the artist was in some way connected to the house and that they were made shortly before the First War. That's when your mother was in service there, wasn't it?'

Norah frowned. 'One of the family was a painter, my mother used to say. Master Charles, she called him.'

'I've learned a little bit about Charles Carey,' said Mel, nodding, and told her about what she had found in the archives. 'But the only person I've discovered with those initials, P.T., was another of the maids. It seems a bit unlikely, but I thought I'd ask if your mother ever talked about her. The name was Pearl Treglown.'

Norah thought for a moment then muttered, 'Pearl. That might be right. Was it Pearl or something else?' She made to get up, but her dog, an elderly Jack Russell called Sinbad, was sitting on her feet and she said, 'If you wouldn't mind, dear. A thin white book. It's on the top shelf over there.' She waved her hand towards a tall bookcase with glass doors. 'Next to the big red dictionary.'

Mel opened one of the doors and read along the spines. 'Do you mean this one?' She held up a large white-covered paperback with a linocut print of a fishing boat on the front. It was called *Voices of West Cornwall* and bore the logo of some small local publisher. Though tempted to open it, Mel dutifully passed it into Norah's outstretched fingers, closed the bookcase and sat down again.

Norah seemed to take for ever, fumbling in her cardigan pocket for her glasses case, having difficulty finding the page she wanted. Finally she got there and frowned as she drew a finger down the text.

'Ah yes, here it is. Pearl. You look, dear. The print is stupidly small. They came to see Mother, ooh, when was it?' Her hand wobbled as she passed the book to Mel.

Mel kept her finger in the page Norah had found while she checked the book's date of publication. '1972,' she said.

It was a collection of oral history and the blurb on the back explained that the purpose of the publication was to record the experiences of those who could remember the First World War and before. She turned to the page Norah had found and started to read.

Jenna Cooper, née Penhale
I went to be kitchenmaid at Merryn Hall in 1907 when I left school. I was only fourteen but back then that's what you did and my mam couldn't afford to keep me home seeing my pa was ill with his heart and she had my brothers and sisters to feed. I missed home at first but I saw them all every Sunday on my afternoon off. They were kind to me at Merryn. There was always something interesting going on – people coming and going and parties and whatnot. My word, though, the work was hard in those days.

Who else was employed? Well, Mrs Roberts the cook, of course, then when I first started there was a butler, Mr Richards, but he retired and after that they had a footman, Jago, who I think had a bit of a soft spot for me. There was a housemaid to do upstairs. First that was Joan until she went to South Africa to marry her boy and we never heard from her again. After that came a girl from Newlyn, Mrs Roberts's niece, Pearl. She was an orphan, down on her luck, but nice, had a bit about her. I remember she liked drawing . . . flowers and such, and we shared a room till she went and married.

It was a good life. The food was better than at home and more of it, but there's no doubting the work was much harder than it is today. Mondays were worst, but Fridays we had to scrub and blacklead all the fireplaces and polish the brass and copper till it shone like Dagwell. I left just before the war broke out when I married Tom. He had come up to me after chapel one Sunday and told me I had a nice singing voice, which I'm not boasting if I say I did. His dad farmed in Buryan parish and I started married life in his family's farmhouse and I didn't see people from Merryn after. Then the war came and nothing was the same . . .

Mel sat poring over these precious scraps of knowledge. *Pearl liked drawing . . . flowers and such . . .* It was really the piece of information she had come to find, wasn't it, and yet it seemed so scanty. How would a housemaid have found the time to draw, let alone the mental space or the energy to exercise her talent? How would she have afforded materials even? And what was Pearl's background, that she was 'down on her luck'? Whom did she marry and what happened to her then?

After a while, she became aware of the curious eyes of Norah and Carrie upon her.

'Well?' said Norah. 'Any help, is it, the book?'

'Oh yes.' Then, of course, Mel had to explain it all to them both. 'Can you think of anything else your mother said about Pearl?' Mel asked Norah, who thought for a moment before shaking her head.

'She only started to talk about those times when she was quite old,' she said. 'When the lady came who wrote that all down for her. She was proud of being in that book, you know.'

'I can imagine,' said Mel. 'But if Pearl *is* the artist I'm searching for, I need to know more about her. For this book I'm writing, you see.'

Norah Varco sat silently for a moment, thoughts passing across her wrinkled face as Sinbad, at her feet, whimpered in his doggy dreams.

'There's something,' she said finally. 'It's a long way back, but when I was a child we lived in Buryan and there was a boy at the school who lived at Merryn. I'd have to think of his name. No, I can't remember now, but maybe it'll come.'

Mel thought this sounded a long shot. 'Never mind,' she said, and scribbled on a page she then tore from her notebook and gave to Norah. 'Here is my number where I'm staying. If you think of anything else useful, I'd love to hear from you.'

Chapter 21

March 1913

Pearl looked around swiftly to check no one had seen her, then rapped on the stable door and called, 'Sir, it's me,' in a low, urgent voice. Hearing a muffled response, she gripped her sketchbook under one arm, hauled the double-door ajar and slipped inside, pulling it shut behind her.

She stood in the coolness of the stable, her eyes adjusting to the patterns of light and shadow.

It always surprised her every time she saw it, Charles's studio. From the outside it was just another ordinary stable in the block, with the doors of a small hayloft visible above. Inside, it still smelled like a stable, of earth and leather, hay and the sweet, not unpleasant, hint of manure. But this was now over-laid with a strong odour of linseed oil. Against the wall rested several canvases wrapped in brown paper – finished paintings, Pearl knew, destined for an exhibition in Truro that she would never see. And at a workbench at the back of the room Charles stood measuring canvas from a roll across a wooden frame the size of Aunt Dolly's favourite tea tray.

'You're in my light,' Charles grunted without turning, and

Pearl skipped sideways out of the slatted square of spring daylight that poured down through a flight of open steps from the hole in the ceiling above. There was a ripping noise as his knife sawed through the canvas, then a scuffle and a thud as he put down his tools.

'Well, that'll do,' he said more gently, turning towards her, brushing his hands on his jacket.

It was odd, she thought, not for the first time, how the building absorbed all echo so that his voice sounded intimate, for her alone. Unlike in the corridor of the house, where a dozen other sounds competed, or in the garden where the wind carried his words away.

He moved towards her, his eyes shining in the gloom. She clutched her sketchbook closer to her chest.

'Let's see what you've done.' He held out his hand and after a moment she gave him the book. 'Come,' he said, and she followed him as he climbed the steps into the brightness.

The old hayloft where Charles painted bore no trace of its previous purpose. Charles had seen to that. He had, he told her when he first brought her there the previous September, asked for the building when he arrived at Merryn.

He flipped up the tails of his jacket to perch on a four-legged stool, where he sat leafing through the drawings Pearl had made in snatched moments since her last lesson, the previous Sunday.

'I had no time, sir. Only an hour on Wednesday when Cook—'

'It's very fine,' cut in Charles, narrowing his eyes at a portrait and smiling swiftly. 'You've caught her in a few lines.'

'Jenna sat for me, sir, but she only gave me a moment and she would wriggle like a dying fish.'

A shout of laughter from Charles. 'Like a fish, eh? A prize one, I'd say!'

He closed the book and returned it to her with a slight

flourish, then reached out and touched her shoulder in a tender gesture. For a moment he appeared lost in thought, one arm across his chest, the fingers of his other hand stroking his moustache. Long, strong fingers, the nails scrubbed clean and cut straight across. Pearl longed to hold them, to stroke the fine hairs on the back of his hand.

'Today we will see what you make of me,' he said.

'You'll sit for me, sir?'

'I will. And the Knights will be struck by the likeness.'

She looked hard at him. 'Are you sure they don't laugh at me, sir?'

'No, no, girl. I told you – they admire your work. They applaud your ambition.'

'My ambition?'

'Yes, and mine. To encourage your talent. Get you started as a painter.'

'But . . .' Pearl's raised shoulders, her upturned hand, communicated hopelessness.

An elderly chaise longue draped with a faded blue velvet curtain sagged at the back of the room, beneath the window cut in the roof, and it was here that Charles sat himself now, one leg crossed over the other. To one side stood an easel, and as she dragged over the stool Charles had vacated, she glanced at the painting propped there.

It was half-finished, but the very young woman in a wide hat, standing in a garden, the ground a riot of spring flowers, her raised hands full of primroses, was already clearly recognisable as Elizabeth. Pearl's gaze dropped to the pile of sketches on the floor of Elizabeth's face and hands. She looked up again at the painting and a stab of jealousy passed through her like a physical pain, seeing the light play across the girl's lovely face, her countenance of pure joy, innocent of pain or real suffering.

What did Elizabeth know of life? What had *she* ever lacked or lost? Then Pearl remembered what had happened to the girl at Charles's party and the look of jealous dislike Elizabeth had sent her, and her bitterness shrivelled and died. She turned back to her task, selecting a pencil from the pot on Charles's desk.

'Will this do?' asked Charles, settling into the couch. Pearl began to sketch, but in two minutes, his eyelids began to flutter and soon his even breathing told her that he slept. And finally she could concentrate on her task.

First she outlined the long oval of his face, as he had shown her how to do. She imagined her fingers tracing the graceful lines of his high cheekbones, stroking the fair waves of hair. How would it feel? Mrs Carey's hair was dry and thinning. Jenna's curls, which she had often brushed for her, were springy, wiry. Charles's hair would not be thick and smooth like her own – it looked too fine for that. Perhaps it would feel as soft and silky as the mistress's little dog.

Her pencil caressed the paper, as she glanced back and forth between Charles and her work. His blond lashes were long like a girl's beneath the thick brows, his nose, a straight sweep – like this – but narrow, unlike the typical Carey snub. It was when she came to draw his mouth that the longing intensified. Beneath the lush moustache, his lips bloomed full and red and well-defined.

Half an hour passed. Pigeons squabbled in the roof, whirring wings scraping against wood. She was finished but he slept on, so she quietly turned a page and started again. His head had slipped onto one shoulder now and his body shifted into a more comfortable position, so she rotated the book and her fingers soared across the page, capturing the long lines of his body, the legs curved diagonally in a graceful S to the floor – Charles never did anything untidily

She drew the contrasting lines of the chaise longue and waited, watching him sleep as the afternoon sun edged across the floor and a horse in the next stable began to whicker and stamp. Wood creaked in the rising heat and Charles awoke. Immediately he arose, groaning and stretching, and limped over to see her work.

'This is excellent!' he exclaimed, staring at the drawings. 'Your shading is sure and I can almost see myself breathe. Is my nose really that shape?' He ran his fingers down his face and laughed.

She laughed, too, and nodded.

'We must get you proper training,' he said, beginning to pace the floor, her book in his hand. 'How can it be done?'

'I don't know, sir.' Confusion whirled in her, passion, anger. She half-stood and the stool spun away across the floor. He turned and stared.

'How can I be anything else?' she cried. 'Look at me!'

His gaze took in her worn dress, the plain white collar, the cracked leather boots. *Only a servant*. The words were unsaid but the voice in her head was Mrs Carey's. The gulf lay open between them.

His eyes, concerned, met hers, which brimmed with tears.

'Oh, my dear girl,' he whispered, and in two paces he had crossed the gulf, standing before her. Their eyes locked. Her lips quivered but no words came. He lifted a blunt forefinger and caught a welling tear, studying it, fascinated, before it dripped from his finger to the floor. In a sudden savage movement he grabbed her shoulders and pulled her towards him, hugging her tightly as she sobbed.

It was a matter of seconds before her hands finally felt his soft corn-coloured hair and her lips met his full warm ones. The sketchbook tumbled to the floor, but neither of them cared.

Chapter 22

'I can't think why we haven't been along here before.'

Mel refastened the gate and slipped her hand into Patrick's outstretched one as they set off up the earthen path. They were deep in the valley bottom, under the trees where the millstream flowed – or used to flow. The millpond had almost dried up now, in mid-July, and was home to gunnera plants, like giant rhubarb. The disused mill itself was now a craft shop.

'We didn't know for definite what to look for before. Now, at least we have a name, there's some sense in searching for it in the church.'

'Is Paul graveyard where Uncle Val is buried?' wondered Mel.

'No, there's a family plot in my parents' local church.'

They plodded uphill in silence, enjoying the ancient lane, the stone walls rising on either side, the electric hum of invisible insects intensifying the heavy thundery feeling in the air. They loosed hands after a while, their fingers warm and slippery with perspiration.

A mile of walking, zig-zagging through a patchwork of fields of cattle, brought them to the edge of the village, then on to the church with its high tower. They hesitated in the porch, listening to the ghostly sounds of the organ, then, deciding it was a practice not a service, Patrick turned the door handle firmly and they passed inside.

'Hope we're not disturbing you,' Mel said to the man at the organ, who was now riffling through a pile of music.

'Oh no, that's fine,' he said absently, 'you go ahead,' and began to play a sombre hymn, so they walked around the light-filled church through a sunny haze of dustmotes, reading the memorials and stroking the wooden carvings made smooth by centuries of other hands.

'Here,' whispered Patrick. He was flicking through pages in a ring-binder. 'Look, we won't even have to go round reading all the gravestones.'

She glanced down the lists of burials but quickly saw to her disappointment that there was no Treglown. She ran her finger down the names again, looking for a Pearl. Her finger stayed at one name: *Pearl Boase, 1925.* It was bracketed with another name: *John Boase*, who had died in 1952. The name seemed familiar.

'Boase. Wasn't that the Head Gardener's name in the diary?' The lugubrious hymn had finished and Mel heard her voice too loud in the sudden silence. The organist flipped some pages and started on a rousing processional hymn.

'Yes, yes, it was. But Boase must be a common name round here – look, here's another, and here, right back to the eighteenth century.'

'Let's go and look for the grave.' Mel jotted down the number of the plot with the pencil from the visitors' book and stared at the plan of the graveyard, trying to commit the location to memory. The part across the road behind the church hall, it said.

They smiled at the organist, who nodded and plunged into

Widor's Toccata in F, the baseline to which Patrick began to hum as they left.

'I love that one,' he said in between hums. 'I'd have it at my wedding.'

'Would you?' Mel said, set momentarily off-balance at the turn of the conversation. 'It is stirring stuff. I like it, too.' She waited but he said nothing more about weddings. A seagull cried mournfully overhead.

They passed in silence through a wrought-iron gate into a kind of garden. Only at the far end were there rows of graves. The rest of the graveyard was a neatly mown lawn, the memorial stones removed and propped up against the surrounding wall.

They reached the remaining marked graves and Patrick stepped left off the path along a line of lichen-covered stones. 'Could you start looking over there,' he called back.

She began studying the stone to the right – *Emily Martin and two infants* – but her mind was still on weddings. *Robert Armstrong . . . beloved*. What should she do? She and Patrick never talked about the future and yet in a very few weeks it really would be time for her to return to London and her job, to pick up the reins of her life there. *Eleanor Godwin, may she rest . . .*

Was their time together real, valuable, lasting – or was it a holiday romance, a midsummer night's dream? What should they do? She had only known Patrick such a short time and yet in some ways – in their mutual ease, the closeness of their times together, the intensity of their passion – it felt as though she had known him for ever.

Did he feel the same way? Sometimes she felt he did, but at others he seemed so distant, unknowable. Misery descended on her like sea fog.

Then: 'I've found it!' she heard him shout, and she shook herself out of her mood.

The gravestone of Pearl and John Boase was like all the others in the row, an inverted U-shape, and the words were still clear:

In loving memory
Pearl Boase 1894–1925
John Boase 1869–1952

Mel crouched and pulled back the long grass to read the rest. *Together again at last*. 'Patrick, she was only thirty-one.' She stood up slowly, appalled.

'Very young to die,' said Patrick. 'He went on till – what – eighty-three. They can only have been together a short while.'

'Mmm. Patrick, I've just realised something,' she said, her tone urgent.

'What?' he asked.

'If this was Pearl Treglown and if it was Merryn's Head Gardener she married . . .'

'Yes?'

'Well, wouldn't she have lived at the Gardener's Cottage?'

'I suppose she would.'

Could it be Pearl, then, whose presence she sometimes sensed? Mel shivered. What nonsense! The sooner they left this gloomy churchyard, the better.

Chapter 23

November 1913

'Ignorant fools.' Charles crushed the letter in one hand and threw it into the fireplace. Pearl, fascinated, watched it uncurl, stretch and brown before being consumed by flame.

'What did it say?' she whispered, horrified. She had known it was important by the way he took it from her tray, turned it over in his hands, examining the postmark, and hesitated before ripping it open. The envelope had fluttered to the floor.

'They don't want the painting,' was all he would say, staring out of the window, down the garden, to where one of Boase's men was raking the fallen leaves in long slow sweeps in the pale winter sun.

'That exhibition, you mean,' she said, understanding dawning. 'Oh.' For months of summer Sunday afternoons she had watched the construction of the painting in question, Elizabeth and Cecily posing for him sitting on the rocks below the cliff, staring out to sea. She had pored over the many sketches of their faces, of Elizabeth's still-girlish figure and Cecily's elfin one, the attempts he made to capture the clouds racing across the sky, to find the exact colours of the sea on a fresh sunny day. The result had pleased all of them – but not, it seemed, the grim gentlemen at the Birmingham gallery.

Disappointment followed disappointment. An earlier portrait of Cecily had not been selected for the Royal Academy's summer exhibition, and Charles had failed to find a buyer for it until Mrs Carey had purchased it herself.

Pearl dropped her tray on a chair and moved across the room to touch Charles's elbow in a gesture of sympathy. As he turned, anger fighting misery in his countenance, there was a light knock on the door and they leaped apart.

Swiftly, Pearl danced back one step towards the sofa and bobbed down as though to scoop up the discarded envelope.

'Ah, Charles.' Mr Carey's eyes passed over Pearl, as he came into the room, a slight puzzled frown on his face, and focused on his nephew. 'I need you in the office, if you wouldn't mind. There's a matter concerning the Top Field I wish to, ah, acquaint you with.'

Pearl watched impatience flash across Charles's features, to be doused by cold politeness. 'Of course, sir,' he said, and followed his uncle from the room.

Pearl tossed the envelope onto the fire, drew the screen across and hurried out to the kitchen to prepare tea. But as she piled cups on a tray and cut thin slivers of bread with the neatness and preciseness of long practice her mind was elsewhere.

What to do, what to do, echoed in her head in rhythm to the sawing of the bread-knife.

There was no doubt that matters with Charles were reaching some kind of climax engendered by his thwarted ambition. The trouble was that any future she might have beyond her present position now lay in his hands. What she couldn't discern, and what mattered to her most of all, was how much he cared about her.

The previous Sunday, they had made love in the studio, then

they had quickly dressed for it was getting too chilly there to dally unclothed. He had paced the room in growing agitation, stopping every now and then to prod a discarded canvas with one foot or to stare at one of the many propped on ledges around the room.

'I can't stay here, I can't live this life.' Charles seemed to be talking to himself, but her hands froze on the boot she was buttoning. He turned to her. 'It'll be a prison. Do you see before you a farmer – do you, girl? Can you see me striding the fields examining cows' hooves? Worrying about the price of potatoes? Discussing the weather with sons of the soil?'

Pearl had heard him speak like this before, and it alarmed her. But lately, as failure followed failure, his paintings fetching no market, he seemed more and more embittered.

'Your uncle won't keep you for ever,' she said carefully. All the servants were aware of their master's increasing impatience with his nephew. How could they ignore the arguments over Charles's frequent disappearance to paint, his trips to London.

'I need to travel. France – I'd go to France if I could. To study. Learn new fashions.'

'But how will you feed yourself? Pay your teachers?' Pearl asked in a reasonable voice.

'Someone will show this new painting. I know they will. Then I'll sell it and I'll go.'

Their eyes met – his, wild, challenging; hers immensely sad. *And what about me?* was their message.

'Why don't you come with me?' he said.

'How can I?' said Pearl. 'We have no money. It'd be daft . . .' Her thoughts trailed off. Arles, Paris. She remembered her father's stories, what seemed like so long ago now. Of the intensity of the light, the colours of the landscape, the relaxed pace of life. But that's all they were to her – stories, pictures in

253

books, dreams. Not for her, when all she knew was a few square miles of rocky coast and scrubby storm-swept fields. Here at least she had a home, people who in a funny sort of way belonged to her. And here she had her own dream, to draw and paint. Where was he taking her? What was he doing? It was frightening.

'Don't you love me?' he said fiercely now. 'Don't you trust me?'

'I love you . . .' she said, but couldn't manage to say she trusted him. Something told her he wasn't safe, that she couldn't cross the divide into his world. There were all his promises – that his friends would help her. What were they worth?

'Did you give Mr Knight my sketchbook?' she had asked, soon after the party.

'Oh yes,' Charles said. 'I've got it in my room. I'll return it to you.'

'And what did he say?'

'Oh, he admired the drawings. Said you were to be encouraged.'

'Was that all?' Pride swelled in her throat, but she couldn't live on pride. 'What do I do now?'

'Practise. Practise what I teach you.'

So there was to be no further help from the artists, then. But what did she expect?

Sometimes, if the family was away and discipline lax she would walk on the cliffs and pass one of the Knights or Mr Birch or one of their friends sketching the cove or working furiously to catch the drama of an approaching storm, paint splashing carelessly onto bushes and rocks around. They would glance at her and nod politely, their eyes faraway, and she would strain to catch sight of their work, before hurrying on, too shy to stay and try to talk. To them she must be just some local girl. A servant. No one.

'I do trust you,' she ventured, 'but it's too much, too big. I can't . . .'

He studied her. 'No,' he said. 'I see.'

And what would people think? she wanted to ask. Would he marry her if she went away with him? He hadn't said so. Married – to Charles. She tried to imagine the reaction of the family, of the other servants, and nearly laughed. It wasn't possible. Even if they were away from here – abroad. Free.

Terror engulfed her.

She watched him cross the floor to survey a canvas on an easel standing to one side, alone: her own painting, worked at laboriously over many months, almost finished now. She rose, wrapping her shawl about her, and walked over to hover behind him.

After a moment he nodded slowly. 'It's going well. Very well.'

It was the portrait of Charles in the Flower Garden, first sketched in the summer over a year ago now. She smiled as she remembered how they had waited until a Sunday when the garden was empty, the family on a visit to friends down the coast, Aunt Dolly with a cousin in Mousehole. A year, more than a whole year to arrive at this point.

Charles laughed suddenly. 'Does it really look like me?'

'I think it does, yes,' she said seriously.

'Perhaps you should put in a symbol. Saint Mark is known by a lion, Mercury by his serpent staff.'

Suddenly she saw what he meant. 'A paintbrush,' she said. 'I will give you a paintbrush. That will be your sign.'

What to do, what to do, rang in her head. The wafers of bread fell from the loaf like discarded leaves from a sketchbook, like useless hopes.

She couldn't leave this place, her place of safety, and travel with him, could she? Why couldn't she? In her heart of hearts she knew

255

the answer. She didn't quite trust him. Oh, why couldn't every-thing stay as it was now for ever? Why did it have to change?

'I've remembered the name, my dear,' came the quavery voice down the telephone line. 'The boy at my school who lived at Merryn. It was Peter. Peter Boase.'

Norah Varco had rung Mel the very evening after she and Patrick found Pearl's grave.

'That is the most extraordinary coincidence, Mrs Varco,' said Mel, and went on to explain what they had discovered that day.

'Peter would have been their boy, then,' agreed Mrs Varco. 'He was one of the oldest when I started at the school. I don't remember much about him. He walked back a different way and his family didn't go to our church or anything. He was a quiet boy. Not stupid, no. Just kept his thoughts to himself. We didn't take much heed of him. His name and that he was one of the quiet ones, that's all I know.'

'When was this, Mrs Varco? What year are we talking about?'

'What? Oh, 1927, must have been. That's when I went to school. He'd have been twelve, I suppose, or thirteen for he wasn't there long. Does this help you?'

'It might be very useful. I suppose he might not be alive still – but if we could find out where he lived, whether he had any children . . .'

'It is another clue,' Mel said to Patrick as she finished the call.

Patrick didn't look up from the kitchen table, where he was piecing together her elderly iron, which had given up the ghost.

'Look, I think I've found the trouble,' he said, holding up a piece of burned wire. 'Whoever put this together should be shot . . . Sorry, what's the clue?' He picked up a tiny pair of

256

clippers and shaved more plastic insulation off the copper wire.

'The old lady I met remembers a boy who lived here at Merryn,' Mel explained. 'His name was Boase. I think he might have been John and Pearl's son. And if she had children, she might have had grandchildren. And we might find out more about her.'

He looked at her over the top of his reading glasses. 'That might not be easy. Think of all the Boases we found in the phone book.' Mel had checked through Patrick's directory when they got home that afternoon. 'Ah, just a turn of the screw here, and I'll fit this back on.' He plugged the iron into a socket and at once it started to heat up.

'You're a genius,' she said. 'Thanks.'

'Iron me a shirt?'

'No,' she said. 'But I'll give you a kiss to say thank you.'

And she did.

After supper, Patrick went back up to the house to prepare paperwork for a meeting he had the next day.

It was still light and Mel fetched a weeding fork and went to work in the Flower Garden. It was a beautiful breezy evening and she weeded happily for half an hour. It felt peaceful and secure within these walls. The desolation she had felt in Paul graveyard had faded away. She thought about the Boases living in her cottage with their little boy, maybe other children, too. Now that she was building up information about Pearl, she felt she was beginning to get a sense of her. Sometimes it felt as though she was nearby, watching.

The white bird was perched in a hawthorn bush close by, singing its evening blackbird song. Only when the ginger cat came sauntering into the garden, its tail flicking, did it fly high up into a tree.

Chapter 24

The breakthrough, when it came, was quick and unexpected.

Mel spent a frustrating week towards the end of July chasing fragments of information about Pearl, her husband John and son Peter, through the Merryn archive, in parish register entries for baptisms and burials, old telephone directories, anything she could think of. She had even gone up to London for a couple of days to visit the Family Records Centre.

Even after all this, barely a page of her A4 notebook could be filled. She sat in Patrick's kitchen one Saturday lunchtime and read down the lines. Pearl Treglown had been born in Newlyn in 1894, had married John Boase, Head Gardener of Merryn Hall, in April 1914, when she was already pregnant, as she gave birth to Peter five months later, in September 1914. She had died young, in 1925, cause of death given as pneumonia following an asthma attack. There were no photographs of her in the archive and the only further mention after 1914 in the household accounts ledger was where 'Mrs Boase' was paid small sums in respect of helping with laundry.

'Thirty-one,' Mel told Patrick. 'I still can't believe she died so young.' Such a short life and Pearl's legacy was a child and seven paintings.

Mel had not been able to trace the births of any more children and was reasonably convinced there had been none. The question was, had Pearl pursued her talent any further? What kind of woman had she been? Had there been genuine thwarted ambition there, or had she been content with her lot in life? Were there any more paintings to be found? If she could only track down Peter's descendants she might, just might, find the answers to some of these questions. And she wanted them for her book.

'I know it might all lead to nothing, But you want to find out too, don't you? It's a mystery concerning the history of your house.'

'One of many,' Patrick agreed. 'And I'm glad you've discovered more about the garden. That's really interesting about Mr Carey's father.'

Old Selwyn Carey had been the creator of the garden of Merryn Hall. Mel had found a great wadge of documents, including ground plans, a ledger, lists of plants and receipts, even a notebook record of his thoughts and ideas. It was he who had grown the handkerchief tree that his grandson Charles loved, from a cutting a plant collector had brought him.

'What have you found out about Peter Boase, anyway?' said Patrick.

Mel looked down at her notes. 'He married a farmer's daughter, Sonia Westcott, at Paul church in 1939. He, too, is described as a gardener and they had three children – Richard, Ann and Michael in 1941, 1946 and 1948. I also found his name in Army records. He was called up in 1940.'

'Explains the gap between children. He must have been away most of the war.'

'Yes, and he died in 1985. Then I start to get a bit stuck. I've found the dates of Richard and Michael's marriages but nothing for Ann. Michael moved to St Austell and he's had at least two children. The question is, where are they all now?'

'I see what you mean. Where do you start to look?'

'It's got to be round here, I suppose. Though I don't fancy ringing up all the Boases in the directory. Oh good, is that the postman?'

The sound of a vehicle made her half-rise in her seat to see the van pull up outside the Gardener's Cottage.

'I'll just nip down and see what he's got,' she said. 'The car tax-disc might finally have arrived.'

The postman handed her the brown envelope that she had been hoping for from the Vehicle Licensing Office, together with a small white one addressed to her in shaky biro.

'Going back up to the hall, my dear?' The postman asked. 'Take these and save my old legs?'

'Of course,' she said, grasping the pile of catalogues and magazines that he passed her and pushing them awkwardly under one arm.

She smiled a vague goodbye and, while struggling not to drop Patrick's post, ripped open the white envelope, pulling out the single sheet of paper inside. She unfolded it and saw at once that it was from Norah Varco.

Dear Mel,
I have a niece in Buryan I spoke to on the telephone last week.
Jo Sennen, her name is. She thinks she knows Peter Boase's
son Richard because her friend's daughter was courted by
Richard's son for two years. She rang me back today to
confirm that he is the right Richard Boase and to give me his
address. My hearing, as you know, is not too good, but
Richard was a farmer up Zennor way and I heard the address

as Greenacre Farm, Long Lane, nr Zennor. I hope this
information is of use to you.
     Yours respectfully,
     Norah Varco

Mel refolded the paper with a sense of triumph. She had found him, and only a few miles away, too. The village of Zennor was up on the north coast near St Ives. What an extraordinary coincidence that the letter should arrive now. She read it again. No phone number given. Should she write to Boase first to engineer a visit or look up his number in the telephone directory? The latter would be quicker, she decided.

Tucking her letters into the back pocket of her jeans, she hefted Patrick's post into an easier position to carry. As she did so, a piece of coloured card slid out of the pile and floated onto the path. A postcard. She picked it up and looked at the picture. A reclining nude. *La Grande Odalisque* by Ingres, she recognised. Painted when? She turned it over to remind herself. But the caption was obscured by a large signature – *Bella*, followed by several kisses.

For a moment she stopped breathing. She looked up at the kitchen window. Was Patrick watching? No. She knew she shouldn't but she must. She read the flamboyant handwriting quickly.

Dearest Paddy . . . Paddy?

I saw this and thought of you, as they say. Remember that day in the Musée d'Orsay? I've got news. Ring me or I'll ring you.

Love, Bella xxx

She flipped the card over again and stared at the picture, that soft flawless skin, the doe eyes of the Odalisque, luscious, tempting, waiting to be found. Something else struck her. *I saw this and thought of you.* Patrick used that phrase occasionally. So it was *their* private joke, his and Bella's.

She stomped up to the house, shoved open the scullery door and dumped the pile of post onto Patrick's fortunately empty plate, the postcard uppermost.

He stared at her with a slight frown. 'What's up?' he said.

'Nothing,' she answered sharply, nodding pointedly at the postcard.

He looked at it and must have recognised instantly what it meant because he picked it up, glanced at the writing side . . . and got up to stash it in the overflowing letter-rack behind the kitchen door.

She stared at him in astonishment. He was just going to ignore the issue, then? She fought for words, but none came.

He started ripping open plastic and pulling out magazines – *The Spectator*, *PC World*, seed catalogues.

'Well?' she said.

'Well what?' He started flicking through *The Spectator*.

She sounded out each syllable. 'Why is she writing to you like that?'

'Oh, that's just Bella's way.'

'That's just Bella's way.'

'Yes.' And then he said, 'Oh really, Mel, if you could hear yourself. We're grown-ups, aren't we? We can't pretend we haven't had other relationships. I'm not going to expunge people from my life merely because I used to go out with them.'

'Fine.' She hadn't heard him use this tone of voice before. Cold, dismissive. Why wasn't he comforting her, telling her he loved her, ripping the card in half, saying Bella was silly.

But he did none of those things.

'What was in your post?' he said, tossing some junkmail into the recycling box. 'Did your tax-disc turn up?'

'What? Oh yes.' She forced back the tears, cleared her throat and pulled her envelopes out of her jeans pocket. 'And there's good news. I've found Pearl Treglown's grandson.'

That night they slept in the double bed in Val's old room, where they usually slept now because Patrick complained that the bed in the cottage was too lumpy. At first Mel had thought the room creepy. 'Don't worry, he died in hospital,' Patrick had said. 'And anyway, he didn't sleep in this bed the last few years. He had a special orthopaedic job with levers to get him up and down.'

Patrick fell asleep almost as soon as the light was out, worn out by the day's gardening and a slight cold. But Mel lay there sleepless in the darkness, trying to block out the sound of an owl outside and to stay her babbling thoughts. Why was she afraid of Bella? Because, she had to face the truth, Bella still had some kind of hold over Patrick. Because Bella was his business, his secret, and he wouldn't talk about her, hadn't done since that night nearly two months ago, when he had confessed to Mel about his heartbreak.

Besides, she knew that she was just as capable as he was of keeping secrets. He would never know how much she still thought about Jake.

But that doesn't mean that I'm still in love with Jake, does it? Merely that thinking about him helps me get him out of my system. I'm working him through, digesting him.

Was that what Patrick was doing, too, with Bella? Just how often was Bella in touch?

Half an hour passed. The owl must have gone off hunting somewhere, but still she couldn't sleep. Her stomach rumbled and after a moment she slid out of bed, pulled on her dressing-gown and padded downstairs. The darkness pressed up against her and it was a relief to flip on the light switch in the kitchen. She poured herself some milk from the fridge and fumbled in a tin for a biscuit. Her eye rested on the overflowing letter-rack.

No, she mustn't. She bit into the biscuit.

Yes, she must.

She lifted out the pile of letters with both hands and sat down with them at the table.

When she had finished riffling through them, relief fought an odd feeling of disappointment. There was only one communication from Bella – the postcard that had arrived today. She shoved everything back in the rack, hoping it looked the same. Then she sat sipping her milk and feeling both ashamed and relieved.

Chapter 25

The next afternoon found Mel's car bumping down a potholed lane to a remote stone farmhouse standing lonely on the side of a hill near Zennor.

The house had that same deserted look of many of the windswept buildings on the peninsula, as though they had long ago dispensed with the bother of keeping up appearances. Crouching firm in the face of winds and stormy weather took up all their strength. As she raised a hand to lift the door-knocker, a bolt cracked back and the door opened to reveal a stocky, white-haired man with a face as weathered as his home.

'Mr Boase?' Mel said.

'Come in, my dear, come in,' he said, opening the door wider and waving her inside. She followed his unsteady, bow-legged figure into a sunny living room with whitewashed walls and a large open fireplace. The only pictures on the walls, she noticed with disappointment as she settled herself on a small sofa, were a framed Victorian sampler and two prints of country scenes. Nothing that looked to be by Pearl.

Richard Boase lowered himself into a battered armchair by the fireplace, then made to get up once more, a dazed expression on his face.

'I'm sorry, I should offer you a cup of tea . . .'

Mel demurred quickly, offering an excuse.

He sank back in the seat, then clasped his hands together against his chest, as though in pleading prayer. 'My wife always . . .' His eyes flickered to the empty armchair opposite. A needlework box stood on the small table beside it, too tidy, unused.

Mel guessed immediately. 'When?' she asked gently.

'She passed away three months ago,' said Boase, studying his calloused hands, touching the overlong nails. Mel tried not to notice that his shirt wasn't ironed.

'I'm so sorry,' she murmured. 'I'm intruding on your grief. Perhaps I shouldn't have come.'

'No, no,' he said, his tone firmer now. 'I like to see people. My daughter, she lives in Canada. Came home for the funeral, but had to go back. Got her own family to look after, you see. My son comes sometimes but it's a long drive from Bristol.'

'Did Mrs Sennen say why I'm here?' When she had telephoned that morning, he had been expecting her call. Norah's niece, it appeared, had given him due warning.

'About my grandmother, is that it?'

'Yes, Pearl Boase.'

He nodded. 'Never met her, of course. Died when Pa was a boy.'

'Did your father ever talk about her?' She explained the purpose of her visit briefly. 'Do you mind if I ask you a few questions? I'm sorry, perhaps it's not the right time for you.'

'I don't mind,' he said. 'I can't stop thinking about what's gone. Nice to have someone to tell it to. My grandmother . . . Pa didn't remember her well, but my grandad used to talk about her. But he didn't tell Pa the most important thing of all, not till he was dying. What he had to say would have been a matter of shame, of course, back then.'

266

'What would?'

'What Pearl did, what I'm about to tell you. I know you young ones don't find these things shocking any more, but when I was a boy you kept quiet about 'em . . .'

'What do you mean?' asked Mel, confused.

'John Boase, the man I called Grandfather, turned out he wasn't my pa's real father at all. When Pearl married him, she was carrying another man's child.'

Mel stared at him, bemused. She had pulled a notebook and pencil out of her bag, but now they lay beside her, forgotten. Another man's child. So this would explain the short five months between Pearl's marriage and Peter's birth.

'Seems the man in question was a young gentleman from Merryn Hall.'

'One of the other servants, you mean?'

'No, one of the master's family. Not the master himself – I don't mean him. His nephew. Name of Charles Carey.'

'Charles? I know about him,' breathed Mel. The image of the good-looking young man with the moustache rose in her mind.

'Course, he couldn't marry her. His family wouldn't let him. But my grandad, John, was Head Gardener there. He was in love with her. Didn't mind about the baby. Always treated Pa like his own lad. Pa was torn in half when he heard the truth. My ma told me he seemed changed after that. Unhappy.'

'It must have been a terrible shock,' ventured Mel. 'Suddenly having to reevaluate everything about himself.'

'Specially since he lost *his* ma so young,' said Mr Boase. 'She didn't have any living relatives. Born the wrong side of the blanket herself and them both dead, her ma and pa.'

Mel finally picked up her pencil. 'Pearl was illegitimate, too? Do you know her parents' names? Where they were from?'

The old man looked into the empty fireplace, unseeing. Then

he said, 'No. But my pa reckoned her father was one o' them artist chappies.'

'What?' Mel put down her pencil again, trying to make sense of this. 'At Lamorna?'

'No, down the coast at Newlyn.'

'But that's extraordinary. Mr Boase, did you know that your grandmother was an artist? I mean,' she amended, 'that she painted?'

'Yes, course I did,' he said simply. 'My sister in London, she's got some of the paintings. That's what she is – didn't you know? Ann's an artist, too. It's her you should be talking to, not me.'

Chapter 26

February 1914

'I have to talk to you.' Pearl had placed a fresh pot of tea on the table before Charles and began, with quiet movements, to load a tray with abandoned breakfast plates. Charles, last down to breakfast this frosty February morning, lowered his newspaper and looked at her, wary. Pearl averted her eyes under his scrutiny and continued to stack cups and saucers, then picked up the tray and waited for what seemed like a long moment for the nausea to pass. Running footsteps outside. She said, in desperate tones, 'I must see you, please, sir.' Then, like a cornered animal, head snapping round as the footsteps stopped. *'Please.'*

The door knob turned.

'The laurels at five,' Charles said in a low voice. 'If you can get away.' The door opened and Cecily bounced in. She stopped when she saw Charles and Pearl, a secret smile on her face; then, her eyes fixed on Pearl, she crossed the room and wrapped her arms round Charles's shoulders.

'Please, Charley,' she said, parodying Pearl's beseeching tone. She knows, thought Pearl, the room starting to spin around her.

But surely she couldn't have heard, she couldn't have heard through a closed door.

'Please, Charley, you will come with us to the Pascoes' tonight, won't you?' *Please, Charley, please, Charley*.

'What's happening at the Pascoes', my sweet?' said Charley, folding his paper as well as he could under Cecily's embrace, his voice to Pearl as if at a distance or in a dream.

'Oh, you *know*. We've been practising and practising. Victoria Pascoe and me and her brothers are doing our Greek tableau. And Elizabeth will be singing. Say you'll come.' Cecily's high voice scraped like metal over stone.

'Pearl, are you all right?' Charles stood up, pushing Cecily aside. The tray crashed onto the table as Pearl swayed and slid to the floor.

'I thought you weren't coming.'

'You're shivering. Here, have my coat. I'm sorry, I was over at the Birches' and forgot the time.' The mantle of rough wool settled heavy on her shoulders, then he dropped down beside her on the stone bench and they sat in the secret darkness amongst the laurel hedges, listening to the sounds of the garden settling around them, the restless play of wind in the branches, the rattle of a blackbird's cry.

'Are you all right? After this morning, I mean. I was worried.'

His arm around her in the darkness was comforting. They would go away together. They'd have to, now that she knew for certain.

'You're breeding, girl, ent you?' Jenna's voice reverberated in her mind. When Pearl had fallen, fortunately it was Jenna who answered Charles's urgent bell-ringing, who had summoned Jago to clear up the broken crockery, had helped Pearl upstairs. It felt worse if she lay down, so Pearl had sat on her bed, fighting the sick empty feeling, puzzling at the tingling in her breasts. Jenna sat opposite her on her own bed and studied her.

'Your face is like pastry and you've a look in your eye. You're breeding, ent you? Who? How far along is it?'

Pearl shook her head.

Jenna came and knelt down and grasped the girl's arms, not ungently, and thought a minute. 'It can't be long. We both had our courses at New Year, remember? You had the gripes, didn't yer? I should have noticed you'd missed.' It was impossible in this small space not to be aware.

'Who's done this to you, girl?' She thought a moment and said in a wobbly voice, 'Not Jago?'

Pearl shook her head, her eyes filling with tears.

'Who then? Who? You've got to tell me,' said Jenna, 'so I can help you. I'll think about what to do. Listen, there are ways, you know, if you don't want it.' She stopped. 'It wasn't one o' Boase's men?'

'No.' Pearl formed Charles's name in her mouth but couldn't bring herself to utter it. It would make it real. But in the end she didn't need to say it. She staggered upright and went to her chest of drawers, pulling open the top drawer and sliding out her sketchbook. She turned the pages until she came to the picture of Charles, asleep in the studio.

After a long moment, Jenna nodded slowly, recognition and anger dawning in her eyes. She dropped her hands from Pearl's arms and said savagely, 'So it's him. Only painting, you said. That's what you were up to all the time. You must of thought I was daft.'

'It's not what you think. I *have* been painting. This . . . it hasn't been going on for long,' Pearl cried. 'And we were careful.'

'You're a fool, you know that? A fool. Look, I'll think about what you can do. If it's not that long, maybe it'll go by itself.

271

Sometimes they do, you know. But you mustn't tell anybody. Anybody, you hear? Not yet, leastways.'

'Cook,' Pearl whispered in panic. What would happen if Aunt Dolly guessed? Would she go straight to the mistress? And what about Cecily? She might be too young to interpret the evidence, but she might have seen or heard something that, if she repeated it to anyone . . .

'Cook don't need to know yet, though she might guess, she don't miss much. Listen, I'll tell her it's the guts ache. Have you been sick?'

'No, but it feels bad all the time, like I'm going to.'

'Stay up here for a bit then. I'll tell her it's your guts.'

An hour later, still dizzy but slightly less nauseous, Pearl had hidden her sketchbook away, this time in the wall cupboard she had found behind her bed, crept downstairs and gone back to her tasks. Mrs Roberts regarded her with a thoughtful look in her eye but, for the moment, seemed to accept Jenna's explanation of a stomach-ache. 'Keep away from the food or you'll give it to the rest of us,' was her only comment.

Pearl turned Jenna's words over in her mind. *Do something about it.* That meant get rid of it. She had heard stories. Jenna had told her that her mother had deliberately miscarried a baby once before her father became so ill. Even then they couldn't afford another mouth to feed.

But perhaps, just perhaps it would work out. She would go away with Charles after all . . .

'I reckon I'm having a baby,' she whispered to him now.

'What?' he said, the arm dropping from her shoulder. '*What?*'

'I'm having a baby.' It became more horribly real as she said it. Suddenly she saw it all clearly. She couldn't stay. She would lose her position. What would happen to her then? She didn't know for sure, but they'd likely send her away, take the baby from her and she would have to start again somewhere else. Whichever way she looked at it, she would have to leave Merryn, this place which had become home, where she was happy. How could she have thrown that happiness away?

'Are you sure?' he hissed. 'How can you be? We tried . . .'

'I know,' she cried out. 'But it didn't work, did it? And now we'll have to go away.'

Charles leaped to his feet, and she had to snatch at the coat to stop it falling. Then he sat down again and she heard him rake his nails across his bristly jaw in the darkness and sigh.

'Pearl? Pearl! I'll skin you. Where is the girl when I need her?' Mrs Roberts's voice carried out across the garden, half-snatched away by the wind.

'I must go,' she said.

'Yes.' His voice was dull.

She stood up, letting the coat fall, and turned to him, leaning her knees against his. His arms encircled her thighs and he pulled her towards him, burying his face in her abdomen. 'It's all right, it's all right,' he breathed. 'I'm sorry.'

She wrapped her arms around his head, rubbing her cheek against his silky hair, the part of him she loved most, his beautiful hair and his vulnerable mouth. She forced his head up towards her now and kissed that mouth, tasting salt and a faint, masculine hint of smoke. Her womb contracted with desire and she gasped as a tender pain rushed through her breasts.

'Can I see you on Sunday?' she said, releasing him. The stable studio was freezing cold now, but Charles had rigged up an oil heater there. They could only work until the daylight faded.

'Pearl? Where in God's name . . .?' Jago's voice now. Pearl felt her way back through the laurels up to the lawn, where the soft oil lights from the house picked out the path. By the Flower

Garden, she stumbled. Suddenly a black shape loomed, a hand reached out, catching her. Jago? No.

'Whoa, girl.' Mr Boase then, steadying her as he might a frightened pony. A basket bumped against her hip; she inhaled the rich smells of earth and vegetable and her gorge rose.

'Here, take these with you,' he said. 'You came to ask me, remember?'

'What?'

'Tell them you were waiting for these,' he said.

She grasped his meaning and took the basket, calmer now. 'Oh. Yes. Thank you,' moved past him and hurried across to the Hall.

'Where you been, girl?' said Jago roughly from the scullery doorway, then his lamplight fell on the basket of potatoes.

'Who asked you to get them?' said Cook from the stove, as they walked into the steam-filled kitchen. 'Though come to think, a few more will be useful.'

'We can go away. I can't stay, can I?' Her voice rose, shaky.

'Pearl, listen to me. We cannot go away together. Don't you see? We have no money to go gallivanting off abroad.'

'But what do I do?' Pearl, trembling, tearful, stared into the dusty chaos of paper and cloth and canvas on the floor of the studio as though seeing her own future. *And the mermaid. Where has the mermaid gone?* Someone had searched her possessions – not Jenna, it couldn't have been Jenna. Jenna was her friend.

Charles stood at the heater, his back turned to Pearl. 'Can't you get rid of it?' he said.

She stared at him, startled. 'I've tried,' she muttered. 'Nothing's worked yet.'

On Wednesday, Jenna had escaped home and collected a brew of herbs under her mother's instructions. She had given the infusion to Pearl late that night, but all that had happened was that Pearl had been very sick.

'There are other ways,' Jenna said the next morning as she mopped her friend's sweating brow, 'but we couldn't do them without Cook or someone else noticing. Shall we wait and see what happens – or tell her?'

'Wait,' moaned Pearl, shivering violently as she tried to pull on her dress. 'Thank God she's going off to market this morning.'

'Isn't there some doctor who could do something?' Charles said now, desperation in his voice.

'What?'

'To get rid of it.'

'Is that all you and Jenna can think of, getting rid of it?' she said, suddenly stubborn. 'It's a baby. Our baby.'

'It isn't, it can't be – don't you see, Pearl?' He almost spat the words at her.

'See what? We could go away. You could get a job, couldn't you?' We could marry, get a home together, she wanted to say, but hadn't the strength to spell it out.

'Pearl, I can't. The Careys, they'd throw me out. And who would give me a decent job if . . .' He didn't need to say the words. If he were with her, married to her. A black rage engulfed her.

'So it's come to that, has it?' She staggered to her feet now, proud, confronting him. 'All your talk about being equal, all those things your friend Kernow says – I've heard you. It means nothing, does it? Nothing. I'm not good enough for you, is what it comes down to.'

'Pearl . . .'

'So why have you given me so much hope, taught me to do this?' She snatched up a sketch from the rolls on the floor and ripped it across. "You can be a painter, Pearl. We can do it together", you said. "My friends will help", you said. But they haven't, have they? I don't think you've even asked them.'

'I have,' Charles said. 'But what can they do, really? You're . . .'

He broke off and turned away.

'Just a servant!' she shouted. 'Go on, say it, just a servant. Well, I am just a servant. But I thought I counted with you, that you were different. That you . . . well, that you loved me.'

'I do love you,' said Charles, clutching at her and imprisoning her with one desperate movement.

She shoved him away. 'But it isn't a big enough love. It is not a love that conquers all things, like it says in the Bible. You won't sacrifice anything for me, will you? Nothing at all. So damn all your big ideas about changing the world. You're the same as all the others. No, you're worse than them. You've made me hope. And now you're throwing it all back at me.'

'I'll give you money, Pearl. I don't have much, but I'll give you what I've got. Look.' He delved into the inside pocket of his jacket and held out some notes. 'Take this now and there'll be more. I'll get it from somewhere. Don't say anything to anybody yet, please. I'll think . . .'

I curse your money, she opened her mouth to say, but something in her head said, *Take it – what else will you have?* The voice sounded remarkably like her stepmother's.

She snatched the notes, eyes blazing, and it gave her some slight satisfaction to see him flinch.

Chapter 27

My sister is an artist. Boase's words rang in Mel's head as she steered the car back down the unmade lane and joined the narrow road that wound its way across the desolate countryside to Lamorna. The more she thought about the revelation, the more she was gripped by a sense of rightness. Pearl herself had not managed to fulfil her ambition, but the granddaughter she never met somehow had. And, even better, Ann Boase – she used her maiden name – had more of her grandmother's pictures. Suddenly Pearl's whole story was opening up. Mel must organise a trip to London as soon as she could.

London. Another thought arose unbidden. Here she was at the end of July, the start of term only – what – seven, eight, weeks away? *Too far away to think about.* But it wasn't really. She and Patrick would have to talk about it sometime. She would make him.

The holiday traffic on the main road slowed her down and by the time she arrived back at the Gardener's Cottage it was late afternoon. Making herself a mug of tea, she took it outside to sit in the sunshine. Because the air was thrumming with the distant sound of holiday traffic, she didn't pick out the well-mannered engine of a Mercedes purring up the front drive of Merryn Hall.

A man's voice – deep, confident – called, 'Hello?' and she watched him come round the side of the cottage, one hand shading his eyes against the sun.

She stood up, wondering who he was. He was well-dressed in an expensive-looking jacket and trousers, polished brown brogues. Fiftyish, she guessed, noting the greying dark hair well receded from his handsome forehead. Someone Patrick knew, she supposed.

'Can I help?' she said.

'Sorry to trespass, but just thought I'd check. I was looking for Mr Winterton, and I didn't get any answer from the house.'

'He should be back from the office any minute.'

The man looked slightly bemused. 'The office?' he said. 'I imagined he was retired, somehow.'

'No . . .' she said uncertainly. 'Look, are you sure I can't help? My name is Melanie Pentreath.'

'The name's Weldon. Greg Weldon.' He put out his hand. A faint bell began to ring in Mel's head. Was he a friend of Patrick's? Had Patrick mentioned him? His forehead was glistening with perspiration. He pulled out a handkerchief and dabbed at his face.

'Have you come far?'

'London. Started early this morning.'

'Look, I'll get you a drink while you wait. Patrick shouldn't be long. I'm a friend of his, by the way.'

He opted for ginger beer and sat with her in the garden.

'I hadn't thought of Mr Winterton still working. He had been described to me as elderly.'

'Oh,' said Mel, with a flash of understanding. 'The old man. Were you looking for Val Winterton?'

'Is that his name, Val? You said Patrick just now.'

'Yes, Patrick lives here now. He inherited the house from Val. Didn't you know? Val died last year.'

'Ah.' The man looked anxious.

'I'm sorry if it's a shock,' Mel said, wondering who on earth this man was and why he didn't know about Val. 'Did you know him well?' He couldn't have done if he didn't even know Val's first name.

'Er, no, not at all. In fact, it's not really a Winterton I was look-ing for. It's my wife.'

'Your *wife*?' Suddenly she remembered where she had heard the name Greg recently. Irina.

'And my daughter. Are they still here? Irina and Lana?'

Mel's hand went to the pendant at her neck. Her face must have betrayed her unease, because he said in a low, urgent voice, 'You do know them, don't you?'

'I – er.' What should she say? 'I – yes.' The truth would be simplest.

'Where are they? Do they still live here? Please tell me.'

'How do you know they came here?' she blurted out, playing for time.

Greg Weldon regarded her as though assessing how much she knew. He seemed to decide to play it safe. 'Oh, she has writ-ten to me. She might have told you, we are . . . separated. But I have to talk to her. It's three years since I've seen my child. Do they still live here?'

'No,' admitted Mel. At least that part of the truth didn't endanger Irina. 'But – well, I do know her slightly. I'm not sure that she wants to see you.' Her mind was working quickly. How had Greg discovered Irina was in Lamorna when Irina had only written with a Post Office box number?

His demeanour changed then, for a second nakedly vulnerable, then hard. He drained his glass and, standing up, handed it to her.

'Thank you, that was most welcome. Well, Ms Pentreath, it seems you have already decided about me.'

Mel stood up too and faced him. Suddenly she saw exactly what Irina had meant. He was a man you should not cross lightly – powerful, used to getting his own way.

He faced her, arms folded. 'Irina has kept my daughter from me without cause for several years now. And I will search for them until I find them. Do they still live close by? I think they must do, from the letter.'

Mel toyed with the idea of lying but gave it up straightaway. Greg was the sort of man who would spot a lie a mile off.

'I'm afraid I won't tell you any more. If you want to wait for Patrick and speak to him, that's fine, but otherwise I'd really advise you to go back to London. Perhaps I can tell Irina you've been looking for her.'

'And away she will fly . . .' said Greg Weldon softly. 'I don't think I need to trouble Mr Winterton. Is he the old man's son, then? My source was a little light on facts.'

'His nephew.'

He nodded. 'Well, good day. And thank you again for the refreshment.' He touched his thumb to his forehead as though he were wearing a hat, an old-fashioned courtesy that belied his anger, and walked up the slope, around the Hall, and was gone.

Mel sat down in a state of turmoil. Then stood up again. Irina. She had to warn her.

Irina's home phone rang several times, then clicked onto message mode. 'Irina, this is Mel,' Mel said fiercely. 'This is to warn you, your husband has been here looking for you. I haven't told him where you are, of course. Ring me.' She put down the phone and looked at her watch. Five-thirty. She picked up the handset again and with her other hand riffled through her diary until she found a number scrawled against the name Carrie. The phone in the hotel was answered on the fifth ring. A man's voice.

'Is that you, Matt?' she asked. 'It's me – Mel.'

'Hello, how are you?' came Matt's voice. Warm, friendly again, good old Matt.

'Is Irina there?'

'Sorry? Just a moment, the other phone's ringing.'

She heard him pick up another call and some discussion ensued. He finished that call, then she heard him say, 'Good evening, can I help you?' and a man's voice, deep, polite, asked, 'I wondered if you had a room for tonight.' It was Greg Weldon.

What should she do? She shouted, '*Matt!*' The receiver was picked up and she heard Matt say to Greg, 'Just one moment, sir.' Then he said down the phone, 'I think she's upstairs. Do you want to speak to her? I can go and find her in a moment, when I'm less busy.'

'Matt, I can't explain now, but that man who's come – you mustn't let him know where Irina is, mustn't let him see her.'

'*What?*'

'I think the man there in front of you is Irina's husband. And she doesn't want to see him. You mustn't tell him where she is.'

'Right, right, certainly,' he said, and his changed tone caused her a wave of relief. 'I'll hand over the message and I'm sure my mother will ring you back later. Goodbye.'

'What did you do?' she breathed when Matt called back half an hour later.

'Simple,' he said. 'I just said that we didn't have a room. Sent him up to Mrs Penhaligon's at Buryan. A shame though, because we'd just had a cancellation, but there we are.'

'Matt, thank you. Have you seen Irina?'

'Yes, of course. And I've told her. Heck, Mel, I had no idea about this situation. I thought she must be divorced or something but this sounds like some soap opera plot.'

'Yeah, I know. How did she react?'

'Well, very shocked.'

'You didn't send her home, did you? He'll find her there – someone will tell him.'

'Of course not. When the other receptionist gets here I'll take Irina to fetch Lana from her friend's. They can stay here for a bit, maybe, while she decides what to do. She's just upstairs calling Amber's mum. Look, Mel,' he lowered his voice, 'she hasn't told me much. Do you know what it was all about?'

'No, not entirely. Only a bit and – well, it sounds unkind, but I'm not sure she's told the complete story. Certain things don't tie up.'

'Okay. Look, I've got to go now. With you in a moment, madam, just finishing this call.'

'I'll ring later on,' said Mel, then impulsively, 'bring them here if you need to.'

'Great. Okay, bye.'

'How is she?' Mel half-rose as Irina came into the drawing room at Merryn later that night.

Irina stood twisting her hands and said, 'She sleeps now.'

Matt had brought Irina and her daughter to Merryn Hall as the safest place Irina could think of just now, then left, promising to come back after dinner was over at the hotel.

'Mum's not been too well today. She won't be able to manage if I don't go back.'

Explaining the situation to Lana had proved beyond Irina's capabilities. First of all she had tried to say nothing of Greg's arrival. 'I thought it would be nice to stay with Patrick for a little while. For a change.' Even Mel had been embarrassed hearing Irina lie so blatantly. Lana had seen through that story straight away.

'Something's wrong, isn't it, Mummy? It's something to do with Daddy, isn't it? I heard you talking to Matt.'

'Yes. He has come here, but we can't see him.'

'But why can't I see Daddy? I want to see him.'

'Lana.' Irina tried to put her arms around her daughter, but Lana pushed her away.

'You never let me see him. I want to see him.' Lana's whinge rose into a wail.

'Lana.' Irina tried to sound firm, but her voice wobbled. 'I have told you so many times. Your father loves you, I'm sure he loves you, but I do not love him and I cannot be with him. He has not been kind to me.'

'But I want to see him.'

Lana looked at Mel and said in a low voice, 'They were close, you see. He gave her presents. She was his little princess. It's very hard for her.'

Mel stared at Irina, restrained by Lana's listening ears from asking any of the multitude of questions swirling in her mind.

'I'll go and see about the beds,' she muttered, and fled the room. 'Are there more sheets somewhere?' she asked Patrick, who was keeping out of the way in the kitchen, cooking supper.

He frowned as he turned pieces of chicken in the pan. 'Try the old chest on the landing if you can't find any in the airing cupboard. How is it going in there?'

'Badly. It doesn't look very simple to me. I know it's always impossible to tell what someone else's marriage is like from the inside, but Irina has run off with Lana and effectively cut her off from her father. It doesn't seem quite right.'

'Why would she have done that?'

'I don't know, except she's obviously afraid of Greg. From what she said just now I don't think Greg mistreated Lana. Lana sounds really fond of him. I suppose Irina believes Greg would take the child from her, that she wouldn't be allowed to see her.'

'Maybe.' Patrick opened an oven door and, with a fork, prodded the pudding baking inside. 'Wonder if there was a legal arrangement . . .'

At this moment, they both froze as the sound of sobbing reached their ears.

'Lana!' they heard Irina shout, this followed by running footsteps in the hall, up the stairs.

Mel moved into the hall at the same time as Irina emerged from the drawing room next door. Irina raised her hands in a gesture of hopelessness. 'She hates me,' she said in a choked voice. 'Says I've ruined her life.'

'Would you like me to try to talk to her?' Mel offered. 'Not that I'm sure what to say.'

'Thank you, but it's best to leave her to cool down. She'll have gone up to her old room. I'll follow her in a minute.'

Patrick put his head out of the kitchen. 'Supper's ready whenever. Glass of wine?'

'A large one, I think, please.' Irina was looking exhausted. She fumbled in her bag for a packet of cigarettes. 'Look, do you mind?' she asked in a desperate tone.

Patrick nodded amused assent.

Mel ran up the stairs two at a time, which did little to relieve her feelings of frustration, and pulled open the door of the airing cupboard. Whilst she sorted through the piles of old curtains, towels and bedspreads for suitable bedding, she felt someone watching her and turned to see a dejected figure standing in a bedroom doorway.

'I'll pop these on the bed for you,' she told Lana. The girl shrugged and wandered back into the room.

'Will you help me? Here, catch this end.' Lana picked up a sheet corner with two fingers and draped it over the bed in a listless movement.

'Don't be too hard on your mum,' Mel said gently, as she straightened the sheet and tucked in the edges. 'She's only trying to do the best for you.'

Lana mumbled something. 'Sorry?' Mel said.

The girl slumped down on the half-made bed and drew an arm tiredly across her face. 'I want my daddy, but she won't let me.' She fell silent.

Mel crouched down beside her. 'I am sure it can be sorted out, darling. Don't worry. Come and have some supper and then we'll get you to bed.'

But as she followed Lana slowly down the stairs she hoped she hadn't made an empty promise.

'She cried until she fell asleep,' Irina said, where she sat hunched miserably on a sofa. She had been restless all evening, smoking cigarette after cigarette and starting at every sound from outside, staring anxiously out of the windows.

'It sounds as though she really misses her father,' Mel said, just as Patrick came into the room and sat down in an armchair.

Irina wouldn't look at her. 'Yes, I know,' she said roughly.

'Is there no way you can sort it out between you, you and Greg?' Mel went on. 'Couldn't your solicitor help you?'

Irina reached again for her cigarettes, fumbled them and the packet fell to the floor. She cursed in her own language and picked them up.

'That is the trouble. Greg is supposed to see the child half the time. He was told to buy me a house in London and to pay money to keep us. But he threatened me. Said he would take Lana from me unless I stopped it all and came back. So . . . I had to keep her away from him.'

'Can he do that – take her away, I mean? Why did you believe him?' Was Irina telling the full story even now, Mel wondered.

'You don't know Greg.' The other woman shook her head sadly. 'He does what he wants.'

What about what Lana wants? thought Mel, looking meaningfully at Patrick.

'How did you come to marry him, Irina?' Patrick asked. 'There must have been a time when you weren't frightened of him.'

Mel remembered the powerful stance of Greg's body, his direct, ruthless gaze.

Irina finally lit her cigarette, took a long drag and said, 'Yes, a bit, but I didn't know what else to do. You know I come from Dubrovnik?'

'Yes, of course,' said Mel. 'I saw the photograph of your hotel. You said your brother runs it now.'

'I can never go back there. I never want to see my brother again. *Never*. I will tell it to you. I was twenty-four when it happened. I had started work as a teacher and my fiancé, Goran, we were saving to get married. Goran was a journalist on a political paper. Unfortunately, his newspaper had opinions that many Catholics, and that included my brother, did not like. When the fighting began, Goran and the others on his paper became targets. It was not safe to be with him where he was hiding and my parents were very worried for me. My brother was angry that I still intended to marry Goran. But I tell you, I did not agree with everything my fiancé wrote, but he was a good man. He had radical beliefs, that is true, but he really wanted to help people. He wanted to stand up to the bullies.' She fell silent for a moment, lost in the past.

'What happened?' asked Mel.

'He was betrayed,' Irina said, tears welling in her eyes. 'Some men found his hiding-place and shot him and the two others with him. Just like that, in cold blood. Goran had never hurt anyone in his life and they did that to him.' She stabbed the cigarette, only half-gone, into the ashtray and shivered, turning once more to look nervously at the windows, though the curtains were drawn now against the dusk.

'Then one night a friend told me. It was my brother who gave away Goran's hiding-place to those . . . those thugs. My brother who had caused the death of the man I loved. A man who had done him no harm.'

'Oh, Irina.' What else could Mel say? Patrick was leaning forward in his chair, listening intently but saying nothing.

'You hear that people can go mad with grief. Well, I was mad for a while, quite ill. When I got a little better, I knew I could not stay there with my family. I could not bear to see my brother ever again, or his friends. And there were others we knew who believed my brother had done his duty as a patriot, as a Catholic. I did not belong there among them any more.'

She sighed, twisting her nail-bitten fingers together in her lap. 'Well, there was a man staying in the hotel, a businessman from Britain. He said he would help me. He said he was in love with me. I tell you, I was not myself. And he seemed so strong, so safe. He knew what to do, how to talk to the right people. He took me on a plane with him to England. I have told you the rest, haven't I? How we married and Lana was born.'

'Yes – yes, you have. But,' Mel wrestled with how to ask the question, 'why did you have to marry him – if you didn't love him, I mean. Was it so you could stay in Britain?'

Irina shrugged. 'Partly, but I tell you, he can be very charming. And to feel safe, cared for, after so many bad things, you cannot imagine how grateful I was. And he was very gentle with me at first.'

At that moment there came the sound of footsteps outside. Someone knocked on the back door.

'It's him.' Irina stood up, poised for flight, her face deathly white.

Patrick hurried out of the room and in a moment came the sound of voices. The women listened, anxious.

'It's all right – it's Matt, I think,' whispered Mel, and Irina dropped back onto her seat.

'I'm sorry,' came Matt's voice from the doorway. 'We've been very busy tonight and I had to send Mum up to bed she's so tired. Irina, how are you doing? How's Lana?' He nodded to Mel and hurried across the room to sit next to Irina.

The woman explained in a low voice how upset Lana had been.

'What are you going to do? Stay here for the moment?' Matt asked.

'You're most welcome to stay for a few days if that helps,' said Patrick gruffly.

'Thank you,' said Irina.

'But Irina,' Matt said, 'your husband will be back and you'll have to talk to him. I don't see how else it can be.'

'We'll be here for you,' said Mel.

'I know I must talk to him,' said Irina, sighing. 'But I would like to know that you are nearby.'

It was past midnight before Matt left and they all got to bed, Patrick patiently checking all the windows and doors were locked to allay Irina's anxiety.

Patrick fell asleep quickly, but Mel lay awake troubled by all the events of the day.

In semi-consciousness, drifting towards sleep, her mind

slipped back to her conversation with the old man that afternoon, of what he had revealed to her about Pearl. Another woman seeking sanctuary at Merryn, who had risked everything and gained – what?

Chapter 28

April 1914

'Is it true, girl, what they're saying? It's no good lying to me.' Shocked into immobility, Pearl finally dragged her gaze from Mrs Carey's half-dressed hair to meet her furious eyes in the dressing-table mirror.

'Yes,' she said hoarsely, making to continue to brush the woman's hair.

'Yes, *Mrs Carey*.' The mistress did not wait for Pearl to correct herself, but half-rose and snatched the hairbrush from her. Her voice rose sharply. 'And you blame my nephew for it, I gather?'

'No, I didn't say that, mam, Mrs Carey!' Pearl cried out. How on earth had the mistress known that, and where in this deepest trouble had she, Pearl, summoned the strength to protect him?

'It is him though, isn't it? Don't think I don't know. I have my sources, you know.'

Cecily. She thought of the spying girl. It could only be Cecily who had told her mother, who had searched her possessions and stolen her mermaid.

'You wretch. You, with your big eyes and your airs above

your station. We've all been wrong about you. Well, they say it's the quiet ones you have to watch, don't they? *Don't they?*' She stood, hands on hips, a picture of rage, but slightly ridiculous with her hair on one side in pins and the other tumbling around her shoulders.

'He . . . he said we could go away together.' Pearl's howl was heart-wrenching.

'Go away together? What a simply ridiculous idea.' The woman threw the hairbrush onto the rug. 'Where would you have gone away *to*, I ask you? And who would pay for it all? He couldn't have expected a penny from us and I can't think of anyone else who would help him after cutting himself off from family and friends in such a low, despicable manner.'

Pearl felt the spit of 'despicable' on her cheek and flinched.

'How far on is it?' her mistress snapped. 'This . . . baby.'

'Might be three months now. My courses—'

'Spare me the details. Three months. I suppose you've tried . . . yes, well.'

'I have, mam, yes.' Pearl stared at the floor. 'It wasn't any good.'

The anger seemed to go out of Mrs Carey suddenly, and a shrewd, calculating look came over her face instead. She sat back on her chair again and gestured to Pearl to continue with her hair.

'Well, I suppose we've time to think about it.' Pearl's hand froze halfway, reaching down for the thrown hairbrush. 'You'll have to go, of course.'

Pearl's eyes filled with sudden tears. 'Yes, mam,' she whispered. Then said, 'I've nowhere to go. Nowhere.'

'Well, you should have thought about that earlier,' Mrs Carey said viciously. Then, seeing the shock and distress in the maid's eyes, added more gently, 'I'll have to find out what happens in these cases. The important thing is that nobody outside these walls learns a thing.'

'Charles? Master Charles?' The stable door was padlocked but Pearl hammered on it anyway. It was useless. Where was he? She had tried his bedroom, hurried round all the rooms downstairs.

A shadow fell across the garden. She looked up, shivering in the sudden coolness, to see a veil of dark cloud cover the sun.

The garden – she must try the garden. She turned and began to run down the path past the house, her heart banging in her chest, her head reeling. She tried the summerhouse first. It was deserted but for a book of poems by Robert Kernow forgotten, dusty, on a chair. She picked it up and flicked the pages, remembering Charles reading her the purple descriptions of the Cornish landscape and the passionate repressed spirit of the people.

Throwing down the book, with such force it bounced onto the floor, she ran outside. With her skirt bunched up to dodge the rose thorns that reached out to snag her, she slipped through the gap into the laurel maze. The seat was empty, and her panic grew. Down to the ravine she ran, then back up the path past the fountain, her breath rasping in her throat, the sky darkening like black ash now overhead. Thunder rumbled.

She halted, looking round madly. No one in the Vegetable Garden. Thunder crashed suddenly and she jumped fair out of her skin. A silence, then every bird in the garden started as one, calling warning.

'Charles,' she called. 'Master Charles!' And fled under the arch into the Flower Garden, searching the greenhouses then going to stand in the corner where he had posed for her painting, the painting she had now hidden deep in the cupboard in her attic.

A footstep on gravel and she whirled round. 'Charles,' she breathed, but it wasn't Charles, it was John Boase. He carried a shovel, which he leaned carefully against a wall before coming over to her, taking off his hat and standing before her.

His look was of deep pity.

'He's gone, miss,' he said gently. Then, 'I'm sorry.'

'Gone?' What did the man mean?

'In the trap to Penzance. Zachary's orders is to put him on the London train.'

The London train? Why? She couldn't ask Boase – no, she couldn't.

Boase cleared his throat awkwardly, then said in a hoarse voice, 'They've sent him away, Miss Pearl.'

'No,' sobbed Pearl. 'He wouldn't have gone without . . .'

She stopped. He wouldn't have left without saying goodbye, surely? But he had. Shock hit her like a dash of freezing water. Then a clamour of voices started up in her head, and black childhood nightmare images of shrieking bats swooped before her. When they finally receded, she stood in a choking fog of desolation, desertion and despair.

Through the madness came a gentle voice. 'I can help you, Pearl, if you'll let me.'

'Help me? Of course you can't help me. You don't know . . . How can anyone help me?'

And she pushed at him, darted away under the arch as the rain started to fall in great soft drops, the air soon a torrent of tears running down her hair, her face, her body. Gasping in panic, she grabbed her skirts and made for the gate, out into the road – which way? Down to the sea.

Slipping and sobbing, she stumbled alongside the stream, the lichen-daubed branches of trees catching at her hair, and shadowed its rushed and noisy course down the valley to the home that called it, that was calling her. The wide open arms of the ocean.

A shout. She looked behind her. John Boase was running after her. She darted past the jetty and up to the right, through the narrow gap in the rock onto the cliff path. Soaked by rain and spray, gasping with cold, she scrambled up the zig-zag path, her heart bursting in her chest. Up and up, slithering on wet stones, scratched by gorse, she clambered higher and higher until she reached the cairn where the painters sat, though no one was there today, then further along the cliff edge to where the sea boiled and hurled itself over vicious black rock below. There she teetered for a moment as the universe held its breath.

'Pearl.' Boase's voice carried over the wind, but he stayed up by the cairn, not daring to come on in case she gave in like many a hunted creature and jumped.

So there she waited on the edge, looking out over the water, the storm washing away all her thoughts until she was just an empty husk, exhausted.

Charles had gone. They had sent him away. He had gone without saying goodbye, probably leaving no message. He wouldn't have had time. But he hadn't fought for her, she knew that in her heart of hearts.

And once more she was alone again, and soon she would be homeless.

She gazed down at the boiling water beneath, knowing how a toss of a white-crested wave could dash her fragile body against the cliff face, crack her skull like a nut. It would be so easy.

Alone.

But no, she wasn't alone, was she? She touched her belly, still as slim and tight as ever, hiding a life within, another heartbeat.

It wasn't much of a hope, having this baby. Maybe it would

be taken from her, and grow up abandoned as she effectively had been, too. But she and it would have to make the best of it somehow. *Where there's life there's hope*, her stepmother's voice rang in her mind.

And when she turned at last to go back, it was to see John Boase waiting for her, watching out for her, as she realised he had done ever since he had first set eyes on her, standing under the Davy statue in Penzance on market-day, all her worldly possessions in a shabby bag at her feet.

'And so he married her,' said John Boase's grandson, ninety years later. 'Married her, and when the baby was born, took her little boy – my father – to be his own. They lived in the Gardener's Cottage until she died. And if my grandfather is to be believed, they were very happy for the short time God gave them together. He was a good man, kind and gentle.'

A romantic story, thought Mel. Very heartwarming. But was it really like that? Didn't Pearl still love Charles? Wasn't she heartbroken when he left? This was John Boase's side of the story, not Pearl's. But perhaps it wasn't possible to learn Pearl's.

She didn't feel she could say this to the moist-eyed old man who had recently lost his wife and sought comfort in the past, those mythical golden days of youth when happy ever afters seemed possible. Instead she said, 'I'm surprised Mrs Carey let them live in the Gardener's Cottage. Why didn't she turn them out to avoid Pearl's secret getting out?'

'Maybe she didn't want to lose a fine Head Gardener. Especially once the war started and so many downed tools to go and fight. And maybe no one else knew the secret. If it was all under the carpet, maybe she wasn't bothered.'

'A pragmatic lady. So what happened to Charles?'

But here Boase shrugged. 'Called up after the Somme. Went missing sometime in 1917, but Dad said he thought he survived after all. Don't know what happened to him after that.'

'I suppose it's possible to find out,' Mel said doubtfully.

'Don't think I ever cared that much, frankly,' said Boase, flexing arthritic fingers stiffly on the arm of his chair. 'Dad always said John Boase was his father, didn't want to hear about Charles Carey. There's a lot more to family feeling than a bunch of DNA, you know. Seems like Carey gave up any right he had.'

'That's true,' said Mel, thinking of her own father who had abandoned them.

As she pondered these things, lying next to Patrick in the darkness, finally she drifted into a deep sleep.

Chapter 29

The phone rang the next morning during an otherwise silent breakfast. Irina, looking pale and distant, sat sipping black coffee. Mel sliced large chunks of soft white bread and Patrick spooned boiled eggs, which Lana loved, into eggcups.

'Can you pick it up?' he asked Mel, who did.

'Mel? It's Matt,' came the voice down the line. 'Listen, I'm worried about Mum. I told you she was tired last night? Well she didn't sleep. She's very breathless and her chest hurts. I've made her stay in bed, but she's pretty distressed.'

'Have you called the doctor?'

'Just now, yes. And he said . . . well, there's an ambulance on its way. And of course I'll have to go with her to the hospital.'

'Oh Matt, that's awful. Poor Carrie. But that leaves you . . .'

'I know. I'm on my own here apart from Ella and George.' Ella was a shy middle-aged woman who came to chambermaid every morning. Whilst utterly dependable in her unchanging routine, she would not be happy answering the phone or dealing with a customer complaint. George, a cheerful stocky pensioner whose jobs were portering and maintenance, would know little about the administration of a hotel.

'What's the matter, Mel?' Irina broke in.

'Just a minute, Matt.' She cocked the handset away from her ear. 'Carrie's ill – she's going to hospital. Matt's a bit desperate for help at the hotel.'

Weariness and concern fought for position on Irina's face. After a moment she sighed heavily. 'Give me the phone, please.'

'Irina . . .'

'No, they are my friends and I want to help.' She held out her hand for the receiver.

'Hello, Matt,' she said. 'It is Irina here. No, no, I am all right. Tell Carrie not to worry, I am coming now.'

There must have been protest at the other end of the line because Irina repeated firmly, 'No, no, I will come. You haven't seen Greg again, have you?' Her shoulders relaxed at Matt's response. 'Well.' She looked at Lana and then beseechingly at Mel and Patrick. 'Lana might have to come with me.'

Mel, impressed by Irina's resolution, readily picked up the hint. 'Don't worry.' She smiled at Lana. 'Patrick's giving me a lift into Penzance this morning to do a few errands. Would you like to come, Lana? We could go shopping and maybe have lunch out.'

Lana slipped the last spoonful of her eggs into her mouth and nodded, her sulky expression suddenly gone. 'Please, Mum?'

'Of course, angel . . . Matt, I'll come right away,' Irina told him. 'And . . . give Carrie my love, poor lady, if the ambulance comes before I get there.' She replaced the handset in its cradle and took a large gulp of her cooling coffee, a picture of strength and purpose. Mel watched her in some surprise; her behaviour was such a contrast to that of the previous evening.

'A woman of many parts,' said Patrick, eyebrows raised, as he closed the front door when she left.

'I think it will help her to have something useful to do,'

replied Mel, 'rather than sit around worrying. And Carrie and Matt do need her. She likes being needed.'

'Let's look at the elephant I bought you. He's so cute, isn't he?'

Mel and Lana had walked up and down the streets in Penzance, browsing in the shops and – Lana's choice – had sat down to eat an early lunch in a Cornish pasty shop.

Lana pulled a paper bag out of the plastic carrier hooked over her chair, unfolded the top and carefully withdrew a carved wooden elephant with a blue and gold howdah in which perched a tiny Indian boy. She had spent ages choosing the present, going from ethnic craft emporium to gaudy gift shop, fingering plastic 'shark's tooth' necklaces and enamel flower brooches before settling on this.

They had hardly spoken about anything unrelated to their shopping, but now that Mel was facing the child across the table, it was difficult to avoid conversation of some sort. She longed to ask Lana what she felt about everything – her father, her music – but was too nervous of destroying their easy companionship. The girl would tell her what she wanted in her own way, in her own time.

Lana ate stoically, looking around her at the other diners. At one point, like a small animal alert to danger, she froze in mid-mouthful, her gaze focused on something outside. But whatever the danger was, it passed and she continued to eat. She was a reserved child, Mel decided, but one with a strong interior life. It was delightful, for instance, to see Lana's free hand dancing a pattern on the edge of the table as though she were hearing a violin in her head.

Lana stopped and looked up at her and said gravely, 'I thought I saw my daddy just now, but it was someone else.'

'Have you been looking for him all the time?' Mel said quietly.

Lana nodded and took another bite. Then she said, 'Mummy shouldn't be so frightened. I want to be here and live with her, but I'd like to stay with him sometimes, too.'

'Does your mother know that?'

'I have told her. I told her again last night.'

'It's very difficult, isn't it,' Mel said carefully, 'when grown-ups don't get on. You know it's not because of you, don't you?'

Lana nodded. 'I know all that,' she said with the air of a woman of the world. 'But she's making it not fair for me.'

'She looks after you very well, doesn't she? It's because she loves you, she wants to protect you.'

Lana sighed and put down her pasty. 'But there isn't anything to protect me *from*. Daddy's okay. He was just frightened that she would go away. And she did, so he was right, wasn't he?'

'I fear it isn't quite as simple as that.' If you love someone, set them free. Maybe that's where Greg had gone wrong. He had trapped pretty Irina, like a terrified little bird, and thought he could keep her in his cage.

'That's what grown-ups always say. As if I'm stupid.'

'I'm sorry,' said Mel, holding her hands up, palms outward. 'I don't think you're stupid at all.' Lana was, in fact, alarmingly discerning. 'I'm really not on anyone's side, you know, just trying to understand.'

Lana looked solemn, pulled off a piece of crust, discarding it on the plate and said, 'You like Patrick, don't you?'

What would this child come up with next? 'Yes – yes, I do, very much.'

'I think Mum liked Patrick for a bit.'

Mel stared at Lana. 'Did she? Really?'

'Yes, she kept talking about him and inviting him to supper, but he didn't invite her back or anything, and once

300

she cried on the phone to him, so I suppose he didn't like her enough.'

'He's always very kind to your mother,' said Mel, her mind working overtime. This revelation might explain some of Irina's prickliness towards her and Patrick. 'I'm sure he's her friend.'

It didn't feel right to let this conversation go any further. 'Have you finished? Yes?' She consulted her watch. 'We've got two hours before we can go and find Patrick to drive us home. Shall we go down to the sea-front? We can buy an ice cream on the way.'

In the car on the way home, Mel rang Irina's mobile but found it out of network range, so she tried the hotel switchboard. Matt answered immediately.

'We're on our way back with Lana,' Mel said. 'How's your mother?'

'A little better, thanks, now she's in hospital. It's a mild heart-attack, a bit of a warning really. They're keeping her in for a few days. My aunt's with her and I'm going back again later. Sorry, what?'

There was some muttering in the background, then Irina came on the line.

'Mel, thank you for having Lana. We are managing without Carrie, but something happened. Greg came.'

'Really? What did you do?'

'It was okay. Matt was here. I made Greg speak in front of him.' She sighed and added, 'I told Greg he could see Lana. Is it all right if he comes tomorrow morning to Merryn? I don't want us to be alone, you see. Can you be around?'

'Well, I suppose so, Irina, if you think that's the right thing.'

When they arrived back at the Hall, Patrick picked up the hanset in the kitchen to see if there were any messages. He listened intently, and Mel saw him frown and scribble something down on an old envelope, which he put in his pocket.

Mel only realised this afterwards, but Patrick was quiet, self-absorbed that evening. While Mel and Lana played Monopoly with an ancient set Mel found in a cupboard, he went off to his study in the old estate office.

'Sorry I've kept her up so late,' she told Irina, who rang the doorbell at half-past nine, 'but she wanted to see you, and we lost track of the time. Goodness, you look exhausted.'

'I am. Hello, darling,' she said to Lana, giving her a hug. They sat in the drawing room while Irina drank tea and told them about her day, how hard they had all worked. Mel waited for her to mention Greg, but she didn't. Finally, she said, 'Come on, angel, tidy up the game now, it's time for bed,' and accompanied Lana upstairs, where, Mel imagined, she would explain to the girl that she would finally be seeing her father the next day, the first time for three years.

Patrick must still be working. Mel turned the lights off and sat for a while looking out onto the garden as it fell into darkness. The distant sky swirled with wispy cloud like the surface of a milky coffee. A bat darted at the window, swerving away at the last second, but making her jump. The stars were huge tonight. Strange to think how they had looked down on this garden nearly a hundred years ago, how Pearl would have gazed at them as Mel did now, how they would be here staring down, long after Mel and Patrick were dust.

How long would it be before she was gone from here – back to London? She didn't know. Perhaps she would start talking about it to Patrick tonight. No, best get Irina's meeting with Greg out of the way first. Perhaps talk to him about it tomorrow night then.

She squinted at her watch in the semi-darkness and yawned,

then walked into the hall and down the corridor to his study. Patrick was sitting on the floor there surrounded by great piles of paper, sorted roughly into piles. The whole room was a jumble of open boxes and files.

'Just trying to make order out of chaos,' he said, looking up, frowning. 'But I keep finding other things that need doing. Look, here's the quote for the buildings insurance.'

'It's awfully late,' she said, leaning against his desk and nudging the computer mouse around with one finger.

'With you in a moment,' he said, distracted, returning to his sorting.

The screensaver cleared and Patrick's Inbox was on display. Out of the list of names, one jumped out at her. It appeared three, no four times. Arabella Blake. Patrick had received four messages from Bella. Once the shock faded, Mel glanced at Patrick, but he was looking at the old envelope he had pulled out of his pocket. She moved away from the computer, alarmed that Patrick would notice her snooping.

But Bella was there, between them.

'By the way,' said Patrick, trying to sound nonchalant but failing miserably, 'there's a slightly tricky situation.'

'Oh?' Like a stone, dropped into the silence.

'There was a phone message earlier. From Bella.' He rushed on. 'She's in this neck of the woods for a few days, staying with some friends near St Ives. Wants to call in. I've suggested tomorrow. After all, I won't be able to go into work, will I? The tree surgeon is coming and we've got this Greg business. Thought you might like to meet her.'

'Oh,' said Mel. 'Did you? Right.'

'After all, you'd have to meet her sometime, since she's an old friend.'

Their eyes locked but it was Patrick who looked away first.

Chapter 30

Mel awoke late the next morning with the feeling that something was badly wrong. The bed beside her was already empty. Scum had formed on the cup of tea that waited on the bedside table. The room was stuffy and her head ached.

A roar and a series of crashing noises vibrated through the house. She hauled herself out of bed and slipped across the landing to the window of Patrick's old room. The tree surgeon's lorries were arriving, trailers, shredders and all. This truly was to be an industrial job.

Wearily, she returned to sit down again on the side of the bed, sipped her tea, put it down again with a *moue* of distaste and contemplated the day ahead. Noise and bother all day and for days to come, someone else's marital drama to witness and, worst of all, an underlying dread that filled her throat and stomach: the arrival of Bella.

Once again, anxieties began to chase their tails around her head. What did Bella want? How could she just be 'in the area' in remote West Cornwall? Why had Patrick taken several hours to tell Mel she was coming, and what were all those emails doing in his Inbox? She wished she could have read them. Or perhaps that would have been worse. Ignorance is bliss, she told herself firmly. *Yeah*, said her brother William's cynical voice in her head, *and the truth will set you free*.

When she arrived downstairs after a hurried shower, Patrick was busy making a trayful of tea for the lads outside, Irina was sitting at the table, morose and smoking furiously, while Lana trailed in and out, whingeing, 'When's he coming?' Then, 'Oh, I want my violin here, Mum, can't we go and get it?' And, 'I can't remember what he looks like. Why haven't you got a photo?'

Mel caught Patrick's eye as he came back from delivering the tea. He looked utterly fed up, and just glowered at her. She glowered back. How could he? How dare he? It dawned on her that he was wearing his smartest cords and that his shirt was neatly ironed. Gulping down a couple of paracetamol she had found in the bathroom, she picked up the fresh cup of tea Patrick had passed her wordlessly, and said, 'I'll be working down at the cottage this morning. Call me when Greg comes, Irina, if you need me.' She gave Patrick a beseeching look, to which he seemed oblivious, and stomped out, banging the scullery door behind her.

At that moment, the bangs and crashes gloriously ceased. They're taking their tea break, of course, she remembered. She hoped it would be the first of many, if they were going to be making that racket. When she reached the cottage, instead of unlocking the door and going inside, she stood sipping her tea, looking out over the peaceful garden. The ginger cat stalked past and off towards the rhododendrons.

How dear this place had become. Her own flowerbed was blooming now with poppies and mayweed, though she'd neglected it recently. Beyond, Patrick had nearly finished rescuing the summerhouse from its pall of green. They had both ripped away great banks of bramble and the green, sour-smelling ivy that rampaged everywhere in these parts, uncovering the sandy path that led round the ghostly concrete-edged rectangle that had once been the pond. Patrick was still digging out the silt.

The atmosphere was different now. The garden was awakening, throwing off its blanket. The muffled sound was gone. Instead it was full of birdsong. An agonising thought struck her: soon it wouldn't need her any more. The time was coming when she would have to leave, and who knew, she thought sadly, thinking of Bella and of Patrick's moodiness, whether she would ever return.

As the screech of a mechanical saw rose once more into the morning air, Mel rubbed her stiff neck. She set her empty cup on the doorstep and dug in her jeans pocket for her door key. But as she wiggled it into the lock, there came a grinding of metal on metal and the roar of an ancient engine as Jim the gardener's rickety van bounced up the lane.

'Mornin',' Jim said, getting out, tipping his battered hat and shambling round to release the tailgate and drag out the lawn-mower. 'Still on yur 'olidays, I see.'

'What? Oh, not holidays, I'm working,' said Mel, 'if I can think for the noise.' They stood and listened to the sawing and the crashing of falling branches then, in a brief silence, she thought to ask, 'What did you mean the other week when you said something about "her" being in the garden? Who was her?'

A puzzled look crossed his face. 'Did I say that?' Then his expression cleared. 'When I was a young 'un, I played hur, I told you.' Mel nodded. 'Well, there was once or twice I saw her.'

'Who?' repeated Mel.

'The woman in the garden. I never do see her again, but sometimes I feel she's hur watching.'

'Watching? Like a ghost, you mean?'

He shrugged. 'Dunno, could be. This is Cornwall. Sometimes

things be how they be and it's no use askin' a packet o' questions.' He turned away.

As he fiddled with the mower and yanked fruitlessly at the starting cord, there was a sudden violent twittering and screeching. Both of them looked up. The cat had reappeared, batting at something that skittered about the grass. Feathers floated into the air. The white blackbird.

'Get away, get out of it. *Sssssttt.*' Mel ran at the cat, which turned and streaked off up the garden. She crouched down to inspect the injured bird as the old man came up to stand beside her.

The bird tried to fly off, but staggered around in a circle, one wing trailing. The man bent down stiffly and scooped it up in his hands, cradling it in such a way that it couldn't peck him, manipulating the broken wing. He made soothing noises and stroked the small body until its quivering lessened.

'Bluddy cat,' he said.

'Do you know whose it is?' asked Mel, putting out a finger to stroke the bird's head. Its pink eyes were half-closed and she was curious to see the yellowish blotches on its beak.

'Ay, it's mine. Or not mine – more like *I* belong to *it*. A stray, found me out. I feed it but it's never at home. Often comes hur, I reckon.'

'Can you put a bell round its neck?' she sighed. 'It's always killing birds and mice.'

'Ay, it's a good mouser,' the old man said, nodding glumly. 'I'll say that for it. Look, if you've got a box I'll take him home, this 'un. Soon fix his wing like new, poor begger.'

Trying to work was torture, what with the mounting heat, the noise of the saws and the dark whirl of her thoughts, and yet writing up the next chapter she had mapped out seemed the only thing to keep Mel tenured to sanity that morning.

There was no summons to the house. The only phone call was from Rowena, asking her to confirm some details about next term's teaching. The woman said something about teaching a course unit herself, but Mel didn't ask her about it. She was too caught up in what was happening here and now, and forgot about Rowena as soon as she put down the phone.

As the morning wore on and the phone didn't ring again, she relaxed. Either Greg had arrived and all was progressing for good or for bad, or else he hadn't turned up. At least she hadn't been required to guard Lana against a kidnapping father or to comfort a sobbing Irina. Gradually the writing absorbed all her attention.

It was satisfying finally to incorporate the new part of Pearl's story she had learned into her narrative. In fact, the maid was to form only a small part of a chapter, but she stood as a metaphor for Mel's theme about the mountain that women artists had to climb, and she was able to go back and slot Pearl's case into her introduction. And as she gave the maid her tiny place in history, once again she felt a twitch upon the thread. For both women Merryn had been a haven after a storm. And in turn had become the arena for the testing of their strengths.

Bella. Mel's concentration evaporated. She pressed Save and rubbed her eyes. The computer clock flicked to 12.31 and the sawing and crashing up the garden ceased once more. Must be lunchtime. She closed down the laptop, splashed cold water from the kitchen tap over her hot face and arms then opened the fridge door. She stood there thinking for a moment, then let the door swing shut. Curiosity had won. She must go up to the house and see what was happening.

The heat rolled in heavy waves across the garden, the midday sun beating down so brightly it was hard to see. But when she reached the Flower Garden she heard the sound of voices. She peered in under the half-arch.

Over by the far wall, under the shade of the beech trees, stood two figures. It took a second for her to register that one was Patrick, this crisply dressed figure, jacket draped over one shoulder, his other hand in his trouser pocket, white shirtsleeves rolled to reveal arms now brown from the summer's gardening. He was standing close, too close, to a slim pretty woman, in earnest conversation. How fresh she looked in her pale-blue shirt-dress, kitten-heeled sandals and with a small neat white handbag hooked over one forearm. The sun glinted on her shoulder-length fair hair. At one point as they talked, the woman put her hand up to her face in a vulnerable gesture and Patrick reached out and rubbed her shoulder as though in comfort. Mel watched for a moment, agonising jealousy swelling inside. They looked so – right – together, those two, Patrick tall, so well-turned out, his skin glowing against the white shirt. Was it standing next to Bella that gave him that gloss? Mel suddenly wanted him so much it hurt.

Tears pricking, she was turning away, when Patrick called out to her. He said something to his companion and began to walk quickly across the garden.

'Hi! We were about to come down and find you.'

Mel stepped forward uncertainly, her smile feeling pasted on. Bella busied herself donning a pair of sunglasses and waited, as Patrick put his arm around Mel and drew her over.

'I didn't know she'd arrived,' whispered Mel, and allowed herself to be received by Bella like a subject by a queen.

Patrick, having watched them coolly shake hands, seemed to feel he had done his bit, for he merely stood, looking from one to another in wary silence.

'I'm really pleased to meet you,' said Bella, her eyes invisible behind her sunglasses. 'Patrick's been telling me all about you.' She put out her hand and gave Patrick a playful pat, her manicured fingertips resting briefly on his shoulder. 'He does keep things to himself, doesn't he?'

'Does he?' said Mel faintly.

'It's part of his attraction, of course,' she went on. 'He imagines we women never know quite what he's thinking. But we do, of course. Men are so funny sometimes, aren't they?'

Mel merely smiled. Bella was very pretty, but it was a cultivated, well-groomed attractiveness. But when Mel glanced at Patrick, she was shocked to see that he was gazing at Bella as though fascinated by every word dropping from her lips.

'Where are you staying?' asked Mel, to steer the subject to safer ground.

'Oh, just with some friends at Hayle, near St Ives,' said Bella. 'I'm there for the week actually.'

'That's nice,' said Mel. 'Hope you get good weather.'

'So perhaps we can see something of each other.'

Patrick stared unhappily at the ground, prodding at a large dandelion plant with his shoe.

In the end he suggested they go down to the Wink, the old pub in the village, for lunch. They crossed the Flower Garden, Bella carefully watching where she placed her exquisitely sandalled feet. Patrick fell behind.

Glancing at the house, Mel suddenly remembered Irina and hung back to ask in a low voice, 'What's been going on indoors? Did he come?'

'Greg? Yes, arrived about eleven. I let him in.'

'How's it going?'

'Fine. Lana was a bit shy at first. I left them all to it. In fact, look.' They had passed back through the arch and Patrick gestured down the garden, shading his face against the sun. There, near the rhododendrons, Greg and Lana stood hand-in-hand, Lana chattering nineteen to the dozen, looking up into her father's eyes, her face alive. As for Greg, all his grumpiness had gone. He gazed down at his daughter, an amused smile on his face. Patrick walked across the grass to speak to them. When he came back he said, 'Irina's gone back to the hotel to help Matt. Greg's taking Lana over there later.'

'Well, thank heavens that seems to have gone well,' breathed Mel. He nodded and moved forwards to speak to Bella. Left looking at his back, she thought, in a sharp reversal, it was her life that seemed to be unravelling instead.

Chapter 31

'Do you remember, Paddy, when we stayed at Lois's cottage that time? And Lois left the brake off on her car and it ended up in the sea and you and Geoff had to haul it out? It was *so* funny, Mel. You wouldn't believe how cross he was, weren't you, Paddy?'

Mel merely continued eating her baked potato, which tasted like ashes in her mouth.

Bella turned out to be one of those people who can prattle amusingly about anything, without allowing the conversation to deepen. At first Mel had thought she was doing it deliberately, trying to exclude Mel by reminiscing about the past, but it only took her a short time to realise that Bella wasn't really interested in Mel. Mel's role was audience, and she had to grin and bear it.

She could hardly bring herself to look at Patrick, who was laughing and joshing Bella with his own stories, though every now and then he would ask Mel if she was all right.

Bella really was very attractive, Mel had to admit to herself, taking little glances at her from time to time, noticing her small high breasts, her lovely neck and glossy hair, and trying not to dwell on the thought that she, Mel, needed to visit a hairdresser, and was wearing faded jeans. The only comfort Mel could find was that, now Bella had taken her sunglasses off in the pub, the shape of her nose and the set of her pale blue eyes gave her the look, just very slightly, of a surprised sheep.

Bella had asked only two questions of Mel during lunch. One, what she did for a living, and the other, how long she proposed staying in Cornwall. Otherwise the conversation had been about things she and Patrick had done together, news of people they had known, funny stories about people buying and selling property in Chelsea where her offices were. Occasionally she would draw in Patrick, touching his arm and asking, 'Paddy thought it was hilarious, didn't you, Paddy?' or, 'Do you remember Hugo in the office, Paddy?' and chasing off after some new anecdote.

Mel, stirring a cup of coffee, longed for the meal to be over. Finally, it was, and Patrick suggested they walk down to the cove.

'I'd love to but it's so hot and I've only got these stupid shoes,' sighed Bella, flexing a pretty ankle. Mel, whilst contemptuous of the fashionable sandals, had to agree with her about the heat and so they laboured their way back up to the Hall to where Bella had parked her Clio behind the tree surgeon's lorries.

They stared in fascination at the wide area of garden already cleared of trees and undergrowth. 'I'm planning a lawn here, you see,' Patrick interjected between the noises of the machinery.

'It's all changed so much since I saw it last,' replied Bella, as they went into the house. 'Do you know,' she said to Mel, 'it was such a dump. I simply couldn't imagine anyone wanting to live here, let alone me.'

'I love it,' said Mel in a dull voice.

'Oh, it's going to be beautiful – I can see that now.' Was her expression wistful, or merely polite? 'Well, it's been so nice,

Paddy, but I really have to go. We're due over at Rick Stein's restaurant this evening.'

'Bit of a trek, isn't it, Padstow?'

'I know, but it's Lois's birthday and she booked it months ago. Do you remember, you were going to come. Before . . .' She trailed to a halt, meaningfully.

'Of course, her birthday, I'd forgotten.' Patrick's distress seemed genuine. 'Send her my love, won't you, Bella?'

'I will. Mel, if you don't mind, is there any chance Paddy and I could meet, you know, for a drink later in the week? I'd really appreciate a proper chat with him.'

Patrick turned to Mel and said in a casual tone, 'We're not doing anything much, are we? Would it be all right, Mel, if I went?'

'Up to you,' said Mel, shrugging.

'I don't suppose you're free tomorrow, Paddy?' said Bella. 'We're going to a play at the Minack Theatre the following evening, and I think there's a meal out planned the night after.'

'Sure. Where should we go?'

Mel said abruptly, 'Nice to meet you, Bella. I'd better be getting on,' and slipped out of the front door. When Patrick came to the cottage shortly afterwards, she had gone out for a long walk. When she returned she found a note that said, *Supper at eight. Px.*

That evening, as Patrick was cooking, Irina rang. After a moment he passed the receiver over to Mel.

'Where are you?' Mel asked.

'Home,' said Irina. 'Lana's here, too, watching TV in the other room. We're going to meet Greg at the hotel for dinner. Listen, I wanted to say thank you both for helping these last few days.'

'That's okay. How did it go earlier?'

Irina sighed. 'He has been most reasonable. Says he's sorry for everything. That we can work something out. He seems to have changed. More gentle. What can I say?'

'He seemed, well, very genuine about missing Lana.'

'Yes.'

'So, what have you agreed with him?'

'It's difficult,' Irina said. 'I am still nervous. But Lana wants to see him, so what can I do? I can't risk her turning against me.'

'No.'

'So we have dinner together and I see how things go. But . . . I feel tired of running now. I have run from my family in Dubrovnik, I have run from my husband. Now I want the quiet life and I want Lana to be happy. Maybe it will work.'

'I hope so.'

'Thank you, Mel.'

'It seems a happy ending might indeed be in sight there,' Mel said, putting down the phone.

'Thank heavens for that,' was all Patrick said from the stove where he was furiously stirring a roux. He seemed distracted this evening, and had made no reference to Bella's visit. Bella was like a sheathed sword between them.

Mel watched him as she sipped her wine, noticing afresh the sure movements of his body as he reached for utensils or crouched down to check the pie baking in the oven, the unconscious way he would stroke the back of his neck whilst thinking. Just as she was recognising fully how dear he was to her, he seemed to be growing further away, absorbed as he was in his own thoughts, hardly looking at her. A lump swelled in her throat. She knew instinctively it was the wrong moment to speak. But in the end, it was no good, she couldn't stop herself.

'Patrick,' she said hesitantly, 'do you have to go out with Bella tomorrow?' The blade, drawn from its scabbard, flashed menacingly.

He looked up from stirring, his blank expression unnerving. 'Well, that's the arrangement, yes,' was all he said. His voice was strange. He moved the saucepan off the heat and turned to face her, arms folded.

'You could ring her, couldn't you, say you're busy after all?'

'Why should I do that?' he said. 'What's this all about, Mel? You weren't exactly friendly to Bella today. She was a bit upset about it. You're not still jealous of her, are you?'

'*She* was upset!' Mel gasped. 'What about me? Don't I get any consideration here? And no, since you ask, I'm not exactly jealous, just . . . furious. You're with me now, aren't you? You can't expect me to be exactly delighted about you spending a cosy evening with your ex-fiancée.'

Her anger ignited his own.

'Mel, what d'you imagine's going to happen? That I'm going to leap over the pub table and ravish her senseless in front of the locals? We're only having a drink, for goodness' sake and, anyway, she's going out with whatshisname, Ed, back in London.'

Mel remembered Bella's adoring expression, the way she hadn't been able to take her eyes off Patrick.

'I don't trust her,' she said. 'Even if there is an Ed waiting in the wings.'

'That's a horrible thing to say. Come on, you're worrying about nothing. I can't let her down, she gets very depressed sometimes, she needs someone to talk to.'

Mel couldn't quite believe that Bella was depressed. Manipulative, self-centred, yes, she thought bitchily, but she didn't seem to be someone who was deep enough even to be aware of the concept of cosmic angst, let alone to suffer from it.

'Doesn't she have other friends who can help? What about this Lois person and the others she's down here with? Why does it always have to be you?'

'I imagine it's because I know her so well – she doesn't have to explain everything. Look, Mel, this is quite an accusation, that you don't trust me.'

'I didn't say that.'

'It's what you've virtually spelled out.'

'Oh, go and see her, then. I don't care. I don't want to be responsible for her jumping off a cliff at Land's End.'

'Mel,' Patrick said, and she was suddenly terrified of the cold steel in his voice. He stopped, took a step towards her. 'It's not going to work if . . . Listen, we're neither of us spring chickens. I can't drop all my old friends, pretend they never existed, just because I've met you. What about this Jake chap? I'm not always asking about him, am I, thinking you're still lusting after him?'

'But I'm not seeing Jake,' Mel said, nearly spilling her wine as she shakily set it on the table. 'And you *are* seeing Bella.'

'You'll see him when you go back to college, won't you? Every day.'

'Patrick, this is ridiculous. You can't make the comparison.' They stared at one another. She couldn't bear his fury and looked away.

When you go back to college.

'Patrick,' she said, again unable to stop herself. 'This might not be the moment, but what are we going to do when I go back?'

'What do you mean?' he said mildly.

'About us, of course. It's only a few weeks before term starts. I've got to go back to my job, my flat, my old life. But where are *we* going, Patrick, you and I? This time has been so special to me. What does it mean for you? Has this just been an enjoyable break from real life? Am I just a holiday romance? Or is it more important to you than that?'

He moved forward suddenly and pulled her into his arms, started kissing her desperately, then hugged her hard and she felt his hot whisper in his ear. 'Don't be such an idiot. Of course you're important. It's just . . .'

'What?' she said, pulling back to look at him. He broke the gaze first.

'Nothing,' he answered, then smiled at her. Once more their mouths met. When next they came up for air she said, 'Oh Patrick, I'm sorry.'

'Oh darling.' He hugged her tighter. 'Come on, don't let's quarrel. It'll work out, you'll see.'

'Will it?' she sighed, realising that he hadn't given an inch over Bella.

'Of course it will.' And once again he began to kiss her, passionately, almost angrily. But he hadn't said that he was sorry, too.

Chapter 32

Looking back on that night many weeks later, Mel was to wonder if she had somehow sensed, even then, that it was to be the last time she and Patrick were to hold one another. There was a deep sense of sadness, of urgency about their lovemaking, as though they had been told the world was about to end. At the time she had put these feelings down to grief, the knowledge on both their parts that she and Patrick were captives of their own pasts, clinging together for comfort. Of course, they were mature adults; they had learned from experience the motions they had to go through to plaster emotional wounds, to find closure, to go on with life. That night, however, they seemed as vulnerable and needy as young children.

How then, after the intensity of that experience, could the events of the very next evening ever have taken place?

The day started normally enough – if you can call being woken at 7.30 a.m. by rumbling lorries and the screech of mechanical saws normal – though Patrick was very quiet. Mel came downstairs to find him standing at the kitchen window, staring unseeing across the garden. She caressed his shoulder briefly as he made way for her to fit the kettle under the tap. She filled it to the brim, realising he hadn't yet made tea for the workers.

'Better go into work today,' he muttered, pouring himself some cornflakes. 'Do you mind being catering manager today?' He nodded his head towards the front of the house, where the noise was reaching teeth-jarring level.

'Should be all right. I'm planning chapter thirteen today,' said Mel, buttering toast. 'About the arrival in Lamorna of Alfred Munnings and Augustus John.'

'How many chapters are there?'

'Fifteen. Then lots of fiddly stuff. Appendices, footnotes, that sort of thing.'

'You've nearly finished, then?'

She had considered how long it would take her once she returned to London, visiting the British Library, and a couple of museum libraries, a conversation she needed to have with a curator at the Tate. A month's concentrated work, she calculated. But that would be if she could find everything easily. Waiting for people to answer emails, especially in August, was frustrating enough. And once she returned to work, the teaching would intervene.

In addition, there was an important visit to make, to Ann Boase, Pearl's granddaughter, to see other pictures by Pearl, to find out what more Ann knew about her grandmother, to learn Ann's own story. No, she certainly couldn't consider her paper finished until she had spoken to Ann. Yesterday she had tried ringing the number Richard Boase had given her, but it just rang and rang without ever awakening an ansaphone. Possibly Ann was away. She visited the States a great deal, her brother said.

Wasn't it funny, was her gloomy thought, how everything was conspiring to draw her back to London? Rowena's recent call had seemed at the time a slight annoyance, but even that was worrying her now. Rowena, it seemed, would still be teaching at the college next term. Why?

Kissing Patrick goodbye quickly – 'I'll get some food in on the way home,' he said – she walked down to the cottage, immediately wilting in the scorching heat. There, after debating the relative demerits of heat or noise, she opted for the sound of the saws and opened both front and kitchen doors to get some air moving through the house. The computer was feeling the heat, too – it took ages to boot up – and while she waited, the feeling of dread that had ebbed and flowed inside her all morning, swirled into a ghostly manifestation. *Bella.*

Why did she feel so anxious? Patrick would see Bella tonight, and at the end of the week, she would be gone. But as she called up her own Inbox she thought of two nights ago, when Bella's name had shown up on Patrick's computer. What had she written to Patrick? If only Mel had looked.

Even Bella was momentarily forgotten as two emails popped into her box. The first one was from Chrissie, the second from Jake.

She stared at Jake's name for a moment, then looked at the heading. NEWS, it said. It had to be for her only, not a round robin this time, as this was her personal email address.

He's either getting married again or he's got another job, she thought. That's why he's writing. Bracing herself, she double-clicked on his message. It seemed an age before it opened up and she read:

'Hi, Mel,

Are you still in the back of beyond? Hope you're having a wild time, whatever. Must send you this as it's so funny, I can hardly believe it myself. Anna and Freya are great – would send you their love if they knew I was writing. Helen's taken them to Spain with her new man.

Good for Helen, thought Mel, genuinely pleased for her. She read the website link Jake had sent her. It was for a publishing magazine and when she opened it up she read:

Sirius Books wins British Dan Brown. Yesterday, Sophie Wright of Conway & Eaton Literary Agency concluded a 'high six-figure' deal for two thrillers by poet and Creative Writing lecturer Jake Friedland, based on a partial manuscript and synopsis. Sirius Editor Bill Meek describes the first of these, *Deciphering Delacroix*, as 'an intriguing and fast-paced tale about an international art conspiracy that puts Dan Brown in the shade.' Sirius plan to publish . . .

Mel closed the link, the initial sense of surprise fading and a smile spreading across her face. He had done it. Good old Jake. Two thrillers, eh? Well, there would be a certain amount of twittering in the staff bar, about it being commercial fiction rather than the erudite satire of the art world he had been working on for so long, but there would be envy, too, she knew. A high six-figure sum. That meant at least several hundred thousand pounds. How many years' salary was that for most of her colleagues? Even she was being paid only a pittance for her book. It was extraordinary!

Clicking on Reply, she tapped out a quick but heartfelt message of congratulation. She squeezed her eyes shut as she pressed Send, and when she opened them, immediately regretted what she had written. What devil had possessed her to suggest a celebratory drink in the same message?

Slightly cross at her recklessness, she stabbed the mouse twice on Chrissie's email, which turned out to be mostly about some paperwork connected to their mother's affairs that needed Mel's signature, then finished: *Can we come for a few days in August when the day nursery is closed?* She replied to that, agreeing to do the first and promising to check with Patrick about the second.

She sighed. In some ways it would be lovely to see Chrissie

and the boys. And yet she also wanted to be on her own with Patrick. Which made her think of the intruder. Bella.

Concentrate, girl, she told herself, and forced herself to open up the document labelled *Lamorna book*.

Two hours later, she became aware that the sound of the saws had ceased, glanced at the time and cursed. She had forgotten the next tea break. She could feel the sun burn through her on the short journey round the house to check that the men hadn't all died of dehydration.

Patrick arrived home in the early evening, hot and irritable, with several carrier bags of shopping. Mel mentioned Chrissie's request, and he seemed pleased at the idea of seeing her. Then she was able to tell him that Irina had rung again.

'It still seems unbelievable, but apparently she and Greg have sorted everything out. Or rather, Lana has.'

'Lana?'

'Yes. She instructed her parents at dinner last night that she wanted to live with Irina, but go to stay with her father often. And since her parents were both sitting there at her mercy, and neither wanted her to view them as responsible for further conflict, they agreed. Oh yes, and he's happy to pay for her music. *Voilà*. Sorted. Irina sounded very proud of her.'

'Out of the mouths of babes and sucklings . . . wisdom. She is an unusually mature little girl, isn't she? Still, I'm surprised Greg agreed to it just like that.'

'Yes, he's a tough nut, isn't he? Though, if Lana is really his little princess, perhaps she winds him around her finger.' Like someone else I know, Mel thought resentfully of Bella but just said, 'So what time are you going out tonight, O Master?' If she made a joke of it, perhaps the whole thing would turn out to be as inconsequential as he pretended.

323

'Meeting her at eight at some pub in St Ives.'

'You'd better get a move on then. It's seven already.'

When he left, he kissed her lightly, but once he was over the threshold, Patrick didn't look back.

Mel drifted around the house and wondered what to do with herself while she counted the hours until his return.

Ten to eight. He'll be nearly there now.

Five to eight. He'll be finding somewhere to park. Patrick had left a T-shirt draped over the back of a chair in the kitchen. Mel cuddled it to her and breathed in the smell of him – earthy, slightly sweaty.

Eight. He'll be meeting her, unless she's late. Was Bella the sort who would be deliberately late? Mel thought she might be.

She tidied up, stuffed a great heap of clothes in the machine, did some ironing, taking particular care over anything of Patrick's. After that she tried to read a novel, but couldn't concentrate so she gave up. Switching on the television, she watched the first twenty minutes of a romantic comedy, but she'd seen it before and, anyway, the repartee didn't seem funny any more. Love going wrong and right again. Why should it be the subject of such amusement? She knew all about love going wrong – the feelings of rejection, desolation, the death of hope, the sense that the future has been taken away. There was nothing funny about any of it.

She slouched into the darkening hall, intending to make yet another cup of coffee. Or she might see if there was an open bottle of wine in the fridge.

But as she turned towards the kitchen, her eye was caught by a strange glow in the dark recesses of the hall and her heart gave a jolt. It only took a second or two for her to realise that Patrick must have left a light on in his study.

She took several steps down the corridor, telling herself she would just turn off the light and march straight back on her mission to the fridge, but when she looked into the doorway of the old estate office, she saw that the light was from Patrick's computer, which he had failed to shut down properly.

A little nagging voice inside her, that she tried very hard to shut out, started shouting at full volume. *Look at the emails, look at the emails!*

It would be wrong. She would hate it if Patrick turned on her machine and started going through her Inbox – saw those messages from Jake and jumped to the wrong conclusion. She cringed at the thought, whilst a priggish part of her stridently protested that there was nothing of blame in her correspondence.

But if there was something going on with Bella, really going on, she had to find out – didn't she? Her sanity was at stake.

She pressed a few buttons and she was in, clicking on his email Inbox, staring at the screen.

She scrolled up and down quickly. Every now and then was an email from Bella. In the last couple of weeks there had been five or six. She turned to the Sent box. There were as many responses from Patrick.

She sat down on the chair and started to read.

The final one, dating from several days ago said, *I don't know what to do, I really need to speak to you. Love, your Bellaxxx*

The one before said, *Your advice is good as always, but I can't decide. Can we meet in Cornwall next week?* So he had known that she was coming, even before the phone call two days ago.

Some way up the screen, at the beginning of the previous week, had come the email she had been dreading.

I'm going to tell Ed I can't be with him any more. We just don't see things the same way. I thought what he and I had was special, precious, but he doesn't take me seriously enough. Not the way you used to. And he's quite selfish. When he works late he doesn't think about me being on my own in the flat, and you know how I hate that. I wish I could see you, Patrick. I don't mean to mess you up all over again, but you're very comforting, you say all the right things and I just need you at the moment – a friend until I pull through.

How manipulative the woman was. Mel went down the list of Patrick's replies, heart in mouth. She read them all and then she sat dazed from the blow she had in effect inflicted upon herself.

The hours passed. Ten o'clock, eleven o'clock. At half-past eleven, she had had enough of sitting in the dark morning room, nursing glass after glass of wine, watching for car headlights to play across the wall.

She wouldn't hang around for Patrick. She wouldn't sleep here tonight, she'd go back to the cottage. Her own hidey-hole.

She was just locking the front door with a key Patrick had given her weeks ago, when his car purred into the drive. She stood on the steps as he parked, snapped off the headlights, and got out. The night was moonless, warm, the air still.

'Sorry I'm so late,' he called in the darkness. His voice sounded weary.

She said nothing, waited as he slammed the car door and stumbled up the steps.

'A good evening?' Her voice was precise, her words like shards of glass.

'No,' he said. 'Going back to the cottage? I'll walk with you.'

There was something flat about his tone. Alarm bells started to ring in her mind. She set off around the side of the building, picking out her way with the narrow torchbeam, aware of him struggling to keep up some way behind.

Outside the cottage, she scrabbled in her bag for her key but dropped the torch, which went out.

'Damn,' she said, and stood listening for Patrick, standing somewhere behind her in the opaque darkness. 'Just looking for the key.'

'Mel,' Patrick said, behind her. His voice still sounded odd. She froze.

'It's not fair. I have to tell you.'

'I know what you're going to say.'

'No, you don't.'

'Yes, I do, Patrick. You're going back to her, aren't you? She's given up the other bloke and wants you back. And like a great wuss you're going to do it.'

'I'm not going back to her, I'm not. I'm . . . confused, that's all. I need time to sort myself out.'

'Well, I'm not hanging around to see what happens. Can't you see through her, Patrick? Can't you? She's the sort who'll bleed you dry.'

'Don't talk about her like that. You make her sound like a kind of vampire.'

'My point exactly.'

'She needs me. She thinks she might have made a mistake in leaving me. We've still got things to work out.'

'And what about me? Don't I need you?'

'Not in the same way. You're a survivor, Mel. That's one of the things I love most about you. You're your own person.'

'Of course I'm a bloody survivor. That's what being grown up is all about. That doesn't mean I don't need you. I do.' Her voice cracked suddenly.

'Mel, I'm sorry, this is so difficult and I'm not putting it well. You wouldn't understand about Bella and me. I've known her so long. She's like a part of me. It's very hard to walk away from her.'

'Why? She's mucked you around so much.' *I read those emails,*

327

Mel wanted to say, but she didn't dare admit to it. Phrases from his responses drifted into her mind. He had tried to be strong: *I'm with someone else now, Bella . . . I want you to meet Mel . . . She's very special to me*. But Bella had been insistent. And now, it seemed, she had won.

'Patrick, I don't have the strength for this,' she said in the darkness, trying her hardest not to cry. 'I'm not going to wait for you to sort yourself out. I have my pride. It's her or me, you can't have both.'

'Mel, it's not as simple as that.'

'It is. Her or me. If you want to be with me, you mustn't see her again.'

'Mel, don't be silly, I can't do that. Not at the moment. Really, if you were to see her, she's very distressed. She's finished with Ed and—'

'She seemed fine yesterday.'

'She was putting up a front. She's good at that. But this evening she was able to let down her guard . . .'

'Patrick,' she broke in. 'We can go round in circles, but I've had enough tonight, I'm shattered. You don't want me to say something we will both regret.' She finally located the key and jiggled it into the lock. 'We'll talk about it tomorrow.' And she went inside and shut the door, leaned against it.

'Mel. *Mel*. Please.' He rattled the door. 'Don't be like that. Open the door, for God's sake. Mel, I love you.' He waited.

Inside, Mel slid down the door to the floor. After a long moment she heard his footsteps, uncertain, on the gritty path, and a curse, then silence.

She covered her face with her hands and cried in the stuffy darkness until she could cry no more. Then she crawled up the stairs and lay on her duvet, too exhausted even to undress. Seconds later she fell into a sleep like oblivion.

'I can't, I can't, don't make me.'

'Lie down, girl, sshh, I won't hurt you.'

'No, no, the baby, you'll hurt the baby.'

'Ah, the baby.'

He sighs; his body, huge and heavy, hangs over me, not like Charles at all – a stranger, this man, another country. Then he gives up, crushes my thigh as he rolls away. He struggles, panting in the darkness, then rests, the pulse of his blood pounds in the silence. I lie flat, still, willing myself invisible like a hare in the grass. An ocean lies between us, an ocean I do not wish to cross and he cannot. My husband. No, I cannot say it.

Aunt Dolly, shaking me. 'You've got to do it, girl. Take him. There's no choice, and you could do much worse.'

'I don't love him.'

'You can be kind. All the pretty talk in the world is no good if there's no kindness. And believe me, I know.' What happened to Mr Roberts? She never speaks of him, but before I can ask she rushes on, 'It would have come to nothing, Pearl. Even if Miss Elizabeth hadn't found out.'

'Miss Elizabeth?'

'Aye, it was her told the mistress. Who did you think?'

Not spying Miss Cecily, then. Miss Elizabeth, who wanted him too. Now we've both lost him.

Charles. My whole body aches for him. And now the tears come, slowly, silently at first, then faster, a torrent, the sobs racking my body, cries of anguish rising in my throat.

Mel couldn't breathe, struggled her way up towards the surface and awoke with a cry. It had been as though a great satanic beast lay on her chest, growling, its eyes glinting inches from her own.

Was it still there? She closed her eyes and pushed at it in panic – the bunched-up duvet unfurled and her sweltering body was free. She lay motionless, heart thudding, her skin prickling all over. Outside, thunder rumbled once more.

A cry. Someone was crying. Where? Was there someone else in the room? The darkness pressed in, mummifying her, smothering her very breath. Suddenly lightning flashed and she squeezed her eyes tight as the brooding hulks of furniture lit up around the room. The cry rose to a wail – inhuman, terrible.

Patrick! she screamed in her head. *Patrick, help me!* But he wasn't here. He'd gone away, far away. Like Charles. *Charles.* The crying rose to an unholy shriek. There was someone, something else in the bed. She could feel their heat beside her. Thunder crashed and lightning flickered on her closed eyelids. Don't open your eyes.

Charles.

Patrick.

Good Lord, deliver me, Good Lord, deliver me.

A sob rose in her throat, but was stifled by another sound. Whispering, pattering. Rain on the roof, tapping on the window, hissing through the trees. Gentle cooling blessed rain.

Gradually, the pressure of the hot darkness lightened. Outside, a bird began to tune up.

The ginger cat gave up yowling to come in and slunk off amongst the trees.

Inside, Mel lay sleepless in the old double bed, gripped by the certain knowledge of what she had to do.

Very early the next morning, exhausted and tearful, she tumbled all her possessions into cases and boxes, packed up the car and set off back to London. It was like driving down a tunnel into a deep black hole. Cornwall was where she had lost herself. She left without saying goodbye.

Chapter 33

'You can't switch courses without going through the appropriate channels, you must know that,' Mel told the arrogant-looking young man in the green fedora whose name was not on her register. 'Go and see Gina in the Enrolments Office as soon as the seminar's over and get the forms signed.'

And I suppose you *must* wear that awful hat in class, she was tempted to add, but didn't. She had long ago learned that commenting on student apparel was dangerous territory. Combating ringing mobile phones and private conversation in class was a more essential use of her energies, anyway.

'This handout describes the programme for the term.' And she handed a sheaf of paper headed '*Symbol and Psyche – the Origins of Surrealism*' to the intense young Asian woman on her left and waited as the twenty students passed the depleting pile from hand to hand. One boy's hair fell across his forehead just like Patrick's . . .

A dull pain gnawed at her stomach and for an instant her mind went blank. 'Are you all right, miss?' asked a pale girl who handed back the spare sheets. Mel looked up. Twenty pairs of eyes were staring at her.

'Yes, just a headache. Now if you'll look at next week's session . . .' *Keep talking. It was all right when she was talking.*

It was the first day of the autumn term.

'Are you sure you should be going in?' Chrissie had said on the phone last night. 'Can't that Rowena person do it instead?'

'I refuse to give her the pleasure,' Mel said. 'Anyway, I told you, it'll be good for me. Get me back into the routine.'

'Well, if you're sure . . .' Chrissie said doubtfully. 'But I bet the doctor would sign a sick note for you without any hesitation.'

'I've had enough of doctors,' said Mel.

She could hardly remember the journey back from Cornwall, six weeks ago, just that she had pitched up at Rob and Chrissie's late at night, having somehow made her way through the terrible August traffic, denting the front of the car badly in a lapse of concentration just outside Exeter. She hadn't been injured, but she was wild-eyed and quivering by the time she reached Islington and when Rob hauled her off the doorstep and half-carried her to the living-room sofa, she collapsed into its yoghurt-and-chocolate-stained cushions and burst into hysterical sobs.

Neither Chrissie nor Rob could get out of her what was the matter. Rob went to find the car to bring in her luggage and to check she was legally parked, fingering the dented bonnet in puzzlement. Chrissie finally coaxed Mel to drink some sugary tea and they put her to bed in the small guest room.

In the morning they couldn't wake her, and when she finally came downstairs mid-morning, she still wouldn't say a word, but sat staring into the distance, hardly noticing Rory who had climbed into her lap.

'Hello, Aunty Mel. You look sad today.'

'She's not very well, Rory,' said Chrissie, disentangling him. Mel merely slumped over the table, still dressed in yesterday's clothes.

Chrissie rang their brother William for help, but could only reach his secretary. On the basis of her advice, however, Chrissie soon afterwards contacted her own GP.

'It's a natural reaction to too much psychological stress,' the doctor told Chrissie. 'The mind shuts down for a bit to distance itself. We'll leave it a day or two and see how she is.'

Then she rang Patrick.

Chrissie thought over their conversation.

'She just took off,' he said. 'We'd had . . . an argument, you see. I expect she's told you.'

'She's told me nothing,' snapped Chrissie. 'She hasn't said one word since she got here. If you've dumped her, and so soon after Jake . . .'

'I didn't dump her, as you so sweetly put it. It wasn't like that. She didn't like me seeing—'

'What?' said Chrissie, smelling a rat.

'Bella came down,' Patrick said shortly.

'Ah. And Mel got the wrong idea. Or was it the right one? Patrick, if you've mucked her about, I'll kill you, you know.'

'It really wasn't like that, Chrissie. I can't explain exactly. It's just . . . a misunderstanding. Chrissie – I want to speak to her. I rang her flat. I hadn't realised she was with you – I should have thought. Can I come up?'

'Don't think there's a lot of point at the moment, Patrick. I'll let you know when she's a bit better.'

When she put down the phone, Chrissie's hand was shaking. The bastard. How could he have done this to her little sister, he of all people? Chrissie always thought of Mel as 'little', had always looked after her. And she'd look after her now. And that meant keeping Patrick out of Mel's way if necessary. She felt no hesitation about doing that.

She had explained all this to the doctor in a low voice when he had arrived.

'She's been recovering from our mother's death, and from the break-up of her relationship. She was on the rebound, really, going out with this old friend of mine, and she's obviously gone in too deep.'

The doctor nodded as though he'd heard it all before, many times, but his expression was compassionate.

'I think you'll find she will be all right,' he said, 'but she must have someone with her. Can she stay here with you?'

'Yes, of course. I've rung up work. They'll let me have the time off.'

On the second day, Mel slept late again. She ate half a piece of toast and a chocolate biscuit, but her eyes showed she was still far away, somewhere deep inside herself. She slept on and off most of the day, Rory watching her anxiously.

Patrick rang again, but Chrissie was short with him, told him she'd call when she had some news.

On the third day, Mel was still tired, but she watched television for short stretches, ate a light meal and mouthed words like, 'Yes,' and, 'Thanks,' in answer to Chrissie's enquiries. She smiled at Rory when he chatted to her about his day. Patrick rang again and had a long talk with Rob. When Chrissie took the receiver she advised Patrick not to ring again for the moment – it would only make things worse. She decided not to tell Mel about the phone calls for the time being. Mention of Patrick seemed to send Mel deeper inside herself.

The following afternoon, Mel sat down at the table and helped Rory draw tigers. These he painted with gloopy black and orange paint that ran, making him stamp his foot with rage.

Mel painted her own picture, a beautiful garden with smiling flowers and small shy animals. Rory, enchanted, forgot his bad mood.

Chrissie hugged her, elated that she seemed to be returning to the world.

But this proved only the beginning. It was a slow recovery, punctuated by long periods of depression, days when unexplained pain shot through her body and her head ached.

Grief, the doctor said.

Later, as the black periods shrank in length and intensity she took to walking the streets, covering miles in a day, exhausting herself in her efforts to channel all her energies into physical exercise so that she wouldn't have to think.

By the beginning of September, three weeks after she had arrived, Mel was a thinner, paler version of her normal self, but she was herself again. Aimee had come to supper, and after they had finished eating Mel said, 'It's time to go home again.'

'Are you sure?' said Chrissie. 'You're welcome to stay, you know.'

'Absolutely,' added Rob, putting his arm around the back of her chair. 'We love having you.'

'I'll keep an eye on her,' said Aimee. She only lived a couple of streets away from Mel. 'She can always stay with me if she feels like it.'

It was Aimee who drove Mel back to Clapham the following evening, in Mel's car, now mended after Rob had haggled with the insurance company and the garage.

She helped Mel in with her luggage and left her wandering around her garden wilderness while she went down to the corner shop for supplies. When she returned it was to find Cara from upstairs perched on the sofa chattering away while Mel sat at the table sorting the mound of post Cara had brought with her.

'And he came two, maybe three times,' Cara was saying, waving her hands around, her eyes shining with the drama.

'Who, Cara?' said Mel urgently, looking up from her search for any interesting post amidst the bills and the mail shots. She had quickly established there was nothing from Patrick. But had she really expected anything? After all, it seemed that all the time she had been unwell, he had never rung once. But now hope was momentarily revived. 'Who came?'

'Your man, Jake, ringing on the doorbell,' squealed Cara. 'Who else? How many men do you have?'

'None, at the moment,' said Mel, forlorn. 'What did you tell him?'

'That you were away in Paris, staying with your French lover, what else?'

Mel rolled her eyes. Just the sort of thing the excitable Cara might indeed have said. 'Thanks for dealing with the post, anyway. Hope it hasn't been a pain.'

'No, no. Good thing your sister rang to tell me where you were or, whoosh, another lot of letters would have flown away to your holiday place.'

'It wasn't a holiday, Cara,' said Mel. 'But thanks. I'm really grateful.'

'So, Jake has been looking for you!' said Aimee, after Cara had left. 'Have you been in touch, you naughty girl? Come on, spill the beans.'

Mel explained about Jake's book deal but said she hadn't had any communication with him since. 'Mind you, I haven't looked at my emails for ages.'

While Aimee made them both some tea Mel turned on her laptop and found that Jake had, in fact, emailed her twice. *I thought we could meet for that drink before term started*, he had written in the first message, then, *Sounds stupid, but I've lost your mobile number. In fact, I've lost my mobile. Ridiculous, isn't it, how much your life depends on a small hunk of metal.*

'He wants to meet up,' she told Aimee.

'Mel.' Worry made Aimee's small pretty face crease up like a King Charles Spaniel's. 'Be careful, won't you?'

'Yeah, sure.' Her voice sounded flat, and Aimee put out her hand and touched Mel's arm.

'It's not him you're thinking about, is it?'

'No,' said Mel, and gazed out of the window to where a plastic carrier bag stuck flapping in a dead tree in the garden of the dilapidated house opposite.

Aimee sighed.

'Perhaps I should contact him,' Mel whispered, almost to herself, then she shivered, remembering Bella, remembering that last night. 'No. I don't think I can. I mustn't.' The plastic carrier bag flapped frantically, as though trying to break free from the tree.

'Mel.' Aimee's face was an unreadable mix of emotions. 'It's probably not the moment, but there's something I want to tell you.'

'What?' She felt her own smile grow, a pale reflection of the grin that split Aimee's face. 'It's Stuart, isn't it? Come on, tell me everything, you dark horse.'

'I didn't like to. Not with you . . .'

'Oh, never mind about that. I need cheering up. Tell me. You're getting married, aren't you?'

Aimee's smile faltered. 'He's asked me, yes.'

'And what have you said?'

'That I want to say yes, but—'

'But what? I thought you were keen.'

'I am, I really am, but . . . well, Callum doesn't like the idea. I don't blame him really. It's not all that long ago since his mum left, and now his dad wants to marry his teacher. *Bleaugh.*'

Mel laughed at Aimee's impression of a disgusted teenager.

'But if Callum wasn't in the equation, would you want to marry Stuart?'

'Yes, I would. He and Maria, his wife, only stayed together for so long because of Callum. Then she found someone else, so that's why they broke up in the end. It's all surprisingly friendly.'

'Does Callum see his mother?'

'Oh yes, but he didn't like her new bloke. That's why he stayed with his dad.'

'And now that's changing, too. I see. Poor boy.'

'What should I do?'

'I don't know. Stick it out. Perhaps it's a question of Callum getting used to you.'

'I suppose that's what I think. But what happens if he doesn't?'

They were silent for a moment.

'Come on,' said Aimee, leaping up and gathering up the mugs. 'You can't stay here – I've decided. I'm due at Stuart's for supper. You're coming, too, and then you and I, we'll go and stay at mine. No arguments.'

Twelve o'clock and the students swirled around Mel like the tide around a rock. Not that she felt very rocklike at the moment, more like a pebble rolled over and over by the current. Somehow she had taught her first seminar since March, and it had gone well, she had detected their interest. But now the black feeling swelled in her again, and she picked up the rag to wipe the whiteboard as though it weighed pounds.

Everything had changed, it seemed to Mel, as she had walked into the college last week. David's friendly face had gone. She had missed his retirement party in the summer. In his place was

John O'Hagen, brisk, militant, too ready to exercise his new found power by making unnecessary changes, the more long-standing members of Faculty grumbled. The second change was that a full-time post had been created for Rowena.

'Student numbers are up. The Art History courses are very popular,' was how John put it to Mel a few days ago.

'Glad to see all the work I've put in over the last few years has paid off,' she pointed out. 'But you might have consulted me.'

'You weren't here,' he retorted.

'I was an email away,' she snapped, but John's attention span was short.

'I'm sorry if you feel that,' he said, getting up to indicate the interview was over, 'but what's done is done and I'm sure we'll all be glad of Rowena's help. She has many useful suggestions.'

Mel was thinking over this conversation as she finished wiping the board.

'Got a moment?' A head poked around the door: a halo of blonde curls held back by an Alice band with a big tartan bow. Rowena.

'Mel, how did the seminar go? You look shattered, dear.' Rowena's light voice with its sibilant sounds could only be called simpering. And that bow, Mel loathed it. All right on a ten-year-old girl, but . . . The worst thing was that her innocent looks completely belied her poisonous nature.

'It was fine, thank you, Rowena.'

'Good. I've just been to see John. I thought I'd share these with you.' She passed a couple of printed emails over to Mel. 'I have some ideas, you see, about how we could improve the ways these seminars are taught.'

Annoyance lashed tiredly inside Mel. She glanced down at the emails. *Student evaluations agree . . . Reshape . . . new technology . . . could be more inspiring . . .* The phrases leaped to her eyes.

'Why didn't you discuss this with me?' she said to Rowena coolly.

'Well, that's what I'm doing now,' said Rowena, with a stagy act of being stung. 'John thought you should see them.'

Suddenly, Mel didn't care about treading softly.

'Rowena, I'm sure you're acting for the best, but let me be frank. I have been here teaching these courses for ten years. You have been here for precisely five minutes.'

'As you know, I was covering your classes when you were off a couple of years ago. When your mother—'

'But that hardly gives you the right to go behind my back and try to change everything.'

'I'm sorry, I didn't think you would see it like that. I was only trying to help.'

'Well, don't.' She sighed, then said, 'It's not that I'm against the idea of change. I suppose we'd better sit down together sometime, but your ideas are not as straightforward as you think. You need to know the background.'

And the last thing I need is you and John caballing behind my back, she thought fiercely as she grabbed her bags, nodded to Rowena and marched out. She walked down the corridor, seeing no one and nothing, unlocked her office door, slipped inside and shut it behind her. She dropped onto her sofa, glad to have a few moments to herself.

Almost at once there came a knock on the door. 'Hello,' she called wearily and the door opened. It was Jake.

He seemed to fill the doorway, his electro-magnetic aura as highly charged as ever. He had grown his blond hair and wore it neatly cut, brushed back, but otherwise he was just the same.

Placing his forearms on each side of the doorway like the chained Samson about to push apart the pillars of the Temple, he said in a mock American accent, 'Welcome back, Miss Elusive. How've you been?'

Mel stood up and crossed her arms, regarding him steadily. 'I've been busy,' she said.

'Got time for that drink this evening?' he said, and she was amazed at the ease with which he asked, as though they were back at the beginning of their courtship rather than exhuming the decayed remains.

'No,' she said shortly. 'I've a lecture to prepare tonight.' Which was true up to a point, but the lecture was already prepared – all she had to do was replace a couple of slides on the Powerpoint presentation since she had found better examples.

Jake tapped the doorway impatiently and glanced at his watch. 'Tomorrow then. Wednesday – no, busy Wednesday, I think. Thursday?'

In the end she agreed to Thursday.

'A drink,' she told him, fixing stern eyes upon him. 'To celebrate your book deal.'

He looked slightly disconcerted, then said uneasily, 'Sure. See you then,' and moved away. Getting up to shut the door, she watched him prowl away down the corridor, like a graceful leopard.

It was a warm September evening, so she ate a paltry supper of scrambled eggs and beans on the last crust of bread and went out to scrutinise the garden. Rowena, Green Fedora, Jake. The irritations of the day whirled round her head. Hard work was the remedy.

It was satisfying taking out her feelings by ripping at the tangles of weeds, hacking back shrubs. After a while she tuned in to the variety of sound around her – the thud-thud of distant music, a man and a woman next door over the fence arguing in some harsh language she didn't recognise, a football crashing against wood and concrete, the shriek of a drill on brick or stone in some house across the way.

All so different from the peaceful garden at Merryn and yet, as she grew calmer, she noticed the twittering of a blackbird, the primitive smell of the earth, the sharp stink of sap. All served to take her right back to Lamorna.

It was hard not to think about Patrick. In truth, she never stopped, though she worried sometimes that her body's memories were mixing him up with Jake. The times, for instance, when she awoke in her wide bed and reached out, half-expecting there to be someone beside her: was it Patrick or Jake she was looking for? When she arrived home, part of her wouldn't have been surprised to find that her flat door wasn't double-locked, that there was someone waiting to welcome her. Who?

But when she lay awake at nights, hugging a pillow, waiting for sleep to overcome her, it was Patrick she imagined close to her, kissing her, his particular smell of wool and spearmint toothpaste that flooded her mind and caused her tears to flow. And she would wonder again why he had never written, never phoned, never come to find her, then decided she knew why, really. *I must get over it, over it*, she would tell herself fiercely.

And now she allowed her mind to drift on to Jake.

Thinking of him confused her. Jake, Patrick, Patrick, Jake. As one drifted out of focus, the other clarified in her mind.

As twilight deepened, she put away her tools and stamped down the culled weeds to squash them into a bin bag which she tied up and set aside for recycling. When she went inside, the phone was ringing. It was her father.

'Dad? Is everything all right?' She hadn't heard from him since the French postcard.

'Mmm? Yes, yes, of course. Hadn't spoken to you for a while, so I thought I'd ring and see how you are. Will said you'd been unwell.'

Master of the understatement, her father.

'A rather stressful summer,' she admitted, knowing he wouldn't want the messy details. 'But I'm fine now.'

'Good, good,' said her father. 'I'm coming to London next week for a conference,' he went on. 'Thought we might have dinner one night.'

'All right. When?'

'Tuesday?'

'Yes,' she said, flicking through her diary, seeing with a little jolt, Jake's name scrawled in for this coming Thursday.

'I'll ring you when I've booked somewhere,' he said.

'Fine. How's Stella?' she asked politely. She liked her poised, carefully coiffed stepmother, but had never really got to know her well.

'Stell? Fine, fine, busy with some blasted charity ball we have to go to this weekend. House is full of boxes of stuff and the telephone doesn't stop ringing with women wittering on about flower arrangements. I'm a stranger in my own home.'

Well, no surprise there, said Mel to herself as she put down the phone. He never was around much for anyone. What might he be wanting to see her for now?

Chapter 34

'There's a new place opened near the tube station,' said Jake as he collected her from her office at six o'clock on Thursday. 'If you don't mind the walk.' They glanced out of the window to see grey London drizzle and Mel reached for her ancient umbrella.

The wine bar was already filling up with groups of young people from local offices but Jake effortlessly staked a table and signalled to a waitress who came over at once. Mel had noticed the girl's eyes fall on Jake from the moment they walked in.

Had he always fussed so much over the wine list, she wondered, sitting back and letting him argue the relative merits of the St Remy over the house Cabernet Sauvignon. Patrick had always studied the list quickly and made a snap decision. In the end she broke in, saying, 'I should really be getting this as it's a celebration,' and ended the discussion by ordering champagne.

'It's really brilliant about your book deal,' she said, after the waitress brought over the bottle in an ice-bucket, with two flutes. 'Here's to you,' and they clinked glasses.

'And to you, too,' said Jake quietly, engaging her eye. 'Your return to the real world. I've missed you, you know.'

Mel swallowed a great gulp of champagne and the bubbles

went up her nose. Coughing and spluttering, it was a while before she recovered.

'Sorry,' she said, taking the wad of rough paper serviettes he offered her. She remembered Patrick's soft handkerchief, which he lent her the first time they met, and a shaft of misery pierced her heart.

'Well, I have missed you,' Jake said, amused and just slightly petulant. 'At least I still have a dramatic effect on you.' He made a theatrical gesture.

'Good,' she said vaguely, feeling some answer was called for, then hastily added, 'Tell me about the book. When did you get the idea?'

'It was down to Sophie, actually,' he said, sitting back in the chair. 'She's a smart girl. She'd been having lunch with a publisher who had bemoaned the fact that publishing had been taken over by the *Da Vinci Code* phenomenon, and saying what a pity it was that there wasn't a British author capable of that kind of thriller-writing. Anyway, this bloke had turned down *Painting for Pleasure* but wanted to see more of my work and Sophie suddenly had an idea. She suggested I try out a synopsis. I had to concentrate on storytelling, she said, and just write the thing. I was a bit unsure about it to start with, I have to say, but then I picked up a copy of the Dan Brown on the way home and decided I could do better. So I bit the bullet and had a go. *Et voilà!*'

'Well, I hope you achieve even half of Dan Brown's sales,' Mel said jokingly, and he laughed, too, but there was a look in his eyes that made her think she had touched a nerve. Once ambitious for literary fame, he was now after the bestseller lists.

'There have been one or two bitchy comments at the college, but, hell. If this first book works out, I won't be hanging around there, I can tell you.'

'Mmm, that was going to be my next question,' Mel said.

'How's your own writing going?' For once Jake sounded genuinely interested in her successes and breathed, 'Oh, well done,' when she told him she had only one chapter left to write.

He lifted the champagne bottle out of the bucket and refreshed their glasses with an elegant flourish, then leaned back in his chair and looked at Mel meaningfully. 'God, it is good to see you again.' He raked his fingers through his hair, shaking his head slightly. She saw him catch his reflection for a microsecond in a mirror on the wall.

'It's lovely seeing you,' Mel told him lightly. He was as charming and energising as ever, and she felt warmed by his attention. But it was as though passing time had laid a patina of objectivity between them, like a plate of thin glass separating her from her feelings about him. What an odd thought, but there wasn't time to analyse it now.

'How are the girls?' she asked. 'And Helen?'

Did she imagine the moment's hesitation before he answered?

'Great, the girls are just great. Anna's started horse-riding. I have to take her down to Surrey every Saturday to watch her trot round in circles. She's so grown up. And Freya does ballet now.'

'And Helen?'

'Ah yes, well, you haven't heard about the wonderful Igor, have you?'

'Igor? Is this the boyfriend?'

'Certainly is. Straight off the Russian Steppes. Or Moscow, anyway.'

'How did she meet him?'

'At a kids' party, can you believe it. He has a little girl, too.'

He looked a little sad suddenly, and Mel said, 'Are you jealous, Jake? That Helen has someone, I mean?'

'I don't know. It's just – odd. Seeing her with another man.'

But you've had other women, she thought. How must that have been for her?

'And the girls like him?' she asked.

'Oh yes.' And now he did sound wan.

'And what about you?' she said. 'Do you . . . have anyone?'

'No, since you ask,' he said, examining his fingernails. Then he looked right at her. 'I haven't, not really, since you.'

How many one-night stands did the words 'not really' encompass, she wondered. But she felt flattered all the same.

'You're a hard act to follow, Melanie Pentreath.'

She laughed and waited for him to ask the same question of her, but he didn't and she felt unaccountably annoyed. Didn't he expect her to attract anyone else?

'I . . . did meet someone. In Cornwall. But it didn't work out,' she said hurriedly.

'You're . . . not together now?' he asked, leaning forwards and staring at her intently.

'No.'

His sigh, as he sat back in his chair again, sounded satisfied. He appeared to expand, relax. 'Another?' His fingers closed around the neck of the bottle.

'No,' she said, shaking her head. 'My head's spinning already.'

'Something to eat, then?'

'No, Jake, thanks. I ought to get home now.'

When they stepped outside, it was still raining slightly. He waited as she put up her umbrella, then said, 'I'll walk you home.'

'No, really, Jake, I'll be fine.'

'It'll be no trouble.'

'Jake . . .'

His shoulders slumped slightly.

'It's been lovely seeing you,' she said, holding the umbrella over both of them, watching a raindrop wend its way down his cheek. He reached out and pushed back a lock of her hair, his eyes scanning her face. He looked hopeful, vulnerable, and part of her very much wanted to let him lean forward and kiss her. To feel safe again. But it felt wrong. There was too much to clear out of the way first, and she didn't know where to start. What she was determined about was that they didn't end up jumping into bed together merely because they were both lonely and had had too much to drink, getting stuck once more in a groove of failed expectations.

'Can I see you again?' he asked, shy as a boy. 'Like this, I mean – I know I'll see you at work tomorrow.'

She laughed. 'I expect so.' He brushed her cheek quickly with warm lips and was gone. She watched him striding away between the puddles to the tube station. His trousers, she noticed, strangely touched by the fact, were just slightly too short.

She walked home slowly, trying to puzzle out her feelings. Was she still attracted to Jake? Yes, emphatically yes. So why did she feel herself holding back? Was it because of Patrick? She supposed it was. She still felt dull, dead inside, like a garden in December.

Chapter 35

On Friday, her father rang to say that he had booked a table at a French restaurant in Covent Garden for their dinner the following Tuesday.

It was exactly the sort of place he would choose, Mel observed as she put down the phone. Authentic French food cooked by an authentic French chef and served by authentic French staff. No doubt, during the evening, there would be heated discussion with the authentic French *patron* – in her father's atrocious French, of course – about some aspect of the menu. She cringed inwardly.

How rare it was ever to be able to see her father on her own ground and to talk to him honestly about things that mattered to her. But what she wanted to say were deep concerns of the heart, and the irony was that while her father was an expert at all aspects of the physical organ, he steered clear of its emotional associations.

Emerging from Leicester Square tube at 7.30 p.m. on Tuesday evening, she made her way slowly up to the restaurant, wandering into bookshops on the way. Her mind was not on books, however. She was going over the lines she planned to say.

'Dad, why did you leave Mum on her own with three small

children all those years ago?' That was one she had tried asking in various ways from time to time. And the answer had always been? A cold one. As though the end of their marriage was like a company demerger.

'Your mother and I found we didn't suit each other, it's as simple as that. We had grown up together, but we both changed, came to have different aims in life.'

Which in her father's case had not included the burden of day-to-day responsibility for three children. It was interesting that he and Stella had never had children – and not, Mel was sure, since Stella had in genteel fashion hinted to her once, because they had not been able to. It was the intimacy, the constant barrage on his emotional equilibrium, the messiness of children from which, in the end, he had probably fled.

If she and William and Chrissie were with him and any of them started bickering, pinching one another or calling each other names, their father would simply walk away. It was so different from the way their mother would deal with their squabbles, by jollying them along, joining in the argument, helping them work their way through their differences.

Five to eight. She put down the book of Egon Schiele nudes she had been flicking through without really taking in the extraordinary power of the drawings, and hurried out of the shop. It was raining again, and she had to dodge into the road to elude the umbrellas of the early-evening crowds around the theatres. She walked quickly up Upper St Martin's Lane, reaching the restaurant exactly at eight.

As she pushed open the door she could see that her father, predictably punctual, was already seated in one of the best tables near the window. There was something rather grand, patrician, about him, she thought, with an unexpected rush of admiration. His long body gave him the false effect of height when he was sitting, an effect exaggerated by his large face with its high forehead and the wing of thick grey hair that belied his seventy years.

He was wearing a formal evening suit and Mel was relieved that she had chosen her black jersey dress to wear with a soft silver scarf and had taken the trouble to pin up her hair.

'Hello, Dad.' He looked up quickly over the top of his glasses, then unhooked the spectacles from his ears and stood up in an awkward movement that caused the magazine he was reading – it was *The Economist*, she could see – to shoot to the floor.

'Mel, dear, you look beautiful.'

It was his vulnerability that stabbed her. She hadn't seen him for – what – eight or nine months, and he seemed less steady somehow. He kissed her quickly on the cheek, patting her shoulder, then sat down carefully. Yet by the way he nodded curtly at the waitress who rescued his magazine and ordered Mel a gin-and-tonic, she saw that none of his presence, his authority, was gone.

'I will have *les escargots*,' he said to the waitress imperiously when she came again later to take their order. '*Soupe à l'oignon* for my daughter here, and then *Suprème de Poulette*, and I'll have the *Bar Cuit à la Vapeur Tartare d'Huitre*, if you please.'

He frowned over the wine list, deciding on a Bordeaux, and sat back in his chair to answer Mel's question about his business in London. It turned out to be a conference at which he was merely an observer, since he had now been retired from surgery for several years.

'And what have you been up to? he asked in turn. 'Gather you've been in Cornwall. Didn't look up Gillian in Bodmin, did you?'

'No, I suppose I ought to have done.' Gillian was her father's elderly cousin, and Mel felt a rush of remorse, having completely forgotten the woman's existence, though Bodmin was the other side of the county from Lamorna. 'I was writing, in fact. And gardening. Helping restore an old garden.' She wondered what it looked like now. Had Patrick continued the work without her? Would the leaves be turning now, the beech trees scattering nuts across the grass and the blackberries ripe? And how was Carrie, and Matt and Irina and Lana? She felt sad that she had forgotten them so easily, so wrapped up had she been in her own problems.

'So I heard from Chrissie yesterday,' her father went on. 'She said you hadn't been at all well lately. I'm most sorry to hear that – though you look all right to me. Between you and me, your sister does over-dramatise.'

'What else did she say?' asked Mel, narrowing her eyes.

Their first courses arrived at this point and her father became taken up with fussing with the snail scoops and summoning the bread-basket.

'So, how are you now?' he said, peering at her before sticking his special fork into the largest snail and bathing his rubbery prize in garlic butter. 'Come to think of it, you do look a little, well, peaky. Mmm, this is really very good. How is the soup?'

'Everything's fine, Dad,' Mel said shortly, and allowed him to think that she had answered both questions with the word. But this time, to her surprise, he didn't let the matter slip by.

'Chrissie said it was to do with a man,' he went on, glaring at her sharply over his spectacles before returning his attention to his dinner. He trapped the second shell and worried at its occupant with his fork. 'That's a pity. You haven't had much luck on that front recently, I think.'

He chewed slowly, looking straight at her for a moment, and she felt like the snail, prodded, trapped and chewed up. She froze, wondering what to say next. Did he really expect her to confide in him?

'Don't let them all go by.' What was he mumbling? She watched as he caught the next shell, then he put down his fork and, taking off his spectacles, rubbed the lenses furiously with his napkin. 'Mustn't let my example ruin things for you,' he said, gazing at the results, his eyes small and pale, defenceless without them. 'I worry, you know. That it has.'

Mel stared down into her bowl. The soaking lumps of bread looked unappetising now, the smell of onion and garlic was making her stomach turn.

'Is that what you believe?' she said thickly, looking up. 'That because you left, I expect men to leave, that I let them leave? It's not my fault that things don't work out, you know.'

Isn't it? A voice in her head hammered out. Her father's voice.

'Cod psychology.' Her father shook his head, then his voice softened. 'Still, I'm not too much of a fuddy-duddy to know these things can have an effect.' He snared the last snail, put it quickly in his mouth, chewed, swallowed and then dabbed at his mouth with the edge of his napkin.

'Why did it not work out with Mum, Dad?' she burst out. 'I've never really understood. Was it because of . . . us?' She thought of Jake, suddenly, leaving Anna and Freya. 'Did having children change things with Mum?'

Her father appeared to think about this and said finally, 'It came down to passion, it's as simple as that. I loved your mother very much, but then I saw Stella and I knew she was the real thing. I've never wanted anyone else since.' He looked at her and his pale-blue eyes glowed with unusual intensity. 'I had to have her. I knew it meant leaving you all, I knew it would hurt you, hurt your mother, but at the time I couldn't do anything else. It was a lover's pure selfishness, I realised that later. Everything else receded in the light of Stella and me.

"The world well lost for love", isn't that what the great lovers say?'

It was the longest speech and the most revealing he had ever made to her. His words struck her right in the heart.

'And so you had Stella,' said Mel, pushing her soup away. 'You had her and you lost us. And Mum.'

'I did lose you, I saw that very soon.' The waitress came to take away their plates, looking disapprovingly at Mel's rejection of the food.

'I felt guilty for a long, long time. I didn't want to have any more children, and fortunately, Stella felt that way, too. But now, I think she regrets it. Well, we make choices, don't we? And we have to live with them. But that's what I mean about you.'

'What, Dad? What do you mean?'

'That you must make your own decisions, paddle your own canoe, as they say. Don't let what I did affect you. I'm an old buffer now who's made a lot of mistakes and undoubtedly caused pain. But I won't have you blaming me for your own choices, I can tell you. None of that therapy rubbish. You're responsible for your own decisions in life.'

'Well thanks, Dad, that's nice to know.' Mel's voice cracked. 'But strangely, it's not that easy. Maybe you're right. You've taught me that men leave and that's what I've found in life. Men. Leave. End of story. Why's it *my* fault?'

His eyes glittered. He shoved his napkin on the table. 'That's rubbish,' he said. 'Look at Chrissie. She's all right with that Rob chap, who's nice enough. Will's happy with Sandra. You've got to take your chance – and don't go expecting perfection. You won't find it. Choose someone you really love and stick at 'em.'

'Like you and Mum?' Mel said in a small tight voice.

'Like Stella and me,' he corrected.

What did that mean for her? Jake or Patrick? Patrick or Jake?

The waitress brought their main courses and for a while, they ate in silence, Mel suddenly hungry, anxious to fill herself with hot, comforting food.

Her father asked her about her book, and her teaching, talked about an art exhibition he and Stella had visited in Birmingham, described a recent outing to London Zoo with Chrissie's children. He sounded a doting grandfather and Mel was surprised to understand suddenly that he would be there when she, too, had children – if that were ever to happen.

Later, outside the restaurant, as they parted – he to return to his hotel in Bloomsbury and she to the tube home – he hugged her and kissed her forehead, and again she was aware of his physical unsteadiness.

'My little Melanie,' he said, and patted her arm. 'Always my little Melanie.'

'Oh Dad,' she said, sighing, her anger at his lack of tact this evening tempered by compassion. 'Wait, there's a cab. I can't have you walking all that way at this hour.' The taxi stopped and, after some grumbling about being treated like an old man, he climbed in. She shut the door and waved as it moved off into the dark, leaving her standing alone.

Chapter 36

'Mmm, you smell gorgeous.' Jake's kiss hello lingered and she felt the shock of an invasion as his hand brushed lightly over her hip. She thrust the bottle she had brought firmly into his hands and stepped away, busying herself removing her jacket. He got the hint, standing back for her to enter the living room.

Jake's flat, a two-bedroomed, first-floor apartment in a gated development in Kennington, looked exactly how Mel remembered it, but tidier. As he went to check the progress of his lasagne, she sipped white wine so cold the glass misted over, and surveyed the books and ornaments on the white shelves that covered two of the walls of the living area. The large black and white studio poster of Anna and Freya leaping in the air, now hanging over the fireplace, was new, so was the pile of hardback thrillers under the window.

She was touched to see the two photographs of herself still on display, albeit in new places – had he left them there since February, or had he whipped them out of the store cupboard for her visit? She was horrified at her cynicism, but soothed herself that it was natural to feel wary.

These last few weeks it had been as though he was courting her all over again. They had revisited the wine bar where, this time, they had eaten. Then she had accompanied him to a book launch at Kensington Roof Garden, where he had tactfully introduced her to people as his 'friend'.

If nothing else, the party had proved useful because she had been introduced to a literary agent who had been most interested to hear about her book and had given her his card. 'In case I can be of use with future projects,' he said.

On this, as at all their meetings, Jake had been charming, attentive, but not overly so, his kisses of greeting tender rather than passionate. Until tonight. Friday-night dinner at his flat. Already the atmosphere felt charged with seduction.

The latest Kate Bush album, which he could only have bought because he knew she liked it, was playing in the background. The magazines and mounds of paper usually piled up around the room had mysteriously vanished as had, she noticed when she used the unusually pristine bathroom, any evidence of dirty washing or shaving scum round the basin, both matters that had caused bickering in the past. A brand new cake of soap lay in the dish and the hand towel – a hand towel? When had he acquired a hand towel? – hung lopsidedly in the metal loop by the shower.

A peep through Jake's bedroom door on the way back from the bathroom revealed a newly-made bed instead of the usual jumble of duvet and pillows . . .

'It's ready to eat now!' he called through from the kitchen.

She took her wine and walked through. And stopped to stare. The small table was set with a cloth, napkins, candles, a small jam jar of freesias. She smiled, eyebrows raised, and met his eyes, where he stood holding a chair back for her. For a moment he glanced away, sheepish, but then he stepped over to her and took her into his arms.

His kiss was like the unleashing of a floodgate of passion in her. She was startled by the intensity of her response. His hands were everywhere, stroking, rubbing, squeezing, until her whole body was on fire and tears leaked from her eyes.

'Oh God, Mel,' he growled in her ear, and his lips were on her hair, her face, her neck, and his body pressed against her.

It was all as she remembered – the way he raked his fingers through her hair, massaging her scalp, and she waited for the butterfly kisses on her eyelids that she loved, but he didn't do that and then she realised with a little shock that that was Patrick, not Jake. *Patrick*. She thrust the thought from her and kissed him back intensely.

'C'mon,' he said, pulling her none too gently through the doorway.

'But the food . . .' she protested.

'Can wait. I can't.' And he pushed her onto the sofa and moved on top of her, so his hardness dug painfully against her pelvis. His fingers were on her, then he was fumbling with his clothes and then suddenly alarm bells went off in her head and she panicked.

'No,' she said. 'No.' And went rigid.

He froze. 'What?' he said. 'What's wrong?'

She pushed at him until he rolled off her and fell onto the floor.

'Christ,' he said heavily, shifting around. 'I'm sorry. I thought you wanted to. What on earth's the matter?'

'I don't know,' she whispered, her forearm over her eyes, not wishing even to look at him. 'I just don't know.'

Jake ate his portion of cold lasagne, but Mel hardly touched hers; the painful lump of emotion in her throat prevented her swallowing anything.

'I suppose I'm not ready,' she said in a quivering voice.

'No, clearly not. I'm sorry,' he said gruffly.

Anger shot through her. 'I can't just take up where we left off, Jake,' she said, glaring at him. 'I don't want to go through the same thing again, to get hurt like last time. It's not the same now. There are things to talk about . . .'

'I know, I know,' he said, putting down his fork. 'But it's different now, for me. It's all clearer. Now the future's sorted out I feel we could make things work. Get that house together. Maybe even . . .' his voice failed for a moment then he muttered '. . . think about a family. One kid might not be too bad.' He laughed nervously.

Mel studied him, astonished, trying to make sense of what he was saying. A year ago, she would have thrown her arms around him or danced a jig on the table. But now, now, she just felt tired, broken inside.

Jake was still talking. 'Seeing Helen,' he went on, 'with her new man – you were right, it's made me think. It's time I moved on, got settled. And I've missed you so, Mel. I never thought I'd miss you so much, but I do.'

Mel was watching him. Had his eyes always been so red-rimmed after a couple of glasses of wine? He was starting to look older. His face was sculpted, hollow, his hair was definitely retreating slightly at the temples. Not that this mattered, she told herself hastily. After all, she had earlier that evening plucked several silver hairs out from amongst the red of her own hair, and stared at herself in the mirror, wondering whether the colour was quite as vibrant as it used to be.

'Jake,' she said steadily, 'you let me down. You didn't want me enough to stay with me. And you slept with someone else to hurt me. It was cruel. You can't expect me to . . . pick things up where we left off.'

'So why did you come tonight? You must have guessed the way we were going.'

Why *had* she come? To discover the truth of her feelings. She said carefully, 'Because I thought that, despite everything, you and I might have been possible. I needed to find out what I thought about you, really thought about you.'

'And what do you really think about me?' He looked half-crazed now; his nose was white and pinched with emotion.

'I . . . I'm fond of you, I really am. And I find you amazingly attractive.' Was there anything else there? Her father's words came into her mind, to grab love where she could find it, not to look for perfection. Was Jake, with all his imperfections, worth it? She was confused.

He flashed her a smile. 'That's something then. Something we can build on.'

She shook her head. 'I don't know. Let's see.'

'Will you stay?' he asked. 'I'm due to have the girls tomorrow. I told them there might be a surprise.'

'Me, you mean? *I* was the surprise?'

'Yes. I thought—'

'Jake,' she said softly, shaking her head. And now she knew the truth of her feelings. 'It's not fair on them, it really isn't. I would love to see them, but . . . I couldn't make them think, hope, that we were together again.'

'I see,' he said. He rolled his head back, eyes closed, a gesture of defeat.

'I'm sorry,' she said, putting out her hand to touch his on the table. He pulled it away.

'I'd better go.' She waited for him to move, to beg her to stay, anything.

He lowered his head. 'Okay,' he said in a dull voice. He got up and shuffled into the hallway. 'I suppose I'd better drive you home?'

'No, Jake. I'll get a cab!'

The twenty-minute wait before the minicab arrived was one of the longest of Mel's life. She sat on the sofa in her jacket, trying not to listen to Jake, who was clearing up, deliberately noisily in the kitchen. She was furious, absolutely furious. He was like a spoiled child who couldn't get his way, withdrawing his attention from her.

The intercom buzzed and he came to stand in the doorway of the kitchen, watching her listlessly. She stood up and took a long, cold look around the flat she knew she would never see again. Her eyes fell upon the photographs of herself. She couldn't bear to think of them there, a piece of herself still in his possession. She marched across the room, snatched them both up and, clutching them to her chest, nodded at him, said a curt goodbye and let herself out of the flat.

Walking down to the gate where the taxi waited she looked back up at the window. He was watching her, but when their eyes met he turned away without even waving goodbye.

As she rode back in the scruffy minicab, clinging to the seat as the driver raced down dark residential streets, cars parked on both sides, she waited for the familiar deadweight of despair to descend once more.

Chapter 37

The weeks passed. October ended, November began. Mel spent the darkening evenings writing the final chapter of her *Radiant Light*, arranging the footnotes and appendices, then considered the illustrations she would recommend that her publisher include. She was reluctant to call the book finished, though, before she saw Ann Boase, whom she still needed to track down.

Bonfire Night and a cold, rain-sodden one. Five pairs of Wellingtons set off from Chrissie and Rob's house down to the local park, one black industrial size, one cream, one green and two Thomas the Tank Engine ones, the owner of one of these pairs, two-year-old Freddy, riding high on his father's shoulders.

This council firework display was to prove one of those ritual events for which the British stoically turn out to say they've marked the occasion, insisting that they are enjoying themselves. Rory squeaked throughout that he couldn't see anything, and indeed, the fireworks at ground-level were invisible to anyone not at the front of the crowd. Freddy cried, terrified by the bangs. A safety poster on the gate had announced that sparklers were forbidden in the park, so Rob couldn't light the ones he had brought to delight the boys, and the queues for hot dogs were so long none of the grown-ups in the party could be bothered to join them. Halfway through the show, the rain began to fall again, steadily, in thick heavy drops.

'Let's go home,' grumbled Rob as soon as the last rocket had fallen to earth and the bonfire had finally been coaxed into life. 'Get something to eat there.'

'Want hot dog,' Rory started up, a plea that instantly turned to a high wail, so Chrissie took Freddy and it was Rory's turn to be carried by his weary dad. 'Hot dog, hot dog, hot dog,' he repeated tearfully in time with Rob's footsteps.

Lost in thought, Aunty Mel plodded along behind carrying Freddy's Wellingtons after they fell off one by one. Guy Fawkes felt like another marker of time passing. Last year it had been the first without their mother, this year it took her further away from Patrick.

The previous few weeks, since her last disastrous evening with Jake, had been relentlessly dreary, but without the despair she had feared that night, riding the minicab through the grid of narrow London side streets.

She should feel desolate, she told herself. After all, her emotional life had closed down on her yet again. But even when she reached home, she had merely felt dog tired, had stumbled straight into bed and slept dreamlessly until morning. When she had awoken there was no crushing black beast of depression. Instead, she had felt strangely free.

She was lucky that the following week was half-term – a full nine days in which she didn't have to bump into Jake at the staff pigeonholes or, come to think of it, Rowena, who was still prowling around, making trouble. For the first few days she left her mobile switched off and waited every time the flat phone rang for the caller to leave a message, so she could check out who it was. But the days passed and Jake didn't call. At first she felt relief, then as time drifted on, this darkened into resentment. That's how little Jake valued her. He had obviously already moved on.

Wednesday night of half-term was supper at her friends Sally and Mike's, with Aimee and Stuart and another couple she hadn't met before. When Sally had issued the invitation a couple of weeks ago she had asked if Mel wanted to bring anyone. Mel had thought for precisely one second before saying no.

She hadn't invited Jake, she realised, because she had known then, deep down, that he wasn't going to be a part of her life again. And admitting that helped her accept the fact that he hadn't been in touch again.

Sally, tactfully, hadn't invited some spare man to make up the numbers, but, more inspiringly, a woman she had met recently who organised new exhibitions at a North London art gallery and reviewed for a website that tracked new work in the capital.

The woman, Judith, asked Mel about her work, and Mel told her about the book and then, somewhat hesitantly, about her discoveries about Pearl in Cornwall. She spoke of Merryn and, suddenly, sitting there in the crush of the small hot London sitting room, memories of Cornwall, the garden, Pearl and Patrick washed over her in one great engulfing tide.

'Are you all right?' asked Judith, and Mel realised she was staring into the distance.

'Yes, yes – I was just thinking about it all,' she said, 'and telling myself that I only have a few more weeks to finish the book.' The end of the year was the publisher's deadline, but it would be hopeless to expect to do much in December, what with essay-marking and preparations for Christmas.

'Have you much to do?'

'Tidying, mostly. But there's a missing part of the jigsaw – someone I've got to see.' How could she have left it all so long? 'Do you know – have you ever heard of an artist called Ann Boase? I'm not even sure what medium she works in, but she must be in her early sixties.'

To her surprise, Judith instantly nodded. 'Yes, I've heard of her, seen her work, too. Big abstract canvases with paint and collage. A great feeling of light and air and the sea. I believe she's particularly popular in America. All those big corporations with huge boardrooms to decorate, I imagine. Why?'

'She's Pearl's grand-daughter, and I think she might have succeeded where Pearl couldn't.'

The next day, she looked up the number Richard Boase had given her, and dialled. This time a crackling ansaphone message invited her to leave her name and number so she did.

Later that evening, she answered the phone and a woman's gravelly voice said, 'Melanie Pentreath? My brother said you might call, dear, but that was back in August.'

'I know,' Mel said, 'I'm sorry. Things . . . got in the way. May I come and see you?'

'I was so hoping you would,' said Ann Boase, 'but I'm off to the States again tomorrow for six days. How about meeting the second week in November?'

Now, as she traipsed back to Chrissie's from the fireworks, Mel remembered. Next Thursday morning – she wasn't teaching until mid-afternoon – she was due to visit Ann's home and studio near Waterloo. And then she would finish her book and send it in to Grosvenor Press – Mel caught little Freddy's sock as it fell from his foot – and after that, well, who knew what she would do after that.

*

'Has Patrick really never tried to call you again?' asked Chrissie, after everybody had wolfed down thick vegetable soup and home-made hot-dogs. Rob had wearily offered to put Rory to bed – Freddy had pegged out on the sofa in front of *Pingu* – and Chrissie was brewing coffee. Mel had just told her what had happened with Jake and added grumpily, 'Don't say anything, Chrissie, I know what you think already.'

'I wasn't going to,' said Chrissie, petulant. 'I could have told you . . . But I'm surprised that Patrick has never been in touch. I thought he would have been.'

Chrissie had long ago told Mel about the phone calls he had made during what they now jokingly referred to as Mel's Dark Period, as though she were a painter whose emotional life was reflected in her art.

'Well, he hasn't,' said Mel in a toneless voice, as she stirred a forbidden spoonful of sugar into her coffee.

They were silent for a moment, then Chrissie said, 'Oh, I quite forgot. I was on the phone to Dad earlier in the week. He rang to ask what Rory wanted for his birthday. We were discussing whether he and Stella would come down and see us, and, do you know, in a moment of madness I asked them if they'd like to stay at Christmas, and he said they would.'

'That's a turn-up for the books,' said Mel. 'I don't remember when we last saw them at Christmas. Actually on Christmas Day, I mean. Won't it be a bit weird?' Chrissie was watching her closely and Mel guessed she, too, was thinking about their last, grim Christmas Day, the first without their mother.

'You will come to stay as usual, won't you, Mel? Apart from anything else, Rob would be grateful to have you.'

'Will you have enough space for us all?'

'Of course, if you don't mind having the Z-Bed up in the nursery. Then Freddy can go in with Rory.'

Mel smiled. 'Only if I can have the Spiderman duvet cover,' she said.

It was a shock to return to her flat the following day to find Cara had taken receipt of a small, tightly-packed Jiffy bag addressed to Mel in Patrick's flowing handwriting.

Mel opened her front door, propped it back with her overnight bag and returned to pick up the packet from the shelf in the communal hall. In the kitchen she opened it carefully with a pair of scissors and drew out a small battered hardcover notebook. She turned the yellowing lined pages, studying the large, scrawled italic hand, rather like Patrick's own. Still jammed in the bag was a white envelope addressed to her, from which she pulled a single folded sheet. It was a letter from Patrick. She stood for a moment staring, unfocused, mustering the courage to read.

Dearest Mel,

At last an excuse to write. I've been wanting to so much, but haven't known whether it would be welcome and I wasn't brave enough to find out. Forgive me.

The enclosed arrived a few days ago. Read the letter inside and everything will be explained. I'm sure it clears up some of the mystery about Pearl.

Otherwise, what to say? I miss you, Mel, I really do. Our time together was so short, but now I look back I know it was wonderful and I think about it constantly. I can't believe how I messed up and I'm sorry. I have to tell you about Bella.

First, the most important thing is that Bella and I are not together and never will be. I realised that, very soon after you left. I began to see her differently. There was a time when she was precious to me, and I must have been grieving for the loss of her all the weeks that I spent with you. I felt so muddled, I'm sorry. I suppose the bottom line is that it was the wrong time for you and me. When you left, I was devastated, but took it as a sign that I had to find out the truth about me and Bella. Whether it would work. And we tried, but it became clear fairly soon to both of us that we were chasing after a phantom. I realised that what I felt for her was a pale shadow of what I felt for you. I've told her I can't be in contact any more, that what she and I had is firmly in the past now and must be left there.

Mel, I don't know whether you ever want to see me again. I couldn't blame you if that is the case, I have so let you down. But I do hope that it is otherwise, that, given time, you might offer me another chance.

The garden is shutting down for winter now. You have missed the leaves turning russet, the sweet wild apples, the scent of smoke from the eternal bonfires – Jim makes some damn fine bonfires. It is dark and foggy here, sodden and lonely. I rather like it.

There's little news. Carrie's condition is stable, but they're waiting for her blood pressure to come down before they operate. She's also on a diet, which makes her irritable. Matt is running the hotel with Irina helping him, though fortunately, it's low season. Greg is sometimes a guest. He has come several times to spend time with Lana. But this week, half-term, after much wringing of hands and asking everybody's advice until we were sick of it, Irina took her up to London on the train and left her there with him. All week she's been like a cat on hot bricks. He will bring Lana back this weekend, please God promptly, for the sanity of us all.

Write to me, please.

All my love,

Patrick

Mel read the letter again, stopping and mulling over *I miss you, Mel, I really do. Our time together was so short, but now I look back I know it was wonderful and I think about it constantly.* A feeling of such relief flooded through her that she leaned against the work surface for support. She read the words again and, for the first time for many months, knew the gift of joy, that soaring certainty that the world is a wonderful place in which we are special and infinitely precious. 'Thank you, thank you,' she whispered, though whom she was thanking she couldn't tell.

It occurred to her, and she was shocked, that seeing Jake again had never given her this joy, and now she knew for certain that with him again those few weeks she had been a sleepwalker, going through the motions. But Patrick . . . suddenly all she wanted to do was speak to him, see him, be with him. She turned to pick up the phone and dial his number, but something stayed her.

She read the rest of the letter once more and caught its warning. *Given time.* Patrick sounded fragile, she thought, sad, and she knew he must have been treading a similar path to hers these last months. And as she reread what he said about Bella, the firework sparks of elation died and fell to earth. All that time he was with Mel, part of his mind had been with Bella. What did this mean? Could she ever trust him? Would he, if he knew she had tried again with Jake, trust *her*?

Given time. Time heals all wounds. She had never quite believed that one. There were some injuries, surely, that were too deep – the loss of a child, for instance, or a partner after many years of marriage. The skin might grow over, the pain might dull, but the scars remained, occasionally to be prodded into agonising pain. Both she and Patrick were battered, wounded. Perhaps they should wait for the scars to form and harden. Time gave other things. Perspective. 'All in good time,' her mother used to say when Mel whined for a toy she'd seen, fashion shoes she was too young for, permission to go to a late disco. What was 'good time'? Perhaps she was about to find out. She wouldn't ring him yet. She had to think.

Mel pulled out a chair from the kitchen table and sat down. For a moment she was deep frozen in thought, but then she put the letter to one side and drew the notebook towards her. She opened the front cover, picked up the folded piece of cream writing paper tucked into a worn-out piece of elastic inside and glanced at the handwritten inscription at the top of the first right-hand page of the book – *Charles Carey*. Charles Carey! This was extraordinary.

She pinched open the letter.

It was close-typed, without margins, on a manual typewriter with a jumpy 'e'.

Dear Mr Winterton,

I encountered my second cousin Susan Granger, for the first time for many years, at a family funeral last week. Susan is the daughter of Elizabeth Goodyear, née Carey, who was raised at Merryn Hall where you live, and she told me you had written in quest of family papers. I am wondering whether the enclosed is of interest to you. My father Duncan and Elizabeth, rest their souls, were first cousins to one another and to Charles Carey, who wrote this journal, I believe, in 1934, when he was dying in a TB hospital in Surrey. I don't remember Charles, being only six when he passed away, but my grandmother, Margaret, whose nephew he was, used to speak of him. He was a painter, not a terribly good one, I'm afraid, and my grandmother helped him when he fell on bad times after the First War. This book I found in my father's

papers when he died. It's a queer story, but perhaps of interest
to you in your inquiries. My children appear to have little
interest in the family history, so I'm happy if you want to place
it with the Carey archive when you've finished with it.
    Yours sincerely
    Jane Merchant (Mrs)

Charles Carey. The photograph she had seen of him in the archive rose in her mind. A carelessly good-looking young man with a cap of soft blond hair and a moustache, slight but graceful, lounging against the car. And in Pearl's painting, the same elegant figure, holding a . . . and now she knew. He was holding an artist's brush. The symbol of his trade, though if Jane Merchant's opinion was anything to go by, he was not a success at it. Mel wondered idly whether any of his work had survived.

The elderly binding creaked as she opened the notebook at the first page. The ink, faded to sepia, was hard to decipher, the curls and flourishes of Charles's pen frequently rendering ys and gs, ss and fs indistinguishable from one another. But she was used to puzzling out handwritten sources and slowly she began to pick out the sense.

A month I've been in this damn place, and now I understand fully why they call us patients, for to be sure, boredom will kill me before the disease gets me. Aunt Margaret visited today with a fine-looking fruitcake, the first decent food I've set eyes on for weeks, not that I have much appetite after all these potions they pump into me. She's the only one who comes now. How hunched she's grown. Not one word from Uncle Stephen's family, all these years.

Charles had clearly felt this was the wrong approach, because a

371

few lines' space followed and he started again on a different tack.

I have made many mistakes in my life, but there is one wrong that I regret above any other. The chaplain who came again today with his chubby fingers and his air of tired resignation could not make me speak of it and so he advised me to write it down, to consider the matter prayerfully and to ask God's forgiveness and peace. I have never had much to do with God, but peace – ah well, that is something we all seek and it has eluded me always.

My father died when I was a boy of ten, leaving me and my mother but her small annuity to live on, her own parents having died some years before. She did her best by me with the help of money my father's brother and sister sent. By the time I was sixteen, she recognised that I was not meant for university, not least because I passed my spare time drawing and painting instead of studying. She begged Uncle Stephen to pay for me to attend art college in London near to where we lived. Unfortunately he would not, his letter pointing out that this training would offer no certain way for a boy in my reduced circumstances to earn a living, but he invited me to make my home with them in Cornwall and learn to farm, for he had no sons to follow him. My poor dear mother did not want to let me go and she saw my reluctance to do so and the strength of my vocation. Eventually she took work as companion to an elderly lady and persuaded Aunt Margaret and her husband to contribute to my education, though they had their own large family to feed.

Two years into my course, disaster struck. My mother was killed in an accident in the street involving a runaway horse and carriage. With her death the annuity my father

372

had left her ceased. Soon, I faced a straight choice between paying the rent and buying food, so I was forced to give up our shabby rooms. At first I stayed with my aunt, but I was made to share a room with her two eldest boys and her crotchety husband resented my feet under his table. There came a time when they could no longer pay my fees, and when my uncle wrote again inviting me to Cornwall, it seemed an answer to please everyone. His wife, Emily, added a charming postscript to offer me my own studio if I wished to pursue my 'daubings', and at the time Lamorna, in a county of artists, sounded a land of opportunity for a tyro like myself.

I loved Merryn from the moment I set eyes upon the place. Cornwall seemed Paradise to me after the fog-filled streets of our capital city. And Elizabeth and Cecily, my two cousins, were biddable and amusing, Elizabeth promising to grow into pale willowy beauty, little Cecily a dark solemn faery child who could yet be coaxed into merriment when teased. Elizabeth, I believe, came to develop some feeling for me, and a tacit agreement hovered in the air that, should in time matters progress further between us, her parents would not stand in our way. My Aunt Emily was a lively, restless woman, champing at the bit with which Fate had tamed her. It could not be denied that Uncle Stephen, whilst a devoted husband and father, was a dull man, and how they came to marry I could not guess, though I knew her family were moneyed parvenus, and my uncle a socially established landowner in need of hard cash. He was bewildered by my Aunt Emily's pretensions in society, flustered by the grand dinner parties she held, critical of the 'fripperies' she ordered down from London, though she was not reckless, instead taking care to account for the money she spent to the final penny. His main interest was the farm, but this was the rock on which my relationship with him was to founder.

If Uncle had had his way, I would have spent every hour of every day shadowing him in his work, pacing the acres he kept under plough, inspecting livestock, administering the estate, keeping accounts, wrangling with tenants and lawyers and bankers. He insisted on involving me in all these tasks. How it all bored me.

There came a time when my pretence to go along with it began to flag. I made mistakes with simple addition, rode a valuable horse when it was lame. One night I refused to coun-tenance going out in the pitch darkness in search of some wretched lost beast and his exasperation with me grew.

Still, if something else much more tumultuous hadn't happened, I might have ridden this storm. But the seeds of my downfall were planted with the arrival of Aunt's latest project.

Her name was Pearl Treglown, and she was meant to replace Joan, the chatty sparrow of a housemaid who had set sail for South Africa in search of her sweetheart. But Aunt Emily had further ambitions. Pearl was to be trained up as Aunt's personal maid, to titivate her hair, look after her gowns. She was no common farmworker's daughter, this one, she carried herself like a duchess, albeit one fallen on hard times. Later, she told me how she believed her father to have been a gentleman, one of the artists who had visited Newlyn, and there was something about her that made me believe it, too. Not least her ability to draw like an angel.

I was very young then, and entertained the radical ideas that many young men have, that romantic love conquers all, that humble birth should be no barrier to success, that beau-tiful words and high-minded ideals, passionately held, are worth more than the common virtues of hard work and faithful duty that any dolt can possess.

And so I, too, conceived a new task in life. Aunt might turn Pearl into a lady's maid, but I would turn her into an artist. She proved an easy and willing pupil.

Despite lack of time, for a long while we made progress. Pearl was a wonderful miniaturist, could record the tiniest details of a flower stamen and charge the slightest blush of a petal with her brush. And soon she was drawing likenesses of faces alive with expression, faithfully reproducing the faint lines that betray character, the glint of knowledge in her subject's eye. I showed her sketchbook once to Mr Knight and he studied it intently and pronounced the drawings fine.

Where all this might have led, I don't know. I had vague thoughts that perhaps the Knights and their friends might take Pearl under their protection, encourage her, perhaps give her money, but the reality was that they didn't have much themselves and, anyway, they couldn't see her as I did then. They knew her only as a shy presence who served them tea or lemonade, not as one of themselves. Still, something might have worked out, had not tragedy struck.

The tragedy was that I fell in love with her.

I had gradually become aware that she doted on me, followed me with those great dark eyes of hers, hung on to my every word. I was used to Elizabeth's attentions, of course, the giggling, the flirtatious glances, but Elizabeth was only an innocent girl, trying out her grown-up tricks on the first safe man she had come across after her father. Pearl, with her quiet still ways that hid deep passion and suffering, was a woman.

It's an old story, isn't it? The master taking advantage of the servant. But it wasn't like that, I tell you, it wasn't. She wanted me as much as I came to want her, but she craved something else, something she couldn't take for herself, something which in the end I couldn't give her: to escape from her present life. And it's that which, most of all, I blame myself for awakening. Her ambition.

Even before our affair was discovered the knowledge grew inside me. How could she, a penniless young woman from a lowly background – yes, despite the tales of her siring – with little education and a country tongue, expect to become independent, to earn her living and the respect of society without a husband of means or the patronage of wealthy friends? We talked of going away together, to France, maybe, or Italy, where no one would know us, where we could forge our own future. But without money, all this was a silly dream. What in the end could I, with no more than tuppence to my name, do to help her or even to help myself?

Marry her? I could not have married her and kept my place at Merryn. Even my gentle London aunt would have closed her door to me, horrified by my choice of bride.

When Pearl told me she was with child, I knew at once our idyll was over. That night, I dreamed. Of working as a clerk in a dreary office with dreary fellows, stumbling home in the dark each night to gloomy rented rooms full of whinging brats, my disappointed wife with no time but to wash and scrub and dandle. We would be miserable. Poor, miserable and frustrated. I awoke in a sweat, crying out in anguish.

In the end, the decision was taken out of my hands, for we were spied upon and betrayed, and I was packed off, back to London on the train with my bags and trunks and canvases, without being allowed to say goodbye, back to throw myself upon the mercies of Aunt Margaret and her lugubrious spouse. She found me rooms and a job – not a clerk's job, thank God, but piecework illustration for a publisher. Light servitude, perhaps, but servitude all the same.

Then fell the great shadow of war, blotting out every young man's hopes. I will not speak of those years still to anyone. Sufficient that, even now, I dream some nights that I am trapped in a long dark tunnel where the screams of men in agony are only muffled by gunfire and exploding shells.

I would see the same knowledge in the eyes of other men I met, men less lucky than I, wheel-chair bound, limbless, and men who appear whole but aren't.

There came a time when, on a mission into enemy territory, my nerves shattered by shellfire, I became separated from my platoon and wandered aimlessly for many miles in the ruined countryside, somehow, miraculously, evading capture. Eventually I sheltered in a tumbledown barn and fell into a sleep like death – the deepest sleep I had had for months. There the farmer found me and took me in, nursing me for what must have been many weeks. My dreams were filled with horror, of blood running down ruined faces, of corpses blown into gobbets of meat. To calm myself in the moments of sanity I would think of Merryn where, I knew now, I had been happy. And Pearl's face would rise before me, oh God, beautiful but ravaged with sadness and pain, her arms lifted out for help uselessly. How I writhed with guilt and misery, in the knowledge of the hurt I must have done her. What had happened to her? I had no idea.

When I recovered I knew I must return to the Front or risk being branded a deserter. But when I followed the farmer's instructions and tried to find my way back, I was taken prisoner by an off-duty patrol. The rest of the war I spent in a German camp.

It was March 1919 before I found myself at the docks in Dover in a worn set of working man's clothes that hung off my wasted body and boots two sizes too big. I had money in my pocket and my freedom, but nowhere to call home. It was obvious to me that I should go straight to Aunt Margaret, especially since theirs was a house of mourning. A letter from her had finally caught up with me in the camp, expressing relief that I was alive and conveying the news of the loss of my two former roommates, her eldest sons, in France. Her youngest son, Duncan, had returned home wounded.

On the train to London I overheard a young officer mention Penzance to the train guard and so I asked him if he knew Lamorna and we fell into conversation. He knew many of the places so dear and familiar to me, so that by the time we reached London I was sick with desire to see Merryn, to find out what had happened to Pearl. And so, cruelly deserting Aunt Margaret in her own time of need, I crossed London with my new friend, stayed in lodgings in Paddington overnight and took the early train down to the West Country.

What possessed me to do this thing, to return to the place of my sins, of my humiliation, like a murderer to the scene of the crime? *You're crazy, you're mad*, mocked the sound of the train's wheels as my new friend and I chain-smoked cigarettes or devoured the great hunks of cheese sandwich we had bought at the station and rejoiced in the simple fact of being free to do so. The Careys wouldn't want to see me. I had heard nothing from them, the whole of the course of the war. But something drove me on, a perverse desire to face the past, to make reparation if such were possible. Or perhaps I'm fooling myself even now. Perhaps I merely wanted to see Cornwall again and the place where I'd been happy.

I left Merryn in disgrace all those years ago and returned like a thief, begging a lift from a carter on his way back from market. I skulked down the last mile of rutted track, my feet sliding in my capacious boots, keeping alert for curious eyes, but saw no one. The peace of the English countryside that late afternoon, broken only by birdsong and the distant lowing of cattle, was like a balm to my spirits after the eerie quiet between explosions or the mutinous silence of the camp. I walked slowly, drinking it in gratefully, still so weak from my confinement that even this short walk was exhausting.

When I stood at last at the gateway to Merryn, it was for a moment as though the years rolled back. I had come home. And yet as I surveyed the long Georgian windows of the house, the lawns rolling up to the courtyard, I could see something was wrong. The grass had been trimmed, but the vast banks of shrubs around were starting to roam untamed and, here and there, weeds were growing up through cracks in the courtyard flags. The house itself seemed empty, dreaming, and as I crept around the border of the lawn, hiding in the shadows of the trees, I saw that the curtains were drawn across the windows, that the stableyard was clear, swept clean, the stables themselves a blank row of closed doors.

Curiosity overcoming caution, I slipped round the side of the house and stepped under the arch into the Flower Garden. To be struck by a scene of desolation.

By now the beds should be dug, ready for planting, but it was clear that they had been left untouched for many seasons, covered as they were by the remains of several generations of weeds. The greenhouses were empty, closed up. Only the espaliered fruit trees, dotted with emerging blossom, seemed pruned and the paths kept clear. This garden, like the house, was sleeping, its vital signs checked, waiting to be awoken – when?

Glancing towards the gardener's hut, I noticed the door

was ajar. And at that moment I was startled by a sound somewhere behind me. A shout followed by laughter. There was a
child playing somewhere further down the garden. Quickly
stepping back out of sight, I skirted the wall of the house and
peeped around the corner.

Down near the Gardener's Cottage, a boy ran across the
grass after a ball, dressed in brown with a mop of fair hair.
Behind him, a tall dark woman lugged a heavy bucket over to
a flowerbed and swung the contents over some shrubs, her
movements stiff and tired. She stood, pail in hand, watching
the child who was now throwing the ball high in the air and
trying to catch it.

'Keep your eye on it, Pete,' she called, as he missed the
catch for the third time and at the sound of her voice, the
scales fell from my eyes.

I fell back against the wall, heart juddering in my chest,
and for a moment must have lost all sense of self. How had I
not recognised her?

To be sure, she had changed, shockingly. She was
scrawnier of figure and the years since I had seen her had
worn away the bloom of her cheeks, sculpted hollows in her
cheeks. I thought of her stiff movements. Was she ill?

When I looked again, they were moving away towards the
little house, throwing the ball between them, the child still
sometimes dropping it, making a play of tumbling to the
ground with a shriek of delight when he chased it.

How old was he? I'm no good at gauging such things. He
had lost the chubbiness, the rounded tummy of the very
young, yet the way he wound his arms around his mother,
and pressed his cheek into her belly, told me she was still his
entire world. Five years old, perhaps, or six.

Why did it take so long for the truth to strike me? I peered at him as he ran, somersaulted, leaped and rolled. His hair was like mine in a photograph I'd seen of myself at that age, but his eyes were fine, dark, like Pearl's. There was something about the shape of his head, his profile, that struck some note deep in my mind. Then I knew beyond any doubt, and once more shock prickled my limbs and I shuddered, and put up my hands as though bracing myself against a falling object. I slid down the wall and crouched, arms over my head. The child was mine. And, oh grief, not mine.

When I looked once more, they had gone inside, but as I staggered to my feet I became aware of someone else nearby. I looked back towards the Flower Garden to where a man stood under the arch, frozen stock still, one hand clutching some long-handled tool. I knew him at once. The gardener, Boase. We stared at one another for a long moment and his expression turned from shock to pain and anger.

Suddenly, I could endure the fellow's surliness no longer. I looked away, busying myself with lighting a cigarette to steady my nerves.

A movement. I glanced up and saw him stride towards me, noticing his white-knuckled grip on the hoe, which I eyed warily.

'What are you doing here?' Every word spat out. The insolence.

I told him, 'I've come home.'

'Home, is it? Well, they're gone.'

'Where?'

Boase sighed then changed tack. 'Did you not hear, then?' His eyes raked my face and body, narrowing as he registered my workman's clothing.

'Hear what? I've heard little news where I've been.' I stared at him hard then, challenging him, the young soldier's contempt for the old man stuck useless at home. He caught my meaning well enough.

'No, I suppose not,' he said, with a sharp intake of breath. Then, 'Your uncle. Sick, very sick. In the hospital at Plymouth. They're all with him. Been away months.'

Aunt Margaret had said no word of this in her letter.

'So there's nothing for you here.' His words ended in a sort of barking sound. The sinews stood out in his neck.

'No,' I said, but he must have seen my glance back to the cottage.

'Leave her,' he said in a strained whisper. 'She's suffered enough. Leave her alone. Go.'

'The boy . . .' I started.

'Go.' His great hand tightened around the hoe. 'Get out of here.'

I went.

I never returned to Cornwall again, and now I never shall. But I often think of him, little Peter. He will be a man now, of course, and I imagine how he must live. Perhaps he's a gardener like his stepfather or works on Uncle's farm, though Uncle died the following year and the land came to be broken up and sold. My son has probably never heard of me, or if he has, I wonder what he's heard, how he's imagined his real father to be? A cad? Or a romantic dream. I fear the former.

I've been a failure, I face that bitter fact daily. No use to anyone, a burden. And now I'm dying, though they won't admit that to me, these doctors with their talk of research and new miracle treatments. Peter is all I have. The memory of that beautiful child, the hope of him. When I think of Pearl and how I betrayed her trust I am weighed down with remorse. But when I remember Peter I'm not sorry. Not sorry at all.

For a long while after she had finished, Mel sat at the kitchen table, staring out at the desolate November garden, tears drying on her cheeks. She hadn't been able to read Charles's account straight through, as part of her mind kept wandering back to Patrick, but somehow she had stumbled through to the end. So Charles had tried to help Pearl – but failed – and had nearly destroyed her instead. What would have happened to her if Boase hadn't been there to help? Dismissal, probably. Then where would she have gone if she had no family? But Boase *had* been there. A strong man. A good, kind man, if his grandson's account of him was accurate. Pearl's defender. Did she ever find out that Charles had come looking for her? Boase should have told her, Mel decided. She wasn't a child to be protected from real life. But what would she have done? Gone away with Charles? Who knows? She had a young child. Her options were few and she must have learned not to trust Charles. Would she have chosen safety, stability, the dull solid virtues of Boase?

Her mind drifted to Patrick and once again, relief and thankfulness flooded through her like a beam of golden light. What should she do? Nothing, she decided. Absolutely nothing. Not today, anyway. She had to think.

Aimee, Stuart and three other friends were due to come for supper that night. All afternoon, as she chopped vegetables and mixed desserts, she remembered cooking with Patrick, he in his butcher's apron, humming to Miles Davis in the large dingy kitchen. What was the garden like in November? Sodden, his letter had said, and she mourned those spring and summer days, life burgeoning rudely all around them. Now, in the dying weeks of autumn, it would be dark, isolated, lonely. But Patrick didn't mind that, being alone. He had told her. After all, his family were nearby, so were old friends. And it sounded as though he saw something of Matt and Irina. Would Mel find it lonely, cut off? Probably. But would it matter if she were with Patrick? Something else she didn't know.

That evening, though she had felt like being alone, she enjoyed herself. The food was nicely cooked, the balance of her guest-list was perfect. Even Stuart demonstrated a previously hidden gift as a raconteur and it was well after midnight before they all departed, to the sound of late fireworks exploding all around. She loaded the dishwasher and scrubbed saucepans – jobs she had denied her guests, peaceful in her own company, enjoying the fact that everything was in its place because she had put it there, appreciating that rare sense of total control. Then she went to bed and slept dreamlessly until nine the next morning.

When she woke up she knew what she should do.

She had to start it three times, but finally she read her letter through and was satisfied.

Dear Patrick

It was lovely to hear from you, more than lovely.

We have both been through so much since we last saw one another. You've had to find out about Bella. I had to see if Jake still meant anything to me, and he doesn't. He just doesn't. Meeting you changed everything. I'm feeling so bruised though, so lacking in confidence, though I'm better than I was, and I can't just rush into something else.

It seems strange in a world where we no longer have to wait for anything, where computers and mobile phones put us instantly in touch, to say that I would like to see you, but not yet.

384

I need more time, Patrick. We both need more time. I know there is risk involved in any relationship, but now I'm looking for something that will last, something that is worth waiting for. I don't know if it will take weeks or months but hope that you will wait.

Charles's journal is an extraordinary find and provides many missing details. I hope it's all right with you if I show it to Ann Boase, Pearl's granddaughter, whom I will see in a few days. I'll return it as soon as I can. This book has been hanging over me for so long, I'm determined to finish it very shortly.

Send lots of love to Carrie and Matt, to Irina and little Lana. I miss them all and Merryn and, most of all, I miss you.

All my love,
Mel

Chapter 38

Walking south over Westminster Bridge, Mel paused to watch a pleasure launch emerge from one of the arches beneath, the swell smacking against its bows as it ploughed its way downstream. There was something cheering about all the boats coasting the little waves, something fine about the mêlée of buildings thrusting their clean lines up into a skyline dominated by the giant wheel.

A shame the view upriver was blocked by builders' screens, she noted, before carrying on towards the frowning black glass and steel monstrosities of Waterloo. Somewhere in the midst of which, if Mel could find it, lived Pearl's granddaughter, Ann.

Since receiving Patrick's letter she had found herself looking at London with new eyes, the eyes of someone who might soon be parted from it. This wasn't the result of conscious decision-making, rather the sense that something inside her was working away by itself, processing pros and cons, muttering to itself, like a computer program into which she'd fed a long list of complicated data before pressing Go and leaving the room.

If she were to be with Patrick again, what should she do? Live in London and go down to Cornwall at weekends? Give up her job and live in Cornwall? She had enjoyed writing her book. Perhaps there could be more? Or maybe Patrick would move back up to the city? She was annoyed at her inner self for taking liberties. After all, she didn't even know what it would be like if and when she saw him again, how she would feel, how he would feel, whether they really had the chance of a future together. But this didn't seem to stop her inner self from hoping.

Mel negotiated a huge roundabout and eventually came to a narrow street heading south away from the river. She checked the name of the road against the scribbled address in her diary and started down it.

As she waited for someone to answer the bell of number 64, she felt with alarm the ground beneath her feet vibrate, then the door opened and the gravelly contralto she recognised from the phone sang out, 'Come in, come in.'

Ann Boase was a short, stocky woman, dressed in a beige safari-style top and trousers. Her hair was dyed brown and held back by a multi-coloured scarf twisted into a hairband, her black eyeliner applied with more enthusiasm than judgement. Mel followed her down a narrow white-painted hall, through a cheerful modern kitchen and out into a huge studio room with a high glass roof. Warm light poured down, reflecting off the pure white walls. The effect was exhilarating, if slightly spoiled by a strong smell of turpentine.

'It's wonderful,' she gasped, looking round at the large bright canvases on the walls, the stripped hardwood floor, stained with paint and glue and blobs of Plaster of Paris.

'Not always as tidy as this,' said Ann, straightening one of the pictures – a furious swirl of midnight-blue paint on which was superimposed strips of white tape forming jagged shapes. Like a thunderstorm, it occurred to Mel, and she wondered if that was what it was meant to be. 'I swept up before I went to

Chicago, but I'll be knee-deep in dustsheets and rubbish again by the end of next week.'

Once again, the floor began to vibrate slightly and this time Mel heard the rushing sound of a fastline train.

'The railway line's down in the cutting there,' said Ann, moving to the French window. Mel joined her. The studio took up most of what used to be garden, and only a few yards of scrub and a line of fir trees separated the studio from a stout link fence and the hidden trains.

'Never much interested in gardening, as you can see,' Ann said, as Mel surveyed the yard outside. 'And you get used to the trains.'

'I was brought up with them,' said Mel. 'The way they sounded back then was comforting.' When had the old gentle trundling sound become this horrible startling modern roar? 'How long have you been here?'

'Since . . . seventy-eight, I think. My daughters are always trying to talk me into moving, the darlings, but I like it here. Come.'

They walked through another door into Ann's living room. More stripped wood floors and comfortable old sofas, the bookcases studded with photographs. Ann crossed the room to an alcove by the fireplace and stood beneath a painting about three feet square in a wide plain gold frame. It was a watercolour of a small boy on a beach, the child fully dressed but with bare feet, digging the sand with a wooden-handled spade.

'It's Pearl's, isn't it?' Mel whispered after a moment.

Ann nodded, her eyes soft with pleasure. 'Isn't it just adorable?'

'And . . . is that . . . Peter, your father?'

'Yes, that's right. He gave it to me shortly before he died – because I was the artist in the family, you see. There are two more over here.' On the wall behind the door hung a pair of small oils. One was the portrait of a middle-aged man, with a kindly face weathered by the sun. 'That's my grandfather. I always think of him as my grandfather, you know. My brother's told you Pearl was a naughty girl?'

Mel, conscious of Charles's journal lying like a dark secret in her handbag in the kitchen, nodded.

'And this is the naughty girl herself.' The final painting was gloomy, an interior setting. The lines of a mirror framed a pale square face, the black hair pulled back. Great dark eyes burned intensely out of the picture, the lips curved in the faintest of Mona Lisa smiles. Pearl, finally, rising out of the past. Mel was mesmerised. She moved back until the painting fell into clearest focus and stared at the eyes that stared back at her. She'd seen that face somewhere before, she knew she had. Mel looked over at Ann. The woman, too, had fine dark eyes, but they twinkled while Pearl's were solemn, and where Pearl's face was square, Ann's, the bone structure sharpened by age, was small and heart-shaped. No, it was somewhere else that she had seen Pearl. Was it in the Gardener's Cottage, or in a dream?

She went back to the picture of John Boase, then across the room again to little Peter, eternally digging.

'And I found one of her sketchbooks for you.' Ann picked up a padded landscape notebook lying on the coffee-table next to a packet of cigarettes and a lighter, and offered it to Mel.

'Sit down and have a proper look,' she said, seeing Mel turning the book over in her hands in astonishment. 'I'll make us some coffee.'

The first page of the sketchbook was inscribed: *For Pearl Treglown, from Arthur Reagan with true affection, 1910*, and it was filled to the last page with drawings and watercolours of plants, faces; studies of hands, the folds of clothes, a flower growing from a drystone wall. There were some that caught Mel's particular attention – several pencil sketches of a man's face instantly recognisable as that of Charles and, close to the end of the book, sketches of little Peter from babyhood on, including studies for the beach picture that met her eye when she raised her head to compare.

'We think Arthur Reagan was her father,' said Ann, returning with a tray of coffee. 'She told my grandfather – John, I mean – that he was a painter, but we've never found out anything much about him. Did you say this was all relevant to something you're writing?'

Mel quickly described the scope of *Radiant Light*. 'I'm hoping to include more about Pearl,' she said. 'I don't know how you feel about that – in particular, whether you would allow me to reproduce some of these pictures. I mentioned the ones we found at Merryn? I'm sure Patrick Winterton, the current owner of the house, would want you to see them at some point.' She bit her lip, wondering whether there might be some dispute over ownership of those paintings. If they had been accidentally left in the house, could Patrick legally claim them as his? She didn't know.

Ann was nodding as she poured the coffee and lit a cigarette, which she inhaled, causing her to cough throatily. 'You told me on the phone. I was fascinated to hear there are more pictures. I'd adore to see them. Do you think Mr Winterton would mind me calling in when I'm next in Cornwall?'

'I'm sure he'd be delighted to show you. He's been almost as interested as I am in your grandmother.'

'How marvellous. And of course you can use these ones. I've got slides of the paintings, but perhaps you might like to take your own. You know, I can't tell you how delighted I am at this interest in Pearl. She must have only a small place, the tiniest of footnotes, in the art of the period, but it would be so splendid for that to be recorded.'

'I think so, too,' said Mel. 'Oh, and I've got something for you.' She put down the sketchbook carefully on the table and went to fetch her bag from the kitchen. 'I don't know whether you know anything much about your grandfather – your biological one, I mean. But this is an account Charles wrote when he was very ill – dying, I think.' She had typed out a transcript of the handwriting, and this she passed to Ann with the small journal.

'How simply fascinating. Thank you.'

'It tells the story from his point of view, of course. And was written twenty years after the events. So we must take his interpretation with a pinch of salt.'

In truth, though she didn't like to say this to Ann, parts of Charles's account lacked the ring of sincerity. Worst of all was the passage about the time in the war when he had gone missing. Had he really been delirious or had he temporarily deserted? And what were the circumstances surrounding his capture by the enemy? She suspected there was a story to be told there, though she couldn't see how she would ever be able to find it out. Or whether Ann and her family would want her to do so.

And Pearl. Had a part of him – the good part – hoped to reclaim Pearl or at least to check that she was happy? She remembered how thin and gaunt he had found her when he had sneaked down to Merryn at the war's end.

'Your grandmother died young, didn't she?' she asked Ann.

'Yes. An awful tragedy. Marked my father for life, the loss of her, it really did. I think it was asthma complicated by pneumonia. Something like that. I remember Grandfather hinting that she had had a very difficult time giving birth, that she wasn't the same after the baby. I always used to wonder what that meant until I had children myself. Damage to the entire pelvic area, I suppose. Most uncomfortable. Anyway, she was told not to have more children. Then she nearly died of the Spanish flu in 1918, poor thing, and never really recovered her health. Terribly sad. You don't have children yourself yet?' Ann's glance was suddenly curious.

'No,' said Mel. But she found Ann's quirky raising of eyebrows sympathetic rather than intrusive. 'Waiting to find the right man.'

'Don't leave it too long. I'm afraid I never found Mr Right, just several Mr Right-I'm-Offs, but I never regretted for one moment having my two girls.'

Mel laughed out loud. 'I'll remember that advice,' she said.

Was that the answer, she wondered after she had said goodbye, leaving with promises to meet again soon. She walked back up the road following signs to Waterloo Station, as she was due in college that afternoon. Was she being unrealistic, desiring a proper father for any child she might have? After all, her own father had proved a 'Mr Right-I'm-Off'. She remembered that conversation she had had with Patrick soon after they had met. She knew he wanted children, wanted to be there for them. She sighed. Too many ifs, not least about Patrick, but Ann was right. She shouldn't leave it all too long. She wouldn't.

When she arrived home that evening, Cara came downstairs bearing a cardboard box with *Fragile* stamped on every side. She watched Mel unpack it on the kitchen table, chasing the small zig-zags of polystyrene that burst out everywhere. The box contained a little teapot, just big enough for two cups. It was decorated with a pattern of clocks with funny spout-nosed faces and spindly legs in red and blue shoes. Woven in between the clocks were repeated the slogans, *Time for tea*, *It's teatime*, *Time to put the kettle on*.

Cara, who was a romantic, stared at it, bemused. 'Who is send you this?' she said, searching for a label, but there was no name.

Mel laughed. 'A very good friend of mine,' was all she offered by way of explanation.

'A man?' Cara's face was disbelieving.

'A man, yes.'

'I know what I say to a man who send me something like that,' said Cara, hands on plump hips. 'What about flowers or, mmm, something sexy for the bedroom?'

Mel laughed. 'It's exactly what I wanted from this man,' she said. She would write him a note to say thank you.

That evening, Mel opened her laptop and started to thread into her book the new details she had learned that day about Pearl Treglown. Three days later, she judged *Radiant Light* finished and emailed the script to Grosvenor Press. She felt bereft after it had gone, as though a chapter in her own life had closed.

Chapter 39

'Time costs money even at Christmas,' quipped Rob as he handed Mel a visitor's parking permit for her car. 'The warden will be looking for his last bonus before the great shutdown, mark my words. Here, let me take the case and that box. Can you and Rory manage the rest?'

It was lunchtime on Christmas Eve, and Mel had arrived to stay three nights at her sister's with a car boot full of luggage.

'We'll be fine, thanks, Rob.'

'I'm taking the presents in for you, Aunty Mel,' Rory said with a solemn air, dragging a box over the lip of the boot.

'Oh, Rory!' Mel saved the contents from disaster just in time and helped him carry the box the dozen yards to the front door, through which she could see Rob vanishing upstairs with her suitcase.

'Tell Chrissie I'll be up in the loft,' he called behind him.

Chrissie hurried up the stairs from the kitchen, her hands covered in stuffing for the turkey, and she and Mel kissed hello, no hands, like shy children.

'These must go under the tree,' shouted Rory, and started pulling parcels out over the living-room floor.

''Eddy, too.' Freddy stumbled up the steps behind Chrissie

394

and ran in to start a tug of war with his brother over a long thin present tied with a large silver bow.

'Boys, stop,' Chrissie said, helplessly waving her mucky hands. 'You're tearing the paper.'

'It's a kite!' shrieked Rory. 'For me from Aunty Mel.'

'No, me,' echoed Freddy.

'It was for Rob, actually,' sighed Mel. 'Your presents aren't in there, kids. Oh, I've left my handbag in the car. And all the doors unlocked.' Casting a helpless glance at Rory's activities she rushed out into the street.

She shouldered her bag and set down a second box of presents on the pavement so she could lock up. It had taken ages yesterday evening, wrapping and decorating them all with ribbons, bows and stickers until they looked too good to open. A silky nightdress for Chrissie, a sports biography for Rob to supplement the jokey present of the kite, a critically acclaimed travel memoir plus a scarf for her father, some pretty china for Stella. Several parcels each for the children, the fruit of a happy morning in Hamley's toy shop with Aimee, who had chosen the latest computer game for Callum.

The only person close to her Mel hadn't bought a present for this year was Patrick. Try as hard as she might, she hadn't been able to think of anything suitable, anything that felt right given the circumstances. Men were difficult to buy presents for at the best of times, she told herself, so what did you get for somebody you thought about all the time but with whom you didn't, at the moment, actually have a relationship? Aftershave? Too clichéd. Books? She wasn't sure which. Music? Ditto. A tie? Socks? Too boring.

Worst of all, she hadn't even heard from him since the arrival of the teapot back in mid-November. At first it hadn't seemed to matter, she passed her days with the thought of him tucked away in her mind like a special secret. But as the weeks crept on and there was no communication from him, her brave confidence began to flag. Had he forgotten her? Or had, maybe, his view of her altered? Perhaps, it occurred to her, lying awake in the darkest hours of the night, he had even found somebody else. But surely he would have said, if that was the case. Wouldn't he? Surely by now they had built some modicum of trust between them.

I should have written to him again since thanking him for the teapot, she decided as she reached into the boot to rescue a bottle of Rob's favourite whisky that had rolled to the back. Shouldn't have left things so long, unresolved. And yet space, silence, is what they had agreed to grant one another, wasn't it?

She leaned against the open boot, suddenly devoid of energy. In the end, she had made him a beautiful card with folding cut-outs of gold and silver angels, and had inscribed it, *Darling Patrick. Wishing you a most wonderful Christmas and New Year. PS: I'm at Chrissie's with the children as usual. How about you?*

She had dropped the card in the postbox two weeks ago and gone to the door hopefully every day since, looking for something from him amongst the scattering of cards from friends, old colleagues and rarely-glimpsed aunts. But nothing came. Nothing, nothing, nothing.

Where did this leave her? Nowhere. Worse than nowhere. In a black hole.

'Any sign of Dad and Stella?' asked Mel as, presents tucked safely under the huge Christmas tree, she joined Chrissie in the kitchen.

'They got here an hour ago and went straight out to the off-licence,' said Chrissie, her arm halfway up a huge turkey carcass, Freddy meanwhile was clamped to her leg, whining.

'Anything I can do?' Mel said faintly, staring round the chaos of the kitchen. Something in a preserving pan was bubbling furiously on the stove, there was flour spilled on the floor. On every surface lay food in various states of preparation.

'Can you turn down the ham? Then there's that Yule log over there to decorate – chocolate icing's in the fridge – and the spuds to peel. I should have done some of it earlier but there were the refreshments for Rory's Christmas show and they gave me an extra shift at work this week, which made me furious. I still haven't made up the beds, can you believe it – never mind wrapping presents. Oh Freddy, darling, don't dig your nails in, that hurts.'

Freddy gave another wail at his mother's sharp tone, and Mel, after turning the gas to 'simmer', reached down to scoop him up. 'Come on, monster,' she whispered into his ear and he turned to snuggle into her.

'Actually, Mel, can you go and ask Rob to come downstairs. He's been looking for the star for the top of the tree half the morning, and we really can live without it. Maybe he'll occupy the boys for a bit, hang up the stockings and make paperchains or something.'

The doorbell rang.

'Oh, that'll be Dad and Stella.'

'We'll get it, won't we, Freddy?' sang Mel and started up the stairs to the hall, nuzzling the little boy's head. He smelled deliciously of chocolate, babywipes and sleep. Last Christmas, she remembered, he could only crawl and had been more interested in wrapping paper than presents. How quickly everything changed. Had it really been a year ago that they had all sat mournfully around the dinner-table as William, in his somewhat pompous manner, toasted 'absent friends'. William and his family were spending the day with his in-laws, this year. It would be strange having Dad instead . . . she hoped he wouldn't be irritable.

The doorbell rang again. 'Coming,' she called and, with her free hand, helped Rory open the door. It wasn't her father on the doorstep but a young man with a motorcycle helmet at his feet, juggling a long rectangular box and a clipboard.

'Sign for this?' he said, holding the clipboard steady. Mel scribbled her name and took the package, which felt lighter than she somehow expected, wishing him Happy Christmas. Rory shut the door shouting, 'Goodbye, man.'

In the gloom of the hall she peered at the label to see whether the parcel was for Rob or Chrissie. Instead she was surprised that it read *Ms Melanie Pentreath*. Why would someone send her something here? The box was really quite light. Not a bottle, obviously, and the wrong shape for chocolates.

She and the boys climbed back down to the kitchen. Chrissie, wrapping foil over the turkey with a ghostly rattling, looked up, eyebrows raised. When she saw the box and Mel said, 'It's for me, oddly,' she gave a curiously knowing smile. 'What?' Mel said.

'Nothing,' said Chrissie, dropping the turkey back in its roasting tray and coming over to see.

Mel slid Freddy into his high chair with the cardboard roll from the foil to play with, then sat down and started to ease out the flaps of the box. It was then she noticed the address on the courier's label: Cornwall. She lifted the lid, folded it back, then pulled apart the layers of cellophane and tissue to reveal . . . a neatly tied sheaf of daffodil buds – no, not just daffodils, but *sol d'oeuil*, narcissi, bedded in damp cottonwool. The faint perfume, the dewy green freshness, rose from the box to transport her out of this hot ham- and onion-smelling, steam-filled kitchen back to the garden at Merryn, the only sound the songs of the birds, the salt-tinged breeze on her face. It was too much. The tears pooled in her eyes and spilled down her cheeks.

Patrick hadn't forgotten her. He was calling her back. Merryn was calling her. Perhaps it was time.

'Why are you crying, Aunty Mel?' asked Rory, more interested in adult tears than the flowers.

'Aunty no kie,' wailed Freddy.

'Because I'm happy,' whispered Mel.

There was a card tucked into the cellophane and she pulled it out. Across it in black ink Patrick had scrawled: *From the garden, the eternal promise of spring. Happy Christmas, darling, all my love, Patrick.*

When Mel's father and his wife returned five minutes later, Stella, elegant in navy and white twinset, took one look at the chaotic kitchen, at Mel sitting crying over a box of flowers, Chrissie trying to comfort her, the children yelling as they fought over the foil roll and, with tactful authority, she took charge. 'I can make lunch, if you like, Chrissie,' she said, 'whilst you deal with the more important tasks.' And before long, soup, cold meat and salad, were laid out on the table in the dining room whilst Rob poured sherry and listened attentively to his father-in-law's views on the parlous state of the Health Service.

'Dad seems quite at home here,' Mel whispered to Chrissie as they took the dirty plates down to the kitchen and gathered up the fruit salad and ice cream for pudding.

'He does seem more relaxed than he used to, doesn't he?' Chrissie agreed.

'It's really been since Mum . . .' Mel didn't finish. Perhaps he was expanding into the gap that Maureen had left.

'I was thinking the same,' put in Chrissie quickly. 'Rory and Freddy have hardly seen him, you know, and there he was before lunch, getting down on the floor with Rory's train track. I don't recall him ever doing that with Will.'

'Don't you?' Mel said. 'You can remember him when he was still at home with us. I can't, you see. I only really remember when we visited him. And he was with Stella instead of Mum. It was dreadfully confusing.'

'And Mum kept crying all the time.'

'I don't remember that, either. But when I try to, I feel this horrible heavy sense of sadness. All locked away inside, I suppose.'

'I wonder if that's what it was, back in August,' Chrissie said suddenly, staring at her sister.

'You mean the thing with Patrick triggering off memory?'

Chrissie shrugged. 'Could have been, couldn't it?'

'Because I thought Patrick was rejecting me, like Dad? Oh, come off it, Chrissie, that's a bit too neat.'

But was it? Did her sister have a point? Mel thought back to that last nightmare night at Merryn. There had been her own distress, yes. But also her dreams . . . the atmosphere in the cottage. That was someone else's memory she had tapped into. *Pearl's*. And if that was really what had happened, surely tapping into her own memories would be easy.

'Do you feel all right now, Mel?' asked Chrissie, standing, bowl of fruit salad in hand, turning anxious eyes on her. 'Not too sad or anything?'

'No, especially not since the flowers arrived. Did you know they were coming?'

'No, I didn't, honestly,' said Chrissie, smiling. 'Well, he rang to check the address, I hoped he'd send you something. Have you spoken to him? Why don't you give him a ring?'

'I might later,' Mel said, offhand.

Chrissie took the hint. 'Oh well, it's up to you.'

After the dessert was cleared away, Mel slipped upstairs to Rob and Chrissie's bedroom and rang the number for Merryn Hall. She listened to his voice on the ansaphone. It didn't sound like him – formal, polite, lifeless – and this put her off leaving a message. She considered ringing his mobile but network coverage was patchy and, if she did get through, she imagined him answering from the midst of a group of friends, or at lunch with his mother sitting there, a cold observer, and lost courage. Anyway, Rob was calling her down for coffee.

'We thought we'd try the crib service at the church,' said Chrissie as they sat in the living room. 'It's at five and I'll be sorted out by then. Some friends of ours go and they say the new woman vicar's very good.'

'We'll come, won't we, darling?' said Stella, patting her husband's hand.

'Of course. Maureen and I used to take you three when you were little,' he said to Chrissie and Mel, 'but perhaps you don't remember. Mel tried to take one of the crib lambs home one year.' He winked at her.

'I do remember,' they said simultaneously, Mel surprised by the sudden flash of recovered memory.

'My granny died,' Rory told Stella solemnly, coming to place his hand on her lap. 'She was very sick and then she died.'

'I know, darling. It's so sad, isn't it?' said Stella, brushing back Rory's hair.

'Are you a granny, too?' he asked.

'I can be your granny if you like, darling. And Freddy's.' She waved at Freddy, who sat squarely on the floor, legs splayed out in front, rolling toy cars onto a transporter. 'You can call me Granny Stella or just Stella.'

Rory nodded and looked satisfied. 'I'll call you Stella,' he said. 'But you'll be like my granny.'

Stella gazed into his eyes as though she'd fallen in love.

Mel and Rob and her father took the boys down to the swings and slides at the local park, whilst Stella helped Chrissie with the beds.

'Are you sure?' Mel asked them.

'Oh goodness yes, you go and have a chat with your father,' said Stella. A suspicion grew on Mel that this 'chat' was not unplanned.

'It's all dads out here, isn't it?' Mel said laughing as they reached the fenced play area, which was heaving with small children. 'We can guess what the mums are all doing on Christmas Eve.'

Men slouched smoking on benches, talked into mobiles or tiredly pushed tinies on the swings.

They don't talk to each other like the women do, she thought.

Whilst Rob patiently stood beneath Rory who was scaling the heights of the climbing frame, Mel grabbed a free baby swing and slotted Freddy into it. Her father started to push him gently, as though frightened the child might fall out.

'More,' bellowed Freddy and Grandad tried a little harder.

'Didn't do much of this when you were young,' he said to Mel. 'I like being a grandad.'

'Do you see much of Will's kids?' Mel asked. Will only lived twenty miles away from him and Stella, in Birmingham.

'We try to. Now that I'm retired it's a bit easier. And with your mother gone . . .' He gave Freddy's swing a harder shove than he intended.

'Wheee,' shouted Freddy, shooting up into the air. 'More, more.'

'Well, it just seems more important somehow. They're nice kids, all of them, and Stella's chuffed that they like her. I think she should have had some of her own, you know.'

'She'll be an excellent grandmother,' said Mel.

'Down, down,' commanded Freddy. 'S'ide.' Her father grabbed the swing before Freddy could clamber out into mid-air, then helped him to the ground and safely over to one of the little slides. There Mel stood behind Freddy as he climbed the half-dozen steps on hands and feet, monkey fashion.

'Have you taken my advice yet?' her father said, his blue eyes fierce upon her.

'What advice?' said Mel to buy time.

'That young man Chrissie told me about.'

'Patrick, you mean.'

'That's the one.'

'Dad, it's all right, you know. I'm not a little girl any more, I can make my own decisions. There's plenty of time.'

'Time is what there's not, Mel. Remember what I said. If you love him, don't look for faults. None of us is perfect and he might slip away.'

'I won't let him, Dad, I promise,' she said, squeezing his shoulder. 'Not this time.'

And they both rushed forward to rescue Freddy, who had fallen off the bottom of the slide with a bump. ' 'Gain,' he said stolidly, looking up at them with satisfaction.

They're all conspiring, Mel concluded, as they sat in a pew halfway down the Victorian church, which was filling up rapidly with children, parents and old people. For some reason they have all decided, my family, that Patrick is the right person for me. Yet my father has never even met him.

'He must have caught the vibes from you,' said Chrissie, with a smug expression when Mel recounted the conversation she had had with their father. 'Yes, of course he's asked me about Patrick, but nothing I could say would make him seem the right person for you. It's just what we see, how happy the thought of him seems to make you, that's all.'

'Different from how I was about Jake?' sighed Mel.

'Very,' said Chrissie. 'You never seemed truly yourself around Jake. You were always watching him, you know, never relaxed.'

'I don't remember that.'

'Well, I do.'

The organ started up, playing softly 'Away in a Manger', as parents removed toddlers from buggies, peeled off children's coats, craned to see whether anything was starting to happen. It wasn't. Mel glanced to her left. Rob was shushing Freddy on the seat next to him and on Freddy's left Rory was slouched kicking the kneeler hanging on the hook in front of him. Next to Rory Chrissie chatted to her father and at the far end of the pew Stella was kneeling, her face in her hands, praying.

Perhaps I should, too, thought Mel, though she hadn't ever had the habit of it. She knelt on her tapestry cushion and closed her eyes, her mind blank.

What should I say?

There was nothing in her mind at all and so she sat listening to the music and the murmur of voices around her and finally a wordless rush of peace and thankfulness seemed to flow through her. *Oh, let me do the right thing*, came the words in her head, though what did that mean – *right*? Right for me, I suppose, she sighed, pushing herself back up onto the pew.

It was a short and simple service, the words of the old carols, which Mel had sung every year of her life at one Christmas celebration or another, suddenly fresh and resonant in a way they hadn't been for years and years, as though they spoke directly to her, and she listened intently to the older Sunday School children reading passages from the Christmas story.

When the Vicar asked for volunteers to carry the wooden nativity figures and to place them in the stable, Rory's hand shot up instantly and he was one of the first to be chosen. Chrissie went to help him lift the ox and to arrange it to one side of Mary and the crib. He skipped back up the aisle with a huge grin on his face.

The final carol, unusually, was not 'O Come All Ye Faithful' or 'Hark the Herald Angels', but 'It Came Upon the Midnight Clear', about the strife-riven world stopping in its tracks to listen to the song of the angels, 'Peace on the earth, good will to men', and looking forward to the time 'when peace shall over all the earth its ancient splendours fling.'

And then the service was over and the lights went up and the church, full of strangers who for this short moment at Christmas became neighbours, were catching one another's eye and wishing each other Happy Christmas, and children were dancing around in excitement at the thought of Baby Jesus and stockings and Father Christmas.

'Well,' said Stella, as they emerged into the cold evening, 'I thought that was simply lovely.' And it was.

Whilst Chrissie and Stella were laying out tea, Mel slipped upstairs once more to use her phone. Patrick was still out, but this time she left a stilted message of thanks for the flowers. Then she called up his mobile number and stared at the printed number on the display until the backlighting faded, before pressing Call. It rang and rang, then switched over to Voicemail. Rather than leave a duplicate message she rang off.

Perhaps she should ring his parents. But she rehearsed the likely prickly conversation that would ensue if his mother answered and decided against it.

Finally, on an impulse, she called up the number for Carrie's hotel. Matt answered on the second ring.

'Mel!'

'Matt, hi. Is this a bad time? Are you madly busy?'

'Not too busy to talk to you. Thanks for the card, by the way. Sorry, we've been a bit behind with cards this year.'

'Oh, don't worry. Just didn't want you to think I'd forgotten you. Matt – oh, it's so good to hear your voice. How are you all?'

'Good, very good.'

'Your mother?'

'Not bad. She's going back into hospital after Christmas for a bypass op. We're trying to stop her bossing us about in the kitchen. She's sitting in the lounge at the moment, chatting to guests. We're pretty full this year as we advertised a special lunch.'

'That's wonderful. How's Irina?'

'Oh, she's somewhere around. She's really great. She'll be pleased to hear you've called. When are you coming to see us?'

'I'd love to quite soon. Actually, I have been trying to get Patrick. Do you happen to know where he is?'

'I certainly do. Up a mountain in Austria.'

'Oh, of course, he's skiing.'

'With an old school chum, he said. Flying back next Thursday. He's coming over to dinner New Year's Eve. What about you? Where are you spending Christmas?'

'I'm with my sister's family. My father and stepmother are here, too.'

'Well, have a good time, won't you? Look, Mel . . .'

'Mmm?' Mel was thinking furiously.

'You will come to see us, won't you?'

'Yes. In fact, listen Matt, I've had an idea, if you don't think it too daft.' And she explained her plan.

*

It was the best Christmas she'd had for years, she thought, as she lay in bed at the end of the following day. All right, so Rory had roused everybody with a shriek of delight at 3 a.m., and Freddy had cried and not gone back to sleep. And the turkey took longer to cook than Chrissie had calculated and the kids' jelly didn't set, and somebody else gave Rob the book she'd got for him – but in the end, what did it all matter? Her father was there, more contented than she had ever known him. And Patrick had sent her flowers and a note with all his love. And she was going to see him . . . soon.

When her father and Stella said goodnight to the family at the end of Christmas Day and her father hugged her and said how much they had enjoyed the day, she hugged him back and he murmured in her ear, 'My little Melanie. Always my little Melanie.'

Chapter 40

'Hello? Patrick?'

'Yes, hello?'

'It's me.'

'Mel!'

'Yes!'

'Mel, this is fantastic. How are you? How was Christmas?'

'Fine, I'm just fine. Christmas was wonderful.'

'I found your message. Only got back this morning. I've been in Austria, skiing, with my friend Tom and his wife.'

'Matt told me. How was it?'

'Terrific. Masses of snow.'

'Thank you again for the flowers. They were simply beautiful.'

'I'd been thinking of something to send you, especially after I got your card. I couldn't believe it when I saw them coming up so early. Must be global warming or something. There are dozens of them.'

'I know.'

'You do?'

'I've been looking at them.'

'*What?*'

'I'm here in Lamorna, Patrick. Just a bit up the hill, in fact. I couldn't get a signal down where you are.'

'Mel! Where? Wait! I'm coming.' The sound of a dropped phone.

Mel laughed and started to walk back down the lane to Merryn.

She had driven down to Lamorna the day before, setting off in chill darkness at five to avoid the traffic, taking it easy with several stops, reaching Carrie's hotel just as twilight was starting to fall. They had rushed out into the reception area to greet her, Matt taking her case with one hand, pulling her into a hug with the other, Irina grabbing her next by the lapels of her coat with a shriek and kissing her on both cheeks, Lana hovering in the doorway to the bar, chewing a strand of hair and shyly waving hello.

The lounge was empty except for an elderly gentleman sitting in a corner reading a book and Carrie on a leather armchair, feet up, by a crackling wood fire. She tried to get up, but Mel stopped her, bending to kiss her instead.

'Come and put yourself here,' Carrie said, patting the arm of the fireside chair next to her, and Irina set about fetching them all tea.

'Look at you all,' said Mel, beaming at them. She noticed instantly that Matt stood close to Irina, the unconscious little looks and gestures that could mean only one thing.

'You and Matt . . .?' she whispered when Irina took Mel up to her room. A double bedroom with Edwardian-style furniture, it looked out over the valley, now dark except for points of light that meant other buildings.

'You noticed,' said Irina, smiling broadly.

'How could I not? That's simply marvellous.'

'It happened slowly. We had to spend so much time together here and Matt . . . well, after Carrie became ill, he's grown up, taken charge. He's a lovely man, Mel. Strong but gentle.'

Mel nodded. There was a new air about him, that was certainly true. 'Is he here all the time now? What's happened to his shop work? And,' she remembered, hoping he hadn't abandoned it, 'the photography?'

'He gave up the shop. He enjoys the hotel now because Carrie lets him make decisions. He's been taking photographs of Lamorna, though. I showed them to a gallery in Penzance and they've ordered some prints to sell.'

'Oh, excellent. And what about Lana?'

'Doing well. She got a distinction in her Grade Five, you know.'

'That's brilliant. But, I mean, does she mind about . . . you and Matt?'

'Not really, no. She knows I can never be with her father again and she likes Matt. He tries to be her friend, not her daddy.'

Perhaps in the end this is what would work for Aimee, Mel thought. If she could just be Callum's friend.

Something else occurred to her. 'Does Greg know? About you and Matt, I mean.'

Irina's expression darkened slightly. 'I think Lana must have told him. He hasn't said anything, though.'

'How's it going with Greg and Lana?'

'Better than I even hoped, Mel. She went to him before Christmas for some days, but told him she wanted to be here for Christmas Day, so he brought her down again. He is different now, more gentle, like a wild animal tamed.'

'I can imagine!' Mel walked over to the window to pull the curtains across but stood watching for a moment as the headlights of a car swept over the road below, illuminating walls and

trees. Up the valley only a short distance away lay Merryn, waiting, as she was, for Patrick to come home.

'And how has Patrick been?' she asked Irina, a catch in her
voice.

'He's missed you,' said Irina, shaking her head sadly. 'I don't
know what happened between you, why you left like that, but
he's been through a terrible time. There were weeks when we
hardly saw him. He was working, he told us. Or busy with the
house. The roof's finished, you know, but the garden is still a
mess.'

'It wasn't the right time for us back then,' said Mel.

'Perhaps it is now. Just as it was for me and Matt.'

'Perhaps,' Mel whispered. 'I hope so.'

The next morning, she woke to the sound of rain pattering on
the window. She lifted the curtain to see that the valley was
obscured by rolling fog.

By the time she had had breakfast and helped tidy away –
'You've got to let me earn my keep somehow,' she told Matt,
who had protested at her even lifting a finger in the kitchen – the
mist had lifted slightly. She pulled on her coat and walked down
the narrow lane to the road and turned up the hill towards
Merryn. Patrick wouldn't be back until the afternoon, but she
couldn't resist going to look.

The air was chilly, but not icy. It would be a warm wet New
Year and the lichen-covered trees dripped all around. By the
time she reached the drive that led down to the Gardener's
Cottage, the cloud was lifting from the valley, but she hesitated.
It felt wrong, somehow, sneaking in the back of the Hall. She
couldn't imagine that Patrick had re-let the cottage, but what
happened if he had and she was intruding on a stranger's privacy? She climbed further up the hill to the old gateposts where

the sign *erryn Hal* still hung at exactly the same angle as she had first seen it eight months ago.

She stood looking down the drive and realised with a pang that little else was the same. The front gardens were a desolate wasteland, trees sawn down and cut up where they lay, the stumps ripped from the ground leaving vast rain-filled craters. Everywhere caterpillar tracks scarred the earth as though a battalion of tanks had driven across the land. The shelterbelts around the edge remained, as did a great copper beech to the right of the path, but the self-seeded sycamore and ash, and much of the tangle of vegetation had gone.

The house itself appeared like a wounded soldier, bandaged and plastered and left in a bathchair to dream away his remaining days. The new slate-tiled roof looked too pristine, one side of the house was still splinted with scaffolding, and the granite walls had been stripped of creeper and showed unseemly blotches of white where damage had been made good.

It wasn't her Merryn any more. Suddenly she couldn't stand it, couldn't bear the thought of investigating further – what might she find? She turned and fled back to the hotel.

Only as the gloomy day started to sink into darkness did she return to see his sparkling blue car parked on the courtyard. He was home. And so, she hoped, was she. Would Cornwall be where she would find herself again?

'What are you doing here?'

He was running, zig-zagging down the puddled drive towards her.

'Patrick. I'm sorry, perhaps I should have warned you. Do you mind?' she called, suddenly nervous.

Then he reached her and his arms were around her, crushing

her; his lips pressed against her face, covering her in kisses, made her sure.

'Mind? You amazing, crazy woman. How could I possibly mind?'

They stumbled together up the drive to the house.

'I can't believe you're here. I simply can't believe it.' She had never heard such joy in his voice. 'What finally made you come?'

She forced him to stop so she could look at him again. He was tanned from skiing, but beneath the happiness that illuminated his whole face she could see strain etched. She traced the lines around his eyes, smoothed the worry from his forehead.

'It was the flowers,' she murmured. 'It was as though you and Merryn were calling me. They whispered a thousand words.'

'All of them true,' he said, pulling her to him again and kissing her very thoroughly. 'Mel, I love you, I'm sorry I never told you that properly before. I have missed you so much. I'd almost given up hope . . .'

'You knew I'd come when the moment was right,' she said. 'Surely you didn't doubt me?'

'Not really, not underneath. Every time I lost faith I'd pull your letter out of my wallet – look, here it is, it's practically fallen apart! And then your lovely card came and I knew everything would be all right. So I sent the flowers.'

They were both speaking openly at last, Mel realised joyfully, as neither of them had really done before. They reached the courtyard and stopped to cling together again. When they finally separated, Mel stared back the way they had come.

'The front garden is, well . . . different.' They contemplated the morass of mud and fallen trees.

'It looks awful, I agree,' he said, 'Like No Man's Land. But don't worry – I've got plans, you see. I'll show you the rest of the place if you like. There's less changed there.'

Indeed, the other parts of the garden were little altered from the previous August but lay brown, dripping wet and uninviting. Only, here and there, under the trees, behind the Gardener's Cottage, snowdrops and daffodils were starting to show.

'Let's hope there isn't a frost,' Mel commented. 'You talked about plans – what are they?'

'I'm hoping for a start that they include you,' Patrick said.

'Oh, Patrick.'

They had to stop again while they settled that point in another passionate kiss.

'There's an awful lot to sort out, of course,' she said later, as they lay wrapped in blankets on the drawing-room sofa before a blazing fire.

'There's plenty of time for all that,' murmured Patrick into her neck.

'What were you saying about plans?'

'Mmm? Oh, for the garden.'

'The garden? I thought you meant about us.'

'The garden *and* us. Mel, darling, despite your general perfection, you have one teeny weeny little fault that I'm going to have to correct.'

'What do you mean?'

'You talk too much at the wrong moment.'

'Mmm*mmm*.'

That evening they talked together over a frugal supper Patrick had cobbled together.

'There's so much here to connect us to the past, isn't there?'

Mel said dreamily. 'We've found so many clues – to Pearl and her story not least of all.'

'It is a garden of memories, isn't it?' said Patrick.

'But not a sad one. Not like a garden of remembrance for the dead.'

'Which leads me on to another aspect of my plan. Maybe we could open an art gallery here. Tourists would come to see the garden and the paintings.'

'What a fantastic idea! We could show Matt's photographs. And Pearl's pictures. Although . . .' Mel explained about meeting Ann and how the paintings might morally at least belong to Pearl's descendants. 'But perhaps they'd allow the paintings to be shown,' she finished. 'And, Patrick, there's something else I haven't told you. My editor phoned the other night.'

'She likes the book?'

'She loves it. In fact, they want me to think about writing another, about the St Ives group. You know, Ben and Winifred Nicolson, Barbara Hepworth, that lot.'

'Mel, that's fantastic.'

She was silent for a moment, her mind in turmoil. Would all this really be right for her, giving up her job to the awful Rowena, leaving her lovely flat, her life in London, to come down here to write, maybe find a teaching post? She still didn't know.

Patrick seemed to sense her confusion for he whispered, 'There's plenty of time, you know, all the time in the world to sort things out in a way that makes us both happy. The important thing is that we're together.'

'Pearl didn't have time, did she? Dying so young.'

'No.' His response was sober. 'But maybe she found happiness, married to a kind man and with a child.'

'I wish we knew that, I really wish we did,' said Mel, and told

Patrick about the dream she had had, her last night in the Gardener's Cottage. 'I'm sure it was her I sensed. She seemed utterly desolate.'

'Maybe that passed. Maybe she got through it.'

'That's what her grandson, Richard, thinks. Patrick, I want so much to believe it was true.'

Chapter 41

July 1919

Pearl was sitting on a kitchen chair in the garden shelling peas. It was the late afternoon of a perfect July day and she felt well, for the first time since last year's illness.

It was peaceful sitting here, listening to the birds and the sound of Peter and the miller's boy playing soldiers down the garden. The fresh green of the peas against the white bowl pleased her, as did the cool smooth feel of the inside of the pods. A ladybird glowed red against light green as it negotiated its way over the peas in their bowl, like a child across boulders on the shoreline. How would she paint that green? A white wash underneath could make it glow with life, she was thinking, when a slight noise – metal on stone – made her look up.

John was up near the Hall. He had propped his hoe against the wall and now crouched down to pick up something from the ground. Whatever it was, he held it gently cupped in his hands. She watched as he came across the lawn towards her. His hair was silver now, but thick and glossy against skin as brown as an acorn. So tall and broad, yet so tender towards whatever he carried. Something moved in her throat. Desire.

He came near and she was acutely aware of him, the warmth of his body, the thick hair on his arms, the sweat beading on his collarbone where his shirt gaped open. He carried a small white bird, she saw.

'Is it dead?'

'There's a heartbeat, but very faint and fast,' he said. 'It's stunned. Maybe blinded by the sun off the window.'

'What bird is it, John?'

He shrugged. 'Looks like a blackbird.'

'But it's white.'

'Aye.'

She put out a finger and stroked the top of its head. Its eyes were slits. After a moment it made a feeble struggling movement.

John took two strides over to a flowerbed and laid the bird under a shrub. Its struggles became stronger and as they watched, it recovered and after a while took off, high and away into the trees.

'Well now,' said John, stealing one of her peas and laughing as she slapped him. He set off back to his work, and she watched his receding figure with overwhelming tenderness.

That night, Pearl lay between the soft sheets, turning over the events of the day in her mind, marvelling at these new feelings. Tenderness, desire. She heard John's tread on the stairs, soft so as not to wake the boy, then the door of their room opened and he shuffled about in the light of his candle, readying himself for bed.

John, her husband. Peter's father, in truth, for he loved the boy as his own. She owed John everything, she had recognised that for a long time now. She had come to love him, her love a gentle, frail thing, had submitted quietly to his caresses over the

418

years, had cradled his spent body after he was done.

But this time, as he lifted the sheet and slid in heavily beside her, turned towards her, for the first time it was she who reached out to him, began to awaken his desire. They had never spoken of love, but tonight she would make sure they did. It was time.

Author's Note

Until the middle of the nineteenth century and the construction of the London to Penzance railway line, Cornwall was effectively detached from the rest of the UK. With the trains came tourism and with tourism came the artists. The nucleus of painters who settled around the fishing village of Newlyn after 1870 worked in a distinct style, eschewing pretty landscapes for the portrayal of ordinary Cornish people at home and work, in tragedy and joy, with a sympathetic realism that impressed critics and public alike. Among them were Stanhope Forbes and his wife Elizabeth, Thomas and Caroline Gotch, Charles Walter Simpson and Norman Garstin. They formed a close but constantly replenished social group whose artists, both male and female, produced work of equal quality.

Around 1900, a new generation began to visit Lamorna, a secluded wooded valley several miles west from Newlyn. Laura and Harold Knight, John 'Lamorna' Birch, Dod and Ernest Procter, Alfred Munnings and, later, Augustus John, were more influenced by Impressionism in their choice of subject and style, moving away from the realist tableaux of the Newlyn tradition to capture light, colour and landscape. Both groups helped establish Cornwall as a land of artists, and their sense of freedom and invention contributed significantly to British art of the period.

The following publications have particularly informed the writing of this novel: *Oil Paint and Grease Paint* by Dame Laura Knight, *The Shining Sands: Artists in Newlyn and St Ives 1880–1930* by Tom Cross, *Five Women Painters* by Teresa Grimes, Judith Collins and Oriana Baddeley. Any mistakes in this novel are undoubtedly my own.

The Lamorna Valley retains its breathtaking and mysterious beauty, but I must apologise for taking slight liberties with its geography for fictional purposes. Merryn Hall and its inhabitants past and present exist only within these pages. So too does Carrie's hotel and Jim and Irina's cottages. Sadly, the community no longer has a Post Office-cum-stores, though the Cove café and gift shop near the quay are definitely worth a visit.

Thanks are due to a number of people who have advised or otherwise helped me during the writing of *The Memory Garden*: Tamsin Mallett and David Thomas, archivists at the Cornwall Record Office and absolute mines of information; Paul and Amanda Hook, whose lovely cottage I stayed in at Kemyel Wartha; Barbara and Dick Waterson of Trewoofe Orchard and Maryella Pigott, who showed me their beautiful Lamorna gardens. Juliet Bamber corrected my worst gardening inaccuracies; Dr Hilary Johnson gave excellent editorial advice, and Bob Mitchell is still lending me his laptop.

Great thanks are due to my agent Sheila Crowley and her colleagues at A.P. Watt, to my editor Suzanne Baboneau, copy editor Joan Deitch, junior editor Libby Vernon, publicist Sue Stephens, and the rest of the team at Simon & Schuster.

Finally, thank you Felix, Benjy and Leo who light up my life, and David, to whom this book is dedicated.

RH, 2007

Rachel Hore

A Gathering Storm

**As Lucy listens to the tales of the past, she learns a
secret that will change everything she has
ever known . . .**

Photographer Lucy Cardwell has recently lost her troubled
father, Tom. While sifting through his papers, she finds
he'd been researching an uncle she never knew he'd had.
Intrigued, she visits her father's childhood home, the once
beautiful Carlyon Manor. She meets an old woman named
Beatrice who has an extraordinary story to tell . . .

Growing up in the 1930s, Beatrice plays with the children
of Carlyon Manor – especially pretty, blonde Angelina
Wincanton, Lucy's grandmother. Then, one summer at the
age of fifteen, she falls in love with a young visitor to the
town: Rafe Ashton, whom she rescues from a
storm-tossed sea.

But the dark clouds of war are gathering, and Beatrice,
Rafe, and the Wincantons will all be swept up in the
cataclysm of events that follow. Beatrice's story is a
powerful tale of courage and betrayal, spanning from
Cornwall to London, and occupied France, in which
friendship and love are tested, and the ramifications reach
down the generations.

ISBN: 978-1-84983-288-5
PRICE: £7.99

Rachel Hore

A Place of Secrets

THE
RICHARD AND JUDY BOOK CLUB
BESTSELLER

**The night before it all begins, Jude has
the dream again . . .**

A successful auctioneer, Jude is struggling to come to terms
with the death of her husband. When she's asked to value a
collection of scientific instruments and manuscripts
belonging to Anthony Wickham, a lonely eighteenth-century
astronomer, she leaps at the chance to escape London for the
untamed beauty of Norfolk, where she grew up.

As Jude untangles Wickham's tragic story, she discovers
threatening links to the present. What have her niece
Summer's nightmares to do with Starbrough folly, the eerie
crumbling tower in the forest from which Wickham and his
adopted daughter Esther once viewed the night sky? With
the help of Euan, a local naturalist, Jude searches for
answers in the wild, haunting splendour of the Norfolk
woods. Dare she leave behind the sadness in her own life,
and learn to love again?

'Rachel Hore's intriguing Richard and Judy recommended
read . . . is layered with a series of mysteries, some more
supernatural than others' *Independent*

ISBN: 978-1-84739-142-1
PRICE: £6.99

**SIMON &
SCHUSTER**

If you enjoyed *The Memory Garden*, you'll love these other fabulous novels from Rachel Hore. These titles are available from your local bookshop or can be ordered direct from the publisher.

978-1-84983-288-5	A Gathering Storm	£7.99
978-1-84739-142-1	A Place of Secrets	£6.99
978-1-84739-140-7	The Glass Painter's Daughter	£7.99
978-1-41651-099-4	The Dream House	£7.99

Free post and packing within the UK
Overseas customers please add £2 per paperback
Telephone Simon & Schuster Cash Sales at Bookpost
on 01624 677237 with your credit or debit card number
or send a cheque payable to Simon & Schuster Cash Sales to
PO Box 29, Douglas Isle of Man, IM99 1BQ
Fax: 01624 670923
Email: bookshop@enterprise.net
www.bookpost.co.uk
Please allow 14 days for delivery. Prices and availability
are subject to change without notice.